D1502348

MURDER IS THE CRIME.
SEX IS THE MOTIVE.

SWEET LITTLE HANDS by Lawrence Block

"She stayed there, stayed right there, right on the edge, trembling, trembling, hot and wet and trembling, and waiting, God, waiting, Christ, waiting—

"Another shot. No louder than the first, how could it be louder than the first, but God, it seemed louder—

"She cried out with joy and fell back onto the bed."

SUMMER FOG by Joe Gores

"After a while, Carole fell asleep. It was going to be a fantasy week, lifted out of time, lifted out of their lives. When he was mended, he would leave, and it would be as if this had never happened. Life was goddamned unfair. Jeanne was in love with a dead man . . . he was in love with Jeanne . . . Carole was in love with him. . . . But he was alive. *Alive.* After being that close to taking the dirt nap."

THE GIRL OF MY DREAMS by Donald E. Westlake

"I saw her in all lights and under all conditions. Diving from a tacketa-tacketa long board into a jade-green swimming pool, and framed for one heartbeat in silhouette against the pale blue sky. Kneeling in the garden behind her house, wearing gardening gloves and laughing, with dirt smudged on her nose and cheeks. Driving her white Porsche, her auburn hair blowing in the wind. . . . The dream, the Dream, became much finer than reality."

GATORS by Vicki Hendricks

"He came out and took a hard look down my body. His eyes glinted and I could see satisfaction in the upturn of his lips, despite their being pressed together hard. I knew there was some macho thing mixed in with the caretaking for his sister. In a twisted way, he was doing this for me too, proving how he could protect a poor, weak woman from men like himself."

FLESH
AND
BLOOD

Erotic Tales
of Crime and Passion

EDITED BY

Max Allan Collins AND Jeff Gelb

THE MYSTERIOUS PRESS

Published by Warner Books

A Time Warner Company

This book is a work of fiction. Names, characters, places, and incidents are the product of the author's imagination or are used fictitiously. Any resemblance to actual events, locales, or persons, living or dead, is coincidental.

Copyright © 2001 by Max Allan Collins and Jeff Gelb
All rights reserved.
Copyright information continued on page 352.

 Mysterious Press books are published by Warner Books, Inc., 1271 Avenue of the Americas, New York, NY 10020.

Visit our Web site at www.twbookmark.com

 A Time Warner Company

The Mysterious Press name and logo are registered trademarks of Warner Books, Inc.

Printed in the United States of America

ISBN 0-7394-1660-X

Book design by Stanley S. Drate / Folio Graphics, Inc.

Flesh and Blood is dedicated to our wives,
with thanks for the research assistance!

—MAX ALLAN COLLINS and JEFF GELB

Acknowledgments

The Editors thank:

Dominick Abel
Joshua Bilmes
Michael Garrett
Sheldon McArthur
William Malloy

Contents

Crime in the Flesh

an introduction by Max Allan Collins

My co-editor Jeff Gelb and I would like to welcome you to the first volume of an exciting new anthology series from Mysterious Press—*Flesh and Blood*, tales of erotic noir.

Jeff is co-creator of the bestselling, long-running erotic horror anthology series *Hot Blood*, which took two of life's biggest mysteries—sex and death—and mixed them into a potent cocktail of erotic horror fiction. I was a frequent contributor to that series and, when *Hot Blood* finally came to a close, expressed to Jeff that the next logical step was a new series that shifted to noir. I proposed that we invite the top names in mystery fiction to let their hair down with an erotic crime story.

At the heart of *Flesh and Blood*'s darkness is the reputation for sex and violence that American crime and mystery fiction has deservedly earned, ever since Dashiell Hammett and Raymond Chandler wrested the genre out of the manicured fingers of the Philo Vances and Miss Marples and into the two fists of Sam Spade, Philip Marlowe, and their descendants. Hammett and Chandler and their pulp-fiction contemporaries redefined the all-American detective story as one of hard-bitten males and dangerous females—hot passion and cold blood.

Not that the protagonists of noir fiction are always the detectives: Sometimes they are the perpetrators, and steamy stories of adulterous lust and criminal greed—descending from James M. Cain and the scheming murderous lovers of his *Postman Always*

Rings Twice and *Double Indemnity*—have become the American equivalent of opera.

Mining those two parallel veins of crime fiction, each volume of *Flesh and Blood* will present new stories . . . with one exception, a sort of "classic crime corner," where we select a previously published tale from one of the giants of the genre. (In this volume, one of my mentors, Donald E. Westlake, fills that honored position.) We have made an effort to invite long-established authors as well as the more current crop, and to seek out up-and-coming writers, as well—three generations of crime, men and women who write today's mystery fiction, and who have leapt at the chance to write this kind of story, without inhibition or fear of censorship.

Since sex and violence are at the heart of the genre's darkness, the *Flesh and Blood* series strives to present the hardest hitting, emotionally riveting fiction the mystery world has ever seen. The degree of overt sexuality may vary from tale to tale, but these are stories whose carnal content is key to the conflict at hand. Whether the protagonist is a private eye, a cop, a crook, or just some average Joe caught up in the web of fate or his own self-destructive patterns, the stories in *Flesh and Blood* aim to take noir to the next level.

FLESH
AND
BLOOD

Sweet Little Hands

LAWRENCE BLOCK

Lying there, it seemed to him that he could hear his own cries echoing off the room's blank walls. His heart was pounding, his skin glossy with sweat. Should he be afraid of this? Could a person actually die at climax?

When he spoke, he did so as if resuming a conversation. "I wonder how often it happens," he said.

"How often what happens?"

"I'm sorry," he said. "I'd been thinking, and I guess I assumed you could read my mind. And sometimes I think you can."

For answer, she laid a hand on his thigh. Sweet little hand, he thought.

"My heart's back to normal now," he said, "or close enough to it. But I was wondering how often men die like that. If a fellow had a weak heart . . ."

"My husband's heart is strong."

"I wasn't thinking of your husband."

"I was," she said. "From the moment we got in bed. Longer than that, actually. Since we got here. Since I got up this morning, knowing I was going to be with you this afternoon."

"You've been thinking of him."

"And of what you're going to do."

He didn't say anything.

"His heart is strong," she said. "In a physical sense, that is. In another sense, he has no heart."

"Do we have to talk about him?"

She rolled onto her side, let her hand find the middle of his chest, more or less over his heart. "Yes," she said. "Yes, we have to talk about him. Do you know what it does to me? Knowing what you're going to do to him?"

"Tell me."

"It thrills me," she said. "God, Jimmy, it gets me so hot I'm melting. I couldn't wait to see you, and then I couldn't wait to be in bed with you. We've always been hot for each other and it's always been good between us, but all of a sudden it's at a whole new level. You felt it, didn't you? Just now?"

"You get me so hot, Rita."

Her bunched fingers stroked his chest, moving in a little circle. "If I could get him hot," she said, "so hot his heart would burst, I'd do it."

"You hate him that much."

"He's ruining my life, Jimmy. He's draining me, he's sucking the life out of me. You know what he's done."

"And you can't just leave him."

"He told me what I'd get if I ever tried. Didn't I tell you?"

"You really think . . ."

" 'Acid in your face, Rita. Not in the eyes, because I'll want you to be able to see what you look like. Acid all over your tits, too, and between your legs, so nobody will ever want you, not even with a bag over your head.' "

"What a bastard."

"George is worse than that. He's a monster."

"I mean, to say a thing like that."

"And it's not just talk, either. He'd do it. He'd *enjoy* doing it."

He was silent for a moment. Then he said, "He deserves to die."

"Tonight, Jimmy."

"Tonight?"

"Baby, I can't wait for it to be over. And we have to do it before he finds out about you and me. I think he's starting to suspect something, and if he ever finds out for sure . . ."

"That wouldn't be good."

"It would be the end of everything. Acid for me, and God knows what for you. We can't afford to wait."

"I know."

"He'll be home tonight. I'll make sure he drinks a lot of wine with dinner. There's a baseball game on television and he'll want to watch it. He always watches, and he never stays awake past the third inning. He settles into his La-Z-Boy and puts his feet up, and he's out in no time at all."

Her hand moved idly as she went over the plan, working its way down his chest, down over his stomach, stroking, petting, eliciting a response.

"He'll be in the den," she was saying. "You remember where that is. On the first floor, the second window on the right-hand side. He'll have the alarm set, but I'll fix it so it's limited to the doors. There's a way to do that, in case you want to have a window open for ventilation. And I'll have the window in the den open a couple of inches. Even if there's a draft and he gets up and closes it, it won't be locked. You'll be able to open it without setting off the alarm. Jimmy? Is something the matter?"

He took hold of her wrist. "Just that you're setting off *my* alarm," he said.

"Don't you like what I'm doing?"

"I love it, but—"

"You'll come in through the window," she went on. "He'll be asleep in his chair. There's all this crap on the walls, swords and daggers, a ceremonial war club from some South Seas island tribe. Stab him with a dagger or beat his head in with the club."

"It'll look spur-of-the-moment," he said. "Burglar breaks in, panics when the guy wakes up, then grabs whatever's closest and— Christ!"

"I just grabbed whatever was closest," she said innocently. "Jimmy, I can't help it. It gets me all excited thinking about it." Her lips brushed him. "We may have to stay away from each other for a while," she said, "while I do the Grieving Widow number." Her breath was warm on his flesh. "So I've got an idea, Jimmy. Suppose we have our victory celebration now?"

"A splendid dinner," George said, pushing back from the table. He was a large and physically imposing man, twenty years her senior. "But you didn't eat much, my dear."

"No appetite," she said.

"For food."

"Well . . ."

"I guess it's almost time," he said, "for me to adjourn to the library for brandy and cigars. Except it's a den, not a library, and brandy gives me heartburn, and I don't smoke cigars. But you know what I mean."

"Time for you to watch the ball game. Who's playing?"

"The Cubs and the Astros."

"And is it an important game?"

"There's no such thing as an important game," he said. "Grown men trying to hit a ball with a stick. How important could that possibly be?"

"But you'll watch it."

"Wouldn't miss it for the world."

"Another cup of coffee first?"

"Another cup? Hmmm. Well, it is exceptionally good coffee. And I guess there's time."

* * *

This is crazy, he thought.

There was her house, and there, in the second window on the right-hand side, was the flickering glow of a television screen. The garage door was closed, and there were no cars parked in the driveway, or at the curb. Nobody walking around on the street.

Crazy . . .

He drove halfway around the block, found a parking place out of the reach of the streetlights. He left the car unlocked and circled the block on foot, his heartbeat quickening as he neared her house.

Anyone who saw him would see a man of medium height and build dressed in dark clothes. And he'd burn the clothes when this was over. He'd assume there were bloodstains, or some other sort of physical evidence, and he'd leave nothing to chance.

Impossible to believe he was actually going to do this. Going to kill a man, a man he'd never met. And would never meet, because with any luck at all he'd strike the fatal blow while the man slept.

Not a man, not really. A monster. Acid on that beautiful face, those perfect breasts . . .

A monster.

Was it murder when Beowulf slew Grendel? When Saint George struck down the dragon? That was heroism, not homicide. It was what you had to do if you wanted to win the heart of the fair maiden.

Or he could go home right now and forget about her. There were plenty of women out there, and most of them never asked you to kill anybody. How hard would it be to find somebody else?

Not like her, though. Never anybody like her. Never had been, and he somehow knew there never would be.

Never an afternoon like the one he'd just spent. Never. Drained him, emptied him out—and, even so, just remembering it was getting him stirred up again.

He was at the window now. It was open a few inches, as she'd said it would be, and through it he could hear the voices of the baseball announcers, the crack of the bat, the subdued roar of the crowd. The mindless prattle of the commercial. "Bud." "Wei." "Ser."

He strained to hear more. Movement from the man. The husband.

The monster.

He got up on his toes, hooked his hands under the bottom edge of the window. He was standing in a bed of shrubbery, and it struck him that he was leaving footprints. Have to get rid of the shoes, too, he thought, along with the rest of his clothes.

Unless he gave it up and went home right now.

But how much better he'd feel if he went home in triumph, with the monster slain and the maiden won!

Besides, he realized, he *wanted* to do it. Wanted to thrust with the dagger, to flail away with the war club. God help him, he couldn't wait.

He took a full breath and eased the window all the way open.

She hadn't been able to eat. Now, upstairs in the bedroom she shared with her husband, she found herself unable to sit still. Her pulse was rapid, her mouth dry, her palms damp.

Any minute now . . .

She stripped to her skin, let her clothes lay where they fell. She sat up in bed and gazed down at her naked body, as if with a lover's eyes. And touched herself, as if with a lover's hands.

Remembering:

Crouching over him, she'd reached to probe with a finger, felt him stiffen and resist. Probed again, not to be denied, and felt him open up reluctantly to her. Unwilling to respond, unable to keep from responding . . .

Her own excitement was mounting now. He was at the window now, he had to be, she was sure of it. But she was stuck up here, unable to know what was happening downstairs in the den. His den, George's den, and her lover was at the window, must be at the window, had to be at the window . . .

She looked down at her hands, then closed her eyes, remembering:

"God, Rita, what you do to me."

"I had two fingers in you."

"God."

"First one and then two."

"I wasn't expecting that."

"You liked it."

"It was . . . interesting."

"You didn't want to like it, but you liked it."

"Well, the novelty."

"Not just the novelty. You liked it."

"Well."

"Next time I'll use my whole hand."

"Rita, for God's sake—"

She made a fist, opened it and closed it, opened it and closed it, watching the expression on his face.

"You'll like it," she said.

And he was down there now. She knew he was, she could tell, she could feel him there. She cupped her breasts, felt their weight, then let her hands slide lower. Let her fingers move, let her fantasies build, let her excitement mount . . .

She was close, very close. Hovering there, not wanting to go any further, wanting to stay there, right on the brink—

A shot rang out.

God!

She stayed there, stayed right there, right on the edge, right on the fucking edge, trembling, trembling, hot and wet and trembling, and waiting, God, waiting, Christ, waiting—

Another shot. No louder than the first, how could it be louder than the first, but God, it *seemed* louder—

She cried out with joy and fell back onto the bed.

* * *

She was wearing a blue satin robe. Her feet were bare. She stepped carefully into the den and gasped at the sight of the man lying there. He was dressed all in black and lay sprawled on his back like a rag doll discarded by a spoiled child. One hand was at his side, the fingers splayed. The other still gripped the hilt of a foot-long dagger.

She drew back involuntarily, then forced herself to take a closer look. "Yes," she said, turning from the corpse. "Yes, that's the man."

"James Beckwith," the detective said.

"Is that his name?"

"According to the ID in his wallet."

"I never knew his name," she said. "When I reported him to the police, I didn't have a name to give them. Because I never knew it."

"You gave them a good description," the detective said. "When I called in just now, they read it back to me, and it was all right on the money. Height, weight, age, hair color, everything down to the mole on his right cheek. That was what, four days ago that you reported him?"

She nodded. "Can we go in the other room now? Seeing him there like that . . ."

In the living room the detective said, "You did the right thing, filing the report. He was stalking you and you reported it. It's a shame we couldn't have done anything that might have prevented this, but—"

"You didn't have a name," her husband said. "You couldn't have him picked up, not if you didn't know who he was."

"No, but we could have staked out your house, and we would have if we'd had reason to believe he was planning anything like this. But we get so many complaints of this nature it's hard to know which ones to take seriously. So we wait and see if the guy takes it to a new level, and then we do something."

"It's a shame it came to this," her husband said. "Possibly, with professional help—"

The detective was shaking his head. "My opinion," he said, "a guy's got this particular kind of a screw loose, there's not a whole lot anybody can do for him. You can say it's a shame he got hurt, but the thing to focus on is nobody else got hurt, not you and not your wife. That dagger he was holding, in fact he's still holding it, well, I don't think he was planning on using it for a toothpick. It's a damn good thing you had the gun handy."

"It's usually locked in a desk drawer. Ever since Rita told me about this fellow, about the remarks and the threats—"

"And I believe he assaulted you physically, ma'am?"

"My breasts," she said, and lowered her eyes. "He ran up and took hold of my breasts. It was the most awful violation."

The detective shook his head. "You can call him a sick man," he said, "and say he was emotionally disturbed, but another way of looking at it is he got pretty much what he deserved."

"He's gone," she said.

"He's gone, and the rest of them are gone, and the body's gone."

"The body."

"And they took my gun, but your friend swears I'll get it back."

"My friend?"

"He'd certainly like to be your friend. He couldn't keep his eyes off you. When he wasn't trying for a glimpse of your tits he was looking at your little pink toes."

"I guess I should have put slippers on."

"And fastened the top button of your robe. But I think you were just fine the way you were. Quite fetching, and the detective thought so, too."

"And now he's gone, and we're alone. So tell me."

"Tell you what?"

"Tell me everything, George. I was going crazy, sitting up there and not knowing what was going on down here."

"As if you didn't know."

"How could I know? Maybe he'd chicken out. Maybe you actually would fall asleep—"

"Small chance of that."

"Tell me what happened, will you?"

"He opened the window and climbed over the sill. Clumsily, I'd have to say. I was afraid he'd make so much noise he'd frighten himself off and pop out again before I could do anything."

"But he didn't."

"Obviously not. I opened one eye just wide enough to get a glimpse of him, and as soon as he had both feet on the floor I opened both eyes and pointed the gun at him."

"And he'd already grabbed the dagger off the wall?"

"Of course not. That came later."

"He grabbed it later?"

"Do you want to hear this or do you want to keep on interrupting?"

"I'm sorry, George."

"He saw the gun, and his eyes widened, and he looked on the point of saying something. So I shot him."

"That was the first shot."

"Obviously. I shot him in the pit of the stomach, and—"

"Where? I couldn't really see anything. Where did the bullet enter? Around the navel?"

"Below the navel. I'd say about halfway between his navel and the place where you left your lipstick."

"The place where I left—"

"Just a joke, my dear. Halfway between his navel and his dick, that's where I shot the son of a bitch. It put him down and shut him up and I guess it hurt. Abdominal wounds are supposed to be the most painful."

"And then it was ages before the second shot."

"I doubt it was more than thirty seconds. Say a minute at the outside."

"Was that all? It seemed longer."

"For him as well, I'm sure. But I wanted a moment or so to tell him."

"To tell him."

"I didn't want him to die thinking something had gone horribly wrong. I wanted him to know everything was working out just the way it was supposed to, that he'd been set up and played for a sap. He didn't want to believe it."

"But you convinced him."

" 'A few hours ago,' I told him, 'she had two fingers up your ass. I hope you enjoyed it.' "

"You told him that?"

"It was a convincer."

"And then what? You shot him?"

"In the heart. To put him out of his misery, although he didn't look miserable so much as he looked embarrassed. You should have seen the look on his face."

"I wish I had. That was the one thing wrong."

"That you weren't there for it."

"Yes."

"Well, you could have been waiting in the living room. You could have popped in when you heard the first shot. But I don't suppose it was a total loss, was it? Being stuck upstairs?"

"What do you mean?"

"You had your hands full, didn't you?"

"Well," she said.

"Excited, were you?"

"You know I was."

"Yes, I know you were. My goodness, now that I think about it, those pretty little fingers have been a lot of places today, haven't they? I hope you washed them before you shook hands with the detective."

"Did I shake hands with him? I don't remember shaking hands with him."

"Maybe you didn't. But if you did, I bet *he* remembers."

"You think he liked me?"

"I'll bet he calls you."

"You really think so?"

"Oh, he'll have a pretext. He's not fool enough to call without a pretext. He'll have something to report on the disposition of the case, or he'll want to check on your state of mind. And if he doesn't get any encouragement from you he'll have the sense to let it drop."

"But if he does?" She nibbled her lower lip. "He's kind of cute," she said.

"I had a feeling you liked him."

"I just wanted him to go home. But he *is* kind of cute. You think . . ."

"What?"

"Well, we couldn't do things the same way we did with Jimmy, could we?"

"What, get him to crawl in the window and then blow him away? I don't think so."

"When he calls," she said, "*if* he calls—"

"He'll call."

"—I don't think I'll encourage him."

"Even if he is cute."

"There are lots of cute guys," she said, "and there ought to be a way to surprise them the way we surprised Jimmy."

"We'll think of something."

"And next time I'll be in the room when it happens."

"Sure."

"I mean it. I want to be there."

"You could even do it," he said.

"Really?"

"Look at you," he said. "You're something, aren't you?"

"Am I?"

"I'll say. But yes, you can be there, and maybe you can do it. We'll see."

"You're good to me, George. Good to me and good for me."

"I am, and don't you forget it."

"I won't. You know the one thing I regret?"

"That you weren't in the room to see it happen."

"Besides that."

"What?"

"Oh, it's silly," she said. "But I wish we'd put it off a day or two longer."

"To stretch out the anticipation?"

"That, but something else. Remember what I told him today? That next time I'd get my whole hand inside of him?"

"You're saying you would have liked to try."

"Well, yeah. It would have been interesting."

"Sweet little hands. Maybe you could do that to me."

"You'd let me?"

"And maybe I could do it to you."

"God," she said. "You've got such big hands."

"Yes, I do, don't I?"

"God," she said. "Can we go upstairs now? Can we?"

Dirty Pool

THOMAS S. ROCHE

"**A**re you listening?" Frenchy Carver smacked me on the side of the head, trying with only moderate success to get my attention away from the blonde, who had just smiled at me and made me the happiest man alive. Simple minds, simple pleasures.

I grabbed his wrist. "Watch it, Frenchy. Don't get between me and the next ex–Mrs. Brewster."

Josie's Gin Joint was packed six deep with wanna-bes, gamblers, and mobbed-up pool fans getting pickled in anticipation of tomorrow's big win at the tournament.

"Don't let your dick be your guide tonight, buddy. You got an amateur hour to win tomorrow morning." He pulled his wrist free and lit my Cuban with his Zippo.

"Just enjoying a little eye candy," I said, without taking my eyes off the blonde.

"Well, pay attention, Brewski, because me and Johnny Bourbon and Joey Donato got twenty yards apiece riding on you." He turned to Johnny Bourbon, who happened to walk by at that moment. "Hey, John, what's the name of the guy Brewski's up against tomorrow?"

"Blackie Snyder," said Johnny Bourbon as he walked by. He leaned down to pat me on the back. "The name of the black queen Brewster here's gonna wipe the table with is Blackie Snyder."

"He's a spade?"

"Course he's a spade. With a name like Blackie?"

"And how do you know he's a faggot?"

"He's from Frisco, ain't he?" said Johnny. "Jesus, Mike, don't you read the fuckin' papers?"

I shrugged.

"Look, don't fuckin' make a joke out of it," said Frenchy. "Why do you think I got you over at the Sands? Teddy SouthSide's got a lot of prestige riding on this spade, and so does Big Johnny Frisco. Those West Coast motherfuckers might try something."

"That must be why you got me loaded down like a one-man band, smartass." Frenchy had given me two guns—a compact Glock nine, which I'd duct-taped under my dashboard, and a little Colt .380 in my cue case.

"You'll fuckin' thank me if anyone tries anything. But I don't trust your shooting, Brewski—I saw you at the range."

"I shoot pool, not guns."

"That's why I got Sam and Dave following you."

"That's fuckin' crazy. It ain't necessary."

"Sixty Gs, motherfucker. That's how much we got on you."

"Tell those two Peeping Toms not to get too close."

"I'll tell 'em," said Frenchy. "You're gonna lay the blonde, ain't you, you fuckin' pussyhound?"

"If it's the last goddamn thing I do."

I was watching the blonde again. She had uncrossed and re-crossed her legs, giving me a quick view of the full length of those gorgeous gams.

"You won't try to lose Sam and Dave?"

"I won't try to lose them." I was already looking at the blonde, who had leaned forward against the bar just enough to stretch what little there was of her dress tight across her back.

"You promise," growled Frenchy. "You'll let 'em tail you so nothing goes down. Be serious here, Brewski."

"Yeah, yeah, yeah, I promise." I polished off my Scotch. Frenchy knew I played better when I'd had about two hours' sleep the night before and recently acquired carnal knowledge of some sweet young thing.

I saw the blonde lean close to Josie, the bartender, and then slide down off the bar stool. She started coming my way.

"I see you're about to receive a visitor," said Frenchy, and he and Johnny vanished into the crowd.

The blonde was even more of a looker up close and personal.

"Hello," she said—sexy, but with just a hint of timidity. "You're that pool player guy, aren't you?"

I chuckled. "I've been called lots of things, most of which I can't repeat in the presence of a lady. But 'that pool player guy,' I'm happy to say, isn't one of them. Mike Brewster at your service."

"So it is you! I'm a huge fan," she gushed. "You're all over the news. Everyone knows about you—you're a heck of a pool player."

"Something else I've never been called," I said. "Have a seat," I offered her.

"Oh, I couldn't—I mean, could I? I saw you talking to your friends . . . I hope I didn't chase them away."

"Of course not," I said. "Have a seat. And you are . . . ?" I asked, raising my eyebrows.

"Oh, God," she said. "I'm so rude! Sorry. My name's Ginny Mott. I'm from Florida, but I'm up here on vacation. I didn't think I'd ever get to meet you in person! But now that I have, I'm hoping I can talk to you a little." She sounded really nervous.

I nodded, smiled.

She blurted: "I'm a pool player, you see. I'm in town to see the tournament tomorrow—I just love watching really good pool players!" The girl was positively perky with enthusiasm. "I was wondering if you'd give me any pointers. I've been practicing since

I was a little girl, and . . . well, I hate to say it, but I'm awfully good."

"Your modesty is becoming," I ribbed her, and she blushed. "What do you want to know?"

"Well . . . I just . . . I was wondering how I know if I'm good enough to go pro." Now she was leaning close to me, and I could smell her perfume—something expensive.

"You must be mistaken. I've never gone pro," I said.

Ginny blushed again—this time, just a little. "Oh, I know that, well, I mean, everyone knows why that is."

"And why is that?"

"Oh, you make more money this way . . . you know, under the table money. Everyone knows you're mobbed up—"

She froze, blushed deeper, looked at the floor.

"I'm saying too much," she said. "I don't mean to be rude, Mr. Brewster—"

"Call me Mike," I said, leaning back and puffing my cigar. "No offense taken. Where do you practice?" I asked her.

"My daddy runs a diner. It has a table—in the back room."

I chuckled. "It's no use telling you, of course, that pool is not an appropriate game for a lady to be playing."

Ginny got a wicked look on her face, and smiled.

"Tell you what," I said. "How would you feel about a little mini-tournament, between, say, you and me?"

"Oh my God, are you serious!" She was laughing. "I could never—I mean, I would lose, for sure, right?"

I shrugged.

"Oh, Mr. Brewster, I would love that! Me, playing against Mike Brewster! Would you really want to do it?"

"Oh yes," I said, eyeing her upper thighs. "Only one thing. I have a minimum wager on every game."

"Minimum wager?" Ginny looked suspicious.

"It's modest. Five bills." When she looked blankly at me, I said, "Five hundred dollars."

"But . . . I barely scraped up enough money to fly up here!"

I chuckled. "Well, since you're a beginner, I would be willing to make alternate arrangements."

"Really? You'd do that?"

"No need for you to risk your money on a game of pool. I think we could find something a little less . . . painful for you to part with. In the event that you lose I think you've got something that's worth five hundred dollars."

I took out the five Franklins I'd won from Dakota Joe earlier that night and held them up as Ginny watched, transfixed.

"I'll gladly place my money against your . . . assets."

Ginny just looked at me, horrified, her eyes wide, her mouth open in an expression of shock and disgust. "You can't mean . . ." she began, then lost her voice. After a minute, she managed to croak out: "You mean if I lose to you, I have to . . ."

"If that pretty face of yours isn't worth five hundred dollars, darling, I don't know who is."

I saw the shiver go through her body, as she looked at the ground, pretending to be nervous and embarrassed. But she was enjoying herself, no matter how good a show of false virtue she was putting on.

I figured this was anything but a wager. Rather, it was a way to cut through the bullshit—a way for Ginny to get into bed with me without having to play the does-she-or-doesn't-she game I saw in our immediate future.

Ginny looked back down at the ground for a long time, as if collecting her thoughts.

"You mean if I lose, then I have to go to bed with you," she said nervously, without looking up.

"That's right," I said.

"H . . . h . . . how many times?"

"Just once," I said.

"Would I have to . . . do anything . . . unusual?"

I laughed. "That one's up to you."

She looked down again, and it was ten seconds, twenty, perhaps thirty, before she looked up. With this dark, wicked grin on her face.

"All right," she said. "Let's play."

I gave my money to Bad Check Sammy to hold, so of course I had to tell him what the wager was. And that sonofabitch has the loudest mouth there is. Soon everybody in the bar was crammed into the pool room, standing on tables, pushed against the walls four and five deep.

As Ginny bent over to take her breaking shot, that dress rolled up a little and a series of cheers and howls went up from the crowd. Ginny reddened, glanced back. Then she smiled, obviously loving the attention.

She held her position there for a painful length of time, and with every second the tension increased, till it felt like the crowd was going to explode.

The break rang out like a gunshot. Balls rolled everywhere.

Two balls rolled in—both solids. I almost swallowed my tongue.

I was sweating by the time Ginny took her third shot. She'd downed a third solid—the four—with her second, and she now had a passable shot at the seven, but it wasn't ideal. She put one leg up on the side of the table—a move that wasn't, strictly speaking, necessary, but which pleased the crowd and distracted her opponent more than anything she could have done with that cue. She was wearing red panties, and there wasn't much to them.

She missed her third shot.

My first shot was the ten, an easy shot into the corner pocket. Then the twelve, into the side, and the eleven and thirteen into the same corner. I had practically cleared the stripes when I let my mind wander to the shape of Ginny's ass in that dress.

The shot I missed was an impossible bank, but it still killed me
to miss it. I might have sunk it another time.

"God," squealed Ginny, seeming genuinely impressed. "You're
so good! I've never seen you play in person! You're so much better
than I expected!"

"I ain't the only one," I said with ice in my voice, eyeing her
suspiciously.

She giggled. "You really think I'm that good?"

I backed down. "I'm just bullshitting the competition," I said.
" 'Scuse my French."

In reality, she was better than I thought she'd be—in fact, she
was damn good. It made me more than a little nervous. I had lost
about one game a year for the last ten years, and I didn't want this
year's game to be lost to a college coed in fuck-me pumps.

Ginny had nothing but a crappy shot from one corner of the
table to the opposite, having to bank at the far end to miss the
eight. She took a painfully long time setting up that shot. She
seemed to be doing all the calculations in her head, furrowing her
brow and gnawing on her lower lip.

Then she bent over again, slowly, spreading her legs and hun-
kering down low. The dress rode up high above the lace tops of
her seamed black silk stockings, exposing the lovely framework of
her creamy thighs, and my head swam as I looked at those gorgeous buns in the tight dress in her next-to-nothing red lace underwear.

She made the shot. And the next one. And the next one—each
shot giving Ginny a new opportunity to flaunt those assets of hers.
To me, and to the crowd.

She finally missed a shot. I let out a long sigh. I was on the
brink of a fucking disaster here. Ginny had exactly two solids left
on the table and I had three stripes. She could wipe the floor with
me if I didn't sink the next shot.

I sighed and lined up an easy fifteen-in-the-corner-pocket.
Ginny slyly positioned herself exactly across the table from me,

and half-sat on a stool so she could put one leg up, showing me what I'd be getting if I beat her, no doubt in the hopes that the distraction would make me fuck up. This girl was more of an evil bitch than she appeared. There might be some hope for her yet.

I missed.

I was fucked. Ginny had two more balls to sink and then the eight ball was all hers.

Maybe she *was* better than me. Then again, maybe I *wanted* Ginny to win.

Okay, listen to me for a minute here. I had pulled the "wager-against-your-assets" scam with a dozen girls who happened to be dumb or horny enough to fall for it, and it had never failed. And I *never* felt guilty about it.

Women don't enter into that kind of wager unless they're prepared to put out already and want to do it in the first place. So it just cuts through the bullshit, the "did you have any pets growing up?" crap that nobody, woman or man, wants to waste time with when there's a good fuck waiting to be had.

But it doesn't matter how good a pool player a girl is, I'd never met a girl who could make any serious headway in a game of pool against Mikey Brewster. Not until now.

This shot Ginny had at the six was a real bitch—almost impossible. Nobody could have made that shot, except possibly me, and possibly Clint Boston, and probably Killarney Sean, the craziest, drunkest Irishman I had ever met and one mother of a pool player. Sean was doing time upstate for bootlegging cigarettes. That Irishman could drink a bottle of whiskey and still sink shots that would have made Minnesota Fats drop to his knees and weep. He's the only sonofabitch who ever took me three for three. And I didn't even think Sean could have sunk that shot.

But Ginny did.

*   *   *

"I made it! I made it!" she shrieked, her ample breasts bouncing as she jumped up and down in celebration. She bounced over to me and hugged me, her nipples hard against my skin through my silk shirt. "Guess you'll have to find another way to keep yourself occupied tonight," she whispered, and danced out of my grasp.

The mood around the table was mixed. A lot of guys had money on me for tomorrow, and they were beginning to lose their confidence, maybe think about changing their bets. But they'd seen me wipe that pool table with so many asses, even theirs, that it brought them savage pleasure to watch Ginny beating me. They lavished affection on her and a few guys even shoved twenties into her cleavage, earning them playful slaps. That bitch loved the limelight. She giggled and bounced away to take a drink from the blended margarita her friend Lucy was holding for her.

Josie makes the world's worst margaritas, so that was some small comfort to me.

Ginny lined up the last solid on the table. If she made this one, it was all about the goddamn eight ball.

Look, I already told you, she wouldn't have signed up if she wasn't prepared to do it anyway. It's not like it was gonna be torture for her if she lost, Goddamn it. Plenty of girls . . . oh, fuck it. I was gonna lose this match to a fuckin' girl, and be forever humiliated among wiseguys and hangers-on. In ten fucking years, it was going to be, "Hey, Mikey, you interested in playing some pool? 'Cause I saw some girls from the Catholic school walking by. . . ."

Ginny looked more gorgeous setting up that shot than she'd looked yet—maybe because I knew I wasn't gonna have her. I thought about taking my dick out and wagging it at her the way she'd wagged those thighs and ass at me—but that seemed like it would be undignified, at best.

Instead, I prayed.

God, I thought, *just let her fuck up once, God. Just let me take one shot, and I'll do the rest. Just one shot, Lord, I'll never swindle a twenty-year-old girl out of her virtue again, I promise. I fucking promise, I will be good and go to church and I won't screw on Sundays from now on. I swear it.*

Bending over, one leg up on the table, tight body poised in that tight dress, Ginny looked up at me, smiled, and winked.

I flipped her off, and she laughed, like I was the biggest fuckin' asshole in the world and she was only moderately embarrassed to have to humiliate me like this in front of my friends.

I fuckin' mean it, God. I fuckin' mean it.

She missed.

I leaned down low and lined up a bank shot.

Ginny was on her third or fourth margarita; I was still drinking Scotch, nice and slow, sipping it. Easy. Easy does it. Ginny sat in Lucy's lap, the two of them almost crushing Ugly Dave, who had a pained expression on his face but was looking like he was in heaven nonetheless. Ginny's legs were parted, practically flashing me as I tried to focus on the shot.

You're never going to get to see that for real, I thought. *You're never going to fuck this dame if you don't start playing some pool.*

Then everything fell into place. I sank the nine and the fourteen, just like that—easy as pie. Then I banked the fifteen in the side, a very difficult shot, without disturbing the eight ball that was just begging to be nudged. Ginny stared like she'd just witnessed a miracle. Then her face fell, and she frowned. She wasn't giggling anymore. And she was gulping, not sipping, her margarita.

Now it was just me and the eight ball, and Ginny's fine, sweet ass wrapped around my cock. Bent over the table, I looked up at Ginny, who was staring at me, looking incredibly worried—like a sick feeling of horror had come over her. Like she was about to puke, knowing I was going to dust her and take her home and fuck her like she'd never been fucked before.

"Aw, come on." I smirked, and winked at her. "I'm not that bad, am I?"

The eight ball went in nice and easy, and I had the gall to laugh. I guess I'm a sore winner.

We took my Impala. I unlocked the passenger's door for her and Ginny slid into the passenger's seat, her dress hugging her the way I was gonna be before much longer. I climbed into the driver's seat.

Ginny looked up and smiled at me, wistfully.

"I really thought I had you," she said. "I thought I was going to win."

"You and me both," I said, just a little more coldly than I intended. I started the car but didn't put it in gear. Instead, I stuck my hand under the dash, nice and easy. Brought it back out again.

Ginny gasped when she saw the gun.

"Who put you up to it?" I asked, my voice cold as ice. Ginny looked at me from under those long eyelashes, looking afraid. She pursed her lips, looked at the gun, then at me.

"I don't know his name," she told me. "He promised me a thousand dollars if I would beat you at pool. He said there was a match tomorrow and if you lost to a girl tonight, you'd lose tomorrow. Something about confidence."

I laughed. "Who's 'he'?"

"I already told you," said Ginny, too quickly, "he didn't tell me his name!"

"Describe him," I said.

She shrugged. "Real short, kind of fat. Dark hair. Ruddy skin."

"You know his name," I told her.

She nodded.

"All right. He said his name was Theo."

"Teddy SouthSide," I breathed. "He goes by Theo when he thinks he's being sly."

She shrugged. "Could be. I don't know."

"That son of a bitch," I mused. "Where'd he find you?"

"I'm the college champion at Gainesville. One of his scouts saw me."

"So you tried to play out of your league," I told her, a little cruelly. "And you blew it. You bet your body against his grand and my half a grand. You end up with nothing. And I get you."

She shrugged. "But I'm not a cheater," she said. "I don't play dirty pool. You beat me fair and square."

Then she was against me, her mouth on mine, her tongue working its way into my mouth, her firm breasts against my body. My arms went around her, the Glock in one hand and one of Ginny's firm breasts in the other. The Glock rested easily on the back of her neck, its weight a comfort as she held me. Her hands were all over me, and I could feel myself reacting to her, feel my cock getting hard. I could smell her sweet, musky perfume and I thought to myself for the first time in about five minutes how much I was going to enjoy this. . . .

I pulled away from her, put the car in gear, and floored it.

I finally lost Sam and Dave near the interchange. It just wouldn't be the same with a couple of wiseguys looking up my butt through the window as I screwed Ginny.

I took her to the Rest-Tite off of 95, got a room right on the parking lot. Took her in there and closed the door. Left the light off but the curtains open a crack, so the moonlight streamed in and lit up that body of hers as she stood there looking at me, as if waiting for me to make the first move.

But then she turned, backed up to me, showed me her shoulders as an invitation.

I unzipped her red dress, and she shrugged it off—as it had been begging to come off all evening. It shimmered down her pale body and piled around her ankles. Her red panties were slight, just a string up the back—hiding nothing of that gorgeous, wide ass and smooth-slung hips framed by black garters. Her waist was tiny; I could practically let my fingers meet if I put one hand on each side of it. I did, and pulled her close against me, kissing the back of her neck, tasting the salt of her sweat, and listening to her moan as I kissed up to her ear.

My fingers slipped up her back and deftly unfastened the clasp of her bra; I brought my hands up to feel her large, heavy breasts, pinching the nipples as Ginny turned her body so she could kiss me. She kissed hard, too, with lots of teeth, the way I like it, her tongue battling mine for dominance, her pearly whites nipping at my flesh as if trying to draw blood. I looked into her brown eyes and watched them sparkle—lust, or mischief? Then I felt her hand on my cock, stroking through my pants, and I didn't care. She unfastened my belt. I kindly slipped the Glock out of my waistband and put it in the pocket of my sharkskin jacket.

She turned, and I held her, and she pulled me roughly back onto the bed.

Ginny was worth every goddamn bead of sweat, every instant of terror, when I'd thought I was going to lose the game. Her body was soft, lush, full of smooth and beautiful flesh, and she gripped me like a Chinese finger puzzle. She rode me, I rode her, and she showed me what that smart mouth of hers could do. By the time we lay in bed together, I was exhausted, my eyes thick with the need for sleep. But I slept with one eye open.

Because even as I listened to her even breathing beside me, felt her naked body pressed against mine, something smelled wrong—and it wasn't the tequila on her breath.

I listened to the sounds Ginny made in the bathroom. Then I heard some other sounds—cloth, zipper. I sat up, looked for her dress on the floor, didn't see it.

She'd made it out of the bathroom and gotten the door open before I grabbed my jacket from the back of the chair and whipped out my Glock. Then I dove for her, willy flapping in the wind as I grabbed Blackie Snyder's hair and yanked her back onto the bed, pistol at her head.

I screamed at the top of my lungs, "Drop 'em or I'll kill her! I fucking swear I'll do it!"

Ginny froze, I froze, the shadows in the doorway froze. I could see them clearly—two of them. Trench coats, low hats, Remingtons.

I looked down into her big brown eyes for a long instant.

Then, "Go ahead and do it, you son of a bitch," she said, and ripped at my eye.

I didn't mean to shoot. It just happened—as she scratched me, I pulled the trigger. Plaster exploded everywhere around me and everything went bright red as Ginny kneed me in the balls. The Glock came out of my grip, and as I grabbed it, some guy hit me hard in the face with the butt of a Remington.

I laughed my ass off, lying there on the floor with blood running out of my mouth into a sanguine puddle underneath me. I felt a boot on the back of my neck. Somebody hit the lights.

"Blackie Snyder," I laughed. "Blackie fuckin' Snyder!"

"I don't usually bleach my hair," said Ginny, lighting a cigarette. She sat down in the chair just in front of me, no underwear under her dress, legs slightly parted so I could see the pussy I'd just fucked—or had it fucked me?—still glistening with the remnants of our lust. "Truth be told, though, I got the nickname from losing pool games by sinking the eight ball so many times."

"You've come a long way, baby," I grunted as I felt the cold weight of a shotgun barrel on the back of my skull.

"Yeah, well, I was eight," she said. "I've had ten years to practice. All you had to do was lose to me tonight, and you would have walked out of here with your bones intact. I would have beat you tomorrow, and Big Johnny Frisco and Teddy SouthSide would have been happy. But no, you had to show you're the best fucking amateur pool player in the country. Well, not anymore, mother-fucker."

"Talk about dirty pool," I said. "This shit's filthy."

"It's a filthy world," she said.

"Especially with you in it."

"You know what really fuckin' burns me, Brewster?"

"Knowing I would have skunked your ass tomorrow?"

Blackie Snyder laughed, shook her head. "You're a good fuckin' pool player. I'm sorry to have to do this." Then she nodded to the two guys holding me down, and I felt someone grabbing my wrist, and I tried to fight against his grasp and felt a boot in my kidneys, so hard I saw stars.

And that's when the one guy took my thumb and twisted.

I told myself I wouldn't scream; then I heard a snap, and screamed anyway.

I looked up, through the bleak pain, and saw Blackie Snyder putting on her shoes. She bent low and grabbed my hair, pulled my face up so I could look at her pretty face, at the way her upper lip curled in contempt.

"Nah," said Blackie, standing up. "Not even close. What steams me," she said, her lips a quarter inch from mine, "is that you're pretty goddamn cute, Brewster. I would have fucked your brains out even if you hadn't won the game."

"Thanks," I said. "I fuckin' appreciate that."

Then even through the agony and the sound of my own scream as the guy grabbed my other thumb and twisted that one, I heard Blackie Snyder's laughter.

The guys let me go. I looked up through bright stars of pain and saw one of them dump the bullets in my Glock into his pocket, then throw the gun down on the floor next to me. I lay there, hurting. They left the motel room door open.

Blackie paused in the doorway, looked down at me.

"It takes the soul of a killer to play dirty pool, Brewster. You should consider another line of work."

Then she was gone, and I heard a car start outside, heard her high heels click-click-clicking across the asphalt. I crawled, groaning in pain, across the floor to the chair where I'd laid my cue case; I saw and felt and smelled the detritus of her sweat and perfume on her panties and bra, garter belt and stockings, littering the floor between me and the case. I screamed in pain as I flipped the latches, and I had to hold the Colt .380 with both hands as I limped out, naked and blood-caked, into the night. I heard the car door slam, heard the tires squeal, saw the headlights come on. I stepped in front of them and raised the .380, laughing my ass off.

"How's this for dirty pool, motherfuckers?" I laughed, and pulled the trigger.

Branded

GARY PHILLIPS

Mark Sullivan's tongue had a spongy feeling and tasted like stale cotton candy. Now that was funny, he supposed, moving his thick tongue around in his dry mouth, when was the last time he'd had that sugary treat? Yeah, he grinned like a gibbon, that's right, he was eating something that had reminded him of the confection last night. Yes indeed.

Pictures coruscated through his sweltering brain. The images were like loose film fluttering in front of a fixed light source. For the briefest of moments, the likenesses the film had captured were projected on a sun-bleached wall. She was on the bed, her glorious backside to him, panties down, and he was riding her like a jockey going for the Triple Crown.

He opened his eyes, smiling broadly. Then just as suddenly, a stifling anxiety bolted through the hangover shrouded like a tarpaulin over his pulsing head. The pressed-wood nightstand with its peeling veneer and the Googie-style lamp upon it had thrown him at first, but now it all came back to him—the smell of her, the feel of her, and of course, letting the tip of his tongue cross his chapped bottom lip, the taste of her. Yes, buddy.

He was getting stiff, seeing her again in his mind, now with only her lacy black bra on, riding atop him as he bucked like a Brahma bull. He touched himself and winced. His penis felt sore. "Damn," he chuckled, "she wore me out."

Sullivan sat up in the bed, the mattress surprisingly firm and comfortable. Surprising given he'd spent the night in a motel room off a noisy main drag. He rubbed his whiskered face and groaned loudly. "Oh shit," he suddenly blurted, then scrambled out from underneath the black sheets. He stood on wobbly legs, allowing his eyes to rove the room. He spied his pants draped over the lone chair in the corner. His shirt was crumpled up at its foot on the floor.

Apprehension and guilt cleared his head enough for him to snatch his pants up and plumb the pockets. "Shit," he repeated. His hand touched change and what felt like a folded napkin in the front right pocket. And in the left, his keys. Well, he mused, at least those were still there. His wallet—"Fuck," he fumed—his wallet wasn't in his back pocket. But that could be explained, he rationalized as he continued searching.

But there were no other pockets. Sullivan threw the pants down in disgust, his head pounding from the exertion. Defeated, he sat on the air conditioner–heater unit attached below the curtained window. Idly, he noted the heavy drape was purple, the walls a mild fuchsia, and the floor's carpet a Pepto-Bismol pink.

"Jee-zus," he murmured, taking in his surroundings. "Where the hell did she take me?" He leaned back, taking a deep breath that caused him to hack up mucus and tequila. "Damn," he blared, struggling to his feet. As he did so, he got a glimpse of part of the area beneath the bed frame.

Sullivan got down on his knees and was happy to find his wallet. He sat on the floor, cross-legged, and thumbed through his billfold. It all seemed to be there, so that was one less story he had to work out. One less lie. Sullivan got up and almost fell over. The blood draining inside his head made starbursts flicker before his eyes.

He steadied himself and tousled his brown hair. "Never again," he promised quietly, while smiling smugly. "What the hell was that chick's name?" Remorse and excitement mingled in him as he recalled the woman he met in the bar last night. She was compact, chunky in the hips but packed just right. She was dark haired and wore jeans, platform shoes, and a low-cut sweater top. What had caught his interest, aside from the fact she'd sat next to him on a stool, was the arrow on her breast. It was a tattoo, and the shaft and quill of the arrow stuck out from the edge of her top. It was green against her tawny skin and turned him on like crazy. He just had to see the other end of that arrow. And he had.

"Ow," he said, a sudden pang throbbing along his penis. "Uh-oh," he whispered warily. No, wait, he'd used a condom, hadn't he? Or had he been so drunk he didn't remember or couldn't put it on. Hell, he was surprised he hadn't been too drunk to fuck, the old punk song went. Maybe he had been, but no, he was sure he'd knocked boots. He chuckled, then got serious. This was no time to reminisce about his lustful indiscretion. Had he taken his wedding ring to the bar? No, he hadn't. That was a relief.

First, there was a kidney to tap. As he sauntered into the white-tiled bathroom, he probed his memory in an effort to recall the woman's name. He stood before the toilet, putting the ol' two-finger hold on his johnson, and reacted to the soreness of his member. He looked down and could see the skin had an off-color hue. He sure hoped that wasn't evidence of some new kind of sexually transmitted disease. Naw, that couldn't be.

As he relieved himself, he tried different names. "Mary, no. Roxanne, no. It was short, one of those model/Hollywood kinda things," he mused aloud. There was a mirror tacked to the wall behind the toilet and he caught a glimpse of himself, naked. He smiled. Yeah, the babes still dug him. Shaking himself, the soreness of his penis became apparent again. He looked down, then in the mirror. "What the hell?"

The discoloration wasn't from being rubbed raw due to sexual gymnastics. The tinge on his penis was of a uniform formation. In blackish Gothic letters tattooed in an arc along the circumference of his penis were three letters. Each an inch high.

"Mia," that was her name, he gasped. And she left it on his penis.

Sullivan didn't move for several minutes, trying to comprehend what had happened to him. "I'm fucked," he concluded correctly as a clammy tremor worked up and down his legs. Each letter was finely crafted along his cock, and each was very distinct—as if a neon arrow were pointed at them blinking "idiot," over and over. There was no dried blood, but the area where the letters had been applied was the source of the discomfort.

"Shit," he repeated yet again, sitting on the bed. "Oh, man, what the fuck am I gonna do?" Sullivan closed his eyes and rubbed his face, hoping and praying when he lifted his head he'd be in his own bedroom, the victim of alcohol-fueled pent-up sexual frustration. But such, he intellectually knew, was not the case. He stood, staring at his branded penis as if it were a friend who'd stabbed him in the back.

"It's punishment for sticking it someplace it didn't belong." Sullivan squinted at the letters, trying to come up with a plausible story to tell his wife. "All right, get the ball back, take the high ground and all that pseudo-military, sports macho jargon we throw around at the business." Sullivan took several deep breaths and got dressed.

It was a quarter to eight and he had to do the presentation at ten this morning. He stepped out of the hotel room onto an open-air second-story balcony. Down in the concrete courtyard was a drained pool. A tall blonde in a skirt that by a whisper made its way south of her crotch walked its length in clunking platform shoes. She had blue streaks dyed in her hair. Nope, that wasn't her.

The woman he'd been with hadn't stepped out to get them coffee and poppyseed bagels. And then to return all girly-giggly as she happily related to him how he'd been so smitten, he'd begged her to have her name scrawled in ink on his tool.

"Fuck!" he hollered. The anger that had been lying beneath the surface was finally poking its way through the layer of shock. The woman in the awfully short skirt looked back at him, a wan smile briefly ghosting across her hard face. Then she kept going underneath an overhead arch and out to the street beyond.

Sullivan wasn't paying much attention. He made his way down the stairs and put the mind that had made him sales manager before thirty to work. He didn't stop to settle his bill, as he assumed from the appearance and name of the joint, ubiquitously called the Boulevard Motel, that it was a pay first kind of establishment. Besides, the heavyset desk clerk in her muumuu barely looked at him from inside the tiny glass-walled office.

Out on the street, Sullivan quickly assessed where he was. He didn't know the buildings around him, and therefore was not near the Red Pirate Bar. The bar was an upscale joint and his surroundings told him what he'd already guessed; he was in a part of town where a hot-sheet motel was not out of place. He started walking. The blonde with the blue highlights was across the street sitting at a bus stop. Her great legs were crossed and her dangling foot jiggled to a beat playing inside her skull. A beat-up pickup, at least twenty years old, pulled to the curb in front of her. Two men with hats were in the vehicle.

Sullivan walked to the corner to see the street name. Danziger. This put him farther from the bar and his home than work. He checked the time. Okay, Bob Ward, his immediate boss, kept mouthwash and an electric razor in his desk. At least once every two months or so Ward was kicked out by his third wife for some transgression or another, thus he maintained his emergency grooming supplies. So Sullivan's decision was made for him, it was to the office he'd go first.

There was a pay phone near the entrance of the motel. He went back to call a cab. Amazingly, the phone still functioned. The beat truck had left the curb, the cutie now sitting between the two men. Sullivan was getting the number from information when the truck did a U-turn in front of a coffee shop on the corner, heading toward the hotel. Idly he wondered if she had a special price for two.

"Yes, I need a ride at," dammit, what was the damn cross street, "ah, it's in front of the Boulevard Motel." The truck pulled into the driveway, but didn't go in. "Yes," he stammered into the handset, "yes, that's right, Danziger and Lewis." The company no doubt made several calls a week at the location.

"Ten minutes, perfect," Sullivan said. The driver and the other man in the pickup had gotten out. Sullivan hung up as the two reached him. Each wore a stylish Borsalino hat, in contrast with their jeans and casual shirts. One had a patch over his right eye, the other had his left eye covered. Their look went with the area.

"It's all yours." He held the receiver aloft for the driver.

The man, thick in the upper body with Popeye-like forearms, hit him in the bridge of his nose. Sullivan staggered back, reflexively bringing up his arm. "What the fuck?"

"Where is she," the man's partner snarled.

"Who the fuck—"

The driver swung again but Sullivan was prepared this time. He clubbed the fist intended for his face with the receiver, breaking it in two. As this one yelped, the passenger went into motion. Sullivan kicked him in the groin. He might be a solid citizen of the striving middle class, but that didn't make him a punk. He played hoops at a court where some brothers from the hood came, and he'd learned to handle his bidnez, as they say. And he certainly couldn't afford to be mugged just now.

"Where is that bitch?" the driver demanded again, rushing him. He got his arms around Sullivan and drove him back against the motel wall. Sullivan punched him alongside his temple, his hangover having dissipated due to the adrenaline he was pumping.

The passenger had straightened up and he and his pal were crowding Sullivan. "You mean Mia?"

A grunt was his confirmation from the driver. "Where the fuck is she?"

"That's what I'd like to know." Did this guy have her name on his penis too?

"Look, maybe we can sort this out and—"

"Only thing that's gonna get sorted out is your ass after I'm through with it," Passenger proclaimed.

"Not here it won't." The new voice belonged to Muumuu. She held an old-fashioned six-shooter down at her side. She seemed to have had practice with the piece. "Get to steppin'," she declared matter-of-factly. "I can't afford any more law trouble."

"Look, Shamu," Driver began.

The peacemaker's barrel angled up from her massive hip. "What?"

The two attackers weighed their possible responses. Silently, as if sharing an ESP link, they trod back to the trunk. The blonde watched dully. "It ain't over, motherfucker." Driver backed the truck up and they took off.

"Lady, thanks," Sullivan said hurriedly, trying to get his breathing notched down to normal.

"You just get your ass out of here before Sally Jessy Raphael comes on, you hear me?" She started to walk away.

"Hey, wait," Sullivan started, "do you remember me coming here last night?"

She went around the corner.

The cab came and he left.

"Come on, what the fuck did you do last night?" Ward had that particular bemused smile of his etched on his face. His face and demeanor was that of the bastard son of Peter Fonda and Dennis

Hopper. He was leaning against the rim of sinks in the men's room. Sullivan was shaving.

"She close her legs too fast or what?" He pointed at the swelling prominent between Sullivan's eyes.

He was on his knees, his hands up her dress as she swayed before him. He shook himself. "Let's just get the presentation over with, shall we?" There was no sense concentrating on too many things at once. Everything had to be dealt with in order.

"Sure, Mark, sure." Ward, a rangy, athletically built man older than Sullivan, took off his glasses. He scratched part of his face with the end of the stem. He too tossed the rock at the courts Sullivan frequented. "When you want to talk about it?"

"Got an extra toothbrush?" Sullivan inquired, judging his handiwork and ignoring his friend's question.

"Got one unwrapped from the stop and rob. When you're my age, teeth are real important."

"Listen," Sullivan said, "when this is done . . . well, thanks, man, huh?"

"Uh-huh," he sagely replied.

The presentation was what it was. Sullivan had done most of the preparation beforehand and he and Ward knew what the clients and their boss wanted to hear. It would have been stellar if Sullivan hadn't, despite his efforts at laser focus, been distracted about the letters on his salami.

Twelve minutes later, he and Ward got word the deal hadn't been nailed. "They still want to see how the billboard ads make for the synergy with the banners on related sites." Their boss, a dot-com millionaire younger than Sullivan, gave them his best Kevin Spacey stare. "Let's not lose this in the last quarter, okay, guys?" He removed his Prada-clad body from the doorway he'd been leaning in, leaving the door ajar.

"Doesn't the word *synergy* make you retch?" Ward snorted quietly through his nose.

Unconsciously, Sullivan was looking down at his crotch. "I've got to go."

"You have short-term memory loss, old bean?"

"It's important, Bob. This has everything to do with my"—he waved at his nose—"and what happened to me last night."

"You know he's expecting our synergistic answer, the unfolding connection of the living and the inanimate in the universe, by the morning." Ward peered at him over the rim of his glasses like a professor dressing down a lazy student.

Sullivan was already at the door. "I'll call you tonight. You blue sky some ideas like you're so good at, and I'll flesh them out. Tonight, I promise, man."

"You better."

"Like I got a choice, right?" He walked fast, taking the side exit. Goddamn, he was spotted by that boot-licking clown Crawford, who coveted his job. But there was nothing he could do about it now. If the ass puckerer told the boss, Ward would come up with a convincing lie. We all do when it counts.

But no story was going to explain away a woman's name on his penis. He could get away with it tonight; his wife would be tired from traveling and her visit with her mother and older sister. Katherine's older sister Carey, who'd moved back home after a funky divorce, had been wearing her family out with her tales of woe for months. But what about tomorrow and thereafter? Was he suddenly going to become a prude and never appear naked before his wife? Would they only do it in the dark? Would he never let his wife stroke him again?

"Shit," he swore again for the umpteenth time.

"Sir?" The cabdriver swiveled his head a quarter turn.

"I'm sorry, it's not you, just something on my mind."

The cab deposited him where he'd left his car, in the parking lot of the Red Pirate Bar & Grill. Last night, he'd figured that was a sign of luck to find a spot so near a jumping joint like the Pirate. The place was open for lunch but it wasn't the same crew as the evening shift. He found out those folks didn't come on till four. He had to be moving anyway.

"**S**orry, dude," the tattoo artist chuckled, "but there ain't much can be done until you heal up."

Sullivan stood before him, pants and briefs down, in the man's shop. He'd picked the business because it was in the neighborhood of the Boulevard Motel. There was a woman working there but she didn't seem to mind. At the moment, she was applying a tiger breathing purple flame to a buffed guy's left pec.

"How long does that take?"

"Depends, and 'sides, unless you want me to make it into a sailboat or something, you gotta see a plastic surgeon, you know, for laser removal of the epidermis." He eyed the woman and snickered again. "And you don't know the chick who had this put on you?"

"No." He buckled up.

"Well somebody did a real good job of it. Not much errant tracks or whatnot."

"How come I didn't wake up with that thing poking me?" He indicated the constant soft buzz of the woman's pneumatic needle gun as she composed her skin art.

The man shrugged. "Drunk enough, or maybe a local anesthetic. I use 'em when they want their old man's name on the curve of their vagina or some cat wants a spider web on the tip of his one-eyed beast."

"Look"—Sullivan produced two twenties and tore them in half—"you make a few calls and find out who made a visit at the Boulevard Motel last night, and you get these." He waved the other halves and tucked them away.

"Okay," the man agreed. He stuck the currency in his breast pocket.

"Ow," the man the woman was working on said. She dabbed at the blood dribbling along his arm.

An uncomfortable twinge gripped Sullivan down below. "I'll call you later."

Just as he got out on the sidewalk, the pickup screeched to a halt at the curb. "Hey, we want to talk to you," the man on the passenger side with the right-sided eye patch shouted.

"Damn straight," the driver put in. Between the men sat a passive German shepherd.

"What is the problem with you two?" Sullivan didn't wait for the answer. He was already running toward his car, parked farther down the block. Sullivan prayed the dog wouldn't bite him on his whang.

The passenger stepped out and commanded, "Sic him, Rex, sic him!"

Rex yawned and continued to pant heavily.

"What's up with this dog, man?" the passenger screamed at the driver.

"Fuck I know."

"Damn," the other one said. He got back in the car too fast and knocked his Borsalino off. Rex looked at him and barked. "Follow him," the passenger retorted irritably, leaning out the open door to retrieve his hat.

The driver was already gunning the truck and the passenger fell out, crushing his hat. The driver slammed on his brakes just as a CheapAss.com delivery car was speeding along. CheapAss.com was one of those Internet delivery services you could dial up to have videos, food, and booze delivered to your door within the hour. Their delivery cars were silver Checker cab–type vehicles with a giant angled clipboard listing the stuff you could order on the roof. The Checker loudly crashed into the pickup's fender. The impact tore the clipboard loose from its moorings and it sailed into the display window of the tattoo parlor. Rex got scared and bit the driver on the leg. He screamed and the dog howled, in unison.

Sullivan drove off in a haze. The clock was ticking and his

options were limited. That name, that fucking Mia's name, was down there, silently taunting him, laughing at his folly. Oh, women like her liked to play with your balls, tell you how much a man you were to get you, like the chump you were, to willingly put them in a vise. They make with the come-on and tell you what you want to know, but really, Mia has contempt for you and your entire species. She'd give him those bedroom eyes in the bar, but inside she'd been laughing at his weakness, his all too human desire. She'd practically shoved her breasts in his face. The fuckin' arrow. What a fool he'd been. He loved his wife, for chrissakes. Sure he looked, window-shopped as grandma used to say, but he didn't touch.

"It's not my fault," he uttered, "that I'm a victim of my own testosterone." He gripped the steering wheel tighter as vestiges of the hangover crept behind his eyes. He couldn't do much else, but he could make her pay.

He headed back to the motel, the scene of the degradation. She'd be around, the one with the blond hair and blue streaks. She just had to be around. He parked across the street and waited. He killed more than a hour, but she was a no show. Determined to find her, he got out and walked into the manager's office.

"Hold on, Annie Oakley," he said to the muumuued woman. She was slurping a popsicle and watching Ricki Lake on the portable behind the counter. She'd tensed at seeing him. "I just want a little information and am willing to pay for it." He produced a twenty and placed it before her.

"What?" she demanded, putting the bill away.

"The blonde with blue streaks, what's her name?"

"How the fuck I know?" She turned her attention back to Ricki. The show was about a group called Strippers Anonymous.

"She's a regular around here, isn't she?"

"Hell no. Never seen her till this morning and haven't seen her since."

"What about those guys in the pickup?"

"Mister"—she put a blank look on him—"this is not *Jeopardy!*, okay? I'm not looking to answer questions I don't know or care to have the answer to. Now, unless you're gonna rent another room—"

Excitedly he blurted, "You remember me from last night?"

"Yes," she said indolently, "you happy now?"

"The woman, the woman I was with, did you recognize her?"

"She was standing outside while you paid. Hell, I thought you two were legit, she was carrying a suitcase and makeup kit."

Sullivan tried to comprehend what she'd told him as he meandered back outside. He called the tattoo parlor, using the phone out front.

"Nope, sorry, I didn't get squat," the owner said on the other end. "Far as I can tell, nobody made a midnight run, even though I told 'em there was a sawbuck in it for them."

Sullivan asked, "What about someone, a woman, who has a traveling kit?"

"That's nothing special, man. I've done some of those kind of jobs myself."

"She got an arrow piercing an orange on the top of her left breast."

"Don't ring my bell, and frankly, it ain't worth me making another round of calls for what you're paying."

He hung up, angry the dude was trying to jack up the price, and angry for getting himself in this predicament. That bitch had set him up. It was all part of the game for her to ensnare him and do this to him. But why him? Was he just an easy target, drooling and eyes bugged out at her? Did she do this all the time? Of course, he snapped his fingers. He got in his car and drove back to the Red Pirate.

His cell phone rang. His heart stopped, but he was relieved when it was Ward and not his wife making the call.

"I'm leaving some notes on your e-mail. You are going to tighten this project up tonight, right, old bean?"

"Naturally," he said distractedly.

Ward exhaled audibly. "Yeah?"

"Yes, Bob, I promise. I'm almost done with my . . . the thing I had to take care of."

"As you say."

At the bar the evening shift was on.

"I kinda remember her, sure." She was one of the bartenders and had brought him his club soda with lime. "She was sitting there." She pointed at a stool.

"You see her here before?" The clock behind her read five past five.

"Yeah, I did," the woman remarked. "Ah, about a week before, I think. Seems I recall her having a drink with another woman, both of them dressed nice, you know, businesslike." She went off to fill another order.

Sullivan used his cell phone to call the airport. His wife's plane was due in ahead of schedule. He clicked off, the big hand on the clock seemingly speeding around the dial. The young sales manager walked into the gathering gloom. All right, no sex with the wife tonight. That would be simple enough. Tomorrow night, make sure he took her out to dinner, dancing, they'd be tired. He cheered up; this might work.

Then maybe he'd be healed enough and get the name removed with laser surgery. It was an out-patient procedure, so what was there to sweat? He reached his car when it occurred to him— bandages, he'd have to hide them too. But he could say he got some kind of groin pull playing basketball. Yeah, yeah, that could work.

"Look, motherfucker, stop bullshitting with us."

He'd been so wrapped up in his plotting he hadn't noticed the eye-patch twins parked behind a large SUV. They had him pressed up against the bar's Dumpster.

He was more irritated with than scared of these two zeroes. "What'd Mia do to you?"

"Where can we find her?" the passenger demanded again. "We owe her for something she done to our cousin. We heard from people we know around here said she was spotted last night with you. Now I'm through talking, it's your turn."

"Tattooed her name on his dick?"

The driver, who favored his bitten leg, screwed up his face. "Huh?" He looked at the other one.

"Stop playing stupid," the passenger said, shoving Sullivan.

"I leave that to you." He shoved him back. "I've got more important matters on my mind, moron."

The driver swung, catching Sullivan in the gut. He doubled over and leaned against the Dumpster. The driver had his fist raised to strike.

"I don't know, man, you understand?" Sullivan said quietly, straightening up. "I picked her up in the bar, and we went to the motel. That's the first and last time I ever saw her."

"No shit?" the passenger said.

"No shit."

The two weighed the sincerity behind his words, and then drove off. He checked his watch and drove to the airport.

"Hi, baby." He kissed his wife as she got off the plane.

"I'm glad to see you." She hugged him tight and it caused a lance of pain in his bruised john thomas.

On the ride home, after discussing how her trip went, she asked, "Did you get out any?"

"No, no, I had plenty of work to take care of."

"Oh, poor darling." She nibbled his ear. "I missed you."

"I did too, sweetie."

At home, she became more amorous. She rubbed a hand on his crotch as they sat on the couch. Sullivan just about jumped out of his skin from the raw sensation. He had to pretend he was enjoying the foreplay.

"Aren't you glad to see me?" she teased as her tongue probed his mouth.

"Of course, Kath."

"You seem tense."

"I've been under a lot of pressure, you know, the new account we're trying to land."

"I know what will relieve that pressure." She started to unzip his pants while massaging his tender rod.

He stood quickly. "Ah, I've got to use the bathroom, okay?"

"Sure," his wife said, a sly smile on her face.

Sullivan went into the bathroom, a panic sweat breaking out on his forehead.

"Mark," his wife called sweetly from the living room.

"Yes, dear," he replied from the bathroom along the hall. *Come on, Sullivan, think of an excuse to get out of this.*

"Did you get my present?" she asked demurely.

A chill clutched his spine. "Present? I was supposed to buy you something?" Their anniversary? Had he forgotten?

"No, dear." She came into the bathroom. He was sitting on the closed lid of the toilet. "I mean from Mia, my love."

He felt faint.

She crouched down beside him. "You see, baby, she's a private eye. Her core business is in adultery cases, though she handles the robbery or even murder suspect now and then too."

Sullivan couldn't speak.

His wife batted her sea-green eyes at him. "She did some work for Tracy, you know, Bob's ex?"

Ward had been married twice before. In fact, he'd run his own company but had to sell it when he'd settled with his second wife. Now he knew why, and why his friend didn't talk about it.

"Seems ol' Bob had been paying for this young, gorgeous fashion student's downtown loft. Well . . ." She stood, letting her spread hands finish her sentence. "Anyway, Helen and I get to talking one day at lunch, you know how us women are."

Sullivan dipped his head up and down, gulping.

"She mentioned Mia and her agency. Helen said she was sorry she hadn't found out about her beforehand."

"So," Sullivan began.

"So she lures the husband—properly sauced—with the wandering eye to a motel room. Using some suggestive techniques, she shows him some porno, whispers in his ear, lets him rub on her, plants the right smell and taste." His wife paused and smiled. "But she assures the client there's no penetration. After all, the tattooing takes time and who can do anything once that's done?"

Sullivan stared at his wife, who looked down at him.

"This is a reminder, dear. Marriage isn't easy, but getting some on the side . . ." She wagged her finger. "Now, I'm sure you have some work to finish at the office. That is, I know that's where you'll be heading, right?"

"Yes."

"Good. 'Cause you don't want to even know about the amputation and taxidermy skills of her other operatives." She started to walk out of the bathroom, then turned to beam at him. "I'm sorry to have taken this step, but you'll be all healed in a few days and then we can get the tattoo removed. It's just, well"—she looked regretful—"you know how men are."

You Don't Know Me

ANNETTE MEYERS

"**H**ear them moving around?" She presses her ear to the door.

He doesn't hear anything, and standing in the dark outside her parents' bedroom scares him. What if they come out and catch him and her listening? And they don't know him, don't even know he's in their place. He gets anxious, like he always does when he's scared. He can't help it.

"You're afraid. What are you fuckin' afraid about? They're *my* parents, not yours."

"I gotta go," he says. The sweat is dripping off him, and his glasses slide down his nose. He has to pee.

She's disgusted with him. "You gotta do better than this or you can't hang out with me." She drags him back down the hall to the other side of the apartment. It's this huge place that goes a whole floor with their own elevator stop. She has her own bathroom.

He can't pee while she stands in the doorway watching him, talking about *them*. It's all she talks about. She hates them. "They're always on my case." She makes her voice whiny. "Why do you have to dress like that, Lila? Like you're a boy. You're such a pretty girl, Lila." She changes her voice. "Do you like the way I

47

dress, Anthony?" Raising her baggy sweatshirt, she flashes little apricot tits at him. "You think I look like a boy, Anthony? What do you say, Anthony? Do you think I'm a pretty girl?" She stands there and waits.

"Yeah," he says. He can hardly hear himself. The piss comes gushing out of him. "You're beautiful." He feels like his feet are glued to the floor. His beeper starts going.

She lowers her T-shirt. "Forget it. Call your mama."

She scares him, but everything scares him. He doesn't want her to stop talking. He's never met anyone like her before. She's so free. She does whatever she wants to do, goes wherever she wants, says what she wants. He doesn't understand why she complains all the time.

". . . can't imagine them having a conversation," Lila says. "They never talk about anything real except when they're talking about me, and even then they don't relate to me."

Hands shaking, he zips up. It's after midnight and he's skipped his last pill. Yeah, his mom'll be on his back in a minute. Why isn't he home? It's a school night. And just like that his beeper goes off again. It's going to wake her parents.

But she laughs and lies down on her bed, her arms behind her head, and stares at him. His and his mom's whole place could fit in her bedroom. Her bed has this thing called a canopy over it. Her stupid mother's stupid idea. He feels stupid.

She jumps up and goes, "Let's get some beer and hang out."

The apartment has a back door and back stairs. This is how they get out. She steers him to the lobby's side entrance, the way they came in. The doorman is this tall jerk with no chin and a skinny mustache. Benny, she calls him. When Benny opens the door for them, he gives Anthony a wink, like he knows something.

"Go on, Anthony, what're you waiting for?" She gives him a push. He stands on the sidewalk and looks back. She's passing something to the jerk doorman.

It pisses him off, like she's got something going with the asshole. Anthony wants her for himself. "You getting something on with him?" His beeper goes off. His mom gave him the beeper so she could keep track of him. No one keeps track of Lila. She wouldn't let them.

Lila laughs at him. "Why don't you call your mama, baby?"

Fuck, she makes him mad. He grabs her arm and she shakes him off, gives him a look like he's a piece of shit. "Don't you ever touch me like that," she says, swiping him with the back of her hand. Her ring nicks him on the cheek. She goes off down the street toward the all-night grocery.

It's only two weeks since he first saw her. He'd started hanging out in the park on his way home from school, where a lot of kids his age hung out with hippies and bikers, drinking beer and smoking weed. Sometimes he'd Rollerblade. He didn't talk much, and pretty soon they were making fun of him because he didn't do weed, and didn't drink.

He was on these pills, two different ones, and he was not supposed to, not even beer, but Anthony didn't tell them that. He didn't go to regular public school because he got anxious attacks. But he was doing better at Harrison, where the classes were small and they didn't keep telling him to do better.

He'd come into the park this one day and bladed up and down the trails. When he came to the bandstand, he didn't see the usual crew, except for the two homeless men who were collecting the empty beer cans. They looked at him, then pointed down in the low valley near the lake. Getting closer, he heard the whistles and shouts. The fight was between two kids he knew who hung out. They were really smacking each other around, kicking and rolling in the grass.

"Kill him, slice him!"

Anthony looked to see where the shout came from and he saw a girl in baggy pants and T-shirt on the path going up the hill. She lifted a can to her lips, drained it, and threw it at the fighters. It bounced off the head of the one standing over the other, who was lying on the ground.

The standing kid yelled at the girl, "Fuck you, bitch," distracted just long enough to get an up-punch in the balls from the kid on the ground.

The girl laughed and bladed off.

"Who's that?" Anthony asked Robert Paredes, one of the boys watching the fight.

"That's Lila. She's crazy, man, but she can fight. I seen her hurt another bitch bad."

Anthony followed her but not too close. After a while she began to look over her shoulder at him.

She was crazy. She'd pass people and clip them hard, then go fast so by the time they began to yell at her she was gone. One time she stuck her foot into the spokes of a bike as the biker rode by and the bike jerked and threw the rider into the road in front of a cab. The cab stopped just in time.

Anthony heard her laughing, but he couldn't see her. He kept going on the path, but he'd lost her. He was tired. He sat down on a bench next to a backpack someone had left. He looked around, prodded the backpack, looked around again. He stood, reached for the backpack, and started to go.

"Where you think you're goin' with my backpack, asshole?" She was standing in front of him, holding a can of beer. She took a long drink, then snatched her backpack from him, unzipped it, and offered him a can of beer. He stared at it, then popped it, and drank. This wild, crazy feeling came over him.

After that, he was with her. They bladed along the park paths with her yelling at people, like, "Outta my way, fuckhead," and "When they let you out, crazy ass?" He liked to see the look on people's faces when she did that. She had the power.

They ended up on the steps near the lake with some other kids and some old fart hippie bums with beards and long hair, and bikers, all smoking weed and drinking beer. Everyone knew Lila and looked at him different because he was with her.

"Pass the beer," she said, "I got weed." She took a couple of baggies from her backpack and flashed them. Two bags full of joints.

"We're out," one of the hippies said. "But how about some grass."

She flung one baggie up in the air and they all jumped for it, scrambling over each other.

His beeper went off.

She stashed the other baggie in her backpack. "What're you, a dealer or somethin'?"

He said the truth. "My mom."

"His mom wants her baby to come home," Lila yelled. "Yeah, yeah, yeah."

He felt his face get all hot.

She laughed. "How'd you get those?"

He looked down at the scars on his wrists, and back at her.

"Come on, let's get some beer," she said.

He followed her out of the park to a deli, where he watched her pick up two six-packs and lay down the bills. She had a lot of twenties all wadded up in her backpack.

"You been drinking?" the clerk asked.

"You talkin' to me?" she said.

Out on the street she said to Anthony, "So I'm a drunk, so what?"

They went back to the lake and sat around smoking and drinking till he didn't know what time it was, but it was real dark and the cops kept coming and waving their flashlights and telling them to clear out.

His mom went after him when he got home. "Whatsa matter with you? You missed your medication. Where'd you go? Why didn't you answer your beeper?"

He wanted to say to her what Lila would say, something free, but he couldn't get the words straight in his head, so he didn't say anything. But he knew Lila now and he would do what he wanted, like her, and there was nothing his mom could say to him anymore that would change that.

So now he watches Lila walk away from him, like he's nothing, and he doesn't know if she means it or not. He touches where her ring nicked him and it's wet. He takes off his glasses and rubs his eyes.

"What the fuck you waitin' for?" He hears her screaming from all the way down the street.

He puts on his glasses. He can barely see her in the light of the street lamp. People turn around and look at her. Like she's a celebrity. She's like no one he knows in his whole life. He catches up with her and waits while she buys two six-packs. She hands one to him and they head out to the park.

The sky is full of dark, rolling clouds, hiding the moon. The park has this wet feel though it hasn't rained, and the air lies heavy over them. It's very dark and after closing time, and the cops are making their rounds. Lila sees better than he does and she hisses when she spots them.

The real night people are settled on the steps leading to the bandstand, talking, drinking. He knows most of them by sight now. They're all different ages. Mostly guys. Some have regular jobs, but like to hang out and drink and do drugs. Anthony's seen some do hard drugs and pass out. The drunks always end up puking by the lake.

An old black man lies snoring on the steps blocking their way. He's giving off a big stink. "Move it, nigger," Lila yells. She kicks at him. He groans and clutches the air, but can't keep himself from tumbling down the rest of the steps. He lies at the bottom of the stone steps, then picks himself up and stumbles away.

Anthony and Lila sit at the top of the stairs, and she begins passing out the cans of beer. His beeper goes off. He shuts it down.

"Get the weed," she tells Anthony, who takes some joints from her backpack and gives them to her.

This big, middle-aged guy stands up from a few stairs below. He lifts his beer can to Lila.

"Hey!" Lila looks at him like she knows him.

He gives her another look and comes up the stairs to them. He's wearing this shirt with the sleeves rolled up, half in and half out of his pants. He's carrying a jacket.

"Hey," he says. He sits down on the other side of Lila.

"Remember me?" she says. "I'm Lila from rehab."

"Yeah," he says. "Lila from rehab." He slurs his words and keeps nodding his head.

It's like they're in some kind of private club together that won't let Anthony in. Anthony moves in closer to her. Lila gives him a mean look, like who the fuck does Anthony think he is, and Anthony inches away.

"Danny Boy," she says.

"Yeah," the drunk says, and like he passes out.

Not long afterward a three-wheel cop car comes along with a searchlight that swirls all over. A loudspeaker goes on and the cop tells them to disperse, get out of the park, the park is closed for the night.

Danny Boy twitches and gets up. He gives Lila a drooly smile and goes off on one of the bike trails.

Anthony doesn't go right home. He circles around and follows Lila. If she knows, she doesn't let on. She's put the hood of her gray sweatshirt up over her head. He follows her right to her apartment building, to the side entrance, where the jerk with the mustache is standing at the door. They don't see Anthony.

"Jeez," the jerk says, "you got trouble again. He called 911 and the cops just got here."

"Fuck," she says, and she goes inside and Anthony doesn't see her anymore.

*　*　*

Late the next afternoon, after he does the grocery shopping for his grandmother and carries the bags up the stairs to the fourth floor for her, Anthony blades to Lila's building. He waits for her, smoking a joint out of sight of the doorman.

A lot of people pass him, heading for the park across the street. Joggers and bikers especially, and bladers. It's spring and everyone's out. Across the way the bushes all have yellow flowers.

A taxi stops and the doorman runs over to open the door. Lila jumps out and walks in Anthony's direction. The doorman helps a tall, thin lady in a fitted suit and high heels get out. Lila's mother, though Lila is small and wears baggy clothes so you can't tell she's not thin.

"Lila," the tall lady says, "where are you going?"

"None of your business." Under her breath Lila adds, "Bitch."

"What do you want for dinner?" the tall lady asks, like Lila hasn't talked back fresh to her.

"Leave me alone," Lila shouts. "Don't you see I'm talking to my friend?"

"Ask your friend if he wants to stay for dinner," her mother says.

"He says he would rather die," Lila says real loud. "Don't you, Anthony?"

Her mother ducks her head like she's embarrassed and goes into the building.

Anthony can't imagine talking like that to his mother.

Lila makes him excited, like he's on the edge, going to jump. He touches his cock, feels the swell. It feels good. He's stopped taking his pills. He heard at the clinic they keep you from getting hard. He wants to be with her all the time.

Apricot tits. Little knobs of nipple that connect his tongue to his cock.

"Come on," Lila says, grabbing his arm. "I gotta get my blades."

She takes him into her building past the doorman and another man in a uniform.

"No Rollerblades," the doorman calls to Anthony.

Anthony stops moving.

"Forget it," Lila says. She shoves Anthony forward and he takes off on the smooth marble floor, barely able to stop himself from crashing into her mother and another woman in a hat waiting for the elevator. He bumps into a bench.

The woman in the hat makes a little noise. She stares at Lila.

"See something you like?" Lila says.

"You kids are out of control," the woman says.

Lila comes up and barks like a dog right in the woman's face. The woman backs off and doesn't get on the elevator when the doors open.

"What is your friend's name, Lila?"

"Puff Daddy," Lila says.

"I thought you said Anthony," her mother says.

"Anthony Puff Daddy." Lila laughs, pokes Anthony so he laughs, too.

In daylight, the apartment looks like a museum.

"Would you like a Coke?" her mother asks.

"Puff Daddy and I are goin' bladin'," Lila says. She takes her blades from her backpack and puts them on.

"Lila, please don't upset everyone in the building."

"Why would I do that?" Lila says.

"Come home early," her mother says. And while her mother continues with, "You know your father doesn't like you to stay out late," Lila mouths the same words, making monkey faces.

Anthony can't get over it. She's so free. If he could only be like her.

When they get to her bedroom, she pulls off her sweatshirt and grabs a fresh one just like it from a drawer. Her apricots are stiff. She stops. "You lookin' at me?"

He cringes. "No."

"What's the matter? Aren't they worth lookin' at?"

He's sweating. "Sure."

She pulls the sweatshirt over her head. "Come here."

He crosses to her, trying to conceal the lump in his pants.

"Closer." He's standing right up against her. His cock shivers. She lifts her baggy sweatshirt and pulls it over his head, her tits in his face. He grabs her ass. He's in a dark place, her sweat salty on his tongue. Her knee nuzzles his cock. "Suck them," she says.

He comes, goes limp.

"Schmuck!" She pushes him away.

They blade through the park, drinking beer, and Lila says, "They're always on my case, come home early, don't do this, don't do that." She stops and yells at no one in particular, "We're big trouble!" A middle-aged black woman pushing a white child in a stroller gives her a look, and Lila screams, "What you lookin' at, nigger?"

The woman sits down on a bench. The child begins wailing.

Lila races off, Anthony follows. "My father called the cops on me once," Lila says. "Didn't think I was respectful enough."

"So he called the cops?" Anthony's shocked. "And the cops came?"

"I punched the stupid asshole out. That's when they put me in rehab. A lotta good it did."

It's getting dark by the time they stop at the bandstand. The usual group is there. A couple of the guys are slap boxing, but like they're loaded and they're not moving too fast and not hitting hard.

"Got any grass, Lila?" one of the old hippies yells.

"Yeah," she says. "Got any beer?"

"Not much."

Anthony's beeper goes off. He ignores it.

"Pass it around." Lila gives Anthony the plastic bag from her backpack. He sees her backpack is full of money, tens and twenties.

"Hey, girl." Danny Boy sits down next to Lila and throws his arm across her shoulder, offers her what's left of his Colt .45 malt.

She tilts her head, but there's hardly anything. She shoves the empty can at Danny Boy, and takes out two twenties. "Anthony, get some beer."

"I don't have ID."

"What a nerd," she says real loud to Danny Boy.

Anthony feels hot, dizzy like he's going to pass out. Everyone is looking at him.

"Here." She pushes the twenties at him. "Just do it. You know where. Give him the whole thing. Tell him it's for me."

Danny Boy laughs and raises his empty can at Anthony. "We'll be right here when you get back." Anthony wants to push it in his face.

His beeper goes off when he is leaving the park, and again at the deli.

The clerk at the deli gives him the eye. "Made you her slave I see."

Anthony smacks the twenties down on the counter. The clerk hands over two six-packs. "Well, watch out for her. She's a nut job."

Lila's not there when he gets back, and it's real dark already. He thinks he's going crazy. He goes from one to another, "Where is she? Where'd she go?"

"Get outta here, asshole," one of the hippies says, giving him a push. "She's been taking turns humping everybody."

His beeper goes off, and they all start laughing.

"Try the lake," one of the bikers tells him. "Saw her go that way with Danny Boy. But leave the beer."

Anthony maneuvers his way down the stairs to the grassy slope leading to the lake. There are dim lights around the lake, but he can't see anything. It's like she disappeared. And with that old drunk. He's not watching where he's going and hits a stump and goes flying, lands on his back, wind knocked out.

"Where's the beer?" Lila stands over him swinging her jeans. She's wearing her baggy shirt, and that's all. She sways and the moonlight makes her eyes glow.

"Left it back there."

She drops her jeans on his face, puts a bare foot on his chest, and moves it around slowly. Then she straddles him. He touches her tentatively, her ass is hard and soft at the same time. Just as he is, though he hasn't taken his medication at all in the past week.

"Well, that's the last we'll ever see of it."

She squeezes her thighs against him like she's riding and he's the horse. Her cunt wets through his shirt.

"I'm sorry," he says.

She gets off him. "Let's get some movies. We'll drink my father's shit." She pulls her pants from his face, sits on him like he's a bench, takes her blades out of her backpack, holds them out to him. "Do it."

She has soft feet, like a baby, and short toes. He takes her toes in his mouth and sucks.

"I knew you were a perv," she says, taking her feet from him. She puts on her blades herself, and starts off not too steady, calling back, "Well, you coming or not?"

At Blockbuster she picks out a couple of kung fu flicks and they go into her building by the side entrance, where the jerk is on the door. "Use the stairs," he says.

Anthony takes off his blades, while Lila can't make her fingers work right and tears at hers in a fury, can't undo them, and gets angrier and angrier. "You got a knife? Cut them off me." She claws at him. "You hear? Cut them off."

He takes his knife, pops open the blade. She pulls it from his hands and hacks at the leather.

"You're ruining them," he says.

"Who cares?" Tearing the wrecked blades off, she drops them into the trash can near the back stairs and hands him his knife.

They climb twelve flights and at the back door she tells him to take off his high-tops. "Otherwise," she says, "they'll come out and tell me I can't do this and I can't do that, like I'm a prisoner." She uses her key to get in. It's a kitchen. The cleanest kitchen Anthony's ever seen. Like no one eats in it.

She's jumpy, throws the videos on her bed, starts going through her drawers, searching the floor of her closet. "You got any acid?"

Anthony shakes his head. He watches her acting crazy. She leaves the room and he waits. She's making him jumpy, too. She comes back with a bottle of dark booze and takes a long swallow, then offers it to him. He takes a swallow, chokes, coughs, hands it back to her. Tastes terrible. He's never had more than a beer.

"I gotta have acid," she says. "Let's get out of here."

They're back in the park near the bandstand and there's a big full moon giving off light and a crowd of the night people, many who work regular day jobs and have money for weed and booze and other stuff. He recognizes them now and they know him, because of Lila. He feels powerful because she's singled him out to be with. They accept him now.

Someone passes them a sweet-smelling joint and they drink Zima and do acid, and he lies back on the steps and looks up at the moon, watching it expand and shrink and turn into a leering, snot-dripping face.

"Where'd you go, Lulu?" Danny Boy sits down next to Lila and throws his arm around her, like he owns her or something. "How about a little sugar?" He makes smacking sounds with his lips. He's so drunk he can't keep his head up, and he stinks of vomit.

Anthony feels Lila stiffen up next to him. She gives Danny Boy one of her bad looks. "That's it," she says. "We're goin' to the lake." Anthony follows her, but can hardly feel his feet anymore and she's swinging and swaying like she feels the same as him.

Danny Boy gets up like she's invited him to go along.

Nobody's at the lake yet, but they will be because the cops will start coming around with the searchlights and drive everyone away from the bandstand. The surface of the lake is like one big dark mirror. Anthony stands at the edge and looks into it and it goes red and yellow and purple and ends up making him lose his balance.

"Watch out there, son." Danny Boy grabs Anthony's shirt. He's so drunk, he leans into Anthony, slobbering, and Anthony pushes him away. There's a ripping sound.

"You tore it," Anthony says, looking at his shirt. Everything explodes in his head. His mom'll kill him. He punches at Danny Boy, but the man is already on his knees.

"Slice him," Lila yells. "Where's your knife?"

Anthony takes his knife out, pops the blade. Danny Boy looks up at him, blinking in the moonlight. He tries to get to his feet, but falls down again.

"What're you waitin' for?" Lila screams.

Anthony has his arm low. He underhands the knife. The blade catches Danny Boy as the man comes up. Catches him in the gut. Danny Boy grabs hold of the knife and struggles with Anthony, like he wants to keep it in his gut and Anthony's trying to get it out. There's blood flying, like it's raining, and Danny Boy howls like a jungle animal. Magic music, is what it is, and when Anthony gets the knife out, he plunges it back in, and out, and in, keeping time to the music. It's so good . . . so good. So good. . . .

"Yes," Lila sings. "Yes. Yes. Yes."

Anthony shudders, his body jerks like he's a spastic. The come collects in his pants.

Danny Boy goes over backward and doesn't move.

Anthony holds up the knife to the moon. The blade runs soft and red.

"Don't stop, Anthony," Lila says. "If we throw him in the lake, he'll just float up and they'll find him. We have to cut him up, take his insides out, then he'll sink. I read it somewhere."

Anthony's confused. What's she saying? His beeper goes off.

"Here." She grabs the knife from him. "I'll do it." She's going through Danny Boy's pockets, pulling out wallet and papers. She empties the wallet, throws it and the papers into a trash basket, and follows it with a lit match. The trash basket bursts into flames.

Danny Boy's insides are hanging out of him, all slimy. "Come on, move it," she says. They throw everything in the lake, but the stuff is slippery and maybe they miss some. Then they each take an arm and drag Danny Boy farther into the lake.

"Everyone out of the park," comes over a loudspeaker.

"Let's get out of here," Lila says, taking off.

The footpaths are pitch black and everything gets very quiet, except for Danny Boy's howling that rings in Anthony's ears. He catches up to Lila and they leave the park together, heading for the side door of her building, where the asshole doorman lets them in.

"Jesus H. Christ!" He's staring at them in the dim light. "You been in a fight?"

"We were attacked by a crazy bum," Lila says. "We'll wash up in the laundry room."

"I don't want nothing to do with this," the doorman says. He turns and leaves them.

Anthony and Lila go to the laundry room and begin to wash the blood and slime off them. "Give me the knife," she says. "I'll take care of it."

He gives her the knife. They put their wet clothes in one of the dryers, drop the coins in, and while everything dries, they wait around wrapped in someone's clean towels Lila pulled from another dryer. And all the time Lila doesn't stand still, but paces the room up and down. He gets tired following her and sits on the floor and starts to go to sleep.

"Wake up." She's hitting his head like she's crazy. They get dressed and go up to her apartment the back way, and she tells him, "Take a shower."

The hot water feels good. He'll just get dressed and go home. He can hardly hold his head up.

Lila pulls back the shower curtain and steps in, takes the soap and lathers her hands. She grabs his cock with her soapy hands. "You come too soon, dickhead, and I'll kill you, I swear."

"I won't," he moans.

She jumps him like a monkey, her left hand around his neck, her right hand guiding him inside her. He holds her slippery ass while she puts both arms around his neck and starts banging. He's going to pass out, for sure.

She digs her nails into his back. "Don't just stand there, asshole."

His feet go out from under him and he goes over backward, pulling her down on top of him.

Lila's screams get drowned out by the water that's coming down on them. "Think we made an idiot baby?" She laughs, turns the water on freezing cold, and jumps out of the shower.

After Anthony turns the shower off, he just lies there. He can't move. He hears her talking. Who's she talking to? He gets out of the shower and wraps one of her towels around him. She's on the telephone.

". . . none of your business," she says. "I'm just tellin' you we were attacked by some homeless and I ran and they caught my friend." She hangs up the phone, when she sees Anthony.

"Why'd you do that?" Anthony asks.

"We should've cut his hands off," she says. "I'm gonna go wash my hair."

Anthony lies down on her bed and falls asleep. The pounding on the door wakes him. Some man is yelling, "Lila! Come out of there."

He sees her standing near the bed. She is wearing pajamas. "What do you want, I'm sleepin'," she says. Her hair hangs in her face.

"Come out at once. The police want to talk to you."

"Stay here," she whispers to Anthony. She leaves the room, but the door is half open.

Anthony gets into his clothes, pulls on his Nikes. He wants to leave, but he's trapped. He looks around the room. There's no blood that he sees. He goes into the bathroom. No blood. Maybe he can leave by the back way. They wouldn't be talking in the kitchen. He pushes the door open a crack, and someone grabs his arm and pulls him out.

"Look what we have here, Pierce. Come on out and talk to us."

Anthony can tell he's a cop though he's not in uniform. The cop brings him into a big room where Lila's parents are sitting on a couch, in bathrobes, both looking at the same time angry and scared. Lila is in a chair near the fireplace and another cop, also not in uniform, is leaning against the fireplace. Lila gives Anthony a terrible look, like she wants to kill him. Anthony can't stop shivering.

They sit him on a chair next to Lila, and take out notepads and pencils.

"So where were we?" the cop named Pierce says. "Oh, yeah, you made an anonymous phone call to 911 to tell us a friend of yours was attacked in the park."

Lila doesn't say anything.

"Is this the friend?" Pierce looks at Anthony.

She gives Anthony another look. "I've only known him a couple of weeks."

Anthony has to pee. He can't concentrate. What did she do with his knife?

"Your doorman said you both came in the side entrance a couple of hours ago, covered with blood."

Lila's mother gasps, her hand over her mouth. Her father, a small guy with thin hair, puts his arm around his wife. They both look sick. Lila glows with a kind of light like Anthony's seen around the Virgin Mary at St. Anne's.

"Nice ring," Pierce says.

Lila looks at her ring.

Pierce takes Lila's hand. "How'd you get blood on it?"

Anthony can't believe it, but she starts crying. Her parents rush to her. She's screaming and throwing herself on the floor.

"We were drinkin' and he got jealous and did it." Lila points at Anthony. "I tried to give him mouth to mouth, but it was too late."

"Stop talking, Lila," her father says. "You're incriminating yourself."

Anthony can't move. Did she say he did it?

Lila turns on her father, smacking him. "Get away from me, asshole. You think I don't know they're writin' down what I say? I don't give a fuck."

"I know my daughter couldn't—"

Lila shrieks at him, "You don't know me."

"Hold up your foot, Anthony," Hernandez says. Anthony holds up his foot. Hernandez nods at Pierce. "Blood in the grooves."

"Let's take a walk, kids," Pierce says.

"I don't think—" Lila's father stops.

"You can come along with us, sir," Pierce says. "We're just going to see where the kids got attacked and what happened to their friend."

"You got a backpack or something?" Hernandez asks Anthony. Anthony nods. "Come along, then, and we'll get it." He's putting on latex gloves.

Lila's room looks the same only the bed is rumpled where he slept and there are wet towels on the floor. His backpack is next to the bed. He picks it up and Hernandez takes it from him. "Let me help you," he says, and then he opens it. "Nice blades." And then, "Your knife?"

Anthony stares at the knife. Hernandez says, "Get up against the wall, Anthony, spread eagle." Hernandez pats him down. "Good boy." They go back to the living room, Hernandez holding the backpack. He nods at Pierce.

"Come on, kids," Pierce says.

"You can't take her away," Lila's mother cries. "It's not safe in the park at night."

"We'll be back," Hernandez says. "We're just going for a little walk. And she'll be plenty safe with us." Hernandez takes Anthony by the arm and Lila goes with Pierce.

In the elevator, Pierce tells Lila to stand still, and he frisks her. "Hate to do it in front of your parents," he said, "but it's got to be done."

"What're you searchin' me for, search him," Lila says.

They leave the apartment building by the main entrance. It must be three or four in the morning because it's quiet on the street, and in the park, the moonlight makes Anthony think he's in a movie. Lila's parents stayed in the apartment. Anthony heard her father on the telephone as they were leaving.

Lila leads the way, like she's a dog on a trail, right down to the lake. The moon is so bright it's like daylight, or maybe it's all the searchlights and the cop cars. Anthony sees yellow tape around a place on the edge of the lake, where a dark lump lies half in and half out of the water. And the shadows of the night people beyond the tape, with the cops on loudspeakers yelling for everybody to get out of the park.

Lila is shrieking and crying. "I was afraid of him. I thought he was gonna kill me, too." She looks down at Danny Boy, blubbering and choking. "I tried to help you."

Hernandez puts his hands on Anthony's shoulders. "You have the right to remain silent . . ."

In the City of Angels

DICK LOCHTE

"**J**ee-zus," Wylie said. "He's giving it to her good."

Mace stared at the punk sitting beside him at the window of the dark room, his night-vision binoculars trained on the apartment building across the courtyard. He guessed Wylie was in his early twenties. Twenty-five, tops. Greenish blond crewcut showing black at the roots. There was enough light from the moon and the glowing pool in the courtyard two stories below for Mace to make out the head of a blue and red serpent tattoo poking above the neckline of Wylie's loud Hawaiian shirt. At Pelican Bay prison, Mace used to watch an old con named Billy Jet stick needles full of dye into the flesh of some of the other cons. There wasn't much else to do there, except get tats or watch other guys getting tats. As far as Mace knew Wylie had never served time, so the snake didn't make any sense to him at all.

The window occupying Wylie's attention wasn't the one they were there to watch, but that point seemed to be lost on him. He licked his slightly feminine lips and said, "Oh, ba-bee, don't use it up all at once."

Mace stubbed out his cigarette and picked up his binoculars.

He aimed them at a set of windc vs one floor up and to the left of Wylie's point of interest. The main room was still empty. Angela Lowell was somewhere to the right, probably in the bathroom, since the bedroom was still dark.

"Swear to God," Wylie said, "this sure beats the beater flicks all to hell. I could go for a little hormone fix myself."

"Keep me posted," Mace said.

"Whoa. Here comes Mr. Backdoor Man."

"I didn't know better," Mace said, staying focused on the Lowell apartment, "I'd take you for some snot-nose kid on his first trip to a riding academy."

"Oh, yeah?" Wylie said, obviously stung. "Well . . . go fuck yourself."

"You're the one who's turned on," Mace replied calmly.

"What turns you on? Little boys?"

Angela Lowell entered her living room dressed in a robe, rubbing her dark hair with a towel, her handsome face shiny from night cream. She crossed the room and moved just past the wide window and out of sight.

"Since you asked," Mace said, "professional behavior turns me on."

Angela walked back into his line of sight carrying a thick book. A coffee-table book. Probably an art book, Mace thought. She was an art appraiser, an artist herself.

He liked the way she moved, a graceful glide. He couldn't see her feet, but he imagined they were bare, luxuriating in the soft texture of the carpet.

"You saying what? That I'm not a professional?" Wylie asked, more hurt now than angry.

"I'm saying you should keep your mind on the job."

Angela turned out the living room light. Mace started a countdown. One hundred. One hundred and one. One hundred and two. One hundred and— A light went on behind the bedroom drapes.

Mace lowered his binoculars and placed them on the table. "She's tucked in," he said.

Wylie was glaring at him. "So you don't think I'm a pro, huh?"

In point of fact, Mace thought he was a hopeless jackass. He'd formed that opinion five minutes after meeting him that afternoon. But he didn't know how long they'd be cooping, so he said, "Right now, I'm jet lagged, bone tired, and pissed off at the world in general. If Paulie Lacotta gives you a paycheck, you're a pro. Okay?"

Wylie nodded, but he still wasn't happy. "I'm pro enough to stay out of the joint," he said.

"Good point," Mace said. "Okay if I fade for a while?"

"Do what you want," Wylie said, raising the binoculars.

Mace was on the cot, just starting to drift when somebody knocked.

He sat up and watched Wylie, a gun in his hand, moving for the door. Mace started to call him off, then thought better of it. Maybe the kid would shoot somebody, then Mace could catch the next flight home.

"Me," Paulie Lacotta said from the hall.

Wylie fumbled the gun back into his belt rig and unlocked the door.

Lacotta brought the smell of booze and cigar smoke into the dark room with him. Even in double heels he was five inches shorter than Wylie's six-one or six-two, a stocky guy wrapped in an Italian suit worth a couple thou, cut to emphasize his shoulders and hide a thickening waist. His nut-brown face had once been slick-handsome, but it was starting to sag at the jowls.

It was nine years since Mace had last seen him.

Lacotta approached the cot, opening his arms. "C'mere, you son of a bitch," he said, grinning.

Mace got to his feet and accepted the inevitable bear hug.

When Lacotta was through physically bonding, he stepped back and gave Mace a head-to-toe. "You're lookin' good, amigo."

The tan. The hug. Now "amigo." Jesus. "You, too, Paulie," Mace said. "Really living la vida L.A., huh?"

Lacotta beamed proudly, as if Mace had paid him a high compliment. "You know it, dude." He turned to the windows. "My girl been behaving?" he asked.

"Been in all night," Wylie said, his eyes darting nervously to Mace as if he half-expected to be contradicted.

"Good." Lacotta removed a gray ostrich-hide wallet from his pocket and slipped a twenty from it. He held it out to Wylie. "Go get us some ice cream, willya?"

Wylie took the bill reluctantly. "What kind of ice cream?"

"Kind? Spumoni. That's what we used to eat, huh, Mace?"

Mace didn't think he'd ever eaten spumoni or any other ice cream with Lacotta. "That's the stuff," he said.

"Where do I find spumoni at midnight?" Wylie whined.

"They got a dozen Italian restaurants within shouting distance," Lacotta said. "Just make sure it's got plenty nuts and fruit."

Wylie seemed uncertain. He said, "I'll . . . be back."

Lacotta moved to the window. When he saw Wylie cross the courtyard, heading for the underground parking, he asked, "How's the kid doing?"

"Even at his tender age," Mace said, "I don't think I'd have worn that beach boy shirt on a shadow job. Snake's a nice touch."

Lacotta crossed the room to the cot and sat on it, looking disappointed. Without thinking about it, he adjusted the crease in his trousers. "I don't suppose you could call shit like that to his attention?"

"You're beautiful, Paulie," Mace said, lighting a cigarette. "Not only do you bring me in cold and saddle me with a green punk, now you want me to give him lessons."

"The kid's a legacy. His old man was Leo Giruso."

"Leo, huh? Like father, like son. Where'd he get the name Wylie?"

"I dunno. Read it in a book, maybe?"

Mace rolled his eyes.

"Okay, so you don't like the kid," Lacotta said.

"It's not just him. I don't like this whole setup."

"Hey," Lacotta said with a little heat behind it, "you did me a good thing a while ago, but I figure I kinda made up for it. Your old man kept his ranch in Montana, right?"

Mace nodded.

"And didn't I put some dough aside for you every year you were away?"

"That you did."

"So now I ask you for an assist and you bust my balls?"

Mace moved to the window and frowned out at the night. "Who is this Lowell woman anyway?"

"Since when you start asking questions like that?"

"Since I started sitting around empty apartments, peeping in windows like some goddamn bathroom idiot."

Lacotta got to his feet. "Yeah, well, like Bobby D. used to say, we all gotta serve somebody." He headed for the door.

"Hold on," Mace called.

Lacotta paused and turned to face him, scowling. "Angie and me . . . it's personal, okay? I just want to know what she's up to. Can you handle that?"

"What are you expecting her to do?" Mace asked.

Lacotta winked. Not much of an answer. "You and the kid enjoy the ice cream," he said, heading out.

"**W**here's Mr. Lacotta?" Wylie asked.

"He got tired of waiting," Mace said, slipping into his jacket.

"I had to go all the way to fucking Westwood," Wylie whined. "And it's melting."

"Stick it in the freezer, then. And make sure to keep checking the Lowell window till I get back."

"Where the hell *you* going?"

"Out. Get you anything?" Mace smiled. "Cookies to go with that ice cream?"

Mace parked his rental in a lot behind the Happy Burger on Sunset. He moved with purpose down the Strip, maneuvering around the late-night dawdlers—GenXers with nothing better to do, hookers, pimps, members of the glitterati who'd dined unfashionably late, tourists looking slightly lost and anxious. He counted himself among the latter.

His quarry was sitting alone at a table in front of a restaurant that was called Charley-O's. When Mace had lived in L.A., it had been the Elegant Eggplant. Now there was nothing elegant about it. Certainly not the gaunt senior citizen sipping coffee and keeping his eyes on the passing parade. In the old days, he'd called attention to his remarkable similarity to the sixteenth president of the U.S. by wearing a stovepipe hat and morning dress. He'd conformed to the informality of the times. Mace found it vaguely disconcerting to see a graying Abraham Lincoln in sandals, jogging shorts, and a T-shirt that read "There's a party in my pants."

"Hello, Abe," Mace said, taking an empty chair. "You're looking breezy."

"Mace." The bony, chin-whiskered face broke into a smile. "Welcome back to the Big Enchilada. What can I do to celebrate? Got a sweet sixteener, tender as a mouse's ear."

"Thanks, but what I need is information," Mace said. "I've been out of the loop awhile."

"Heard you went to live on a ranch after you left Pel. For a city boy that could be like prison."

"Not really," Mace said.

"I guess not. How can I help?"

"You ever hear the name Angela Lowell? Midtwenties. Brunette."

"Tits?" Abe asked.

The question annoyed Mace but he managed to reply, "Two, as I recall."

Abe furrowed his brow and stared at his coffee for a few beats. Then he unfurrowed and shook his head. "No bells ring. Want me to dig a little?"

"Yeah," Mace said. "Do I check in by phoning this place?"

Abe reeled off a seven-number combination. "My cell phone."

"Your cell phone," Mace repeated, dumbly.

Abe's long fingers reached into the pocket of his party-loving pants and retrieved a lime-colored cellular phone. "You *have* been out of the loop."

"I'm a fast learner," Mace said, and stood to go. "You used to be a man who could keep a secret. We haven't had this conversation, okay?"

"What conversation?" the gaunt man asked.

Mace was moving his key toward the door lock when he heard grunting and moaning inside the apartment. He opened up, the hall light falling on Wylie and a plump woman banging away on the cot.

The woman's bloodshot eyes popped open and saw him. She didn't say a word, but she stopped writhing under the skinny boy and just lay there. Wylie didn't seem to notice her sudden passivity. More likely, he just didn't care.

Temporarily ignoring them, Mace moved to the window. The Lowell apartment looked unchanged. He relaxed, turned, and noticed Wylie's holstered gun resting beside his pants on the carpet.

The woman watched him fearfully and silently as he freed the gun and pointed it at the back of Wylie's bouncing head. She still said nothing. Mace wondered if she were a mute.

Wylie's snake tattoo stretched from his neck down his back,

curving at his waist and disappearing toward his lower stomach. Mace pressed the gun to a spot just above the snake's tongue and below Wylie's left ear and said, "Bang, you're dead."

Wylie made a noise like "Gah" and pushed in on the woman.

"Feeling better?" Mace crooned. He grabbed Wylie's left ear and gave it a nasty twist. The young man yelled as Mace led him by the ear off the woman.

"Lemme go, you fuckhead."

Mace did let him go, pushing him onto the foot of the bed. He stuck the gun behind his belt and said to the naked woman, "Out."

"But I . . ." she began, not a mute after all.

"But nothing." He bent down and gathered her discarded clothes and six-inch pumps from the carpet. Gripping her by a fleshy arm, he yanked her from the cot.

"Hey. Wait a goddamn min—"

He dragged her to the open doorway. She tried to kick and bite as he pushed her into the hall. He threw her clothes and shoes after her and slammed the door on her curses.

Wylie was sitting on the cot rubbing his ear. "You're a real asshole," he grumbled.

"And you're a real pro," Mace said scornfully. "Yes you are."

The plump hooker began pounding on the door.

Mace picked up Wylie's pants and found his wallet. "How much you owe her?"

"Thirty."

There were two fifties and several twenties in the wallet. Mace took one of the fifties, opened the door, and threw the bill at the woman. "Keep the change," he said, and slammed the door again.

It shut her up.

Mace sat down at the table by the windows and stared at Wylie, who was pulling up his rumpled khakis. "I thought you was out gettin' *your* ashes hauled," Wylie said. Then his pout dissolved. "You gonna tell Mr. Lacotta?"

"What's the percentage in that?" Mace answered.

Wylie picked up his shirt and slipped into it on his way to a kitchenette counter where a bottle of Jim Beam rested next to a set of tumblers. He cracked the bottle.

"Do one for me," Mace said.

Wylie put a couple of inches into two tumblers. He walked to the table and sat, shoving one of the tumblers toward Mace. Mace shot his. The kid followed suit. "Mr. Lacotta says there's a future for me in the corporation."

Mace said nothing. He raised his empty glass. Wylie crossed the room, got the bottle, and brought it back to the table. He splashed a couple more inches of bourbon into their glasses.

"How long you been working for Paulie?" Mace asked.

"Six months."

"Like it?"

"Got me a title: Security Consultant. My own office. Check every week. Free time to screw off. Okay, so I gotta let my hair grow out and maybe burn off my tats. Still a good deal."

"What kinda jobs he been givin' you lately?"

Wylie thought about it. "Surveillance, mainly. Before Angela, I was keepin' tabs on this guy, Tiny Daniels. Me and another guy, we followed him for most of last month, day and night. We went all the way across the state and back again by friggin' car. This Daniels is scared to fly."

"Maybe he's too fat to fit in the seats," Mace said.

"You know Tiny?"

"He didn't used to be that hard to keep in your sights. He weighed in at three hundred pounds and he was in the office between mine and Paulie's."

"No shit? The fat man worked for the corporation? Times sure as hell have changed."

"You don't have to tell me," Mace said. "What's Tiny been up to?"

"Not all that much. Had a meeting at this place just outside Frisco. Commingore Inc."

"They make weapons," Mace said.

"Yeah, I know. Lissen, Mace, about the hooker. If you tole Mr. Lacotta—"

"Don't worry about it." Mace poured himself another shot. "Get some sleep. We'll switch at four."

Wylie nodded and moved to the bed. He sat on it, winced, and pulled a used rubber from under his thigh.

Mace leaned forward. "Oh, lemme get rid of that for you."

Wylie held out the contraceptive.

Mace turned away from him, chuckling at the kid's gullibility.

Angela Lowell is asleep. The thick art book she'd been reading lies nearly submerged in the bed's thick down duvet.

Mace stands beside the bed, watching her. She is only partially covered by the duvet. In peaceful sleep, she is achingly beautiful. Her right arm is raised high on the pillow. Her full right breast has freed itself from the ribboned neckline of her sheer gown.

Something—an intake of breath, the shifting of air—causes her to stir. She opens her eyes. Sees Mace . . . and smiles.

He bends over her. Her arms come up to meet him. Playfully, she pulls him down.

The mere touching of their lips ignites her. Her fingers tighten on his back. She breathes heavily, pressing her body against his. Her tongue, hard and hot and pointy-tipped, slips into his mouth. She begins tearing the clothes from his body. First his shirt, then his belted slacks. He tries to help but, almost angrily, she insists on doing the job herself.

He lies back on the bed as she undresses him. She smiles at his erection, touches it almost playfully, then caresses it.

He moans. It's been so long.

Someone calls his name.

"No," Angela shouts. "Not enough time."

In a frenzy, she straddles Mace, moving down his body eagerly until her body takes him in. He arches his back, feels the velvety softness yield—

"Mace," Wylie hissed near his ear. "Gotta get up."

Mace awoke from the dream to a room filled with glaring sunlight. Wylie whispered, "Mr. Lacotta just crossed the courtyard."

Mace swung his bare feet around to the floor. He was still groggy from the dream. "What time is it?"

"Almost eleven," Wylie said. There was a knock at the door.

"Why didn't you wake me sooner?"

"No reason to. She ain't goin' nowhere," Wylie said, heading for the door.

Lacotta entered, giving Wylie a manly punch on the arm. "How's the boy?"

"Fine, Mr. Lacotta."

Lacotta's grin faded at the sight of Mace sitting on the edge of the cot in his underwear. "You keepin' banker's hours, Mace?"

"Mace had the night watch, Mr. Lacotta. Just hit the sheets a couple hours ago."

"What's on your mind, Paulie?" Mace asked. "Your ice cream's in the—"

"Slip some clothes on. We'll go for a walk."

"Now this is beauty," Lacotta said as he and Mace strolled through Griffith Park. It was green and tranquil, bathed in sunlight. "Not like your friggin' Montana. Too cold in the winter, too hot in summer. I don't know how you can live there."

"Maybe I like extremes," Mace said.

A softball landed at Lacotta's feet. He picked it up, tossed it back into the game. Immediately, he began rubbing his shoulder. "What do you do with yourself back there?" he asked.

"Hunt. Fish. Read. Watch the news, mainly the weather."

"No jobs?" Lacotta asked.

"Not the way you mean it."

"Your time at Pel Bay, guys go bad in there."

"Guys go bad out here in your sunshine," Mace said, annoyed. "What's on your mind?"

"You're different. Maybe it was stir. Maybe playing hermit on your old man's ranch."

"I'm older," Mace said.

"Old age turned you curious, huh?"

"I get it. You've been talking to Abe. Honest Abe."

"You put my business out on the street," Lacotta said.

"If you'd tell me what the hell I'm supposed to be doing, maybe I wouldn't have to."

Lacotta nodded. "Yeah, maybe." He gestured toward an empty park bench. When they were seated, looking out at the softball game, he said, "I told you it was personal between me and Angie. Only jealousy isn't the big problem. Not that I'm Joe Don't Care. Remember the Irish broad who worked at the Raincheck?"

"Let's take it one romance at a time."

"Yeah, right. Well, Angie and me, we're going great until right around when the trouble started."

"You want me to ask what trouble?" Mace said. "Okay, I asked."

"I had this deal going. And it got cocked up. Right around then, Angie suddenly went unavailable on me and I went a little nuts, like I do. I even asked her to mar . . . Hell, I tried everything. She just wasn't interested. Then I went back to being my usual cynical rat-bastard self. I started thinking maybe the two things are tied in."

Mace frowned. "Tied in how?"

"You remember Tiny Daniels?"

"Hard to forget."

"The fat fuck was working for us, but he was cutting all these deals on the side. With the Russkies. The Chicanos. The gooks, even. Montdrago was madder'n hell, but he just let Tiny walk away."

"He suddenly get religion?" Mace wondered.

"Yeah, sure. The big man gets religion when the Holy Ghost gets his own talk show. Tiny tells Montdrago he's got some heavy insurance in place, can put him away. Could be a bluff, but it keeps the fat man breathing."

"And all this relates to Angela Lowell how?"

Lacotta squirmed on the rough bench. "I get word Angie's been keeping company with Tiny. So you see my position?"

"No," Mace said.

"I got to know: Did she have anything to do with the fuckup on the deal I had going? Has Tiny taken over the project? I got to know the answers before Montdrago starts asking me the questions. That's why I need you, Mace. Somebody outside the organization. A friend I can trust."

"How much does Wylie know?"

"Bupkis," Lacotta said. "Even if he does get the drift of things, he's still my guy. He won't fuck me over with Montdrago."

Feeling suddenly restless, Mace got up from the bench. Reluctantly, Lacotta followed behind him. "And if Angela *is* in bed with the fat man?" Mace asked. "You kill her?"

"No way," Lacotta said. "You tell me she's sold out to Tiny, then I'll know for sure what a fucking doof I've been. Then maybe I can get her out of my mind."

It didn't make sense to Mace. There was still more to the story. He was about to press when a tall African-American male, apparently one of the homeless army, staggered toward them.

"You gen'mens got a dolla' y' can spare?" he asked.

Lacotta gave the man a hard, get-the-fuck-away glare. He saw Mace reaching into his pocket and said, "Don't do that."

Mace got out his wallet and removed a dollar. He handed it to the black man who accepted it with a grin. He held the bill out to Lacotta. "Here. This fo' you."

"I don't want your fucking money," Lacotta said testily.

"It's fo' you. A dolla' to blow me."

"What?" Lacotta couldn't believe his ears.

"Man say you a dolla' blow job."

Furious, Lacotta grabbed the black man's coat. "What man?" he yelled.

The black man grinned. His left hand emerged from his coat pocket carrying a small pistol that he shoved into Lacotta's midsection. "The fat man. He say, 'Bye-bye, asshole.' "

With amazing speed, Mace's right foot connected with the pistol, knocking it aside just as it exploded.

Lacotta yelled and fell back, losing his grip on the black man.

Mace grabbed the gun. The black man tried to knee him in the groin, but Mace twisted his body and took the knee on his thigh. With his free hand, he punched the black man once in the stomach, once in the face.

The black man let go of the gun as he bent to the ground. Mace kicked him in the head. Once. Twice. It was all he could think about.

He felt somebody grab his arm. He swung around, fist cocked for the punch, and saw it was Lacotta. Even then, he almost took the swing.

Lacotta backed away. "Let's get outta here," he said.

Mace blinked.

The park was in silence. The ballplayers, the dog walkers, the strollers were all frozen, staring at them. The only thing in motion in the whole park was the black man getting to his feet and running away.

Cautiously, Lacotta took the gun from Mace's hand and slipped it into his pocket. He led Mace toward the parked car.

Mace got in, still dazed.

As they drove away, Mace asked, "You hurt?"

"Naw, maybe some burns," Lacotta said. He smiled, then started laughing. Soon he was laughing so hard tears appeared at the corner of his eyes. "I told you not to give that fuck the dollar, didn't I?" he said between bursts of nervous laughter.

*   *   *

Wylie was gone when Mace let himself into their room. He'd seen Angela Lowell's car in the parking area, but, as cavalier as Wylie was, he couldn't believe the punk would have deserted his post for no reason. He sat down and watched the Lowell apartment for a few minutes without seeing any sign of activity. Then he pecked out Angela's phone number.

When her answering machine clicked on, he hung up and went visiting. He used a pick to enter her apartment. He'd done the same thing the day before, just after he'd unpacked. He liked getting the feel of the place, experiencing the softness of the sofa, the scent of her bath soap, the way the light filtered through the bedroom curtains.

There were several framed pastels on the bedroom wall, signed with an *A*. Her work. A narrow street with book stalls. The statue of a lion. A stern-looking, elderly man wearing a high collar. Her father?

He investigated her medicine cabinet, casually browsed the pill bottles. None particularly interesting. Her two perfume bottles seemed almost untouched.

In the drawer of her bedside table he found an assortment of expensive contraceptive sheaths along with a spermicidal gel and a plastic case containing an IUD cap. There was also a vibrator for those lonely nights.

He made one more pass through the apartment and let himself out.

The rest of the day, he waited at his place, wondering where she'd led Wylie.

The phone woke him.

It was dark. He squinted at his watch. Nine-eighteen.

The voice on the other end was barely recognizable. "I . . . been shot. Tiny picked up the bitch . . . Followed 'em . . . Got jammed."

"Where are you, Wylie?"

"Point Dume." He coughed. "Twelve Oceanside Drive."

"I'll send an ambulance."

"No," Wylie shouted, and began coughing. "No. I'm okay . . . in the car. You come get me."

"On my way."

He pressed the tab to disconnect the call, wondering if he shouldn't just send the damned ambulance. The kid said he was okay. Maybe he wasn't as bad off as he sounded. Maybe a lot of things. He wished he had a gun. Worse came to worse, he figured he could use Wylie's.

The breeze off the Pacific was warm and briny as he turned off the Coast Highway onto Dume Drive. It had taken him nearly thirty minutes to get there. Wylie's car was parked on Oceanside, down the block from number twelve. Wylie wasn't in it.

The metal gate to number twelve was open a few inches.

Mace entered the grounds cautiously, not liking the creak of the gate. He moved down a stone walkway that cut through a Japanese garden to a modern beach house, all stone and metal and glass. As he approached the thick glass front door, a man stumbled toward the door on his way out.

He was short, stocky, and middle-aged. Mace had never seen him before. He was wearing black pants, shiny black shoes, and a white dinner shirt rapidly turning red at the collar. He tried to push the glass door open, but he hadn't the strength. His knees buckled and he sank to the flagstones.

Mace opened the door just as the man keeled over on his side. He'd been shot in the neck, a few inches below his sunken chin. No pulse. It was a near miracle that he'd made it to the door.

Mace patted him quickly, hoping to find a gun. No luck.

In the next room, the living room, he found two other dead men. The one staining the white rug was in his twenties, chiseled features, thin mustache. Also in dinner clothes. Shot twice in the chest. A gun was clutched in his left hand.

Mace had to break his index finger to pry the weapon free. He checked the clip. Two bullets left. He snapped the clip back into the gun and moved on to the other fatality.

It was Tiny Daniels, looking even fatter in death. He was seated on a massive leather chair, a broken wineglass near one of his patent-leather–shod feet. In his tux, he looked like a three-hundred-pound penguin. His eyes were open, giving his puffy face a look of astonishment.

There was a small hole in his black satin lapel. Mace touched his neck to see if there might be some pulse.

The fat man slumped forward, his upper weight tumbling him from the chair onto the carpet. Mace bent over the corpse to look at Tiny's face. Something glinted at the corner of the mouth.

Tiny's teeth were clamped on something. Mace worked a couple fingers between the teeth and pried out . . . a coin the size of a silver dollar. Some kind of specialty item. No writing. Just a man's face in bas-relief. He might have studied it longer, but a door slammed, followed by the sound of running footsteps.

Shoving the coin into his coat pocket, Mace raced through the cottage to the kitchen. The back door was open. It was the screen door that had slammed shut. As Mace went through it, its wooden frame splintered near his hand.

Ducking, he raised his gun. Too late. A tall figure, masculine he thought, slid over a cement wind wall separating the cottage from the sandy beach. Mace was poised to chase the figure when he heard a female voice call out, "What's happening down there?"

He moved back through the cottage to a stairwell and raced up to the floor above. "What's happening?" the voice asked again behind a closed door.

Mace didn't bother trying the door handle. He raised a foot, kicked in the door, and ran into the room, gun held high.

The room was dark. A wind off the water stirred gossamer

drapes. Angela Lowell was in a rumpled queen-size bed. The sheet
that had been covering her had fallen to her waist, revealing her
naked breasts. Caution forced Mace to look away to make sure
they were alone in the room.

That accomplished, he turned back to her. She regarded him
with no emotion showing on her lovely, placid face. "Carlos?" she
asked.

"No. Not Carlos."

"I see that now." She smiled at him. "I'm . . . awake." She slid
to the side of the bed and sat there facing him, completely naked.

"We have to leave here," Mace said. "Put on your clothes."

"What clothes?"

He picked up a black dress from the floor and a pair of white
silk panties. The panties were still warm from her body. He placed
them beside her on the bed.

"Put the clothes on now," he ordered.

"I don't think . . . I . . . ca . . ." She slumped back onto the
bed, eyes closed, breathing softly through an open mouth.

"Damn it," he grumbled and put the gun in his belt. He
jammed the panties in his pocket and began to struggle the dress
over her rubbery body.

He found her shoes and purse, but there were probably other
things of hers he was leaving behind. Fingerprints, if nothing else,
but that wouldn't matter if she was a frequent visitor to the cottage.

He hoisted her over his shoulder. She was a substantial, full-
bodied woman. By the time he got her to his car, he was breathing
like a porpoise. He dumped her onto the passenger seat and used
the safety belt to keep her upright. He tossed her shoes onto the
backseat and got behind the wheel.

Wylie's car was still parked in front. Still empty.

Mace drove away from it, humming a tune. He was surprised
to realize it was "Oh where, oh where has my little dog gone."

Heading back to the coast highway, the girl beside him began
to snore.

* * *

He called Lacotta from a gas station pay phone. "Tiny's out of the picture, permanently," he said. "If he wasn't just blowing smoke about having some life insurance, Montdrago had better call his lawyer or put on his running shoes."

Paulie began to squawk, cursing Tiny, then Angela, Mace, and finally himself. Mace listened for a while, trying to decide if it was an act. After five minutes he no longer cared. "Shut up for a goddamned minute," he shouted into the phone, and was half-surprised when Lacotta obeyed.

"I'm up to my chin in your bullshit," Mace said, watching the car parked just past the gas pumps. The girl's head was still angled forward, eyes closed. "Tell me what's been going on and where the girl fits in. Make it quick and simple."

There was silence on the other end for a couple seconds. Then Lacotta said, "There's this guy I know in Paris—ex-CIA. He came into possession of something very hot. He held this auction and—"

"What part of quick and simple don't you understand?"

"I'm trying to explain. This goddamned formula is gonna take us to a new generation of weapons. Smart bombs, shit. There are gonna be fucking *genius* bombs."

"Paulie," Mace said. "Get to the point in sixty seconds or I head straight to the airport."

"Calm down. Jesus. I'm the guy standing at the fucking precipice. I borrowed a shitpot of company loot to buy this goddamned formula. It was a lock. I'd already got a commitment from Commingore Industries that would net a very sweet profit."

"Only . . . ?" Mace said.

"Only this ex-CIA guy got cute. You know how they are. He baked the formula inside a coin that's made from the same shit the weapons are gonna be made of."

Mace saw Angela's head bob. She was too far away to hear

him, but he didn't want her waking up alone in a parked car. "I'm hanging up," he told Lacotta.

"Whoa, whoa. I used Angie to mule the coin back here. Somehow Tiny found out and intercepted it."

"Why use her?"

"She goes over there four, five times a year, picking up art for her clients. The customs people know her. She's legit. Handles paintings worth big money. Straight as they come."

"Except that she sold you out."

"I'm not sure she did. I sure as hell didn't tell her about the formula. I sent her over there supposedly to pick out some paintings for me. I told you the seller was cute. He was using a gallery for a front. He put the fucking coin in a crate with the art she bought for me. Only it never got to me. Tiny had the shipment hijacked."

Mace felt his pocket getting a little heavier. "I don't suppose the inventor can just strike another coin," he said.

"Well, that's the thing. We're talking exclusivity here."

"Meaning your cute ex-CIA guy made sure there'd be only one coin."

"I tried to tell him that a white coat who could come up with something this valuable might have a few more good ideas in his head, but by then the body was already cold."

"Okay, I get it," Mace said. "Tiny wound up with the coin and the girl. And you wound up waiting for the monthly audit with your finger up your ass."

"Something like that. What the fuck do I do?"

"I'll let you know," Mace said, and hung up.

Angela opened her eyes just as he got behind the wheel.

"Who the devil are you?" she demanded, slurring a little. "Do you work for Tiny?"

"Nobody works for Tiny anymore," Mace said, driving

through Santa Monica, heading east to Hollywood. "Not even Tiny."

"What do you mean? What am I doing in this car?"

"We're headed away from a bad situation. We left three dead men back there. Four if you count Tiny as two."

"My God," she said. "Did you . . . kill them?"

"No, ma'am. All I did was get you dressed and out of there before the cops dropped by."

She looked down at her dress.

He reached into his coat pocket and pulled out her panties. "These yours?"

She took them from him and, without hesitation, hiked up her skirt and slid them on.

"What drug were you on?" he asked.

"I . . . Demerol. I shouldn't drink with them, but sometimes I . . ." She decided not to finish the sentence.

"You didn't hear anything back at the house? Gunshots, shouts, anything?"

"No," she whispered. "Are you sure they're all dead? Tiny and Lew? And Carlos?"

"Tiny I'm sure of. I didn't recognize the other two gentlemen."

He moved the car around a creeper. From the corner of his eye he saw her turn to him. "Why . . . did you help me get away?"

"You didn't seem to be in any condition to be entertaining cops."

They drove in silence for a few minutes. Mace took the La Cienega exit and headed into Hollywood. "What was Tiny to you?" he asked. "Lover? Friend?"

"A friend, I guess. And a client. I . . . deal in art and sculpture. Tiny was a collector."

Mace reached into his pants pocket and got out the odd coin. "Recognize it?" he asked.

She shook her head no. "It looks like a commemorative coin."

He grinned. "Commemorating what, I wonder?"

"Could I . . . ?"

He handed it to her. She studied it.

"Recognize the guy?"

She shrugged. "Nope. Where did you get it?"

"A dark, damp place," he said, holding out his hand.

She placed the coin in his palm and he slipped it back into his pocket.

"Where do I drop you?" he asked.

The Hollywood Boulevard of his memory had not been a particularly lovely streetscape. Now it was incomparably garish and ugly. Dark, looming buildings. Vacant movie theaters. Tattoo parlors. Fast-food joints.

While they paused for a red light, Mace watched male and female hookers hungrily work their way through the stalled traffic, plying their rough trade. The light changed and he started forward, almost hitting a huge man on Rollerblades. He was wearing a pink Mohawk, matching pink short shorts, and tube top, gliding across the boulevard with a boom box under one weight-lifter arm and a pink poodle under the other.

"What do you think?" Mace asked, indicating the apparition. "Too much?"

"Pink is always in style," she said.

The apartment complex was on a side street several blocks off of the boulevard. Pretending he'd never laid eyes on it before, Mace aimed the car into the circular drive and parked by the front doors.

"What now?" Angela said.

"You go inside and get on with your life," he told her. "The police may visit, sooner or later."

"What do I tell them?"

"The truth. You've visited Tiny's often but you weren't anywhere near there tonight."

Her fingers touched the door handle, but she seemed reluctant to leave. "I'd feel more comfortable if you came in. Just for a little while."

"Sure," he said.

They'd barely entered her apartment when she excused herself. He poked around the living room for a while. When she emerged from the bathroom wrapped in a white floor-length robe, he was at the portable bar, fixing himself a gin and tonic. "I'd like one of those, too," she said, leaving him again to enter her bedroom.

When he'd finished building the drinks, he called her name. She didn't answer.

He crossed the carpet to her bedroom.

She was lying in bed, covered by a sheet but obviously naked. Eyes closed. He was amused by how close the situation was to his dream. The only differences were that he was carrying two gin and tonics. And she wasn't asleep.

He placed the glasses on the night table next to the bed. He noticed that one of her pastels was missing from the wall. No surprise. Probably in the closet.

He stared down at her.

Her lips twitched. Then she grinned and opened her eyes. "I'm pretending to be Sleeping Beauty."

"I'm no Prince Charming," he said, and yanked the sheet away.

She grabbed his belt and the top of his slacks and drew him closer. "Charm isn't all it's cracked up to be."

She pulled him down onto the bed. It required very little strength on her part. She began undressing him, not frantically like in the dream, but slowly, sensuously.

He was perfectly content to let her do most of the work until his clothes were off, then he made his contribution. Tongue. Fingers. Exploring her amazing body.

Finally, with a moan, she pulled away and opened the drawer to her night table, extracting a contraceptive sheath. She had a lovely method of lubricating him.

He repaid the compliment.

Then they made love.

"The ice has melted," she said, sampling her drink an hour or so later. "I'll fix some new ones."

She returned shortly with two fresh g & t's. She held one out to him and placed the other on the table. "Have to freshen up," she said. "Be with you in a minute."

It was more like fifteen.

She'd brushed her hair and applied new lipstick. She was wearing a simple skirt and blouse. She looked great. Even better when she smiled. "Thirsty man, huh?" she said, indicating his nearly empty glass.

Mace nodded, but seemed to be having trouble moving his head. Trouble speaking, too. "I . . . I . . . ."

She put one knee on the bed and reached over him to grab the glass before it slipped from his fingers. She paused to kiss him, pushing her tongue past his lifeless lips. It was a kiss more exploratory than passionate. She backed away as he struggled and failed to raise an arm to hold her.

"Relax," she told him. "The paralysis isn't permanent. In an hour or so you'll be good as new, assuming you live that long. Probably not."

He watched her pick up his pants and root through the pockets until she found the coin. She carried it to the light. "We looked all over Tiny's for this. You walk in and five minutes later, it's in your pocket. Well, you're supposed to be good." She held up his empty glass. "But not that good."

Someone called her name from the living room.

"In here," she called back.

Wylie sauntered in. "He drank the shit, huh?"

Angela didn't bother replying.

Wylie moved to the bed, grinned down at Mace. "You can hear me, right, asshole?" He laughed. "Don't bother trying to answer,

Mister Pro-fessional." He turned to Angela. "That trank of yours is a beauty."

"Everything quiet at the house?"

"Well, yeah. So what's our plan now? We gonna have to take him all the way back there?"

Angela gave him a disgusted look. "What do you think?"

"I guess, if we want it to look like he pulled the trigger on Tiny."

"It would have been so much simpler if you'd just followed the plan," she said.

"You were the one said your fucking drug'd keep 'em all under for an hour. That little son-bitch—what's his name?"

"Lew," she said flatly.

"Yeah, Lew. He nearly did me while I was searching for the coin. Shot him in the fucking neck and he still didn't go down. Threw everything off. I wasn't set up for Mace when he showed."

"All you had to do was hold your ground and take him out," she said. "You panicked and ran out to hide in the dunes. Leaving me to improvise."

Anger showed briefly on Wylie's face. His lip curling, he said, "Least it gave you a chance to ride his hobby horse."

"Very poetic," she said. "You going to be able to carry him downstairs if he's dead weight?"

"He a better fuck than me?"

She gave him a look of contempt. "What's that got to do with anything?"

"Was he better?"

"We're poised on the brink of collecting more money than either of us can spend in a lifetime of vulgar extravagance. All we have to do is set up this fool. He and Paulie will pay the price for Tiny and we can walk away without ever having to look back. And you want to know if he was better in bed? Well, sonny, as far as I'm concerned, all you boys are in second place."

"You sayin' you're a dyke?"

She took a step toward him until she was in his face. Through clenched teeth, she said, "What I am is no concern of yours, snake boy. Now I ask you again: Can you carry him to the car or do we have to run the risk of taking him there at gunpoint?"

"I can fucking carry him," Wylie said, drawing the gun from his belt.

"That's Carlos's, right? It's got to look like Carlos shot him before he died."

"I know the goddamned plan," Wylie said.

"Use a pillow to muffle the sound."

"Yeah, yeah." Wylie reached past Mace for the pillow. Suddenly, Mace's right hand shot up and grabbed Wylie by the throat. His left twisted the gun free, not caring much either way if any fingers came with it.

Wylie yelled and Mace smashed the gun against the side of his head. As Wylie fell forward, Mace drove an elbow into the back of his head then leapt from the bed. He raced through the apartment, catching Angela at the front door, struggling with a lock.

"Too late," he said.

Her body slumped and she turned. "The stupid . . . he put on the chain lock."

"Just being cautious," Mace said.

"You didn't drink any of the gin?"

He shook his head. "Your improvising at Tiny's had some rough spots."

"I thought I did pretty well, considering."

"What was the plan? Wylie cleans house, shoots me, and you wait for the cops so you can give them an eyewitness account of my murder spree?"

She shrugged. "We weren't planning on killing anybody. We thought Tiny would give up the coin. But the fat bastard kept his mouth shut."

"That he did," Mace said.

"So, of course, the cool-headed Mr. Wylie had to shoot him.

That's when he decided to set you up. He called you and we started searching the place. We didn't find the coin and one of Tiny's bodyguards woke up sooner than expected. It was a mess. But I thought I put on a pretty good show for you."

"Your panties were still warm," Mace told her.

It took her a second or two to realize what he was saying. "I should have left 'em on," she said. "It would have been okay, me stoned in bed with my panties on. I just thought it'd make a more interesting distraction."

"I was distracted all right," Mace said. "But I was also suspicious."

"Why?"

"I've been in this apartment before. You had a drawing hanging in your bedroom. It's the same guy who's on the coin. You design it?"

"No. I was told whose portrait would be embossed on it, so I looked him up. Did a sketch, just for my own amusement."

"Who's the old bird, anyway?"

"Count Basil Zaharoff," she said. "He was a liar, a cheat, a schemer. Supplied weapons to both sides in the Boer War, the Balkan conflicts, and World War One and wound up one of the wealthiest men in Europe. They called him the Merchant of Death."

"Born before his time," Mace said. "Just think of the fun the two of you could be having today."

"Just think of the fun the two of us could be having." She moved toward him.

"You never give up, do you?"

She licked her lips and ran her right hand up her side, fondling her breast. "I didn't think we were quite finished," she said. The hand went to the top button of her blouse, worked it free, and drifted to the next.

She was something, all right. But her eyes shifted for just the fraction of a second and that was enough.

He took a fast sideways step and the heavy metal sculpture Wylie swung made an arc through empty air and dug a chunk out of the plaster wall. Mace smashed the gun butt against Wylie's skull. The tattooed punk went down, but not all the way. He started to straighten and Mace hit him again, sending him to the carpet.

Angela headed for the door. "You won't make it," Mace warned.

She froze.

Somehow Wylie got to his feet.

"Boy, you're too stupid to live," Mace said, and drove the heel of his hand into Wylie's nose, cracking the bone and sending it up into his brain. Wylie's eyes rolled up in his head and blood spurted down over his lips and chin. He fell backward onto the carpet and stayed there.

Angela stared down at the lifeless man. "You . . . killed him," she said with a hint of wonder.

"It's what I'm good at," Mace said, lifting a cushion from the sofa. He pressed the muzzle of the gun into it and shot her twice in the general vicinity of her heart, assuming she had one.

"Well, that's that," Lacotta said to Mace, snapping his cellular shut and slipping it into his pocket. They were in a nearly deserted departure lounge at LAX.

Mace glanced at his watch. His flight was forty minutes late, which meant he was stuck with Lacotta for a while. "Your guys went over her room, right?" he asked. "I doubt they'll bother to dust it, but still . . ."

"They did a steam clean. You're clear." Lacotta smiled. "We're all clear. That was a beauty idea, putting Tiny and the other two guys on Angie's bill."

"It's what she and Wylie had in mind for me."

"This way, it looks like a lovers' quarrel, her going psycho and being taken down by one of the fat man's bodyguards before he faded. No connection whatsoever to the corporation."

"What are you going to do about the money you blew on the formula?"

"I think I'm gonna get lucky on that. When Tiny's 'insurance' surfaces, Montdrago's gonna have other things on his mind, like how he'll look wearing orange."

"Maybe Tiny was bluffing about the 'insurance,' " Mace said. When Lacotta's smile went sharklike, he added, "Oh, I get it. You'll make sure something surfaces."

"Gotta keep one step ahead," Lacotta said. "That's why I want you to move back here."

Mace shook his head. "That's not going to happen," he said.

"It'd be like the old days, amigo. You and me. Only now, we'll be in charge of things. Hell, I bet we could even find out what happened to the fucking formula."

"You'll do okay without me," Mace said. "And the world will surely be better off without its genius bombs."

He stood up.

"Where you going?" Lacotta asked. "Your plane's not in yet."

"Getting us a couple of soft drinks from that machine," Mace said. "Got some coins in my pocket I'd like to get rid of."

Trophy Wife

JEFF GELB

"You want a lapdance, sweetie?"

I looked up from my soft drink, scanning the young dancer's bikini-clad body from bottom to top, and liked what I saw: muscular calves, smooth thighs, curvy butt. Belly button ring, flat stomach, and thankfully natural breasts, not those bulbous grapefruits that most dancers thought men wanted to see. And the face of an angel, not the usual weathered biker chick or gothic-rock look that most of the girls at Bare Essentials favored.

I grinned at Roy, who had brought me to the club. "Pardon me, pal," I said. "I have some business to attend to."

"Yeah, monkey business," he said.

"You mind?"

"Hey, it's the reason we came here. You're horny as hell because your wife's been out of town for, what, three weeks now, nursing her dad? What'd he have, a heart attack?"

I nodded. "And you're horny because your wife just won't put out."

"True," he admitted. "The Bitch."

I winced at his language. "Have another fight?"

"When don't we fight?"

The dancer grabbed my hand and pulled me away from my best friend. "I'm Brandi," she announced over the loud music, mostly '80s hair-band stuff that somehow didn't sound so dated in this smoky environment.

"Jay," I responded automatically, my heart already pounding in anticipation.

She shook my hand and then placed it on her breast for a quick squeeze. My dick immediately woke up. She giggled.

"See anything you like, Jay?"

"Everything," I said, and that was not a lie. She led me to a room containing about two dozen cubicle-type booths, with swinging doors providing a modicum of privacy. Only a person well over six feet could see what was going on inside those miniature rooms, and I suspect he'd catch an eyeful.

"You ever done a lapdance before, Jay?" she asked.

"Nope. My buddy recommended we try it."

"I think you're gonna like it." She winked. The room was barely bigger than the chair in its center, with just enough extra room for the dancer to straddle me once I'd sat down. Brandi took off her bikini top to reveal soft but perky breasts with gumdrop nipples, and the effect on my dick was immediate. She must have felt it strain against my pants as she squirmed into place, facing me and pushing a small tit into my mouth. I sucked away like a baby, more excited than I'd been in years. This was a beautiful young woman, not much more than a teenager, her soft hair tickling my face, her perfumed body touching me, her nipple growing distended in my mouth as I tugged at it. All this sex within seconds of meeting her was such an aphrodisiac that I seriously wondered whether I would pop my rocks right there.

Perhaps sensing that I was perilously close to climax, she pulled away just far enough so that my mouth wasn't glued to her nipple.

"So what do you do?" she asked, as her bottom half ground slowly against my pants.

"I sell computers." Another lie, though not a big one: I actually sold computer software for Roy's firm, one of the biggest in Silicon Valley.

"Hey, I'm looking for a laptop," Brandi enthused.

"Well," I said as I grabbed one of her pliable breasts and kneaded it, "looks like you found a lap and I found a top!"

We both laughed at my joke, and she made eye contact with me as she lowered a hand to my crotch and started rubbing at it.

"Wow," I panted. She winked as she undid my belt and grabbed at my dick, which was already dripping with precoital fluid.

"Ooo," she enthused. "You are horny, aren't you?"

"Yeah," I said with some embarrassment.

"Not much we can do about that . . . here," she said.

And then the song ended. She winked again, zipped me up, and disengaged from my lower torso. I rearranged myself so it wasn't immediately apparent that I had grown by six inches in the past three minutes, and handed her forty dollars. "That was great," I gasped.

"My pleasure," Brandi said as she put the two twenties in a tiny purse she carried. She patted my cheek. "You're really cute."

She walked away from me and I admired her perfect ass cheeks, swaying in rhythm to her pace.

I rejoined Roy at the small table in the noisy main room. As I sat down, he grimaced. "What?" I asked.

"Couldn't help but notice . . ." he started, pointing to my crotch.

I looked down and was mortified to see a dark spot where I had leaked through my cotton khakis. "Oh shit," I muttered.

"She was that good?"

"She was incredible. Just as the song ended, she was grabbing my dick!"

"Why didn't you do another song?"

"Well, I didn't want to cum right there, you know?"

"So let's take her someplace for a ménage à trois."

I laughed. "Your favorite French words."

"My only French words. So what do you say?"

I shook my head.

He was relentless. "All these sluts fuck the customers on the side. We'll just offer her two-fifty and I'll bet she'll do both of us. Hey, we've always talked about how cool it would be to have a three-way."

"Yeah, as long as you didn't grab my dick by mistake!"

"Listen, if she's as good as you say she is, I wouldn't mind getting some action either. I haven't gotten laid in six months."

"You ought to be seeing a marriage counselor by now—or a lawyer."

He bristled. "I don't need your advice. I get enough of that from the Bitch."

I threw up my hands in surrender. "Sorry."

"So what do you say?"

I regarded Roy for a moment. "You're serious?"

"As a heart attack."

"Well—I don't think two hundred and fifty dollars would cut it. And anyway, where would we go?"

"Your place—Beth is out of town."

"And Amy?"

"The Bitch? Fuck her. She's used to my not coming home after fights. Hell, I've practically got a tab at the local Sheraton."

I sighed. I wasn't sure whether Roy was playing one of his mind games or if he was serious. But the idea was . . . intriguing. "What if Brandi says no?"

Roy leaned into the table till he was inches from my face. "What do you use when you go fishing—bait or a hook?"

"What? I haven't been fishing since I was a kid."

"What did you use?"

I couldn't imagine what Roy was getting at. "A hook, I guess."

"And how many fish did you catch?"

I laughed. "Never caught a one. That's why I stopped fishing."

"Well, that was your problem. Try some bait." He looked up and around the club, spotting Brandi a few tables over. He got up, approached her, and spoke into her ear. I watched as Roy slipped a wad of cash into Brandi's bikini top. She rubbed at Roy's crotch and then turned to me and waved. In a moment, the two were arm in arm and headed back to our table. Roy winked at me conspiratorially.

"Brandi said she's very interested in your offer, Jay."

"My offer?" I said.

"You know—four hundred to do both of us? At your place?"

I bristled. "What?"

Roy kicked my shin. "She gets off in thirty minutes. I gave her directions."

I felt panic setting in, but Brandi leaned over and whispered in my ear, "You ever fuck a girl doggie-style, Jay? While she was giving head to your best friend?" She licked my earlobe and pulled away, grinning, knowing she'd cemented the deal.

"Well, then," Roy said, "we'll see you at Jay's in about an hour."

We were driving back to my place in Roy's Jaguar, the streets of San Jose wet with a sudden spring shower we'd missed while we were in the club.

"Slow down," I complained.

He turned to me and grinned like a kid in a candy shop. "You still mad at me?"

"Hell yes I am. You had no right to do that without talking to me first."

"Why, so you could say no?"

"Yeah. For starters, I don't fuck around on Beth."

"Oh really? What do you call what you were doing back in that club?"

"I didn't know she was gonna be that . . . forward with me."

"Don't bullshit me, Jay. You went there because your body had needs that weren't being met. It's strictly biological. It has nothing to do with Beth."

"What about Amy?"

"I told you, I don't give a shit about the Bitch. She married me for my money and that's all she cares about."

"And you?"

"I care about getting my best friend laid, that's all."

"Hey, don't be so altruistic. You're gonna get laid too."

"Damn straight I am!"

He took a rain-slicked corner on two wheels. I looked over at him. He drove cars the way he drove his company employees. It made him a successful businessman but not a well-liked boss. I had met Roy when I was trying to sell him on using our company's business software. He liked my style, hired me away from the competition, and somehow we'd clicked as friends. Maybe in his mind, I represented the guy he could have become had he not inherited his father's money. Maybe he pitied me. Sometimes I felt he did. Maybe even tonight.

"Slow the fuck down," I groused uselessly. "Anyway, how do you know she'll come? She probably just said yes to get us out of her hair."

"I know these sluts, Jay. I've fucked dozens of them. Hell, I ran a strip club for a while when I got out of college."

"And that four hundred dollars? I can't afford that."

"Who said anything about four hundred dollars?"

"You did, Roy."

"She'll fuck us both for two-fifty and she'll love it."

"What's the point? You've got the money. Four hundred dollars to you is like four dollars to me."

"I told you, I know these sluts. They're all the same. It's not about the money for them, it's about the power they feel when they hold your dick in their hands. The power of the pussy. They're fucking bitches, all of them."

"Well, I don't know . . ."

He put a hand on my shoulder. "When's your birthday?"

"What? Uh . . . November sixth."

Roy shook his head. "Nope. It's tonight."

I was still wrestling with the idea when we arrived at my home, a ranch-style place nestled on five acres far from the noise of the city. Beth and I had been so excited to find the house, thinking it was the perfect environment to start a family.

Roy fixed us drinks to calm our nerves, and Brandi arrived less than an hour later. Outside of the club, wearing blue jeans and a college sweatshirt, she looked like the beautiful campus coeds I had lusted after unsuccessfully for most of the four years I'd attended UC Santa Barbara. Then I'd met Beth in one of my computer classes, and had decided to set aside my *Playboy*-fueled dreams of finding the perfect fuck-bunny and settle for the more realistic goal of landing a good wife and future mother. The wife part had stuck, but we'd found out that there was something genetically missing in Beth that made the baby part impossible. We'd discussed adopting, but our hearts weren't in nurturing someone else's child. It cast a pall over our marriage that made the sex act much less enjoyable for both of us. It was just too painful a reminder of what we couldn't accomplish together. So I guess that's why I was more than ready, after ten such good but unexciting years of marriage, to go along with Roy's crazy early "birthday gift."

"You guys ready for action?" Brandi asked as she stood in the middle of my dining room, took off her sweatshirt, and bared her beautiful breasts. As if we needed a reminder of what we were about to buy. I heard a sharp intake of breath from Roy and realized he hadn't seen Brandi topless. It was really quite a sight.

He approached Brandi and gave her a drink. She tipped the glass to her lips and let the clear liquid drop on her tongue and then drip down till it formed rivulets on her breasts. Roy leaned forward and licked some of it off her nipples before she pushed him back.

"The money, honey," she purred. Roy took out his wallet and slapped a bunch of twenties down on the polished mahogany tabletop. "Ready, willing, and able," he growled.

I wondered whether she was going to count the bills and go ballistic, but she was too busy rubbing Roy's crotch. "You first, big boy?" She knew who was buttering her bread that night. I didn't mind, either. I was still getting used to the idea of what I was about to do, wrestling with my conscience and discovering I was losing the match.

Meanwhile, Roy and Brandi were already in a naked clinch, and he was motioning me to join them. They were both on the living room's soft carpet, which my wife and I had picked out together five years ago when I'd gotten a sales bonus. We'd never used the carpet in the manner it was being used now. Brandi was going down on Roy, her gorgeous naked butt raised high in the air, offering a delectable bull's-eye. Even the sight of Roy's naked body didn't faze me. I had to admit, I was also, as Roy put it, ready, willing, and able.

I slid off my clothes, slid on a condom, and slammed into that tempting target, reveling in her moan of ecstasy—whether real or faked didn't matter to me—and joined in the fun.

The next thing I remembered, I was rolling over on the soft mattress of our bed. My arm slapped cool flesh. I opened one eye and muttered, "Sorry about that," noticing how my words were slurring. "I must have had more of that liquor than I thought."

Next to me was Brandi's now familiar naked form, spooned away from me. I studied her curves, trying desperately to recall how we'd ended up in bed together, or what had happened before that. But my mind was blank. Why pay for sex when you don't even remember it afterward? Furthermore, I was nauseated. I couldn't believe that, for the first time since my college days, I might actually throw up from the effects of liquor. I silently vowed never to drink again and then, laughing nervously, I prodded one of Brandi's ass cheeks. She didn't move. I laughed uneasily and said, "You drank too much too, huh?" No response.

I sat up in the messy bed and willed my vision to focus. "Brandi?" I called out, loud enough to wake the dead. Or maybe not. I noticed a dark pool on her pillow and, heart pumping so hard I got an instant headache, I turned her face toward me. That's when I threw up.

"Oh God, oh God, oh God!" I screamed between barks of vomit. I jumped out of the bed, fluid and food still escaping my mouth, and ran into the bathroom where I finished my work over the toilet bowl.

"Roy! Roy!" I yelled as I struggled back to my shaky feet. *Where the fuck was Roy, and what the fuck had happened?*

I heard a noise behind me and for one terrifying moment I thought it would be Brandi, her head still bashed in, her eyeball still hanging out of its socket on some stringy substance. But it was Roy, fully clothed.

He offered me a towel. "Take it easy, Jay. Just take a few deep breaths."

"What the fuck happened in there?" I managed to say as I wrapped the towel around my waist.

"I'll explain later. Let's get you cleaned up and dressed."

"But how did she . . . ? Who . . . ?"

"Jay . . ." He was uncharacteristically quiet for a long moment. "What are you saying? You don't remember killing her?"

"I fucking didn't kill her!" My legs were shaking like leaves in a hurricane and I felt another urge to lose my lunch. But there was nothing left in my system, so I just stood there, holding a towel rack for balance, tears streaming down my cheeks. "I don't remember anything. . . ."

Roy took my arm. "Get dressed and we'll figure this out. We'll come up with a plan. We'll make this work."

I allowed him to lead me back to the bedroom, but I shielded my eyes from the thing on the bed that had been a living, breathing sexual being just hours earlier. Shakily, I put on a jogging outfit and we retreated to our den, which was originally going to be the baby's room, until we found out there would be no babies.

"I don't understand," I stammered. "Why can't I remember anything?"

"I'm afraid that's my fault," Roy said. "I spiked our drinks with some of that date rape drug, to loosen us all up. Guess you guys drank more of it than I did."

In the dim recesses of my memory, I recalled Roy handing me and Brandi drinks, but I couldn't remember him imbibing. "What the fuck, Roy! You should have told me."

Roy shrugged. "I just wanted you to have a good time, buddy. I knew you would pussy out on me otherwise."

"But I didn't kill her!"

Roy said nothing. His silence spoke volumes. Finally, ready to scream, I repeated, "I didn't kill her, Roy!"

Roy sighed. "It's okay, buddy, I understand. You've been upset with your wife since she told you that you could never have babies. Maybe, in your . . . state of mind . . . you were just doing to Brandi what you must have fantasized doing to your wife."

"That's bullshit, Roy! Maybe that's what you fantasize, but . . ." I shut up suddenly, a sick realization coming over me like the darkest of shadows. "You killed her," I whispered.

"What?"

"I said, you killed her, Roy. You're the one who hates your wife. You hate all women. You said it at the club—women are all bitches, you said."

He smirked. "I thought you couldn't remember anything, Jay. Now you choose to recall the things you can frame me with? Well no way, buddy boy. You killed her. I know because I saw you do it."

"What?" The news hit me like a body blow. I actually backed away from Roy till I hit the wall. "No, no I didn't."

"You did, Jay. I was sleeping in the living room and her screams woke me up. When I got to your bedroom, I saw you beating the shit out of her with the trophy."

"What trophy?"

Roy retreated into the bedroom for a moment and returned carrying a large metallic gold-plated trophy on a wooden base, wrapped in a towel. "Now do you remember?" he asked.

I shook my head. "No. I don't believe you."

"Jay, your fingerprints are probably all over it." He set it down on a desk between us.

"You must have put it in my hand after you killed her."

"Jay, I'm sorry you killed her but I promise I'll help you out. Just relax."

"You set me up, Roy. That's why you brought her here instead of the hotel."

"Bullshit. Your place was closer and I was drunk."

I looked around the room and suddenly thought of Beth. When was she due back in town? Today? Tomorrow? What would she return home to? A husband in jail for murder, a home and life ruined by the bludgeoning death of a stripper?

What was Roy saying? "I have the best lawyers in the city. I know they can help."

I shook my head and felt queasy again. "No, Roy, they won't be helping me because I didn't kill her. You did."

I noticed little beads of sweat building on Roy's forehead. "Jay, you've gotta stop that. I couldn't have killed her, I wasn't even awake when you . . . when she died."

"How do I know that, Roy? How can I believe you? You spiked the drinks."

"That was for your own good."

"I can't trust you, Roy. And now you want me to take the fall for your nasty little murder. You got off fucking her and then you probably got off again when you killed her."

Was it my imagination or was Roy the one who was shaking now, even as I started to feel calmer inside? I eyed the trophy.

He mumbled, "You don't know what you're saying, Jay." And suddenly he jumped to grab the trophy, but I had moved a millisecond earlier, grabbed it before he did, and slammed the fucker into his nose. I heard a sound like breaking twigs, and Roy's groan, and then I brought it down on his head, once, twice, and then I lost count.

I blinked, standing above Roy's slumped, still form, trying to catch my breath. *It was him or me, him or me, him or me.* It became my mantra until my heartbeat slowed its pace and my mind cleared.

I looked around the ruined den. Roy's blood and brains and flesh had turned the place into an abattoir.

I backed out of the room and looked into the bedroom. It didn't look much better than the den.

I walked back to the living room and sank into the soft cushions of our couch. I noticed I still had the gore-stained trophy in my hand. I wiped off the blood and guts so I could read the little plaque.

"To Jay—my best salesman and my best friend—Roy."

My best friend. Well, someone once said you never knew who your best friends were until you were in a bind. In the end, I figured, Roy was no friend at all.

I remembered getting a bonus when I got that trophy. The bed that Brandi had died in had been bought with that bonus money. Beth and I had picked it out. We had planned to make babies in that bed, me and Beth.

Beth. I got up, walked over to a wall calendar by the kitchen phone. I checked the dates and realized that Beth, my precious Beth, would be home later today.

She'll forgive me. Won't she?

She'll believe me. I'll explain everything and she'll believe me. Won't she?

I eyed the trophy. It was still bloody.

She has to believe me. . . .

I hefted the trophy in my hand. It almost slipped out of my grasp from all the gore.

Won't she?

I heard the familiar sound of a key in the front door. I looked down at the trophy. It felt weightless in my hands as I started to swing it, back and forth, back and forth.

Won't she?

Summer Fog

JOE GORES

Francis Romance trudged up the wide carpeted front stairway of the converted Victorian. It was a bright morning in Pacific Heights under San Francisco's retreating summer fog. A discreet three-by-five brass plaque beside the heavy hardwood front door identified it as the office of Caulfield Associates.

At the head of the stairs, Romance paused to catch his breath. He was a lean high-cheekboned man of about sixty-five who would have been handsome in his thirties, and had aged well. Eyebrows like hyphens emphasized fog-gray eyes set deep in a bony face. Silver glinted thickly in his black hair. His dark blue suit and tieless lighter blue shirt accentuated his leanness.

A chubby African-American woman in her midtwenties sat behind a reception desk just inside what had once been the Victorian's broad, homey living room. On her desk was a workstation and printer and fax, but no typewriter. She was the agency's primo Internet genius. Romance was still a typewriter guy. Three men, all under forty, were at other haphazardly scattered desks. Two were working on their computers, one was on the phone.

"Our lord and master got a hot one for you?" she asked.

Romance smiled down at her—he thought of her as a girl, not a woman, but that might just have been his age showing.

"You mean you're willing to believe there's maybe something the computers can't handle, Linda?"

"Romance," Linda said, crinkling up her huge brown melting eyes. "Computers can't handle Romance—with a capital *R*."

He grinned and rapped the knuckles of his scarred right hand twice on her desktop as he went by her into the room, the way a gambler knocks the blackjack table to show he is standing pat with the cards he has been dealt. The scarred knuckles were unnaturally bunched; the hand looked only marginally useful.

Linda's big soft brown eyes followed him toward the door in the rear of the room. None of the other operatives had looked up from his work since Romance had entered.

Romance pushed open the door to George Caulfield's private office—once the formal dining room—with stiffened fingers. Caulfield was tipped back in his swivel chair with one foot on the floor, the other hooked over the corner of his desk. Early thirties, dark hair cut short, dark eyes that snapped and crinkled and winked and didn't miss one damned thing. His wise-guy's face should have been lean and rodential, but it was round, with squirrel cheeks; a hustler on antidepressants.

Romance flopped down in the chair across the desk from him.

Caulfield said into the phone, "E-mail the subject's vitals to Linda, she'll get right at it." He listened, gave a silent shrug. "You want it by five, you got it by five." He hung up to look at Romance. "I left you a message to be here at nine A.M. It's nine-forty-five."

"Held up in traffic," said Romance.

"Don't give me that shit. You live two miles away."

"At your house, fucking your wife's brains out."

Caulfield's other foot joined the one already on the corner of his desk. He frowned almost sadly at the tips of his dull black five-hundred-dollar Mephistos. "She doesn't have any." He interrupted himself to ask, as if he really wanted to know, "Why do you still even bother with this detective shit, Fran?"

"I need the money until Social Security kicks in, then I'll be farting through silk." The corners of his wide mouth turned up slightly. "Here's one for you, Georgie: Why do you keep me on your list of available operatives?"

"You've walked down those mean streets, kiddo. The rest of us . . ." Caulfield gestured out toward the main office. "Can you imagine Ronnie or Jackson or Fonseca out there ever firing a gun? Linda, maybe, but . . ."

"And I work cheap. Per diem and expenses, off the books."

Caulfield abruptly took his feet off the desk and leaned forward to signify that fun and games were finished.

"This one is right up your alley, Fran. An honest-to-God tail job. Our client is Flush Pearson—"

"You know why they call him Flush?"

Caulfield was interested. "You hear stories, but—"

"When he was just starting out, he lost a felony case on appeal. That was when the Hall of Justice was still on Stockton across from Washington Square. His client was a tough Italian from North Beach. When he realized he'd have to do time he stuck Pearson's head in the men's room toilet and flushed. Twice."

Caulfield grinned with his eyes slightly narrowed. He'd figure out a way to use the story to his advantage, Romance knew.

"Flush has a client who wants a woman tailed, starting today." He opened a file folder on top of the desk and spun it around so it faced Romance. "Domestic, her husband's been seen around town with a blonde. But there may be money as well as sex involved. The client has lots of it, hubby none."

Without looking up from the slim file, Romance asked, "Flush's client got a name?"

"Not for us."

"The subject got a name?"

"Not for us."

Romance closed the folder, waggled it while getting to his feet. "If I see some guy getting into her pants, how do I tell if he's our errant hubby or not?"

"For Chrissake, Fran, what do you care? You've got her address there in the file, her description, the make and model and license number of her car, you pick her up at her apartment on Telegraph Hill at three P.M. What the fuck more do you need?"

"A raise," said Romance.

"A raise," muttered Caulfield at the closing door. "A fucking raise."

Romance picked up the unnamed subject at 3:04 P.M. when she came out of her apartment house on the first curve of Telegraph Hill Boulevard below Coit Tower, that tan phallic symbol of Lily Coit's supposed sexual congress with numerous volunteer firemen. Romance was parked on Lombard facing downhill. Any car getting down off Telegraph had to use Lombard.

The subject was driving an old red superbly maintained Ferrari SWB California Spyder convertible. They had stopped making them in 1963. The car shook him. So did his flash of the subject's profile as she went by: like the Ferrari, almost familiar, and momentarily disturbing. Her gleaming blond hair was long, shoulder-length, with the ends curled under.

It was an easy tail. He lay a block, block and a half back as she went down Lombard and then Columbus to Union, up and over Russian Hill and out past Van Ness Avenue to the little Union Street upscale shopping area in Cow Hollow.

When the Ferrari disappeared into the parking garage near the Metro Theatre, Romance dropped his eight-year-old Toyota into a loading zone half a block away. His commercial license plates and the magnetic signs on his doors (ACME ACCOUNTING—THIS VEHICLE CARRIES BOOKKEEPING RECORDS ONLY—NO CASH) let him use white-zone parking without getting ticketed.

The subject walked out of the garage seven minutes later. She wore a black leather coat and black leather jeans so tight the pockets were fakes. She had the body for it. He front-tailed her to the Vietnamese beauty salon a couple of doors down from Fillmore Street where she got her nails done. Romance boned up on antiques in a shop across the street.

At four-thirty the blonde had—aha!—a rendezvous. Except it was with a diminutive Chinese woman about her own age at l'Entrecote de Paris. The glass-enclosed dining area that fronted Union Street was bathed in late-afternoon sunlight. Romance got a table close enough to overhear some of the gossip from the financial district office where the China doll still worked. He knew there was no danger of being spotted by the subject as long as there was no eye contact. Shadowing was simple if you followed its surprisingly few rules.

Girl talk was no longer about clothes, work, movies, boyfriends. *Sex in the City* had changed all that.

The Chinese girl said, "All you ever meet at the gym is narcissists who pump iron." She took a sip of wine, gave a little burbling laugh. "At Marge's bachelorette party last night—you remember Marge—we started wondering who has the longest one in the office."

"Eddie the long thin computer nerd," promptly said the blonde. "I'd bet twelve inches at least."

"Because he's tall and—"

"Because he's got that long nose." She paused, said, "This girl sits on Pinocchio's face and says, 'Lie to me, lie to me.'"

They both went off into gales of not-so-girlish laughter. It was nearly seven P.M. when they hugged on the Union Street sidewalk to go their separate ways.

Looked like a bust, for today anyway. Union Street to shop, meet a girlfriend for a late lunch—all very straightforward. But then, suddenly, the blonde started getting tricky. Back in her Ferrari, she went out to Union's dead end, turned down Lyon to enter the

Presidio at the Lombard Street gate. Then she played hide-and-seek in the countless little roads through the Presidio's countless wooded acres. Thirty minutes later obscure little Kobbe Avenue dropped her down on Lincoln Boulevard where it skirted the cliffs fronting the open Pacific.

Even then she wasn't satisfied. She left the Presidio on El Camino Del Mar, dove into the rich, twisty, confusing streets of exclusive SeaCliff, eventually slipped into Lincoln Park, past the Palace of the Legion of Honor, finally emerged into the Richmond District's gridded streets at Thirty-fourth Avenue. Right on Clement to Seal Rock, left into Alta Mar, Point Lobos for half a block, a left into Forty-seventh. Then into Balboa, tipping over the edge of the city to slide down to Ocean Beach and into the fog starting to flow landward in earnest.

Fran, well back behind her all the way, was thinking that she sure as hell didn't want anyone to know where she was going.

Ocean Beach Apartments, a great tumbled monolith of brown stucco apartments heaped together cubistically to front the Pacific from across the Great Highway, where the Playland at the Beach amusement park had once been? Maybe, but she drove past the entrance in the Burham Building at 825 La Playa.

A block beyond, where La Playa dead-ended at Golden Gate Park, she turned right into Fulton, then right into the Great Highway. Checking out the neighborhood for possible watchers?

The red Ferrari took an angle right into the outdoors parking lot for the Ocean Beach Apartments' tradesmen and visitors, not tenants. They had underground parking. When Romance drove in a minute later, he saw the car tucked into the left front corner of the lot, in the least-conspicuous slot.

The blonde was walking quickly, not looking back, around the side of the apartment block. He drove through the lot and turned up Balboa to glimpse her going into an inconspicuous side entrance beyond a decorative brick turnaround.

Romance circled the complex, reentered the lot. Her car was

where she had left it. He parked his Toyota on the ocean side facing the beach, his side mirror adjusted so he could see the Ferrari with just a movement of his eyes.

A truck going by on the darkening Great Highway blew its airhorn and a flock of brown and white gulls flew up from the beach, then settled down again. From here he could see only the old crumbling seawall with its rebar showing where the concrete had fallen away. Beyond the seawall the Pacific stretched to the darkening horizon. Glistening waves piled in out of the almost-set sun.

A girl went by on her bicycle, black hair streaming in the wind, her handbag hanging down her back with its strap around her neck. Through his open window he could hear the waves pounding the now unpopulated beach. In the deepening darkness he could just read a sign left over from the Playland at the Beach days:

WARNING—RIP CURRENTS
PEOPLE SWIMMING AND WADING
HAVE DROWNED HERE

Memories crowding in on him. In 1966, he had been running the Playland shooting gallery and living in the three-room apartment behind the gallery. Some asshole had gut-shot him when he was serving a routine summons and complaint, the doc had told him to get a sedentary job for a few months. He'd ended up here.

The fog was sweeping in from the Pacific in earnest now, sucking the warmth from his old bones. He rolled up his window, checked his rearview for the red car.

Romance, waiting for some errant blonde as he'd done so many times before. He chuckled, then sobered. This blonde drove a red 1963 Ferrari Spyder just like the one that another blonde had driven, back then. . . . He flexed his scarred right hand. This one even looked like that one, a lot. But this was a third of a century later, for Chrissake.

Playland . . . 1966 . . .

* * *

On the counter across the front of the shooting gallery were eight rifles and two long-nosed pistols and an old-fashioned scrolled-silver cash register. The body of the gallery was full of scummy green water; behind it rows of tiny white rabbits, deer, ducks, and yellow squares moved on conveyor belts across a woodland scene badly painted on canvas in primary colors.

Romance was a cadaverous man of about thirty, wearing a garish aloha shirt outside his black flannel slacks. He picked up one of the pistols from the counter, fired carelessly yet so quickly that the *ting ting ting ting* of the four pellets knocking over little moving tin figures was almost one continuous sound.

He put the pistol down, leaned his elbows on the counter. Across the black-topped arcade the turquoise diving bell hung idle above its circular tank. A lone sailor, nuzzling his cloth-coated shore-leave girl, shivered in his summer whites. At the just-closed concession stand, a fat man sucked a malted milk.

A coughing fit doubled Romance over. Jesus, that hurt his still-tender gut! Fucking fog. Sure, it masked the tawdriness of the games and rides, and it gave their smoky festoons of colored bulbs almost a fairyland quality, but so what? It had also emptied the amusement park of customers.

When he came erect, the fat man was a yard away, still slurping his strawberry malt. He wore a dark gray suit with a blue shirt. His jowls were also blue, and his nose was cruelly hooked. His eyes, which should have been brutish under those heavy brows, were a melting Hershey-bar brown.

"If you'd beef up, my friend, you'd look like Sinatra. You get a rear out of running this nice place?"

"It's a living."

"It won't be."

Romance narrowed fog-colored eyes. "What's the 'If'?"

"If you don't lay off Johnny Dutton."

"I'm not laying on him. Three-by-six of Mexico is—unless they just left him lying at the bottom of the cliff."

The fat man picked up one of the rifles and gripped the stock with both hands. The hands twisted against each other. His fingers, splaying against the wood with effort, were like rolled nickels, his twisting arms like oak limbs. The walnut stock splintered. He laid the maimed rifle back down.

"You've been told, my friend."

Romance shook his head at the splintered stock, sighed, and reached under the counter for the phone to call Jeanne Lazin.

When it had been Romero's supper club, five silver dollars had been sunk into the red concrete of the foyer. After it went topless as Bubbles, the new management had pried them out again.

Romance pushed aside the green curtain to be met by a strident blast of go-go music and the mingled reek of sweat, testosterone, cheap perfume, and weed. The place was blue with cigarette smoke and the shouts of shit-kickers from out of town. At the left wall the bar ended in a raised dais on which two girls danced wearing only spangled bikini bottoms, stiletto-heeled shoes, and a nimbus of sweat. Their hair was flying, their faces were set in rictus grins, their unfettered breasts jounced and whirled as their pudenda dry-fucked the go-go beat.

Romance threaded his way through the packed tables to Jeanne Lazin's. He bent and kissed her on top of her shimmering blond head, slid into the seat across from her. A topless waitress, her nipples covered with spangles to meet the health department code for beverage servers, came to take his order.

"I thought I wasn't seeing you any more," Jeanne Lazin said with a slow smile that made her green eyes sparkle.

"How do you stay so beautiful with the hours you keep?"

"My soul expands after dark, like a cat's."

Jeanne was half a dozen years younger than Romance, with a flawless patrician face—high cheekbones, a straight nose, a generous mouth—and long gleaming blond hair, shoulder-length, with the ends curled under. She wore a pink pantsuit and an ermine wrap that not even her beauty could make shabby.

"Did Johnny enjoy playing piano in a dump like this?"

The waitress brought their drinks. Jeanne let her eyes get misty with memory.

"Know why I keep coming here, Romance? So I can pretend that when the band's set is over, Johnny will sit down with me. . . . I loved the soft way he spoke, his funny little laugh . . ."

"So why didn't you marry the guy, Jeanie?"

"We didn't need marriage. Not Johnny and me."

"I always sort of thought you fell so hard for him because your old man said he was lowlife, but I could be wrong on that."

Her face was instantly cold. "You and I became history the day I met Johnny Dutton, and you can't handle that, Romance."

"I agreed to look into how he died, didn't I?"

"So you'd have a chance to sleep with me again."

"When do we start?"

Her green eyes flashed. "Never. Especially not now, when . . ." She made an abrupt angry gesture. "I want to know all about him. Everything about him. I *need* to know." Her eyes misted up. "He was buried before I even knew he was dead."

"The climate would account for the quick burial. Beyond checking with the Mexican consul general—who says it was an accident—I can't learn much without going down there."

"So go down there!"

"You know I don't work in the field any more. Johnny fell off a cliff near a little place called El Dorado. Only road of sorts is to Culiacan, which has an airport. I've been there, it's on the coast, no electricity, rugged bluffs. Easy to slip and fall in the night, maybe with half a heat on. End of story."

"If you're not going to help me, why am I here?"

"Something happened tonight that made me want to ask the bandleader why Johnny was down there."

"Why do *you* think he was?"

"I think that a lot of dope gets moved up from Baja."

"If you're suggesting that Johnny—"

"Maybe he heard something and was investigating on his own," he said with a total lack of conviction.

But her eyes were shining. "That's just the sort of thing Johnny would do, all right."

"Of course it is," he said soothingly. "Now if you'd get the bandleader to come over here . . ."

The set ended. The bartender plugged in the jukebox, Jeanne went away, returned shortly with Efrain Navarre. He was a stout swarthy man with sniffles and nervous hands, wearing pointy shoes and ripoffs of Carnaby Street's finest.

"Miss Lazin tells me that you are going down to El Dorado to look into the tragic death of poor Johnny. It is a frightful thing to die all alone in Mexico." In a dreamy, faraway voice, he repeated, "All alone. In Mexico. Most tragic."

"I think you've got it wrong about me going down to El Dorado. I'm only mildly curious on behalf of . . ." Romance made the slightest of bows. "Miss Lazin. I hoped you might have some idea what he was doing down there."

"Johnny said it was just a vacation."

That was it. Navarre returned to the bandstand with a detour down the hall to the restrooms and pay phone.

Romance said, "I told you I'm out of the P.I. racket, Jeanne. I'm not going to Mexico. That's final."

For reply, she stood abruptly, swirled the ermine around her shoulders, and left. He sighed, gave her enough time to get her red Ferrari Spyder out of the lot next door, scattered enough money across the table, and left himself. The go-go girls were at it again, sweat flying, breasts jouncing. Far fuckin' out.

Huge breakers smoked out of the wet misted night to crash on the hard sand. Water swirled up the beach, engulfing Romance's shoes before he could dance away from it. He started back up the eroded concrete steps in disgust.

Maybe he should go down to Mexico for a few days after all, soak up some sun, find Dutton's grave. Then Jeanne could make a pilgrimage and put some flowers and a star burst of tears on the careless rectangle of heaped Mexican dirt. And probably sleep with a bullfighter in Calienti on the way home.

Playland was long closed, but DARK MYSTERY brooded through the swirling fog in blood-red neon. Below were the blue misted words, DIFFERENT! EXOTIC! WEIRD! The House of Horrors pulsed with green neon that illuminated a phony stone tiki with a red mouth and yellow eyes and pointed cannibal teeth.

Romance fought with the lock on the folding doors across the front of the shooting gallery. Tomorrow he'd have to graphite it. In darkness he went around the counter and down the narrow catwalk to the left of the water tank. Behind the target conveyor belts was the unlocked door to his apartment.

He flicked the light switch. Nothing. There was the faint smell of cigarette smoke in the totally black room. He felt his way to his broken-down easy chair and the reading lamp beside it, turned the finger switch. Again, nothing.

The front door lock jimmied so he had trouble opening it.

Both lights out though they operated on different circuits.

Cigarette smoke when he didn't smoke.

His hand prowled the reading table beside his chair for the heavy brass ashtray that had come with the apartment. Ashtray in hand, he backed silently into the middle of the room.

Grunt of effort. Romance threw himself sideways, but something struck the side of his neck a numbing blow. He went to one knee, a heavy shoe thudded into his ribs. He went over sideways in a fetal curl, trying to protect his perforated gut. Two men were kicking him.

"Told you . . . lay off . . ."

His right hand groped for the dropped ashtray. There was a

funny little laugh and a deliberate shoe came down on his hand to twist and grind. Only pain kept him from fainting. Then a heavy shoe caught him under the chin, and he went away.

Dawn poked cautious pale fingers between sash and shade. Romance opened his eyes. His nose was pressed against the rug. He moved his right hand, screamed, coughed up blood.

After a rest, he was able to move his legs without moving his macerated right hand. He was afraid if he looked at it, he'd vomit. He started gingerly kicking at the legs of the little round reading table by his easy chair. It went over, the phone fell on the floor near him.

Depress the plunger, release it, dial the number left-handed. Luckily, the receiver had landed near his face. When he heard Jeanne's voice on the phone, his eyes went almost opaque with the effort to be light and carefree.

"Just called to say I'm on my way to Mexico after all."

After an assessing pause, "You're a sweet man, darling."

"We both think so," he said airily, and hung up.

He repeated the phoning process. Another woman's voice, crisply efficient, said, "Kevin Rymer Investigations."

"Kevin there, angel?"

He could picture Carole d'Angelo at her desk, phone in her left hand, scribbling madly on one of her yellow legal pads. Round Italian face framed in almost unkempt black hair, ten years older than he, fifteen pounds overweight. She had trouble keeping her hands off him in her motherly, oddly sexual way.

"On stakeout over in Oakland, Fran. I can—"

"No, that's okay." He rested a moment, said, "Efrain Navarre, N-a-v-a-r-r-e, mainliner, heads the combo at Bubbles. Johnny Dutton, D-u-t-t-o-n, bobbed piano for Navarre until he went off a cliff near Culiacan two weeks ago. Accident, question mark? Have Kevin send a Mex speaker down to talk to the local law if there is any, find any witnesses, photograph the grave."

"Can do." She paused. "Are you okay, Fran?"

"No. I need a ride to a medic can keep his mouth shut—"

"Gunshot?" Her voice was at once professional and alarmed. "With all this heat from Sacramento the doctors are—"

"Stomp job. And I need somewhere to hole up for a while."

"I'll be there in thirty," she said tersely.

Fran Romance woke thirty-nine hours later, nude, right hand in a cast, flat on his back in a strange bed with the stiffened nipple of a large, firm female breast between his lips. A female hand was pumping him erect. He just naturally started to lick the nipple. Carole d'Angelo, also nude, gave a low moan of arousal and thrust down to impale herself on his now distended member.

She tried to be gentle, but soon was reared back, riding him hard, harder, harder yet, faster and faster, she had him close to coming and she was in control. Sweat poured off them.

"Yes yes now now!" she cried.

He growled hoarsely as her vagina contracted rhythmically around him, milking him dry. Finally she went limp and folded down on top of him. She lay there sobbing, while he gently brushed the wet hair back from her forehead with his undamaged left hand.

After a while, Carole fell asleep. It was going to be a fantasy week, lifted out of time, lifted out of their lives. When he was mended, he would leave, and it would be as if this had never happened. Life was goddamned unfair. Jeanne was in love with a dead man . . . he was in love with Jeanne . . . Carole was in love with him. . . .

But he was alive. *Alive.* After being that close to taking the dirt nap.

Romance slept on the satin pillow.

It was two-thirty in the morning. Romance, wearing black fedora and black overcoat, stood at the window of the darkened apartment on Greenwich below Stockton, watching Efrain Navarre cross Columbus toward him at almost a trot. Romance knew a repossession agency was looking for the bandleader's pale gold Fleetwood; he'd probably parked on the other side of Columbus in the almost assuredly vain hope they wouldn't find it.

Fumbling the key to his apartment, Navarre turned on the lights and hurried across the living room to the sideboard against the left-hand wall where he kept his paraphernalia. His frantic unsuccessful hands rifled the drawer.

"I've got your whiz-bang, Navarre."

Romance stepped out of the bedroom. His right sleeve was empty; bulkiness under the topcoat showed he was wearing a sling, also black. He looked deliberately theatrical, but Navarre turned pale. Five inches of shiny aluminum elongated the short-barreled .22 Colt Woodsman in Romance's left hand.

"You are ridden by a very expensive monkey," said Romance. "Always a bad idea to get hooked on your own product."

"I . . . You startled . . . A week ago I thought . . ."

"Thought I was going down to Mexico. Yeah. So you fingered me from the topless joint. Now, I want the fat man."

"The fat . . . I do not know who you . . ."

Romance put his pistol against Navarre's sweaty forehead. "At this range, even left-handed I can hardly miss. One . . ."

"Please . . . I cannot tell you what I do not . . ."

"Two." Fran's finger took up the trigger slack. "Dumdums. Hollow points. Disintegrate on contact. Thr—"

"Jell-O!" Navarre screeched. "They call him Jell-O! He tends bar in the financial district. . . ."

Romance returned the unloaded pistol to his belt, from his overcoat pocket took the flat tin box that held Navarre's eyedropper and bent spoon and small white bindles. He dropped it on the rug. Navarre went down on his knees to scrabble after it.

When Romance came in out of the fog of Bush Street at just 1:55 A.M., another day had died. Canned music flowed through the vaguely Elizabethan Poet's Rest, ceiled with thick oak timbers, cool and golden-hued from pastel lights behind the bar. The walls were dark and wood-paneled, the small windows leaded diamonds of fogged knobbly glass.

Jell-O, immense behind the bar, arms wide, hands gripping the hardwood, had a strained, glassy look. He stiffened and started to pant. His gripping fingers whitened for a few moments. Then he moaned, relaxed, and began breathing deeply.

"Bourbon and branch," said Romance.

A short dark intense-looking girl in her twenties popped up from in front of the fat man. Wiping her mouth with a Kleenex, she looked speculatively at Romance.

"You want one too?"

"I just came from there."

She shrugged. "Sure." She opened the cash register, took out a twenty, lifted a knee-length brown coat off one of the brass clothes hooks behind the door, and went out into the fog.

Jell-O slid the drink across to Romance before coming out from behind the bar to lock the front door. He left the keys hanging in the lock.

Back behind the bar, he said, "On the house, my friend."

Romance toasted with the glass, drank. "You don't seem surprised to see me, Jell-O."

Jell-O brought an army-issue Colt .45 out from behind the beer cooler and set it on the top of the bar. Even his immense paw could not quite dwarf the original 1911 model automatic.

"Navarre called today. All you had to do was take your beating and stay clammed. Now . . . attempted holdup. You came in wavin' that popgun in your belt, I smoked you."

Romance had his coat open and his left hand hanging free.

"How about I smoke you first?" he asked.

"You might teach yourself some swift with the other flipper eventually, but not in a week."

"You weren't really watching me shoot out at Playland, Jell-O. I'm left-handed."

The Woodsman gave four thin splats so close together they were almost one sound. The .45 splashed into the beer cooler. Jell-O crashed to the wood-slatted runway behind the bar where the girl had been getting dusty knees a few minutes earlier.

Romance rammed the .22 back into his belt and looked over the bar at the fallen, cursing fat man. He hummed "Don't get around much any more," said, "Both hands, both kneecaps," pointed at the bullet-starred backbar mirror, added, "Seven years bad luck from the ricochet, Jell-O. All of it yours."

At the tiny telltale sounds of movement, Romance lifted the Woodsman from the arm of his old easy chair and told the closed door, "Come in but easy does it."

After what seemed like a long time, the door drifted open. A lone man came through with his hands at shoulder-level, his eyes on the Woodsman. He was wearing two hundred dollars worth of fawn-colored topcoat with a smear of grease down one sleeve. The knees of his trousers were ripped. Mist glinted in his wavy golden hair. His blue eyes, deep-set in a rugged lifeguard's face that women like Jeanne Lazin always found attractive, were hollow and haunted.

"On the wall," said Romance. "You'll know the routine."

When the big blond man was straddle-legged five feet from the wall, all his weight on his outstretched hands, Romance frisked him. He had no firearm on his body.

"I need help, bad," the man said as he straightened up.

"I guess I'm talking to Johnny Dutton."

Dutton seemed genuinely startled. "How'd you make me?"

"I got warned off for asking around about your death. Then I got beat up just on the rumor that I was going to Mexico to look for your grave. So I sent someone down to snoop around. Nobody had heard of a gringo named Dutton going off a cliff, accident or otherwise. So, you faked your death. Pretty slick."

Johnny Dutton gave an odd little almost embarrassed laugh, said with slightly sour admiration, "You're pretty damned slick yourself, Romance."

Romance felt suddenly tired, bushed, all in.

"Why do they want to kill you after going to all of that trouble to fake your death? Easier just to kill me."

"You weren't the only one looking, so all of a sudden I was expendable." Dutton gestured broadly, sweat standing on his face. "They've already offed Navarre and Jell-O."

Romance wondered if he was sorry at those two deaths. He decided he wasn't. He said, "Why come to me? I've got scant reason to help you. Jeanne's old man has all the money in the world and she's in love with you—"

"Fuck Jeanne. Sure, she'd do anything for me, but she can't do it quick enough. By the time she realizes I'm alive, I'll be dead again. For real this time."

"Now I believe you," said Romance. "So now I'll help you."

Fear still tugged at Dutton's features. "What if they're out there, waiting? I . . . saw that House of Horrors across the midway. You could hide me there, bring your car around . . ."

Romance stared at him for a long moment, nodded slowly.

"If that's the way you want to play it, sure."

They went out the back door of the apartment, two tall indistinct figures in the swirling fog, ran lightly across the blacktop, paused while Romance unlocked the access door. Inside the House of Horrors was dark save for a life-size skeleton with upraised arm and grinning jaws. Its pale phosphorescence glowed dully off the passenger cart tracks curving toward it.

"Ten minutes," said Romance.

He got his car from where he'd left it nose-to against the seawall. Dutton's odd little laugh seemed conclusive, but he owed it to Jeanie to be sure. Either way, he'd need the car. At the House of Horrors he paused outside the door, afraid to die.

"Dutton," he hissed. "I've got the car." No answer.

He went through the doorway in a rush, diving down and to his right even as he felt the sting on the back of his neck. Dutton must have been wearing a knife in a flat ankle sheath; he would have picked up some tricks like that south of the border.

Romance gurgled grotesquely as he came up in a crouch, the Woodsman in his left hand. He breathed open-mouthed for silence. His hand ached in its cast. His stomach ached from the gunshot wound five months before. His neck stung where the knife had just missed the spinal cord. Be sedentary, the doc had said. Yeah, sure.

Three interminable minutes ticked by. He could sense Dutton moving around cautiously, trying to find a body before showing himself in the gray rectangle of the open doorway. The heroin-smuggling ring had been his, of course; when federal heat started coming down, he'd decided to disappear. But Romance had brought him back to life. Romance had to die for the same reason Jell-O and Navarre had died: They all knew Dutton was alive.

Something bit a piece from the skeleton's luminous rib cage. The pelvis and part of a thigh began to disappear. Romance's .22 gave its flat plop. Something abruptly inanimate fell. The skeleton was whole again. Romance duck-waddled forward. His fingers brushed cloth, the side of a face. He had gotten Dutton just above the right ear. No pulse. Curtains for Johnny Dutton.

A phone call should just reach Guido before he left home to catch the changing tide with the rest of the fishing fleet. Romance would get the dead man down to the docks before dawn. Out near the Farallones, a weighted-down Johnny Dutton would go over the side. Jeanne already thought him dead; she would forget him in time. If she never did, well, she would always have Paris.

* * *

An hour after sunrise, Romance parked by Playland once again. The fog was gone. He could smell salt air, the smashing breakers shook even the sidewalk. He'd never been so tired. When he opened his door, Jeanne Lazin opened her eyes and sat up on the couch. Her perfume reminded him of forget-me-nots.

"The door was open, so I knew you were back from Mexico."

He sat down in his easy chair, leaned back, shut his eyes.

"I didn't go to Mexico. I've been sick."

"Didn't go?" Her voice was shrill. She stood over him, glaring down. "You knew how much finding out about Johnny means to me. Last night I dreamed he was still alive. I'll never stop looking for him. Not now. Not when I'm going to need—"

"You need to forget about Johnny. He's dead."

Her face spasmed with rage. She swung her arm, hard. Her open hand left a dull red mark on his cheek.

Romance came back to the new millennium with a start. Something heavy had knocked against his car door. Even through the fog he could still see the red Ferrari parked in place. Knuckles on his window brought his head around. The blonde was standing outside the car, hunched down against the cold, wet ocean fog. She mimed rolling down the window.

He did. Jesus, he'd lost it. Getting made on stakeout like a rank amateur.

"You're Fran Romance, aren't you?" she asked.

Up close like this her resemblance to Jeanne Lazin went through him like a chill.

She confirmed it. "You knew my mother," she said. Her eyes, even in darkness and fog, were that same clear sparkling green. She forestalled his question. "Mom died a month ago. Along with all the money, she left me a letter. She'd never stopped looking for Johnny Dutton, and she finally found an old dying fisherman named Guido who wanted to confess. Confess what he'd done with my father's body." She delved in the heavy handbag that had thunked against the car door. "After I located you, I got her old Ferrari out of storage and . . ." She raised her head. Those clear green eyes drilled into his fog gray ones. Her hand came out of her handbag. "According to Guido, you knew my father, too, Romance. . . ."

George Caulfield sighed wearily, said, "Well, thanks, Benny, I guess," and hung up the phone. To himself, he added, "Aw, shit," and went to tell Linda what had happened.

Flush Pearson stood up when his striking brunette client was shown into his private office in the Trans-America tower. It was high enough up to have a stunning view out over the bay and the two bridges and Alcatraz and Angel Island.

Allison Rockwell sat down in the client's chair across the desk unbidden. Suddenly she looked unsure of herself. She clasped her hands around prim knees and stared at her intertwined fingers. Finally she raised her head to look at him with clear brown eyes from behind light-framed glasses.

"What . . . what did the investigator you hired find out about my husband's . . . private affairs, Mr. Pearson?"

It was Flush's turn to hesitate. He cleared his throat.

"Well, Mrs. Rockwell, we don't exactly know. The . . . our man . . . was found murdered in his car this morning."

"Murdered!" she cried, her face ashen.

"Shot in the head sometime last evening."

She leaned forward in sudden dread. "Please . . . tell me it didn't have anything to do with my . . . my hiring him to . . ."

"I think I can reassure you on that point, Mrs. Rockwell. Those are the chances they take. The police believe it was a random act of violence. He was found at Ocean Beach so I presume he was staked out waiting for the blond woman to—"

"Ocean Beach? But my husband was nowhere near Ocean Beach yesterday!" She leaned back, almost found a wan smile.

"Oh, thank God he wasn't with her!" Then the smile faltered. "What a terrible thing to say! That poor detective is dead and . . ." She ran down with a hopeless gesture.

Flush said smoothly, "Do you want us to continue our—"

She sprang to her feet, eyes wide. "Oh my God, no!" She opened her handbag. "Do I owe anything further for—"

"Your retainer will cover it, Mrs. Rockwell." Thinking, and much more. Romance had done only one day of field work.

She offered a small cool hand. "Then I . . . I think I want to just . . . go home. To my husband."

Allison Rockwell rode the elevator down to the parking garage. She got into her red Ferrari, used the tipped-down rearview mirror to pull off the excellent brunette wig and shake out her own long gleaming shoulder-length blond hair. She curled the ends under with her fingers. The brown contacts hiding her green eyes could wait until she got to her townhouse.

On his way to Pac-Bell Park for the Giants/Dodgers game, Caulfield made an appearance at Fran Romance's wake. He didn't stay for the rosary. The half-dozen old-timers who'd shown up had drifted away, too, leaving only two people in the funeral parlor with the closed casket. Head wounds are hard to conceal even with industrial-strength makeup.

Linda went up to stand with her hand on the casket for a moment. There were two big bouquets of flowers, only one of them hers. She would take his ashes home after the cremation and . . . and what?

"Did you know Mr. Romance well?"

The old woman in her seventies, who had sat in the back sobbing into her handkerchief during the rosary, had come up beside Linda. Her round, age-lined face might once have been pretty in a plump, motherly, Italian way.

"I . . . we worked together," said Linda. She wouldn't cry, she told herself fiercely. "He was a friend."

"Yes." The old lady nodded. "A friend." A wistful, remembering smile lit up her face, momentarily erasing thirty years. "Once, for a week, a great deal more."

As they had been speaking, a tall, striking blonde with a patrician face had come up the aisle with a bouquet of forget-me-nots. She laid the flowers on Fran Romance's coffin. She spoke to the other two women as if they had been speaking to her.

"A friend? No, I only met him once. But he knew my mother." She paused. She smiled. "He knew my father, too."

Candie-Gram

MICHAEL GARRETT

The assassin slumped low behind the steering wheel of his parked car, barely visible in the darkness, watching.

Waiting.

His breath was rapid, his pulse soaring, his temper like a fuse burning closer to the point of ignition. It was almost 10:30 P.M. and she'd been inside the motel over three hours. Her car was parked near the exit door, and sooner or later she would come outside. And when she did, he'd send her straight to hell where she belonged.

The continuous roar of passing interstate traffic prevented anything resembling silence. "I'm going to a movie with Deb," she'd said. Yeah, right. He'd seen through her lie the minute she'd opened her fucking mouth, she'd so obviously avoided looking him in the eye.

As the night wore on, the .38 Special felt small and insignificant, like a toy in his muscular elastic-gloved hand. Such a sissy weapon, he thought. Nothing like the Magnum he preferred. But the .38 couldn't be traced back to him, and was more than enough to snuff her life away. Her boyfriend, too, for that matter. Fucking son-of-a-bitch wife stealer. Whoever the hell he was.

The assassin took a deep breath to calm his nerves. Shit, it was getting colder. The windshield was already iced over and clouds of frozen breath plumed from his nostrils, glowing a ghostly blue from the reflected light of the nearby neon motel sign. He wiped a clear circle in the fogged window, then shifted in his seat, closed his eyes tightly, and slowly shook his head.

He'd warned her a thousand times he'd blow her away if she so much as *looked* at another man, but she obviously hadn't taken him seriously. That was her big mistake. Her *fatal* mistake. *She's mine, and nobody else has the right to touch her!* He ground his teeth together at the thought of what she'd been doing all this time and wondered for the thousandth time how long it had been going on.

Suddenly the metal security door at the end of the motel's central hallway swung open. A tall, skinny man of about her same age held the door open for her and she waltzed into the cold night air as if she had every fucking right in the world to be there, as if she dared anyone to question her presence. She wrapped her full-length fur-collared coat tightly about herself and smiled at the polite son of a bitch. The guy paused, grinning back at her, and watched her hair flutter in the cold breeze as she walked ahead of him. Then he fell in line behind her, stepping quickly to catch up and say something.

From a slow simmer to a bubbling boil, the rage inside the assassin grew. His breath quickened. His heart pounded harder against his chest. A throbbing headache felt like an ice pick stabbing through his skull. He swallowed hard and pulled the door latch, pushing himself out of the automobile and staggering toward her on rubbery legs that were cramped from lengthy confinement inside the car.

"Bitch!" he screamed. "You goddamn fucking *bitch!*"

Her head snapped in his direction, her eyes reflecting the horror of having been caught. Her boyfriend stopped in his tracks, backing away toward the safety of the motel's inner corridor.

But before the cheater could get back inside, the assassin gripped the revolver with the gloved hand at eye level, steadying himself with the fingers of his left hand wrapped around his right wrist. He took steady aim and fired two rounds. The bitch screamed at the top of her lungs as two blossoms of blood sprouted from her lover's chest and he crumpled to the cold asphalt surface. The handgun swung back quickly toward the hysterical bitch and the assassin took deadly aim, smoke still rising from the weapon's short stubby barrel.

"No!" she screamed. "Don't! It's not—"

But the assassin was no longer in the mood for explanations. He'd heard enough already. A roaring in his ears blanked her screams anyway. Pleading for her life was too little too late as far as he was concerned.

He wanted to ask her why she had done such a stupid thing, but he was caught off guard by lights flickering on in nearby motel windows, their draperies parting as occupants peered outside to investigate the noise. In the momentary distraction the bitch suddenly rushed him, still screaming and now pounding his chest, dislodging the fake beard he wore as a disguise. A shrill whistling in his ears hissed louder and louder and he shoved her hard until she fell on her back beside her dying lover.

"Shut up!" he yelled. "This is *your* fault, not mine." Icy tears streamed down his cheeks. "Thanks for making it so easy," he gasped as he emptied the rest of the rounds into her helpless form.

A rattling knock at the door jarred Patrick Pharr awake just past midnight. He groggily opened his eyes, disoriented as his mind slowly recovered from sleep. What was going on? He was in a motel room hundreds of miles from home and someone was at the door. Why hadn't they called instead? Could the place be on fire?

"Give me a minute," Patrick called as he slipped on his pants. Reaching for the doorknob, he paused to squint through the peephole. A uniformed police officer stood in the hall corridor. Puzzled, Patrick opened the door.

"Patrick Pharr?" the stone-faced officer read his name from a dog-eared spiral pocket notebook.

Patrick nodded, then a flash of worry passed through his mind. Could something have happened to Sue or one of the kids back home? Somewhat nervously, he answered, "Yeah, that's me. What's this all about?"

Both officers mumbled their names and flashed badges, but Patrick was too anxiety-stricken to notice. "We'd like to ask a few questions," the first cop said.

Patrick motioned the lawmen inside. Almost immediately he labeled the officers by their differentiated demeanors. The big one, the macho guy who was apparently in charge, obviously considered himself a Supercop. The other, shorter with a more average build, didn't even look like a cop at all. He was the Noncop.

The modest motel room was small and cramped. "Sorry, but there's no place to sit but the bed," Patrick apologized.

"You sit; we'll stand," Supercop said, and as Patrick settled on the edge of the sagging mattress, he began to feel angry. What the hell was going on here? Why were these Dirty Harry wanna-bes waking him from much-needed sleep?

"Where were you at approximately ten-thirty P.M. tonight, Mr. Pharr?" Noncop asked.

Patrick's temper flared. He'd had about enough. "Now, wait a minute," he hissed, knowing that his face must be turning red, as it usually did when he was mad. "I don't appreciate this hard-ass questioning without knowing what the hell is going on."

Supercop took a deep breath and his chest bulged. He was a big, mean-looking fucker, Patrick recognized immediately, and realized his own false bravado would get him nowhere. "Well, excuse us for bothering you, *Mister* Pharr," Supercop spewed sarcastically, "but we either talk here or elsewhere. The choice is yours."

Patrick's shock deepened. He'd never been in trouble with the law in his entire life. In fact, he'd always sympathized with, and supported, the police. There must be some mistake. And now, sitting there in his undershirt and staring up at the standing uniformed policemen, he felt small and inadequate—and vulnerable.

Noncop stepped forward, his expression softening. "Looks like we're off on the wrong foot, Mr. Pharr. I'm sorry." He paused to shake Patrick's hand, then continued. "A man and woman were shot in the motel parking lot just a short while ago. We're questioning all the guests for anything they might've seen or heard."

The news was unsettling. This place wasn't the Waldorf-Astoria, but it seemed safe enough. Patrick had always opted for the less expensive motels to pocket the savings from his travel per diem but had never chosen to stay at dumps. A soft "Wow" of astonishment was all he could mutter in response.

"You here on business or pleasure?" Supercop asked.

"Business, of course," Patrick answered.

"What time did you settle in for the night?" Noncop asked.

"Been here all evening, since about seven o'clock," Patrick answered.

"*Alone?*" Supercop interjected.

Patrick hesitated and swallowed hard, hoping neither cop noticed he'd been taken aback by the question. Candie had been with him most of the evening, and they'd given the room's queen-size bed a real workout. But there was no way he could admit that. Not only did he have a wife and kids at home, but Candie had a husband and three children as well. What if these guys wanted him to testify? He could never admit such a thing on the public record. "Yeah, alone," he reluctantly muttered, avoiding eye contact. "Just watching TV."

The cops paused momentarily, and Patrick felt as if his every move were being analyzed through a microscope. Finally Noncop broke the silence. "Hear or see anything unusual?"

"No, not a thing," Patrick responded quickly.

"No screams, no—?"

"*Nothing.* Nothing at all," Patrick interrupted.

Supercop stepped over to the television set and punched the power button. The picture blinked on at its previous level of volume. "Sound wasn't turned up very loud. You should've heard something. Hell, your room is one of the closest to the crime scene." He stared at Patrick with an expression of doubt.

Patrick scratched his head. "As I recall, I was in the shower at about that time. I wouldn't have heard a bomb go off."

Noncop nodded slightly while Supercop stared blankly over Patrick's shoulder at the bed behind him. "Give us a call if you think of anything," Noncop said as he handed Patrick a card. "We got a lot more guests to wake up before it gets any later."

Patrick forced a smile, but didn't like the way they hesitated with their blank stares. Sure, he'd lied, but not about the crime. Had they noticed his reaction when they asked if he'd been alone? Hell, a murder had just occurred outside the motel. Anybody would be startled by the news of such a tragedy. Anybody would show *some* kind of reaction, wouldn't they?

Once the cops were out of the room and the door closed, Patrick pivoted to face the bed and froze. Remnants of an evening of ecstasy were plainly visible. The bedspread and blankets were tossed aside the way he'd left them when he got up to answer the door, but a stain was clearly noticeable on the bed sheet. Part of a foil condom wrapper lay in plain sight on the nightstand, too. Shit! The cops would've been total idiots not to notice. Now they knew he was lying, and could even consider him a suspect!

Patrick ran nervous fingers through his thinning hair. Damn! Should he find the two cops and come clean? They'd still be around here somewhere. But then they'd also want to question Candie! Oh, *shit!* The two-year intermittent tryst had progressed flawlessly prior to this. Now the illicit relationship seemed dangerously near its end, for reasons entirely beyond their control that could also take down both of their marriages. So much for fucking around. . . .

Patrick sat on the edge of the bed and gazed at the digital clock. It was after 1:00 A.M. now. He'd never sleep a wink, he knew. Finally, he snatched the telephone receiver and called the front desk.

"Hello? This is Patrick Pharr in room 202. Can you tell me anything about this shooting the cops are asking about?"

The desk clerk, whose voice sounded like that of a senior citizen well past retirement, was evasive. "Don't know much. It was a couple that was shot. Woman's dead. The guy won't be dancing anytime soon, either, or so they say."

"Was it a robbery?"

"Don't know. Don't think so."

"Were they guests?"

"One of 'em was."

Patrick hesitated. "Whew!" he finally said. "Have much crime around here?"

"Not in the five years since I've worked here," the desk clerk answered.

Patrick thanked the clerk and sat on the bedside in deep thought, nervous that the fantasy he'd lived could be blown wide open, not to mention the fact that two innocent people had been gunned down practically right outside the door.

As he switched off the light, Patrick noticed a candy wrapper that had fallen to the floor, and memories of only a few hours earlier flooded his mind. Candie was incredibly creative when it came to sex. . . .

Younger than himself by twenty years, she'd never looked more beautiful, so soft, so warm and tender. She lay on her back across the bed, her nude form tantalizing in the dim light with her shoulder-length blond hair fanned out across the pillow behind her head.

"Ready for your favorite treat, sweetheart?" he whispered. She smiled.

Candie raised her eyebrows and smiled mischievously. "Hmm, sounds like you've brought Candie some candy," she answered.

Patrick laughed. "Only the kind you like best, sweetie."

He reached into his overnight bag and removed a cherry-flavored spherical-shaped lollipop. Candie grinned.

Patrick removed the candy wrapper and tossed it toward the waste basket, anxious to administer the treatment she'd taught him so well to deliver. "*Candie-Gram,*" he rang out in a lighthearted singsong voice.

Patrick positioned himself between her long, lean legs and propped himself on his elbows. He watched her facial expression change from wonder to anticipation as he took the lollipop into his mouth.

"Of course, I like the way you taught me to wet my candy better," he said softly.

He lowered his face between her legs and found her smoothly shaven vagina, to no surprise, already wet and inviting. He ran his tongue up and down the folds of her labia and tickled her engorged clit with the tip of his tongue, feeling a tremendous sense of satisfaction when her muscles flinched from the sensation. He took the sucker from his mouth and twirled its white stick between his thumb and forefinger. Candie moaned softly and closed her eyes.

Patrick gently rotated the stem of the lollipop, gliding the globe of hard candy up and down inside her labia, twirling it as it moved. He felt her legs tighten and watched an expression of heightened pleasure wash across her face. Then he removed the lollipop and gently licked away the candy coating. "Ooohh, it feels so *good,*" she moaned as he repeated the process. "You learned well."

He ran his fingertips along her inner thighs and down the backside of her knee to her lower legs, gently massaging her all the way. "I didn't think you could possibly taste any sweeter," he said as he finally laid the moistened candy on the nightstand. "I'll save some of my favorite flavor to enjoy later, after you're gone."

And then he eased beside her and kissed the softest lips he'd ever imagined, and she returned his passion in kind. From there, their lovemaking progressed at its usual pace, slow and sensual, engulfing them both in a passion so strong, so powerful, that neither could imagine anything better.

A truck horn blared outside and Patrick, suddenly jarred back to reality, wondered if he could live without Candie now, should they be forced by circumstance to disclose their relationship. He was clearly addicted to her. He only hoped there'd be a way to protect their secret.

Patrick was awake bright and early, anxious to return home to e-mail Candie with the news about the murders when a hard knock rattled his door again. He jumped in response, his nerves still frayed over the disturbing events. A squint through the peephole revealed Supercop standing again in the hallway.

"Checking out kind of early, ain't you?" Supercop said as Patrick opened the door.

"Not at all," Patrick answered, motioning the officer inside. "Wish I had something new to tell you, but I swear I don't remember a thing."

Supercop stood just inside the doorway with a steely-eyed stare, then exhaled in apparent boredom and reached inside a jacket pocket for a lollipop.

Patrick was stunned. A bizarre coincidence? A cold sweat beaded across his forehead. He tried to speak, but couldn't. Supercop unwrapped the candy and popped it into his mouth. "There was a bald-headed TV cop who used to like these things. Can't remember his name," Supercop said.

"Kojak, I think it was," Patrick offered. "Telly Savalas."

Supercop shrugged but didn't budge an inch. Patrick felt his nerves tense like a coiled spring. What was going on here? Why would this cop want to taunt him this way?

Supercop finally cleared his throat and glanced around the

room. "Ever met a sexy blonde named Candie Burnette?" he asked matter-of-factly, without even looking at Patrick.

Patrick's heart sank. Shit! The cops knew about her already! He exhaled deeply, closed his eyes, and slowly shook his head. "Look, Officer, if this gets out, a lot of innocent people will be hurt."

Supercop offered no sympathy, and instead pivoted slightly to remove the Do Not Disturb placard from the interior doorknob. He opened the door and hung the sign outside, then gently closed the door and snapped the interior deadbolt lock in place. He faced Patrick with his typical deadpan expression and whispered, "I know all about you, Pharr. Your ass is *mine*."

A flush of fear washed over Patrick as if his skin were on fire.

Supercop stared with menacing eyes, then snarled, "You don't seem too upset for a guy whose girlfriend got pumped full of lead last night."

His head spinning, Patrick dropped to a seated position on the side of the bed. No, it *couldn't* have been her! Not Candie! But how? Why?

"Tell me about it, Pharr. Why'd you kill her?" Supercop asked sternly.

"*What?*"

Patrick felt nauseated. The loss of Candie was devastating enough. And on top of losing a woman so dear to him, he himself was accused of the crime! How could anything be worse? He'd lost Candie, and now he'd lose his family, and likely even his freedom as well.

"No . . . I . . . ." Patrick tried to explain but was overcome with grief. "I can't believe it. Not Candie! Who would want to kill *her?*"

"Made it look like a hit from a jealous husband, didn't you, Pharr?" Supercop continued. "Killing the innocent guy as if he was her boyfriend was a stroke of genius, I have to admit." Supercop took the candy from his mouth and twirled its white stem between his fingers. "Poor guy must've just happened to have walked out with her or something."

Patrick couldn't respond, but sat on the bed with slumped shoulders, slowly shaking his head. A jittery feeling swept over him. His fingers shook uncontrollably and he felt sick. Finally he looked up at the hard-nosed cop, tears streaming down his cheeks.

But then he noticed Supercop's nostrils flare. The cop's expression took on an entirely different appearance, a look of hatred with an evil grin beginning to sprout.

Patrick's head began to spin. What was going on here?

Supercop's chest heaved as he slipped an elastic glove over his right hand and removed a .38 Special from his right pocket. "She ever tell you she was married to a cop, Pharr?" he slurred.

Patrick's eyes bulged as he slowly shook his head.

"Didn't think so," Supercop answered with the glove tightly in place. "Most guys ain't got the balls to fuck a cop's wife." Supercop paused and slowly shook his head. "Guess we got a little unfinished business between us, don't we?"

Patrick's pulse raced. His mouth dropped open, but there was nothing left to say.

"Ever thought about suicide, Pharr?" Supercop asked. "I guess a guy like you would be mighty depressed after gunning down two innocent people."

Before he knew what was happening, Patrick felt the cop's muscular arms wrap around him like a human straitjacket, restraining his every move. Supercop placed the gun in Patrick's right palm and circled his own meaty hand around Patrick's, forcing the weapon against the side of Patrick's head. He found no will to fight back; it was hopeless, anyway. Supercop was far too strong. Patrick felt the cold steel barrel pressing against his temple. He suddenly recalled his concern of only moments earlier that things could never be worse.

But he'd been mistaken, of course, Patrick now realized. The situation *could* be worse.

Much worse.

Detour Drive

TERRILL LANKFORD

FRIDAY

Red and blue flashing lights reflected off the face of Matt Clark, his weathered good looks ravaged by a grueling depression. Someone, possibly the lieutenant, wrapped a blanket around his shoulders, but he still shivered in the fading July light.

Someone else said, "Go home, Matt. There's nothing more you can do here. Want someone to give you a lift?"

Matt didn't answer for a long moment, his mind a million miles away. Finally he said, "No. I can handle it."

It was a large bedroom in a small house high up in the Hollywood Hills. Los Angeles was a magnificent panorama through the wide-view window behind the bed, but John wasn't looking at L.A., he was staring down into the face of the beautiful woman who had come on to him in the restaurant not even an hour before. He may have been on top, but the woman was *working* it!

She kept saying things like, "C'mon, Buck, slap it!" and "Give me that cock! Go deep, baby! Deep!"

And John did his best to comply, turning up the heat, but finding it hard to maintain control. He wanted it to *last.*

"Damn, baby," he said. "That's some good pussy. . . . Good pussy! I love your pussy. . . ."

She said, "Fuck it then. . . . Fuck it!"

It wasn't the first time he'd been with a white woman, but it was the first time a white woman had made love to him with the same abandon his black girlfriends could exhibit. This bitch was *hot.*

Matt Clark stood there, in the doorway, lurking in the shadows, watching the lovers. There was no expression on his face. Even if the lights were on it would have been impossible to tell what he was thinking.

The man in the bed was beginning to lose it. "Baby, I'm coming. . . ."

The woman moaned, "Don't! Don't come!" which has a tendency to produce the exact opposite result. And it did. But at least the man tried to explain it as he went:

"I've got to . . . I can't hold it. . . . Your pussy's too good. . . . It's too . . . good. . . ."

He drove deep into the woman and grunted like a dying man. Then he collapsed on top of her.

The woman was incredulous. "You came inside me? Don't tell me you came inside me?"

"Where was I supposed to come?"

"Not in my pussy. Shit. . . ."

Matt Clark, still standing in the doorway, fired up a postcoital cigarette. The voyeur's brand.

The woman didn't move, but she did say, "Oh, fuck. . . ."

Her partner rolled over and looked at the man silhouetted in the doorway, calmly smoking a cigarette. "What? Who the fuck is that?"

The woman turned on a light next to the bed, illuminating the room.

The man in the bed was better looking than Matt thought he would be. Gina had always preferred rough customers. This dude looked like a downright refined black man. Gina looked as pristine as always, even having been freshly fucked. Her long blond hair seemed perfectly in place, her nails perfectly manicured. It didn't look like she had even broken a sweat during the act. Which made sense, because she usually took on lovers more for revenge than for the pure pleasure of the experience.

Gina finally answered her bed partner. "It's my husband."

"Husband?! You didn't say anything about a fucking husband!"

"You didn't ask."

Matt tried to straighten his rumpled trench coat, not wanting to be shown up by the *GQ*-looking black man who had just fucked his wife.

The man looked at his suit draped over a chair equidistant between himself and the big guy in the doorway. He started to go for the clothes.

Matt said, "Don't move, Quickdraw."

The man became perfectly still. "Hey, man, I don't want any trouble! I just want to get my shit and get out."

"Guess I'm going to have to clean up the puddle you left in my bed, that right, fuckboy?"

The man sized up Matt Clark. The stone-cold cool coming off the dude was chilling his spine.

Gina said, "Matt, why don't you just leave? I'll clean up John's puddle and we can just forget all about this, okay?"

Matt dropped his cigarette on the shag rug and ground it out with his heel.

"Wish it was that easy."

John looked at Matt Clark, then at the man's unfaithful wife, Gina, who was lying there naked, making no move to cover up despite the delicate nature of the situation.

John said, "You're both crazy."

"John. You just fucked my wife. I'm not happy."

John started to go for his clothes again.

Matt said, "You get out of that bed and I'll break your goddamn neck."

"All I want to do is get my clothes and leave."

"How do I know you don't have a gun or a knife stashed away?"

"What the fuck? I don't have any weapons. I don't want a fight. I just want out!"

"That's right. You came, didn't you? Now you want to go. You've done your job. Jammed your jizz up into my wife's pussy. Maybe she'll even have your kid. . . ."

Gina snorted. "Fat chance."

Matt ignored her. "Funny what goes on in your house while you're out digging up the mortgage."

Gina said, "Fuck you, Matt. Why are you even here? You're supposed to be at work."

"Something happened. I got off early."

"Great. Well, at least *one* of us got off."

"John, sounds like you still got some work to do. You didn't hold up your end of the bargain, did you? Or did I miss something? How long you been going at it?"

Gina frowned. "You didn't miss anything."

"John, doesn't look like you've done a man's job here. Maybe you better finish up, 'cause I'm sure as hell never going to fuck her again now that you've stunk up the joint."

John stared at Matt, then looked to Gina for some indication of what he should do.

Gina just shrugged.

John put on a hard look, trying to bluff his way out of the room. "Fuck this. . . ."

He scrambled for his clothes.

Matt crossed the room and caught John before he could make

it to the chair, kicking him in the ribs. John tried to put up a fight, but he never had a chance. Matt was like a madman. He threw John to the floor and punched him repeatedly in the face.

Gina didn't move from her spot. She seemed very calm. Nonchalant, even. She dryly said, "Don't kill him."

Matt stomped John in the groin and walked away from him, catching his breath and checking his pulse.

"I'm no running back."

"Feel better?" Gina asked.

Matt listened to John moaning on the floor, thought about it for a moment, and was kind of surprised by the conclusion he reached.

"You know? I do. I really do."

Matt picked up John's clothes and sorted through them, looking for weapons. He noticed how expensive the clothes were. A stark contrast to his own rumpled suit and trench coat.

"Nice threads, Homeboy. What you do for a living?"

"He's a lawyer. I met him at the Epicenter."

"What kind of lawyer?"

John started to answer. Gina cut him off. "Don't. . . ."

But it was too late. John groaned, "I'm a defense attorney."

Matt's face flushed with anger.

"Son of a bitch! A defense attorney. . . . Named *Johnny* even. . . . You are one wicked bitch. You really know how to rub it in."

Matt threw John's clothes on the floor next to the man and unzipped his pants.

John looked up from the floor, battered, bruised, bleeding. "Oh, man, what're you doing?"

"Tit for tat, buddy. Or is it the other way around?"

Matt started pissing on John's clothes.

John said, "Fuck, man, you're rude."

Gina got up and put a robe on. Then she sat on the edge of the bed and lighted a cigarette. "This is a very dignified scene."

Matt went to his closet and found the box containing his

backup Nine. The lieutenant had taken his service weapon at the site of the shoot, as was standard procedure. He slapped a mag into the bottom of the gun and placed the piece in his empty shoulder holster. He pocketed a second mag and said, "I see him leave this house wearing any of my clothes, I'll shoot him." Then he turned and walked out of the room. A few moments later, the front door slammed.

John looked up at Gina and wiped blood from his mouth. "Call the cops."

Gina blew an elaborate set of smoke rings and said, "He *is* a cop."

Morrissey's "Maladjusted" screeched out of the radio as Matt Clark cruised through the night streets. He didn't know where he was going, he just knew he had to *go*.

Tourists were caught up in the biker scene on Hollywood Boulevard; gang-bangers worked the alleys between Hollywood and Sunset, selling crack and whatever else the people needed; hookers hovered under sodium vapor lights at Sunset and Highland. Farther west on the Strip the hype billboards towered over rock'n'rollers trying to get into the hip clubs. Two blocks to the south, Boys Town was partying it up on Santa Monica Boulevard. Matt took it all in stoically. Just another Friday night. But there was an additional vibe to it all, an underlying buzz. Independence Day was two days away. The town was gearing up for the long weekend. They were pacing themselves, but the pace was fierce.

Matt dropped in to Gil Turner's liquor store on Sunset and bought three bottles of booze. Jake, the counterman, wrapped them in three separate paper bags.

"Been a long time, Matt. Where you been hiding?"

"Sobriety."

Jake tried to hand Matt his change. Matt waved it off. "Keep it."

Matt took the bottles and headed for the door.

The counterman called after him, "Good to have you back!"

The bell on the closing door jangled the only response he'd receive.

Out in the parking lot Matt sat the three bottles in a row on the hood of his car. He pointed at them in rotation, playing eeney-meeny-miney-moe, trying to let luck decide where he would begin.

The bourbon won it. He took the bottle and cracked it open. He took a moment to mull the consequences. It had been a while since the demon liquor controlled his life. *Fuck it.* He tipped the bottle up and took a sip.

It was good.

He took another sip. Longer this time.

It was *real* good.

He kicked back the bottle and chugged.

Gina Clark was still in bed, staring out the big window at the city lights down below. The house was situated high up in the Hollywood Hills, above Beachwood Canyon, but the view from the bedroom window was a straight shot to downtown L.A., visibility allowing, and this was one of those clear, clean summer nights that made the high price paid for the place worthwhile. She could see lights twinkle all the way to South Central.

John was in the bathroom, washing his clothes in the sink. He was wearing a pink towel around his waist and muttering under his breath, "Motherfucker . . . Son of a bitch . . . Piece of shit . . . Racist fucking pig . . . I'm gonna kick his ass. . . ."

John wrung the clothes dry and hung them over the shower rod.

Gina said, "If you're smart you'll shut up in there. He might be listening."

John walked into the bedroom, suddenly worried again. "You think he's still out there?"

"Maybe. You never know with Matt. He's unpredictable."

"Is he dangerous?"

Gina looked at him like he had just asked the dumbest question in the world.

John went to the corner of the room, picked up his briefcase, put it on the bed, and worked the combination locks.

Gina asked, "What are you doing?"

"I'm arming myself. I'm not taking any more shit from that pig."

John opened the briefcase, then turned it so she could see inside.

There were two shiny 9mm Colt pistols in custom holsters strapped to the interior lid of the case, which was otherwise filled with legal briefs.

"Why the hell do you have those things?"

"Kind of guys I defend, it pays to be prepared. I don't *win* every time out, you know. I've had to deal with disgruntled clients over the years . . . and their relatives."

"You get into a gunfight with Matt and you'll be defending scumbags at the Pearly Gates. He's a crack shot."

John pulled one of the guns out of its holster and chambered the first shell. "He better be."

Matt continued his sojourn through the city. *His* city. He took a slug off the bourbon, now half gone. He was feeling no pain. Couldn't even remember why he was mad in the first place. Everything so beautiful, good to still be alive, why be angry?

Oh yeah. There was that shooting earlier in the day. But what did he expect? He was a cop. Shootings happen. Friends die. Then there was the black defense attorney he caught fucking his wife. But what did he expect? His wife worked as a paralegal downtown and she hated his guts. Shit was going to happen. It wasn't the first time she had picked up a quick fuck at that den of vipers called the Epicenter. It was a lawyer bar and restaurant a block away from the courthouse and thus always thick with the kind of fixers Matt hated. Gina counted on that. And Matt couldn't blame her—

much. But did she have to bring the fucker to *his* house? To *his* bed?

Time for another sip.

He stopped at a red light, leaned his head back, and almost fell asleep. The light turned green and the car behind him honked. Matt laughed drunkenly and hit the gas.

John was preparing to leave. His clothes were wet, cold, and wrinkled, but they would get him home. And the crazy cop couldn't accuse him of raiding his closet. Maybe he could make it to his car in one piece. He picked up his briefcase and made for the door. He didn't even want to look at the woman who had put him in this situation.

Gina said, "Where do you think you're going?"

"Home."

"Oh no you don't. You're not leaving me here to face him alone. He might kill me."

"Call the police. Or the FBI. But I'm not staying here."

She looked at him like he was a complete prick. It got to him. He knew she was bad news, but damn she had a sweet pussy. It had almost been worth the ass-kicking he took from her husband. He put his briefcase on the bed and opened it again.

"Tell you what, you're really nervous I'll loan you one of my pieces. Know how to handle a gun?"

He pulled the remaining pistol out of its holster and twirled it on his finger.

"Of course I do. But he's a cop. I've got no more chance against him than you do."

"Surprise is a great equalizer, and self-defense a powerful elixir for an L.A. jury. Especially self-defense against a member of the LAPD. You'd probably pocket some coin with that one."

A sly grin crept along Gina's mouth.

"Really? Hope it doesn't come to that."

"You don't love him anymore, do you?"

"What gave it away?"

* * *

Matt approached Boardner's, a hipster joint disguised as a dive bar off Hollywood Boulevard. He was drinking from a bagged bottle of Johnnie Walker Black.

A thick-necked bouncer stood in front of Boardner's talking to some biker pals. He stopped Matt as he tried to enter the bar with the bottle of booze.

"Hey, man, this ain't no 'Bring your own' joint."

Matt said, "Hold it for me, will ya?" and handed him the bottle.

"Sure. . . ."

Matt entered the bar.

The bouncer checked out the bottle. More than half full. He handed it to one of the bikers and they had a laugh. The biker tipped the bottle up, took a big swig.

"Heeere's Johnnie!"

Boardner's was as fabulous inside as the facade outside promised. Eight-by-ten glossies of Hollywood has-beens faded on the walls, CCR's "Fortunate Son" blasted out of the jukebox, and strings of white Christmas lights trimmed the decor all year round. It was dark and crowded and reeked of cigarette smoke despite the state and city ordinances banning smoking in public places.

Matt staggered along the bar, checking out the locals. Bikers, rockers, wanna-bes, punks, drunks, dreamers, sluts, and slatterns. The disillusioned and the ignorantly optimistic. His people. His town. He was home.

The bartender, Jack Barrett, looked up from a flirtation at the end of the bar and said, "Hooooly shit. Look who it isn't."

Jack went over and shook hands with Matt from across the bar and said, "Goddamn, man, where the hell have you been?"

"Among the living."

"Well how the fuck are you?"

"Thirsty."

"Now you're talkin'."

Jack poured a shot of Jim Beam and sat it in front of Matt.

Matt said, "What's wrong? You too good to drink with me?"

Jack smiled, poured himself a shot.

Matt looked at the cluster of black-leather-clad rocker chicks hanging at the end of the bar with Jack's object of desire, a funky beast of a redhead. He raised his glass to the ladies, then looked at Jack and they clinked their glasses in a toast.

Jack said, "To good pussy."

"To good pussy."

They kicked back their glasses and drained them dry.

Matt indicated another pour. Jack hit both the glasses.

"To great tits."

"To great tits."

Clink. Tip. Guzzle.

Again.

"To firm, round ass."

"To firm, round ass."

"What the fuck else is there?" Jack asked.

Clink. Tip. Guzzle.

Matt gritted his teeth, shaking off the burn. "Damn, it's good to be back."

"C'mon. Meet the ladies."

Jack and Matt moved down the bar toward the women.

Jack said, "This is Patrice . . . Diana . . . Vicky. Girls, this is my good friend Matt. . . ."

Matt shook hands with each of them as they were introduced. The last one, the Latina named Vicky, showed immediate interest. She blushed as their hands touched and said, "Nice to meet you, Matt."

"Pleasure's mine. . . . What are you ladies up to tonight?"

"Just the continuing search for the perfect party."

"I heard that."

* * *

Five rounds later and Chris Isaak's "Dancing" was juking the joint. Matt, Jack, and the girls were laughing and having a great time, each of them drunk as horny skunks. They had been making idiots of themselves and the bar crowd had begun to thin out as a result. Jack's bartending skills diminished as his alcohol level increased and Matt's general aura of hostility glowed brighter with every shot. This combination did not create an environment conducive to peaceful sipping by innocent bystanders.

Matt leaned into Vicky and whispered in her ear, "Why don't we get out of here? Go somewhere quiet."

"Maybe. . . ."

A snicker went up somewhere in the room. Matt took notice of the two black guys halfway down the bar who had been staring at him for the better part of an hour. It was beginning to get on his nerves and now they were *laughing* at him. Where would it stop?

One of the men was huge. A linebacker without a team. The smaller of the two was bald, with an intense gaze that could pierce steel. They were both eyeballing him and it was pissing him off.

Matt straightened up, looked at them hard. He focused on the linebacker. "What you starin' at, brother?"

The big man said, "Not your brother, motherfucker."

"Then maybe you should quit eyeballing me."

The smaller of the two said, "Morris looks where Morris looks."

Jack, still behind the bar, took a step toward the two black men. "C'mon, fellas, let's not have any trouble in here."

Morris ignored Jack and kept staring at Matt. He said, "I know your ass. You're 5-0, aren't you?"

Matt leaned back on his barstool, let his coat drop open so Morris and Jamaal could see the gun in his shoulder holster.

Matt said, "That's right, hard-ass. I'm fucking 5-0. Want to make something of it?"

Jamaal said, "That's a stupid thing to do. Go flashing your shit around in some bar. Like you the only one in the city knows how to get a piece. Stupid."

Matt leaned forward. "You want something in particular, banger?"

"I'm no banger, bitch. I'm a businessman."

"You boys know who I am. I must've busted you sometime in the past."

Morris said, "You didn't bust me. You traffic-stopped me 'bout a month ago. Hassled my ass for driving a Mercedes through Beverly Hills. Like a big nigger can't own a Mercedes-Benz."

The event flashed on Matt. "Fuck yeah. I remember you. Wasn't your car either, was it, homey?"

"No, it was my cousin's ride. But he's a big black motherfucker too. You would have stopped him just the same."

"Just doing my job."

"You made me late for a meeting. Cost me money."

"Sorry about that. Jack, why don't we buy these young men a drink? Square things away."

Jack had retreated to the corner of the bar, sweating it out silently.

"Sure thing, Matt. Two more of the same, guys?"

Morris and Jamaal turned their heads and stared at Jack. Jamaal pulled a thick wad of cash out of his pocket, peeled off three twenties to pay their bill, and said, "Fuck you both. And stick the change up your ass."

Morris and Jamaal turned back to Matt, looked at him with dares in their eyes.

Matt said, "Just trying to be neighborly."

Morris said, "You're a fool."

Morris and Jamaal got up and headed for the door. Jamaal kept an eye on Matt as they walked away. Morris didn't even give him that.

Matt said, "Don't go away mad, fellas. I'm sure I'll see you around again."

Jamaal said, "Count on it, bitch."

Matt laughed as they walked out.

Jack leaned into him. "I wouldn't fuck with those guys if I were you."

"You're *not* me, are you?"

Matt looked at the women. They were silent, scared maybe, repulsed, probably. Matt stood up and took Vicky by the arm.

"Let's get out of here."

Vicky didn't move. She looked at him with a touch of fear in her eyes and said, "I think I want to stay here a little longer. With my friends. You know, it's rude to leave them like that. . . ."

Matt looked at her, comprehending the change in attitude. He was not happy about it. "Suddenly I'm a bad guy? What's that about? I'm supposed to sit here and take shit from those . . ."

He stopped short of saying it. Everyone in the bar was staring at him. Vicky looked at the floor.

Matt said, "Fuck this. . . ." He pulled out his wallet, tossed some money on the bar, and hissed at Jack, "Add that to your ass wad."

Matt stomped for the door.

Jack said, "C'mon, Matt . . ." But he was gone. Jack looked over at the ladies and said, "That guy's wound too tight."

Matt staggered out of Boardner's and walked up the street in the opposite direction from where his car was parked. His next destination was only four blocks away and he could use the fresh air.

It was getting late. Hollywood was winding down. The tourists had given up for the night, the homeless were bedding down in the alleys, and the streets were being claimed by crack dealers and their clients. No one approached Matt on his journey. He looked too *unsavory.*

He climbed the stairs of a crumbling apartment building in the heart of Hollywood. When he pulled on the security door it sprung open, busted long ago. Most of the fluorescent lights were burned out in the long hallway and the air was thick with the ghosts of a million Mexican and Indian meals. He found his way to apartment 14 and knocked hard on the door.

After a few moments shadows could be seen moving behind the peephole. A soft voice whispered, "Who is it?"

"It's me. Matt."

The voice took on a stern timbre. "Go away."

"Roz, please let me in."

"Go away."

"Please. I need to talk to you."

Locks turned and the door opened a few inches, still connected to a safety chain. Rosalind looked through the crack. She was an exquisite black woman, even half asleep and out of makeup. A Nubian princess lost in Hollywood.

"I told you I didn't want to see you anymore. I meant what I said."

"I've been having kind of a rough day."

She could smell the booze coming off his breath. "Oh my God, you're drinking again. You've really fucked up this time, haven't you?"

"Some things happened today. . ."

"I know what happened. It's all over the TV. That's no excuse for falling off the wagon."

"Can I just come in and lie down for a few minutes? I'm really tired."

"Go home. To your wife."

"I can't."

"Why not?"

"Someone else is there. A man. She's fucking someone else."

"It's about time she got smart."

Rosalind closed the door. Matt leaned against the wall and rested his eyes. After a long moment the door opened and he entered the apartment.

He had not been in the place since their last argument over a month ago, but nothing had changed. She always kept the apartment immaculate. Her taste was fine, but the furnishings were sparse. She had done what she could with her small income from waitressing at Hamburger Hamlet.

Rosalind was dressed in the sheer blue nightgown he had given her for Christmas. She had remarked at the time that it looked more like a gift for him than for her and it once again produced the desired effect on him. He hugged her tightly and immediately felt a stirring down below.

Matt sleepwalked toward the bedroom. Rosalind grabbed him by the arm and tried to stop him. "You're not getting in my bed."

He wrapped his arms around her and kissed her on the cheek. He tried to kiss her on the mouth but she struggled out of the way and he sloppily got her other cheek.

"Stop it, Matt. I told you I don't want anything to do with your bullshit anymore. I've had enough!"

"Please, baby, don't be like that. Not tonight. I need someone. . . . I need someone to understand."

She looked into his desperate, sad eyes and resigned herself to being his caretaker for one last night. Knowing what she knew about his afternoon, she couldn't rightly turn him away.

They fell into bed and into the familiar patterns that had come to dominate what was left of their relationship. But as the events of the day played through Matt's mind he became possessed by a savage urge to drive into Rosalind with a ferocity that took her by surprise. When he was nearing completion Matt realized that he was replaying the events he had witnessed from the doorway of his own bedroom only hours earlier. It was as if he and Rosalind were a negative image of Gina and her lover. White on black, black on white, he matched them stroke for stroke, caress for caress, and as much as he hated himself for it, the awareness of what he was doing did not stop him from climaxing violently deep into Rosalind's body. He churned inside her until the pressure faded and he felt himself going limp, then he collapsed onto her chest and felt complete for the first time that day. Except for maybe the six seconds it took to fire the rounds that had saved his life.

Rosalind turned on the light next to her bed. She and Matt were both naked and sweating. It had been a good ride. For both of them. The sex was always good with him. It was the rest of it that disturbed her.

Rosalind said, "I guess that's what you mean by 'understanding'?"

Matt gasped for breath and laughed.

"This is the last time, Matt. I mean it. Don't be coming around here anymore. I can't handle the head games."

"What if I told you it was over between Gina and me?"

"You've been saying that for two years. That shit won't ever be over."

"It's been over for a long time. I just never had the energy to get out. But I'm telling you now, I won't stay another second in that house. She can have the place for all I care."

"Keep talking, baby, if it makes you feel better."

Rosalind turned on the TV, flipped around the channels, stopping on NBC. A broadcaster was announcing over a logo, "The following is a rebroadcast of the eleven o'clock news. . . ."

Rosalind said, "You want to see this? I caught the early edition. You're famous. Again."

Matt didn't respond. On the tube a newscaster named Lisa Joyner was speaking into the lens as a logo of a gun firing and the words POLICE SHOOTING floated next to her. "A Los Angeles police officer lost his life today in an exchange of gunfire with two Latino youths. . . ."

Matt took the remote from Rosalind and turned off the TV. "Fucking beaners. . . ."

Rosalind stared at him silently.

Matt touched her on the shoulder. "I didn't mean that the way it sounded."

"Yes you did. You can't help it. It's who you are."

"They killed Harris. They tried to kill me. What am I supposed to say?"

"You can say whatever you want. I'm sure those boys' families are talkin' about you right now in exactly the same way."

"At least those two pieces of shit are still alive."

"Just a few holes to patch up, huh?"

"The fuckers robbed a seventy-two-year-old man and beat him half to death. We pull 'em over and they fire fucking AKs at us. I guess after they killed my partner I should have just asked them nicely to drop their weapons and come on down with me to the station."

"Hey, what do I care? Everybody can just keep on hating every-body."

Matt got out of bed and started getting dressed.

"You're some piece of work. Harris is down at the morgue and you want to have a dialogue on race relations."

"I just think you should acknowledge your racism if you're going to be carrying a gun and a badge around on the streets of L.A."

Matt glared at her. "I'm no racist."

Rosalind laughed. "Please, baby, don't play me."

"If I'm a racist, what the hell am I doing with you?"

"You think fucking me proves you're not a racist? Your great-great-grandfather probably fucked his slaves. That doesn't mean *he* wasn't a racist."

"My family never had slaves. We're from Connecticut."

"They *would* have had them if they could."

"Why does it always have to be about color? I'm with you because of who you are. I don't give a damn about race."

"That's bullshit, Matt. You've been trying to make up for something. I don't know what it is, but I know you've done something bad and you think you can find redemption in my pussy. Well, you're looking in the wrong place. You need to find it within yourself."

Matt considered Rosalind's words. Then he put on his shoulder holster and gun, grabbed his jacket, and headed for the door.

Matt exited the apartment building, huddled up against the early morning chill, and walked the ashen streets of Hollywood. He went down Cherokee, past the darkened Boardner's sign, turned the next corner, and entered the cul-de-sac alley where he had left his car.

The alley reeked of garbage and human waste. One tinted sodium vapor light from the lot next door filtered into the darkness, casting a yellow glow over his vehicle, which was parked at the very end of the cul-de-sac. He was glad to see no glistening glass on the ground around the car. No predator had smashed his windows to get his radio. It helped that the car looked like plainclothed trouble.

Matt fumbled drunkenly with his keys and dropped them. As he bent down to get them he noticed two feet stepping out of the shadows. He looked up.

Morris, the big black dude whose cousin owned a Mercedes, towered above him. Morris said, "Nobody around to help you now, 5-0."

Morris kicked Matt in the face, knocking him against the car door. Matt scrambled to his feet and turned to run, only to find the bald guy called Jamaal standing behind him. Jamaal forearmed Matt in the face, knocking him toward Morris.

Matt reached under his coat for his gun, but Morris grabbed his arm and twisted it around behind his back. "Uh-uh, motherfucker, that's *our* gun. . . ."

Jamaal reached under Matt's jacket and pulled the pistol free. Jamaal looked at the gun, a Browning 9mm, and smiled. "A real

PO-lice gun. Muuuutherfuuuucker. How many niggers you off with this piece, 5-0?"

Matt just stared at him.

Jamaal chambered a shell and pointed the barrel at Matt's face. "Oh, bitch, I want to blow your fucking head off so baaad."

Morris said, "Go right through him and hit me, little brother."

"Fuuuuckk. . . ."

Jamaal pistol-whipped Matt across the face, opening a cut over his eye.

Morris said, "I got an idea. . . . I'm gonna try the choke hold out on him. . . ."

Morris shifted Matt's body and put him in a classic police choke hold. Matt struggled with all his strength, knowing full well that this could be the end of his life, but he couldn't overcome the more powerful man's grip.

Jamaal danced in front of Matt, waving the gun in his face.

"Oh, yassss! Take that motherfucker OUT! Die, you Mark Fuhrman–lookin' motherfucker!"

Matt could feel an overwhelming darkness creeping into his brain. Was this how it would end, killed by a couple of angry barflies in an alley in Hollywood? Was this what he had been working for all of his life, so he could rot in a stink-encrusted cul-de-sac? Would they ever catch these fuckers, or would he go into the cold files as an unsolved homicide while these scumbags played Wyatt Earp with his backup piece? These questions were replaced by a quick moment of existential panic right before the lights went out.

The cop went limp as a rag doll. Morris dropped him to the ground.

Jamaal said, "Is the bitch dead?"

Morris picked up the cop's keys and went around to get in the car. "Who the fuck cares?"

Jamaal looked down at the cop, kicked his body. There was no movement in return. He reached into the cop's pocket and lifted his wallet. Then he aimed the pistol at the cop's head and caressed the trigger.

BANG!

Jamaal jumped as the car backfired, Morris having turned the key in the ignition. Jamaal looked at Morris, who revved the engine and grinned. Jamaal said, "Scare the fuck out of me, why don't you?"

"Get in. I got an idea what we can do with that piece. . . ."

Jamaal stared at the cop. He looked dead already, why waste a bullet? Besides, they ever go down for this it'd be better if Morris was the one pulling the capital time. He got in the car and they drove away.

SATURDAY

Morning light crept into the alley. A mangy dog rummaged behind a Dumpster for food. It came over and sniffed Matt Clark's face, sniffed his clothes, lifted its leg and urinated on his forehead, claiming Matt as part of his territory.

Matt woke with a start, realized what was happening, and screamed from the gutter depths of his soul. The dog scrambled out of the alley, hungry but relieved.

Matt sat up, choking, wiping dog piss off his face.

"Son of a bitch!"

He looked around. His car was gone. He got to his feet, still drunk, rubbed the back of his neck, and tried to remember what had happened. He checked for his gun. Gone. Checked for his wallet. Gone. The only thing he had left was himself, and that was a dubious consolation prize.

Light was beginning to fill the horizon as Matt trudged up Vine, heading for home. Morning traffic had already begun to gather steam by the time he reached Franklin. He stopped at the

ARCO station and bummed a cup of coffee off the Indian behind the counter.

"You look very bad, my friend," the Indian cracked. "Very bad."

Matt made the long, arduous climb into the Hollywood Hills. Beachwood Canyon was coming alive with Saturday-morning enthusiasm. The joggers were hitting it early, limbering up in their expensive sweat suits, their Sony Walkmans and their brand-name bottles of water strapped to their waists. Matt finished his coffee and considered puking on a group of passing runners.

He hated the yuppies in his neighborhood. These were the people he was paid to protect, but they were the first to assume the worst and scream bloody murder any time the media implied that a cop had crossed the line. They took for granted the freedom of movement on these mean streets that cops spilled their own blood to guarantee.

Buying into this neighborhood had been Gina's idea. Even with both their incomes they had trouble making the mortgage every month. The only reason he went along with it was the view. They had a great view of the city from every room in the house. He felt like he could keep an eye on things from up here. If the town started to burn again, he would be one of the first to know.

He took the series of small streets that led to his house halfway up the mountain. He was completely winded by the time he got to the empty lot that overlooked his house. He threw up in the bushes and felt better, then he stood on the crest of the hill, watching the rising sun glint off the HOLLYWOOD sign in the distance. He pulled down his zipper and pissed bad coffee and good liquor in a great arc into the valley below. He wished he could have pissed on the sign itself, but this was as close as he could get in his current state of confusion.

When Matt entered the house, Gina was at the breakfast table, having coffee. A newspaper was folded on the table in front of her. She did not seem startled to see him.

The house was split level. The front door opened on the top floor where the bedroom and bathroom were located. Ten stairs led down to the kitchen, living room, and dining room. Matt stood at the top of the stairs, looking down at his wife.

Gina said, "You shouldn't be here."

"It's my house."

"It won't be for long. I called my attorney. We'll be filing on Tuesday."

"Which attorney is this? The brother who was in my bed last night or some other stud?"

"I'm using Nick Tatum."

"Nick's *my* attorney."

"Not this time."

"You fucking him too?"

"Don't be such a child."

Matt snorted and started to walk down the stairs.

Gina calmly reached under the newspaper and produced the 9mm Colt pistol that John, the horny defense attorney, had given her the night before.

"Just stay where you are," she said. "I have no intention of ending up like Nicole."

"I guess that would make *me* Phil Hartman then. . . ."

"Not unless you push it."

Matt continued down the stairs.

Gina stood up to get a better aim and steady her arms. She took the classic combat stance that Matt had taught her on the firing range when they were first dating. Funny how a mating ritual can backfire on you like that.

"I mean it, Matt. Don't even think about it."

"I need some fresh air. I'm going out to the patio. You want to shoot me, go ahead. I really don't give a fuck."

Gina took a step back, let Matt pass her, keeping the gun on him at all times.

Matt opened the sliding glass doors, went to the rail of the large wood deck that he had built with his own two hands, and looked out over the city. Somewhere down there two black dudes were joyriding in his Plymouth.

Gina stepped into the doorway, pistol lowered to her side.

"What happened to you?"

"What hasn't?"

"I heard about Harris."

Matt didn't look at her. "Yeah? How? The TV?"

"That and about fifty calls looking for you. They're worried about you, Matt."

"That come as some kind of shock to you? That someone could actually *care* about me?"

"The whining male thing won't work this time. Any excuse and you're on a bender."

"Don't flatter yourself. I'm not on a bender. I'm just maintaining an attitude."

"Well maintain it somewhere else. I'm sorry about Harris, but this marriage is over. I'll give you five minutes to pack some things. Then I want you out of here or I'll call your field supervisor."

"Call him."

Gina backed into the house.

Matt stared at the smog-shrouded city in the distance. His eyes were bloodshot, his face bruised. The cut over his eye began to drip. He wiped it away with his sleeve. Los Angeles beckoned with her hungry stare. These were the people he bled for. Did they appreciate him? No. Most of them hated him. Thought all cops were racist and corrupt. Thought Rodney King a hero and Jesse Jackson a prophet. The Rampart scandal had just added fuel to the fire. Like all their evil theories had been proven correct just because some bad cops had been caught breaking the law. That didn't keep Harris from eating pavement yesterday. Matt would have been right alongside him if he had been two seconds slower on the draw. Would he get a commendation for his bravery and his skill? Hell, by the time the fixers were done with the case he'd be lucky if he could stay out of jail for shooting those punks. Like *they* should have more rights than him or his partner. What the fuck was he doing here?

Maybe he could go to Canada. His sister lived in Vancouver. The only racial problems Vancouver had were all the rich Asians that had flooded the place, fleeing Hong Kong. He could live with that. No problem at all. He could work as a security consultant up there and never get shot at again. Never have charges brought against him for just doing his job. Canada. Vancouver. That was it. Next stop: the bank, then LAX. He went back into the house.

Gina was at the dining room table, pouring herself another cup of coffee. She still held the pistol in her right hand.

Matt walked past her and headed for the staircase.

"See you, bitch."

"What about your clothes?"

"Burn 'em."

"My pleasure."

"I bet."

Matt went up the stairs and out the front door.

Gina yelled after him, "*Chickenshit!*"

A shock went through her body after she said it. She knew it had been a bad mistake. Why did she have to push it? There was a moment of silence. Maybe he hadn't heard her? Maybe he didn't care?

No such luck.

Matt suddenly came back through the door. "You always have to have the last word, don't you, cunt?"

He bounded down the stairs in a rage.

Gina dropped her coffee cup, raised the pistol, and aimed it at Matt.

"Stay the fuck away from me, asshole! I'll kill you!"

Matt continued forward, yelling, "Do it! Do it! Do it!"

Gina pulled the hammer back, letting him know she meant

business. She was shaking badly. Matt was right in front of her now, arms down at his sides.

"Come on, bitch! Show me what you've got! You've been killing me slowly since the first day I met you. Let's end it now! Let's go!"

Tears were brimming in Gina's eyes. Tears of fear . . . and hatred.

"Fuck you! You think it's been easy being married to you? It's been a big fucking pain in the ass. And a bore. That's the biggest problem. You just bore my ass! Fucking cop. Think you're better than everyone else. You're nothing but a goddamned storm trooper!"

"You're the one with the gun. Let's see what you're made of."

"I'll do it, swear to God I will."

"What's stopping you?"

Matt pushed his forehead directly against the barrel of the pistol and left it there.

Gina stared at him, crazy with pent-up rage. Seven years of domestic hell was culminating in this moment. But she couldn't pull the trigger.

She lowered the weapon.

Matt sneered at her, the way he had sneered a million times over her weaknesses and failures.

The sneer filled Gina with new resolve.

She raised the gun, aimed it dead center at Matt's chest, and pulled the trigger.

Click.

No flash.

No bang.

There was either no bullet in the chamber or the one that was there was a dud. She was certain she had cocked the gun the night before, then depressed the hammer and put on the safety to prevent an accidental firing while she slept with it under her pillow. She had clicked off the safety while making coffee in the morning and assumed she was properly prepared to defend herself if the need arose. All she had to do was pull the hammer back and squeeze the trigger. So what had happened?

They stood there staring at each other, contemplating what it all meant. She had just done her best to kill him. But fate had saved him and screwed her.

As it sank in to Matt's foggy brain that he should be on the ground bleeding to death, just like his partner eighteen hours earlier, his anger swelled.

Matt slapped the gun out of Gina's hand. "Whore!"

The gun tumbled through the air, end over end, struck the fireplace, and bounced to the floor, hitting *hard*. The gun fired, the bullet finally making contact with enough sharp force to discharge it.

The bullet pinged off a metal heating grate in the wall, ricocheting . . .

. . . off a marksman trophy engraved to Matt, which sat on the mantel, bouncing off and striking . . .

. . . a huge buckle on Gina's purse, which was hanging from a dining room chair . . .

. . . coming off at an angle, smashing through a wedding photo of Gina and Matt in happier times . . .

Final destination: Gina's forehead.

There was a brief moment where their eyes locked and they wrestled with disbelief. What had happened? What was happening? *Could* this be happening? Did a bullet really just go through her/my forehead? *What can we do about this?*

Matt was shocked, but Gina didn't have enough time to fully comprehend the event. She took her stunned expression to the floor with her. She was gone before she hit the ground.

Matt stared down at his dead wife. "Gina?"

No response was possible. Her brains were splattered on the picture window behind her, tainting the nice view. Matt looked at the gun, retraced the circuitous route it took to find his wife, then shook his head in wonder.

"That was a hell of a shot."

Matt Clark washed his face, put a Band-Aid on the cut over his eye, and rinsed the blood off the arm of his jacket. He looked at his face in the mirror. What had he done? Was it his fault? Who would believe otherwise?

He went into the bedroom and rifled through the dresser drawers looking for money. He found a few bucks, some coins, not enough to get very far. He pocketed the dough and rubbed his temples. His head was throbbing.

He went to the top of the stairs and looked down at Gina's dead body, stretched out on the living room floor. The pool of blood around her head had stopped spreading. She looked like an angel with a red halo.

Matt turned and went out the front door.

Concrete stairs led to the streets directly above and below his house. He could either go up the long flight of steps into the mountains above or down into the city below.

He chose the downward path.

Once he reached the bottom of the stairs he took to the surface streets, passing the development exec getting his *L.A. Times* off the front porch of his half-million-dollar bungalow, the young starlet coming home from a long night of auditioning, the elderly couple scraping last night's roadkill off the front bumper of their SUV, the little rich kids tossing firecrackers in their backyard. The neighborhood was in full long-weekend mode, but none of his neighbors would have a weekend as long as his.

As Matt descended from the heights of the Hollywood Hills, heading for the bottom of Beachwood Canyon, he passed a street sign that made him pause and laugh.

He was walking down Detour Drive.

Dying for Sin

WENDI LEE

*T*he gunshots echoed off the cathedral's stained-glass scenes. Screams followed the shots, bouncing around the apse in a ghostly imitation of the real thing. Zoë couldn't move, she could only watch as bits of blood and bone sprayed her pale blue designer skirt and matching jacket. She found herself inspecting her father's expression, a study in beatific suffering and acceptance. She noted the details: the crucifix behind the altar, the crown of thorns, the bowl of pebbles. She remembered Papa's habit of taking a pebble from the bowl at Easter and worrying it between his fingers.

Her brother Rico stood beside her, his hands on her shoulders, keeping her from getting in the way of the assassin's bullets. It was over as suddenly as it began. Papa's body, the shell that once held the man who had raised her and loved her, was falling toward her, arms out in a ghostly imitation of Jesus on the cross, dying for our sins.

Her scream dried up in her throat. Rico held her back and she tried to shake him off, tried to get to her father, but her brother's grip tightened.

Finally able to break Rico's hold, she knelt over Papa's body. No matter how much she pounded on his chest, Papa wouldn't breathe *for her. The scream that had shriveled up in her throat now burst forth. Once again, Zoë was able to breathe.*

Zoë bolted upright in bed, sweaty and trembling. A figure was bent over her in the darkened room, talking to her in a soothing manner. "Zoë. Zoë. It's okay. You're all right. You were having a nightmare." A hand rubbed her back, stroked her hair. An arm went around her shoulders. The scent of White Shoulders surrounded her. Faith. It was Faith who was by her bedside.

Zoë gulped in air like a water-starved goldfish. Her heart was hammering triple-time. She felt the wetness on her cheeks and pulled a corner of her bedsheet out to pat her face dry.

Faith had turned on the small night-light by Zoë's bed, illuminating the room in a golden glow.

"When will I stop having this nightmare?" Her voice was as shaky as she felt, but she managed a smile in Faith's direction. Probably the most horrific aspect about her nightmare was that the details weren't right. Zoë had been seated in the second row, next to Faith. There had been only one shot, not several. In her dream, Papa fell toward her—in reality, he had fallen away from her. She hadn't seen much more than a little blood because she had hidden her face against Rico's shoulder.

"It's only been a few days, Zoë. You can't expect to forget something like that."

In the five years that Faith had worked for Zoë, she had become more than an employee, she had become Zoë's closest friend. Faith was the oldest of Zoë's "girls." A woman of thirty-two, Faith had been a battered wife who had finally summoned up the courage to leave her husband and start a new life. Unfortunately, her husband hadn't wanted Faith to start a new life, and had come after her. Fortunately, one of the nights that he attempted to beat on her in public, Papa De Silva was there. Papa brought her to Zoë's establishment, the Purple Rose. No one ever heard from Faith's husband again.

Zoë had started the Purple Rose seven years ago. After finishing high school, Papa had asked her to think about what she wanted to do with her life. Zoë decided to start a halfway house for young women who needed a way to get back on their feet. The Purple Rose became just such a place: a house of ill repute where the clients stayed the same, but the women kept rotating.

The idea was simple: A woman could work for Zoë's brothel while she went to college. Her room and board were paid for, as well as her education and other incidentals. When she earned her chosen degree, she left "the life" to follow her chosen profession. The only stipulations were that she not marry or have any romantic ties while she was studying, and that she leave at the appointed time—five years from the day she moved in to work for Zoë.

In the seven years that Zoë had been running her offbeat social service, eleven former "working women" were now respectable working women. Three had become teachers; two now operated their own businesses—one owned a restaurant and the other ran a high-society boutique; one was working for the mayor's office; and the other five women were in various high-powered positions within the top industries in the city. One alumna of the Purple Rose had even become a vice president of Stanton Industries. They had proven to be very useful to Papa in their current positions.

Faith would be graduating from college soon with a degree in nursing, and would soon be leaving to work the second shift at St. Francis. One of their favorite private jokes was about the client who liked to have Faith dress up as a sexy nurse and play hospital.

"Bert's getting you ready for your career," Zoë joked.

Faith giggled. "Yeah, I'm going to spend most of my days being chased around a hospital bed by male patients in wheelchairs and walkers."

Looking at Faith, it wasn't hard to imagine that happening. She was a tall honey blonde with intelligent green eyes and a stunning smile. She smiled. "I'm okay now. Why don't you get some sleep."

Faith squeezed Zoë's hand, kissed her cheek, and left.

Zoë reached out to her right for her teddy bear, Abercrombie, the beaten and worn stuffed animal that she had owned since before Papa had taken her into his fold. She had been just eight years old. Her mother had been a no-account crack whore who had come forward, claiming that Zoë was Papa's child. When he offered to take Zoë off her hands, her mother held out for money before turning her over. She sold her daughter to Papa for the kind of money it would have taken her a week to earn with her body.

Then, because she hadn't gotten the original sum she'd asked for from Papa, she turned around and sold Zoë again, this time to Frank Murdock, a purveyor of pornography and prostitution. Murdock was head of the Irish mob, and it was reputed that he didn't care how he made his money, as long as other people were being used to make it for him. He sat back and collected the profits.

Zoë shuddered as she recalled Murdock, the man who insisted she call him Daddy for the first eight years of her life. "Daddy" taught her how to please a man. He sold her services to men who liked little girls.

She didn't know there was a better life out there until Papa, or rather, Rico, rescued her from Murdock's clutches. When Papa finally sent Rico to search for Zoë, he found her, took her home, and showed her that love for family wasn't anything like what she knew from Murdock. She adored Papa—he was the father she had always imagined she would have. She was relieved that he was her real father, not Frank Murdock.

Still, her time with Murdock was etched indelibly in her memory. She remembered every humiliation, every bruise and cut, every time "Daddy" told her to love him. To this day, she couldn't have sex for enjoyment. She ran the Purple Rose, but if any man requested her for the night, she turned him down, preferring to let her girls earn their college tuition, preferring to keep to herself. Zoë remained forever marked by her time with Murdock. All the therapists and psychoanalysts available hadn't been able to erase the horror of her young life.

She fervently wished she could switch Murdock with Papa. Murdock's death would be a favor to the world at large. Papa's death had diminished the world a little bit.

Pulling the covers up to her neck, Zoë tried to go back to sleep, but all that she could think about was the coming war among the factions of organized crime now that Papa was gone. What, in fact, was going to happen to her business? Papa's protection was a large part of what kept Zoë's good works going. Without him, what was she going to do? She liked to think that Rico would allow the Purple Rose to continue.

Emma watched her lover, Lilith Malone, light up another expensive foreign cigarette. Lilith normally smoked only a couple of times a day, but Papa's death had set her on edge and Emma felt helpless to make things right. Lilith was standing in front of the lighted vanity mirror, making sure every hair was in place. She never went anywhere without looking as if she'd stepped off the pages of a fashion magazine.

"The way you're going through those coffin nails, you're gonna have to buy another pack before the funeral service," Emma said as her eyes took in the curve of Lilith's full breasts in the form-fitting black velvet dress. She couldn't help it—she reached out and cupped her lover's left breast, pressing her body against Lilith. They fit so well together. She was tempted to peel off Lilith's dress like a skin of a banana and make love to her, mess her hair, watch a thin sheen of sweat cover her perfect skin, make her cry out with desire and joy, make Lilith want more.

"Why don't you put that cigarette out?" Emma lightly rubbed her hand over Lilith's belly, which curved ever so slightly. Her hand wandered farther down over the curve of a hip.

Lilith closed her eyes and leaned into Emma, clearly savoring the intensity of the moment. Then she opened her dark eyes and shot an amused look at her paramour and bodyguard in the mirror. "Do funerals make you hot, my dear?"

Emma reluctantly stepped back and sighed. Lilith's question was designed to remind Emma of their obligations. And to Lilith, business always came first. "I always desire you," Emma said, favoring Lilith with a playful smile. "I was going to suggest another way to relieve the tension."

A sly smile appeared on Lilith's lush lips. A light went on in her exotic cat's eyes. "Maybe we can do something about my tension later. After we pay our respects to the De Silvas."

Emma stood up and smoothed her more conservative dress, a gray skirt and jacket with black brocade around the neckline, hem, and sleeves. Bold black buttons marched down the front of the jacket, giving it a solemn air. Lilith reached out and Emma dutifully came closer. Her lover pulled her close and kissed her deeply.

Emma pulled away this time and smiled. "I'd better touch up my lipstick."

Emma and Lilith had learned of Papa's death on Friday night while they were working at Lilith's nightclub, the Midnight Rendezvous.

Although Papa's death had shaken up most of the underworld, and a good part of the rest of the city, Emma hadn't had much contact with Papa, except for a couple of times when they'd both been eating at Papa's Ristorante.

Emma knew that Lilith had business dealings with Papa, the head of the De Silva mob, but she hadn't thought that Lilith would react with anything more than a shake of her head and a crocodile tear. She was totally unprepared for Lilith's response—she barely slept or ate for two days, and had gone through three cartons of those fancy cigarettes. Probably most disturbing was Lilith's total lack of concentration and attention to her duties at the club. In fact, she barely made an appearance on Saturday night before begging off, explaining that she had a headache. For a fleet second,

Emma wondered if there was someone else. However, she shook off that insecurity and attended to the duties of running the club.

She went back to her duties, but Emma's mind was on Papa De Silva and the effects of his death on the city. But she knew what was troubling Lilith. It was the same thing that troubled all who were touched by Papa De Silva's untimely death: Who was going to head up the crime syndicates now that Giacomo De Silva was dead?

And now, as the two women readied themselves for his funeral, Emma finally spoke up. It was now or never, she thought. "Darling?"

Lilith was smoothing her hair with a boar's-bristle brush, taking care to turn under the ends so that it was one continuous wave across the back of her black dress. "Mmmm?" was her response.

"Do you think Rico is going to take over as head of the De Silvas?"

Lilith stopped brushing her hair and looked at Emma's mirror image. Emma tried to read her lover's face, but Lilith's expression was impassive. "Of course he will. Who else would? Papa was grooming him for that position."

Emma waited a beat, then asked, "And who will be taking up Papa's mantle as benevolent tyrant, deciding what the organizations can and can't bring into the city?"

Lilith put the brush down, her cold eyes never leaving Emma. A sly smile crossed her luscious ruby-red lips. "Why, I will, of course."

Of course, thought Emma. Who else?

Zoë slid into the place beside Papa's third wife, Giselle, and gave her a hug. Giselle wore a black veil, black gloves, black pearls. When Papa had married Giselle, no one had had the nerve to say anything, even though it was only a few months after his second wife mysteriously died.

Vic, Papa and Giselle's son, sat on the other side of his mother. He turned his head to nod to Zoë, then acknowledged Rico and Faith, who had taken seats in the second row. Before the funeral started, Zoë looked around one more time, recognizing members of the Tong, the Triad, and the Yakuza as well as Freidman's people and Lilith Malone. There were members of the media, members of law enforcement, both the bought and those who couldn't be bought. Zoë suspected that the ones who couldn't be bought weren't there to pay their respects to the De Silvas, but to ferret out his killer, and to make sure Papa was really dead. Cardinal Micelli was missing—he was in the hospital on life support, having collapsed from a stroke on Holy Saturday.

Sweeping the church one last time, Zoë realized that there was one faction missing: Frank Murdock was nowhere to be seen, and Zoë didn't see anyone from his organization. It wasn't a shock—Papa had said many times that Murdock had no class, and Zoë had seen no reason to disagree with him on that point. Almost everyone suspected that Murdock had ordered the hit, and he wasn't smart enough to show up for the funeral in an effort to dispel those rumors. In her heart, Zoë knew Papa had been assassinated by Murdock.

Monsignor Rossi stepped up to the front of the sanctuary and took his place at the altar. Zoë tried to quiet the thoughts that bothered her. Rico would replace Papa, but she knew Papa had been worried about Rico's shortcomings: Papa used to always say that Rico didn't have enough presence. And it was true—Zoë couldn't picture Rico calling a meeting of the mob leaders and conducting business the way Papa had done.

"Giacomo De Silva was a good man, a pious man, a man who knew what was important in life," Monsignor Rossi began. "We are gathered here today to pay tribute to a man who touched all of our lives. He loved family above all else." His sharp eyes took in the front row, sweeping over Zoë, Giselle, Rico.

The door at the back of the church suddenly swung open,

commanding everyone's attention. Frank Murdock strolled through the doors, upsetting the service, upsetting Giselle, who had taken to sobbing uncontrollably, angering Zoë and Rico with his boorish behavior. He was even uglier than Zoë remembered—his hair was gray now, and his bulldog face had sagging jowls. His formerly muscular frame was running to fat. But he was still a larger-than-life presence, and it seemed that when he entered the cathedral, everything stopped.

Murdock had the sense to not push it. He took a seat toward the back of the church and nodded to the monsignor to continue. After faltering slightly, trying to find his place in the sermon, the priest took up where he left off and his passionate delivery assured everyone there that Giacomo De Silva was a fine, upstanding citizen, a man who stood by his children, and a good Catholic.

Giselle brought the black lace hankie up to her eyes. Rico absentmindedly patted her shoulder while looking straight ahead, seeming to be lost in thought. Zoë would have given anything to know what he was thinking. She turned back to the service, and a tear slid down her cheek as the first organ notes of "Ave Maria" filled the air.

Papa's Ristorante was closed for the day to welcome the mourners. Zoë joined Vic, Rico, and Giselle as they accepted the condolences from those who came to pay their respects to the survivors.

Just then, Murdock came in the door. He had a smirk on his face as he surveyed the dining room, his eyes finally resting on Zoë.

Rico took Zoë's arm. "Zoë, be a good girl and circulate." He patted her on the arm and smiled with his mouth, but not his eyes, which glittered with anger. "By the way, the family needs to talk tomorrow. We need to be clear on a few things."

Zoë pulled Rico close and said quietly, "I want Murdock dead."

He pulled away from her. Zoë was sure he could see, by her expression, that she was serious.

"We'll talk about it later," was all he could say before being called away to greet more guests.

Before she had a chance to do more than narrow her eyes at his abruptness, he was halfway across the dining room to check on an ice sculpture that was going to be a centerpiece at the buffet table.

Rico still thought of her as the fragile child he had rescued. He had never accepted the fact that Zoë could stand up to Murdock and show her contempt without breaking into tears and blame. But she could always count on Rico to be protective of her.

As soon as Rico was called into the kitchen to calm down the chef, Murdock approached her.

"You're looking good, kid." His eyes swept her body up and down, lingering on her breasts.

She remembered Papa's lesson: Never let them see your weak side. She wondered again if he had been behind the assassination attempt. "Your condolences are appreciated." If Murdock caught the sarcasm, he didn't show it.

"Yeah, I bet they are." Murdock smirked. He put something into those words, something lascivious that wasn't appropriate, especially on such a solemn day. But she was aware that he was baiting her.

She leveled her gaze at him. "He was a wise and kind man, a man anyone would be proud to call a father. He didn't beat me or do perverse things to me in the name of love. I was very fortunate to be taken into this family."

Murdock actually looked serious for a moment. No, Zoë corrected herself, he looked puzzled.

"I've always wondered," Zoë said, "why Papa didn't have you killed for what you did to me and all those other children."

He reached out and with one finger lifted her chin up so she was forced to look at him. "Don't you know? I had something on him and if anything happened to me, my lawyer would have made Giacomo's secrets public." He grinned as shock registered on her face. He laughed. "What Papa didn't think about is that once he died, I'd be next in line to take over as head of the crime mobs. And I plan to make some changes in your brothel, daughter."

Zoë's face felt like it had turned to stone. "You have no say in the Purple Rose. Rico's in charge, not you."

Murdock grinned. "Maybe, but can you see that wimp calling a meeting to order, let alone heading Papa's organization? And what makes you think he won't change your brothel once he gets a little power? He's always fallen in line with what Papa wanted, but I know he's got ideas of his own."

She crossed her arms, suddenly cold. "How would you know that?"

"We got drunk together once, before you came along. He told me he wanted to expand into prostitution, but Papa nixed the idea. Then you came along, and years later you brought up the same idea with a twist. And were successful. You think Rico won't take it away from you?"

An invisible fist squeezed her heart. Zoë couldn't breathe. No, she couldn't believe that of Rico. He had always been so sweet to her. He was her savior. Murdock was just trying to drive a wedge between them.

Zoë turned away from Murdock and circulated among the crowd to calm down. She found herself catching snatches of conversation when people weren't aware of her presence.

"Who's going to take over for Papa?"

"I don't think Rico's strong enough."

"I predict Murdock's a shoo-in, now that Papa's gone."

"The De Silvas are going to go the way of the Freidmans if they don't watch out."

Rico was talking to Rabbi Seidelman when she approached him.

"Hello, Rabbi." She accepted his brief hug, then turned to Rico. "I need to talk to you now."

The rabbi excused himself and left Rico and Zoë alone.

"I've just been talking to Murdock."

A muscle twitched in Rico's jaw at the mention of his enemy's name. "I was trying to keep you from having contact with him. We'll take care of him later."

A wave of affection and sadness washed over Zoë. "He thinks he's going to take Papa's place. He said he was taking over the Purple Rose." Rico didn't say anything, but there was a wary look in his eyes. "He told me that even if you became the head," she continued, "you'd want the Purple Rose to become just another brothel. Tell me he's lying, Rico."

Rico didn't meet her eyes for a moment. Then he looked at her. "Zoë, we can make so much more money from your business if we don't use it as a social work program."

Zoë set her mouth in a thin line. "Rico, I don't think you're getting the big picture here." She wanted to explain how the women she helped were now in positions to help the Family.

His eyes strayed to the door. "Can we talk about this later, Zoë? This is not the time."

She nodded with reluctance, kissed his cheek, and moved away. She needed fresh air. Donning her coat, she caught Lilith's eye and nodded briefly to her before leaving the restaurant.

Papa had been more than a father to her. He had been her friend, her mentor, her support. It had all been taken away from her with one gunshot, and she wondered where she was going from here. She wanted to find the man who shot him, but even more, she wanted to find the man who ordered the shot.

Zoë looked up for the first time since she left Papa's Ristorante and noticed that she had been wandering toward the waterfront. She hadn't intended to take a long walk, but even now, she sensed that someone was following her.

The streetlights weren't as reliable here as they were near the restaurant. Nevertheless, she spotted the limo even before it pulled alongside her. Zoë tried to ignore it. She hoped it wasn't someone out to harm her—possibly a man who thought she was a street-walker.

She wondered if Rico had sent along a limo to watch her, to make sure she was going to get home all right. The door to the limo opened and the overhead light in the car illuminated a sleek blonde wearing a gray jacket and skirt with black trim. Zoë recognized her as Lilith Malone's right hand, Emma.

Emma smiled. "Need a lift? We need to talk."

As Papa's daughter slipped into the car, Emma couldn't help but feel the timing was inappropriate. But Lilith had insisted. "Feel her out," she'd said.

Emma, arms crossed, wiseass expression firmly in place, had replied, "Literally?"

Lilith had stopped and shot a look of disgust at her lover. "Don't take this lightly. I know this isn't a great time to be talking to her, but I think she's our best chance, and we need to move fast. Murdock is probably mobilizing the Tongs and Triads as we sit here discussing this matter. And Freidman's still on the fence."

Emma had to agree with Lilith. But it didn't keep her from feeling queasy about taking advantage of Zoë De Silva's grief.

Zoë slid in beside Emma, who offered her a glass of red wine. "It's too cold out there to be walking."

"I was thinking."

"Must be tough to lose your dad." Emma took a sip of her wine. She wouldn't know—she'd never had a dad growing up, and looking at Zoë's pain-racked face, she felt lucky.

Zoë looked down into her wine and shrugged. "So what did you want to talk about?"

Over the edge of her glass, Emma feigned surprise. "What makes you think I have an agenda in mind?"

Zoë smiled. "Come on. You followed me in your car for at

least half a mile, and I'm supposed to think you just happened by?"

"Okay, Lilith wanted me to talk to you, find out about your loyalties."

"My loyalty is with Papa," Zoë said without a moment's hesitation.

Emma raised one perfectly arched eyebrow. "I'm talking now that Papa is no longer with us."

Zoë closed her eyes for a moment. "I can't think of that right now. Not until I find out who killed Papa."

Emma sensed that if there was one thing Zoë had learned from Papa, it was patience. Outwaiting the other party was part of the game, something that Rico and, as far as she could tell, most of the other leaders had never learned. Lilith was an exception, which was why Emma felt that her lover had the best chance of taking Papa De Silva's place. She would sit back and watch the others kill each other off until she was left.

Emma put her glass down on the small bar and leaned back in her seat. "So right now your allegiance is with Rico?"

Emma knew that Rico had spoken out against the Purple Rose recently. He wanted more profit and couldn't see the long-term benefits of making other women's lives better. He was as short-sighted as the rest of the men who headed up the various crime syndicates in the city.

"He's my brother," Zoë replied in a carefully neutral tone. "And I hope he will respect my business interests as Papa did."

Emma smiled. "I understand that Rico has not respected your business interests in the past. He was against your idea from the beginning. What makes you think he'll change?"

"We haven't talked yet. I can't make any predictions at this point." Zoë frowned, clearly confused and a little angry. "What's this all about? Did you come here to ask where my loyalties lay or to talk me into switching loyalties?"

Emma picked up her glass again and recrossed her legs. "Lilith wanted to know if you'd consider allying yourself with us."

Zoë made a face. "She sided with Murdock the last time we had a meeting."

Emma sipped her wine. "That was an executive decision. Murdock is inconsequential right now."

"The matter of child prostitution isn't, at least to me it isn't. I don't think we're going to come to an agreement, Emma. But it was nice talking to you." Zoë started to lean toward the chauffeur, but Emma gripped Zoë's arm firmly.

"Just hear me out before making a decision."

Zoë leaned back and crossed her arms. "All right, but you don't have much time. I want to go home and there's nothing you can say to me to change my mind tonight."

"Look, Lilith has built up a nice little empire. She has eyes and ears in all the right places. She likes to help women. You like to help women. Why shouldn't we be partners? You have no loyalty to Rico. He doesn't have the brains to realize what you've built up. He sees green paper as the only valuable commodity. He'll destroy you if you stay with the De Silvas. Why don't you join forces with us?"

Emma could see the thoughts turning in Zoë's mind. "And what if I do?" Zoë asked. "What guarantee do I have that I won't be just a foot soldier in Lilith's little gang of assassins?"

Emma set her mouth in a thin line and narrowed her eyes. But she got herself under control. "Well, as a member of Lilith's little gang of assassins, I can understand your concern."

Zoë looked ashamed of herself. "I apologize for that comment, Emma. I'm—tired."

Emma softened, reminding herself that Zoë had just lost her father. Emma sensed that she and Zoë, in different circumstances, could be very good friends.

Her voice was gentle this time. "You are a very important cog in the De Silva wheel right now. You would have to discuss it with Lilith. Can you meet with her tomorrow?"

"I can't think straight tonight." Zoë looked weary. "Can I think about it?"

Emma gave Zoë a card. "Call me when you're ready to talk. The offer is good until the end of the week."

Zoë was dropped off in front of her house. It was past midnight when she walked in the door. Of course, these were peak hours for the brothel and both clients and girls were enjoying each other's company. The music had been cranked up and several girls were dancing with the clients who had just arrived.

Faith came into the waiting room, dressed in a skimpy nurse's uniform. A tiny version of a nurse's cap was perched on her head, tendrils of hair straying from under the cap, giving her that just-out-of-bed tousled look. The buttons on her uniform barely enclosed her breasts and the skirt didn't even cover her shapely ass. Her long legs were encased in sheer white stockings and a red garter belt held them up. Instead of sensible white shoes that nurses wore, Faith wore iridescent white fuck-me slings with six-inch stiletto heels.

She came over to Zoë.

"You okay?"

Zoë half-smiled. "Yeah. I think I am. I've got a lot of thinking to do, though. Hope you don't mind if I just go up to my rooms."

Faith squeezed her hand. "Let me know if there's anything I can do for you." She sashayed over to Bert, a regular customer, grabbed his tie, and led him out of the social room and up the stairs. "Mr. Smith, you're looking a little feverish. I think we need to take your temperature." She slipped a thermometer out of a pocket and began shaking it down. "I've got a private room in the back."

Zoë grinned, hung her coat up on the rack, and went up to her private suite of rooms. When she closed the door to her suite, she sensed that she wasn't alone. Before she had time to turn on the light, someone hit her, launching her halfway across the room.

A light came on and Murdock stood over her. "Daddy's home," he said.

Zoë touched her jaw where he'd slapped her. "Get out before I call Rico." She got up gingerly and limped over to the phone on a table by the fireplace.

"Oh, I don't think Rico's going to save you this time. I own you, and this place is mine, too."

Before she had a chance to pick up the phone, Murdock was behind her, grabbed her around the waist, and began to drag her into the bedroom. She screamed, hit out at her assailant, and scrambled away. Murdock came after her, kicked her in the ribs, and grabbed her hair. She whimpered as he pulled her into the bedroom.

"Let's seal the deal right now," he said, throwing her roughly on the bed and pulling her dress up.

"Help me!!" Zoë yelled, grabbing the hem of her dress and trying to pull it down. He hit her across the face again and she yelped. She was dimly aware that it was party night and the music was too loud for anyone to hear her.

How had Murdock gotten in here without being seen? Again, party night meant that a lot of traffic passed through the Purple Rose.

Zoë tried to scream again, but Murdock punched her in the mouth, then hit her across the face again. She felt warm blood from her split lip trickling down her chin just before she blacked out.

When she came to, he was over her, undoing his belt. He'd arranged her on the bed with her legs spread wide. She couldn't open her left eye all the way and she stifled a moan so she wouldn't draw attention to herself as she looked around for something to defend herself with. Murdock had her splayed across the foot of the bed, nowhere near her gun, which she kept stored in a special holster built behind the headboard. It was an unusual place for a gun, and Zoë doubted Murdock had found it.

He finally noticed she was awake and it made him grin. "Good. I didn't want to fuck a rag doll. I like my women to fight."

"Screw you!" Her lips felt huge and the split opened again. Blood trickled down her chin.

He laughed. "That's just what you're gonna do, darlin'. You're gonna be just another one of the whores in my place and you need to be broken in. I'm just the man to do the job." He pinned her wrists together with one large hand.

Zoë shuddered. She needed some answers. Maybe if she kept him talking, she'd think of something. Maybe she could distract him. "You said Papa had secrets." Her voice came out as no more than a whisper. "What secrets, Murdock?"

"No reason for you not to know, daughter. Giacomo knew that I was your biological father," Murdock said. "But he kept you anyway."

"But you weren't a real father to me," Zoë managed to say, even though her jaw was killing her.

"Which is why screwing you doesn't bother me. And afterward, I've brought a little crack for you to sample. You might as well learn to like it. Your mother was a crack whore, so you'll learn to like it." He pulled his belt out of the loops. "Once you've had it a few times, you'll do anything for me just like she did before she was used up."

Zoë wanted to throw up. If she could make herself vomit, maybe Murdock wouldn't rape her. She started to convulse.

Murdock cracked her across the mouth again. "You'll choke on your own vomit if you try it. Take a deep breath, baby, and prepare yourself for your first good fuck since you were taken away from me."

"Rico will kill you for this."

He dropped the belt on the floor and pressed his weight on her. His breath smelled like sour milk and whiskey. "Rico and I just made a deal tonight. I get control of the Purple Rose. And you. I thought we'd expand the menu. I've always liked 'em young." He chucked her under the chin. "What were you, eight years old when I broke your cherry?"

"He wouldn't," she whispered. "He wouldn't make a deal with the man who killed Papa." She managed to close her legs. Her face was wet with tears.

Murdock let go of her wrists, grabbed her hair, and yanked hard enough to pull her head back at a painful angle. "You think so, little Zoë?" he hissed. "You think I ordered the hit on your dear papa? It wasn't me. Think again. Who else gains from his death?"

And she did think as Murdock used one knee to roughly part her legs again. He tried to enter her. She moaned. Warm blood trickled from her lip again. Her arm slipped off the bed and her hand touched something. Murdock's belt. Murdock tried again forcefully and she screamed. It hurt. Daddydaddydaddy . . .

Murdock's eyes were closed. It was now or never. She grabbed the buckle, swung the belt around Murdock's neck, and pulled the loop through the buckle. Tight. Tighter. Murdock's face turned red, then purple like a rose. His tongue stuck out and he clawed at her grip on the belt. He tried to hit her, but it took all his strength to try to breathe.

Zoë was feeling stronger now. Very strong. She was screaming. She wriggled free of his weight and dragged him across the room, kicking his head, his shoulder.

He went limp. She kept the hold on the belt until she knew he was dead.

Her first thought was to call Rico. But she couldn't. Rico had betrayed her and Papa. Rico was no longer the brother she had once adored. He was her enemy now. Rico had killed Papa.

She managed to get up, sobbing and hysterical, and stagger into the bathroom. After a long hot shower and a good cry, Zoë knew what she had to do. She would no longer be part of the De

Silva family. She inspected her face in the mirror and applied makeup to cover up the bruises and cuts as best she could. Then she went over to the phone.

Zoë dialed the number Emma gave her in the limo. "Emma? It's Zoë De Silva. I've thought about it and the answer is yes. I've had a bit of trouble tonight and need you to come over. Can you be here in an hour? I have some business to clear up before you get here. Oh, by the way, bring a cleanup crew."

Zoë hung up and went to her bedroom to retrieve her gun. After checking it to make sure it was loaded, she paused in the doorway and looked at Murdock's body in the bedroom. She closed the door. Then she dialed another number.

"Rico? We need to talk. No, not tomorrow like we planned. Now. What's it about? What do you think? Lilith Malone approached me tonight. She wants to know if I'll work for her." She listened for a moment. "I thought you'd be interested. Fifteen minutes? Good. I'll have a glass of brandy waiting for you."

The Girl of My Dreams

DONALD E. WESTLAKE

Yesterday I bought a gun.

I'm very confused; I don't know what to do.

I have always been a mild and shy young man, quiet and conservative and polite. I have been employed the last five years—since at nineteen I left college because of lack of funds—at the shirt counter of Willis & DeKalb, Men's Clothiers, Stores in Principal Cities, and I would say that I have been generally content with my lot. Although recently I have been finding the new manager, Mr. Miller, somewhat abrasive—not to overstate the matter—the work itself has always been agreeable, and I have continued to look forward to a quiet lifetime in the same employment.

I have never been much of a dreamer, neither by day nor by night. Reveries, daydreams, these are the products of vaulting ambition or vaulting desire, of both of which I have remained for the most part gratefully free. And though science assures us that some part of every night's sleep is spent in the manufacture of dreams, mine must normally be gentle and innocuous, even dull, as I rarely remember them in the morning.

I would date the beginning of the change in my life from the moment of the retirement of old Mr. Randmunson from his post as manager of our local Willis & DeKalb store, and his prompt replacement by Mr. Miller, a stranger from the Akron branch.

Mr. Miller is a hearty man, cheeks and nose all red with ruddy health, handshake painfully firm, voice roaring, laugh aggressive. Not yet thirty-five, he moves and speaks with the authority and self-confidence of a man much older, and he makes it no secret that some day he intends to be president of the entire chain. Our little store is merely a stopover for him, another rung upward on the ladder of his success.

His first day in the store, he came to me, ebullient and overpowering and supremely positive. He asked my opinion, he discussed business and geography and entertainment, he offered me a cigarette, he thumped my shoulder. "We'll get along, Ronald!" he told me. "Just keep moving those shirts!"

"Yes, Mr. Miller."

"And let me have an inventory list, by style and size, tomorrow morning."

"Sir?"

"Any time before noon," he said carelessly, and laughed, and thumped my shoulder. "We'll have a great team here, Ronald, a first-rate team!"

Two nights later I dreamed for the first time of Delia.

I went to bed as usual at 11:40, after the news on channel six. I switched out the light, went to sleep, and in utter simplicity and clarity the dream began. In it I was driving my automobile on Western Avenue, out from the center of town. It was all thoroughly realistic—the day, the traffic, the used-car lots along Western Avenue all gleaming in the spring sun. My six-year-old Plymouth was pulling just a little to the right, exactly as it does in real life. I knew I was dreaming, but at the same time it was very pleasant to be in my car on Western Avenue on such a lovely spring day.

A scream startled me, and my foot trod reflexively on the brake pedal. Nearby, on the sidewalk, a man and girl were struggling together. He was trying to wrest a package from her but she was resisting, clutching the package tight with both arms around it, and again screaming. The package was wrapped in brown paper and was about the size and shape of a suit carton from Willis & DeKalb.

I want to emphasize that everything was very realistic, down to the smallest detail. There were none of the abrupt shifts in time or space or viewpoint normally associated with dreams, no impossibilities or absurdities.

There was no one else on the sidewalk nearby, and I acted almost without thinking. Braking my Plymouth at the curb, I leaped out, ran around the car, and began to grapple with the girl's attacker. He was wearing brown corduroy trousers and a black leather jacket and he needed a shave. His breath was bad.

"Leave her alone!" I shouted while the girl continued to scream.

The mugger had to give up his grip on the package in order to deal with me. He pushed me away and I staggered ineffectively backward just as I would do in real life, while the girl kicked him repeatedly in the shins. As soon as I regained my balance I rushed forward again, and now he decided he'd had enough. He turned tail and ran, down Western Avenue and through a used-car lot and so out of sight.

The girl, breathing hard, still clutching the package to her breast, turned to smile gratefully on me and say, "How can I ever thank you?"

What a beautiful girl! The most beautiful girl I have ever seen, before or since. Auburn hair and lovely features, deep clear hazel eyes, slender wrists with every delicate birdlike bone outlined beneath the tender skin. She wore a blue and white spring dress and casual white shoes. Silver teardrops graced her graceful ears.

She gazed at me with her melting, warm, companionable eyes, and she smiled at me with lips that murmured to be kissed, and she said to me, "How can I ever thank you?" in a voice as dulcet as honey.

And there the dream ended, in extreme closeup on my Delia's face.

I awoke the next morning in a state of euphoria. The dream was still vivid in my mind in every detail, and most particularly I remembered the look of her sweet face at the end. That face stayed with me throughout the day, a day which otherwise might have been only bitter, as it was on that day Mr. Miller gave the two-week notice to my friend and co-worker Gregory Shostrill of the stockroom. I shared, of course, the employees' general indignation that such an old and loyal worker had been so summarily dismissed, but for me the outrage was tempered by the continuing memory of last night's wonderful dream.

I never anticipated for a second that I would ever see my dream girl again, but that night she returned to me, and my astonishment was only matched by my delight. I went to bed at my usual hour, fell asleep, and the dream began. It started precisely where, the night before, it had ended, with the beautiful girl saying to me, "How can I ever thank you?"

I now functioned at two levels of awareness. The first, in which I knew myself to be dreaming, was flabbergasted to find the dream picking up as though no day had elapsed, no break at all had taken place in the unfolding of this story. The second level, in which I was an active participant in the dream rather than its observer, treated this resumption of events as natural and inevitable and obvious, and reacted without delay.

It was this second level which replied, "Anyone would have done what I did," and then added, "May I drive you wherever you're going?"

Now here, I grant, the dream had begun to be somewhat less than realistic. That I should talk with this lovely creature so effortlessly, without stammering, without blushing, with no worms of terror crawling within my skull, was not entirely as the same scene would have been played in real life. In this situation, in reality, I might have attacked the mugger as I'd done in the dream, but on being left alone with the girl afterward I would surely have been reduced to a strained smile and a strangled silence.

But not in the dream. In the dream I was gallant and effortless, as I offered to drive her wherever she was going.

"If it wouldn't be putting you out of your way—"

"Not in the least," I assured her. "Where are you going?"

"Home," she said. "Summit Street. Do you know it?"

"Of course. It's right on my way."

Which wasn't at all true. Summit Street, tucked away in the Oak Hills section, a rather well-to-do residential neighborhood, was a side street off a side street. There's never any reason to drive on Summit Street unless Summit Street is your destination.

Nevertheless I said it was on my way—and she accepted pleasantly. Holding the car door for her, I noticed my Plymouth was unusually clean and I was glad I'd finally got around to having it washed. New seat covers, too, very nice-looking; I couldn't remember having bought them but I was pleased I had.

Once we were driving together along Western Avenue I introduced myself. "My name's Ronald. Ronald Grady."

"Delia," she told me, smiling again. "Delia Wright."

"Hello, Delia Wright."

Her smile broadened. "Hello, Ronald Grady." She reached out and, for just a second, touched her fingers to my right wrist.

After that the dream continued in the most naturalistic manner, the two of us chatting about one thing and another—the high schools we'd attended and how odd it was we'd never met before. When we reached Summit Street, she pointed out her house and I stopped at the curb. She said, "Won't you come in for a cup of coffee? I'd like you to meet my mother."

"I really can't now," I told her, smiling regretfully. "But if you're doing nothing tonight, could I take you to dinner and a movie?"

"I'd like that," she said.

"So would I."

Our eyes met, and the moment seemed to deepen—and there the dream stopped.

I awoke next morning with a pleasant warm sensation on my right wrist, and I knew it was because Delia had touched me there. I ate a heartier breakfast than usual, startled my mother—I have continued to live at home with my mother and an older sister, seeing no point in the additional expense of a place of my own—startled my mother, I say, by singing rather loudly as I dressed, and went off to work in as sunny a mood as could be imagined.

Which Mr. Miller, a few hours later, succeeded in shattering.

I admit I returned late from lunch. The people at the auto store had assured me they could install the new seat covers in fifteen minutes, but it actually took them over half an hour. Still, it was the first time in five years I had ever been late, and Mr. Miller's sarcasm and abuse seemed to me under the circumstances excessive. He carried on for nearly half an hour, and in fact continued to make reference to the incident for the next two weeks.

Still, my hurt and outrage at Mr. Miller's attitude were not so great as they might have been, had I not had that spot of warmth on my wrist to remind me of Delia. I thought of Delia, of her beauty and grace, of my own ease and confidence with her, and I weathered the Miller storm much better than might have been expected.

That night I hardly watched the eleven o'clock news at all. I stayed till it ended only because any change in my habits would have produced a string of irrelevant questions from my mother, but as soon as the newscaster had bid me good night I headed directly for my own bed and sleep.

And Delia. I had been afraid to hope the dream would continue into a third night, but it did, it did, and most delightfully so.

This time the dream skipped. It jumped over those dull meaningless hours when I was not with Delia, those hours as stale and empty as the real world, and it began tonight with me back at Summit Street promptly at seven, and Delia opening her front door to greet me.

Again the dream was utterly realistic. The white dinner jacket I wore was unlike anything in my waking wardrobe, but otherwise all was lifelike.

In tonight's dream we went to dinner together at Astoldi's, an expensive Italian restaurant which I had attended—in daylife—only once, at the testimonial dinner for Mr. Randmunson when he retired from Willis & DeKalb. But tonight I behaved—and felt, which is equally important—as though I dined at Astoldi's twice a week.

The dream ended as we were leaving the restaurant after dinner, on our way to the theater.

The next day, and the days that followed, passed in a slow and velvet haze. I no longer cared about Mr. Miller's endless abrasiveness. I bought a white dinner jacket, though in daylife I had no use for it. Later on, after a dream segment in which I wore a dark blue ascot, I bought three such ascots and hung them in my closet.

The dream, meanwhile, went on and on without a break, never skipping a night. It omitted all periods of time when I was not with my Delia, but those times spent with her were presented entirely, and chronologically, and with great realism.

There were, of course, small exceptions to the realism. My ease with Delia, for instance. And the fact that my Plymouth grew steadily younger night by night, and soon stopped pulling to the right.

That first date with Delia was followed by a second and a third. We went dancing together, we went swimming together, we went for rides on a lake in her cousin's cabin cruiser and for drives in the mountains in her own Porsche convertible. I kissed her, and her lips were indescribably sweet.

I saw her in all lights and under all conditions. Diving from a tacketa-tacketa long board into a jade-green swimming pool, and framed for one heartbeat in silhouette against the pale blue sky. Dancing in a white ball gown, low across her tanned breasts and trailing the floor behind her. Kneeling in the garden behind her house, dressed in shorts and a sleeveless pale green blouse, wearing gardening gloves and holding a trowel, laughing, with dirt smudged on her nose and cheek. Driving her white Porsche, her auburn hair blowing in the wind, her eyes bright with joy and laughter.

The dream, the Dream, became to me much finer than reality, oh, much much finer. And in the Dream there was no haste, no hurry, no fear. Delia and I were in love, we were lovers, though we had not yet actually lived together. I was calm and confident, slow and sure, feeling no frantic need to possess my Delia now, *now*. I knew the time would come, and in our tender moments I could see in her eyes that she also knew, and that she was not afraid.

Slowly we learned one another. We kissed, I held her tight, my arm encircled her slender waist. I touched her breasts and, one moonlit night on a deserted beach, I stroked her lovely legs.

How I loved my Delia! And how I needed her, how necessary an antidote she was to the increasing bitterness of my days.

It was Mr. Miller, of course, who disrupted my days as thoroughly as Delia soothed and sweetened my nights. Our store was soon unrecognizable, most of the older employees gone, new people and new methods everywhere. I believe I was kept on only because I was such a silent enduring victim for Mr. Miller's sarcasm, his nasal voice and his twisted smile and his bitter eyes. He was in such a starved hurry for the presidency of the firm, he was so frantic to capture Willis & DeKalb, that it forced him to excesses beyond belief.

But I was, if not totally immune, at least relatively safe from the psychological blows of Mr. Miller's manner. The joyful calm of the Dream carried me through all but the very worst of the days in the store.

Another development was that I found myself more self-assured with other people in daylife. Woman customers, and even the fashionably attractive and newly hired woman employees, were beginning to make it clear that they found me not entirely without interest. It goes without saying that I remained faithful to my

Delia, but it was nevertheless pleasurable to realize that a real-world social life was available to me, should I ever want it.

Not that I could visualize myself ever being less than fully satisfied with Delia.

But then it all began to change. Slowly, very very slowly, so that I don't know for how long the tide had already ebbed before I first became aware. In my Delia's eyes—I first saw it in her eyes. Where before they had been warm bottomless pools, now they seemed flat and cold and opaque; I no longer saw in them the candor and beauty of before. Also, from time to time I would catch a pensive frown on her face, a solemn thoughtfulness.

"What is it?" I would ask her. "Tell me. Whatever I can do—"

"It's nothing," she would insist. "Really, darling, it's nothing at all." And kiss me on the cheek.

In this same period, while matters were unexpectedly worsening in the dream, a slow improvement had begun in the store. All the employees to be fired were now gone, all the new employees in and used to their jobs, all the new routines worked with and grown accustomed to. Mr. Miller seemed also to be growing accustomed to his new job and the new store. Less and less was he taking out his viciousness and insecurity on me. He had, in fact, taken to avoiding me for days at a time, as though beginning to feel ashamed of his earlier harshness.

Which was fine but irrelevant. What was my waking time after all but the necessary adjunct to my dream? It was the dream that mattered, and the dream was not going well, not going well at all.

It was, in fact, getting worse. Delia began to break dates with me, and to make excuses when I asked her for dates. The pensive looks, the distracted looks, the buried sense of impatience, all were more frequent now. Entire portions of the dream were spent with me alone—I was *never* alone in the early nights!—pacing the floor of my room, waiting for a promised call that never came.

What could it be? I asked her and asked, but always she evaded my questions, my eyes, my arms. If I pressed, she would insist it was nothing, nothing, and then for a little while she would be her old self again, gay and beautiful, and I could believe it had only been my imagination after all. But only for a little while, and then the distraction, the evasiveness, the impatience, the excuses, all would return once more.

Until two nights ago. We sat in her convertible beneath a full moon, high on a dark cliff overlooking the sea, and I forced the issue at last. "Delia," I said. "Tell me the truth, I have to know. Is there another man?"

She looked at me, and I saw she was about to deny everything yet again, but this time she couldn't do it. She bowed her head. "I'm sorry, Ronald," she said, her voice so low I could barely hear the words. "There is."

"Who?"

She raised her head, gazing at me with eyes in which guilt and pity and love and shame were all commingled, and she said, "It's Mr. Miller."

I recoiled. "*What?*"

"I met him at the country club," she said. "I can't help it, Ronald. I wish to God I'd never met the man. He has some sort of hold over me, some hypnotic power. That first night he took me to a motel and—"

Then she told me, told me everything, every action and every demand, in the most revolting detail. And though I squirmed and struggled, though I strained and yearned, I could not wake up, I could not end the dream. Delia told me everything she had done with Mr. Miller, her helplessness to deny him even though it was *me* she loved and he for whom she felt only detestation, her constant trysts with him night after night, direct from my arms to his. She told me of their planned meeting later that very night in the motel where it had all begun, and she told me of her bitter self-knowledge that even now, after I knew everything, *she would still meet him.*

Then at last her toneless voice was finished and we were in

silence once again, beneath the moon, high on the cliff. *Then* I awoke.

That was two nights ago. Yesterday I arose the same as ever—what else could I do?—and I went to the store as usual and I behaved normally in every way. What else could I do? But I noticed again Mr. Miller's muted attitude toward me, and now I understood it was the result of his guilty knowledge. Of course Delia had told him about me—she'd described all that to me during her confession, relating how Mr. Miller had laughed and been scornful to hear that "Ronald the sap" had never been to bed with her. "Doesn't know what he's missing, does he?" she quoted him as saying, with a laugh.

At lunchtime I drove past the motel she'd named, and a squalid place it was, peeling stucco painted a garish blue. Not far beyond it was a gunsmith's; on the spur of the moment I stopped, talked to the salesman about "plinking" and "varmints," and bought a snub-nosed Iver Johnson Trailsman revolver. The salesman inserted the .32 bullets into the chambers, and I put the box containing the gun into the glove compartment of my car. Last evening I carried the gun unobserved into the house and hid it in my room, in a dresser drawer, beneath my sweaters.

And last night, as usual, I dreamed. But in the dream I was not with Delia. In the dream I was alone, in my bedroom, sitting on the edge of the bed with the gun in my hand, listening to the small noises of my mother and sister as they prepared for sleep, waiting for the house to be quiet.

In last night's dream I had the gun and I planned to use it. In last night's dream I had not left my Plymouth in the driveway as usual but half a block away, parked at the curb. In last night's dream I was waiting only for my mother and sister to be safely asleep, when I intended to creep silently from the house, hurry down the sidewalk to my Plymouth, drive to that motel, and enter room 7—it's always room 7, Delia told me, always the same room—where it was my intention to shoot Mr. Miller dead.

In last night's dream I heard my mother and sister moving about, at first in the kitchen and then in the bathroom and then in their bedrooms. In last night's dream the house slowly, gradually, finally became quiet, and I got to my feet, putting the gun in my pocket, preparing to leave the room. And at that point the dream stopped.

I have been very confused today. I have wanted to talk to Mr. Miller, but I've been afraid to. I have been unsure what to do next, or in which life to do it. If I kill Mr. Miller in the dream tonight, will he still be in the store tomorrow, with his guilt and his scorn? If I kill Mr. Miller in the dream tonight, and if he is still in the store tomorrow, will I go mad? If I fail to kill Mr. Miller, somewhere, somehow, how can I go on living with myself?

When I came home from work this evening, I didn't park the Plymouth in the driveway as usual, but left it at the curb, half a block from here. My mind was in turmoil all evening, but I behaved normally, and after the eleven o'clock news I came up here to my bedroom.

But I was afraid to sleep, afraid to dream. I took the gun from the drawer, and I have been sitting here, listening to the small sounds of my mother and my sister as they prepare for bed.

Can things ever again be as they were between Delia and me? Can the memory of what has happened ever be erased? I turn the gun and look into its black barrel and I ask myself all these questions. "Perchance to dream." If I arranged it that I would never awake again, would I go on dreaming? But would the dream become worse instead of better?

Is it possible—as some faint doubting corner of my mind suggests—even remotely possible, that Delia is not what she seems, that she was never true, that she is a succubus who has come to destroy me through my dream?

The house is silent. The hour is late. If I stay awake, if I creep from the house and drive to the motel, what will I find in room 7?

And whom shall I kill?

Flowers for Bill O'Reilly

MAX ALLAN COLLINS

If he hadn't been angry, Stone wouldn't have been driving so damn fast, and if he hadn't been driving so damn fast, in a lashing rain, on a night so dark closing your eyes made no difference, his high beams a pitiful pair of flashlights trying to guide the way in the vast cavern of the night, illuminating only slashes of storm, he would have had time to brake properly, when he came down over the hill and saw, in a sudden white strobe of electricity, that the bridge was gone, or anyway out of sight, somewhere down there under the rush of rain-raised river, and when the brakes didn't take, he yanked the wheel around and his Chevy coupe was sideways in a flooded ditch, wheels spinning.

Like his head.

He got out on the driver's side, because otherwise he would have had to swim underwater. From his sideways tipped car, he leapt to the slick highway and did a fancy slip-slide dance, keeping his footing. Then he snugged the wings of the trench-coat collar up around his face and began to walk back the way he'd come. If rain was God's tears, the Old Boy sure was bawling about something tonight.

Private detective Richard Stone of Chicago, Illinois, had spent the afternoon in the rural burg of Hopeful, only there was nothing hopeful about the sorry little hamlet. All he'd wanted was to do a kindness for an old lady, and find a few answers to a few questions. Like how a guy who won a Silver Star charging up a beachhead could wind up a crushed corpse in a public park, a crumpled piece of discarded human refuse.

Bill O'Reilly had had his problems. Before the war he'd been an auto mechanic on the Northside. A good-looking dark-haired bruiser who'd have landed a football scholarship at Notre Dame if the war hadn't got in the way, he married his high school sweetheart before he shipped out, only when he came back missing an arm and a leg, he found his girl wasn't interested in what was left of him. Even though he was pretty good with that prosthetic arm and leg of his, he couldn't get his job back at the garage, either.

Stone and O'Reilly weren't friends, exactly. It was more like friend of a friend. The detective knew the slightly younger man through Katie Crockett, secretary at Stone Investigations (and Stone's fiancée); Bill had been a good friend of Katie's late brother, Ben, who'd died in the war.

And Stone himself, though at six feet a fairly strapping physical specimen, had not gone to war. Due to his bona fide detective's flat feet, Stone had been classified 1-A. He didn't feel particularly guilty about that—at least, he didn't admit it to himself, if he did.

Not so long ago, Katie, sitting in Stone's lap in his inner office, not exactly taking dictation, had said, "Please help Bill out. Help him find work. He gave so much . . ."

"And I didn't?"

"That's not how I meant it, Richard . . . but you *didn't*, did you? Boys like Ben and him made such a sacrifice for their country. . . ."

"You mind not using my lap for a soapbox?"

Katie's pretty mouth tightened and she got to her feet, sandy hair flouncing. She said curtly, "I don't mind not using your lap at all, for anything."

And she had skirt-swishingly clip-clopped her high-heeled way back out into the reception area.

So Stone had tried to help Reynolds out, he had really tried, only Bill—a great guy, a regular joe—had brought back more from the war than just a Silver Star and disabilities; he'd also carried home nightmares, and recurrences of malaria, and a growing tendency to drown his troubled memories in a bottle.

But the last time Stone had spoken to Reynolds, when they'd gone to catch Goliath Murphy take on Jersey Joe at the arena, an on-the-wagon Bill had said things were looking up. Said he had a handyman job lined up in a little town upstate—Hopeful, where as a kid he used to visit a maiden aunt, and where he'd spent so many summers it was like a second home to him, even to where he was known around town, and remembered fondly. This was a chance to go home again, and start over, plus the position was going to pay better than his old job at the garage.

"Besides which," he said, between rounds, "you oughta see my boss. You'd do overtime yourself."

"What kind of boss is that?"

"The kind of boss that's easy on the peepers."

Jersey Joe whammed Goliath a good one and the crowd moaned in collective disappointment; Stone had to work his voice up over the din to get in, "What, are you working for a woman?"

Bill nodded, grinning. "And what a woman." The crowd was settling down and Bill didn't have to work as hard as Stone had to be heard. "She's got more curves than a mountain road."

Stone arched an eyebrow. "Easy you don't drive off a cliff."

That's all they'd said about the subject, because Goliath had come out swinging at that point, the arena crowd roaring, and the next Stone heard from Bill—well not from him, *about* him—he was dead.

It was the morning after Memorial Day when the call came in, a collect call from an Agnes O'Reilly.

"Operator," Stone had said, "I'm afraid I don't know any Agnes O'Reilly. . . ."

But Katie had come scooting in, saying urgently, "That's Bill's aunt!"

Stone, cupping the receiver, gave his cute secretary a wry grin. "Eavesdropping again, baby?"

Mild embarrassment passed over the pretty face, but she said only, "You don't get that many long-distance calls," and pulled up the dictation chair and waited for him to do the right thing.

"I'll accept the charges, operator," Stone said.

The voice was quavery, the connection staticky; you would have thought the call was from the next world and not forty miles north of Chicago.

"Thank you, thank you, Mr. Stone, for taking this call. Bill had your number in his wallet, but I didn't have an address or would have written . . . wouldn't have troubled you with this expense. . . ."

The old girl was weeping through all this.

"What is it, Miss O'Reilly? Has there been an accident?"

"They say there has. They say it was a car."

"Is Bill all right?"

"No . . . no. He's dead, Mr. Stone. After all he survived overseas, and now he's dead."

"I'm very sorry. Can you talk about it, Miss O'Reilly?"

Gradually, he was able to get it out of her. Bill's body had been found in Hopeful's city park. His spine had been snapped.

"I couldn't . . . couldn't afford to bury him properly, Mr. Stone. All those beautiful flowers yesterday in the Hopeful cemetery . . . Taps playing . . . American flags flying . . . I could see it from my window . . . such a lovely ceremony. But not for Bill."

Katie was crying into a hanky; even from only one side of the phone conversation, she could gather what had happened.

"I wish we'd known, Miss O'Reilly," Stone said. "We'd have come to the funeral. There'd have been flowers."

"There was no funeral, Mr. Stone. I'm so ashamed. I have no money. He was buried in a pauper's grave."

Stone swallowed, shifted in his swivel chair. "I'm sorry. Is there anything I can do?"

"No. No, there's nothing any of us can do for Bill except . . . pray. Pray he's at rest and safely in the Lord's bosom. I knew you were Bill's friend. He spoke so highly of you. So I thought you should know."

Stone thanked Bill's aunt, and soon he was holding the tearful Katie in his arms.

"You have to go there, Richard. Right now!"

"Well . . . what is there to do about this, baby? Bill's dead. Tracking down hit-and-run drivers, that's police business. . . ."

She drew away from him slightly and looked at him, her lovely lips quivering. "I want you to claim the body."

"What? Hell, Katie, he's already buried!"

"In a pauper's grave, you said. He was a hero, Richard. It's not right."

He sighed. "I know. We could have gotten him into Arlington, if his aunt had only thought to call me sooner."

Her expression was firm. "I want him buried next to Ben. In St. Simon's cemetery. Next Memorial Day, there will be flowers for Bill O'Reilly."

Chief Thaddeus Dolbert was one of Hopeful's four full-time cops. Despite his high office, he wore a blue uniform indistinguishable from his underlings', and his desk was out in the open of the little bullpen in the storefront-style police station. A two-cell lockup was against one wall, and spring sunshine streaming in the windows through the bars sent slanting stripes of shadow across his desk and his fat florid face.

Dolbert was leaning back in his swivel chair, eyes hooded; he looked like a fat iguana—Stone expected his tongue to flick out and capture a fly any second now.

Stone said, "How does a thing like this happen, Chief?"

Dolbert said, "We figure he got hit by a car."

"Body was found in the city park, wasn't it?"

The chief nodded slowly. "Way he was bunged up, figure he must've got whopped a good one, really sent him flyin'."

"Was that the finding at the inquest?"

Dolbert fished a pack of cigarettes out of his breast pocket, right behind his tarnished badge; lighted himself up a smoke. Soon it was dangling from a thick slobber-flecked lower lip.

"We don't stand much on ceremony around here, Mr. Stone. County coroner called it accidental death at the scene."

"That's all the investigation Bill's death got?"

Dolbert shrugged, blew a smoke circle. "All that was warranted."

Stone sat forward. "All that was warranted. A guy who gave an arm and a leg to his country, wins a damn Silver Star doing it, and you figure him getting his spine snapped like a twig and damn near every bone in his body broken, well that's just pretty much business as usual here in Hopeful."

Under the heavy lids, fire flared in the fat chief's eyes but his voice and demeanor remained calm. "I knew Bill O'Reilly when he was a kid; me and my brother and him used to go swimming out to the gravel pits. Nice kid, Bill . . . but that was the old Bill. Not the drunken stumblebum he turned into."

"I just saw him a month or so ago, and he was on the wagon."

"Well, he fell the hell off, then. That lush was a prime candidate for stepping out in front of a car."

Stone held his irritation in; he needed this fat jackass's cooperation. "You make any effort to find the hit-and-run driver that did this?"

The chief shrugged. "Nobody saw it happen."

"You don't even know for sure a car did it."

"How the hell else *could* it have happened?"

Stone shrugged one shoulder, smiled ever so slightly. "Maybe I'll just take a little time here in your fair city, and find out."

A finger as thick as a pool cue waggled at the detective. "You got no business stickin' your damn nose in around here, Stone."

"I'm a licensed investigator in this state, Chief. And I'm working for Bill O'Reilly's aunt."

Dolbert snorted a laugh. "Working for that senile old biddy? She's out at the county hospital. She's broke! Couldn't even afford a damn funeral. . . . We had to bury the boy in potter's field. . . ."

That was one of Hopeful's claims to fame: The state buried its unknown, unclaimed, impoverished dead in the potter's field there.

"Why didn't you tell Uncle Sam?" Stone demanded. "Bill was a war hero—they'd've buried him with honors."

Dolbert shrugged. "Not my job."

"What the hell *is* your job?"

"Watch your mouth, city boy." He nodded toward the holding cells and the cigarette quivered as the fat mouth sneered. "You may be big shit in the big city—but don't forget you're in *my* world, now. . . ."

Stone stood up, pushed back, the legs of his wooden chair scraping the hard floor like fingernails on a blackboard.

"Good," Stone said calmly. "Then you're just the man I need." He slapped the chief's desk, and papers and other junk on it jumped. "I'm here to reclaim Bill's body. He's going to get a proper burial, in the 'big city.' Put the paper work in motion and I'll get back with you."

The chief seemed suddenly flustered. "Well, hell, that just ain't done. . . . I mean, he's dead and buried. . . . You'll have me swimmin' in red tape. . . ."

From the doorway, Stone said, "What's the problem with that? You can swim. Remember you and Bill out at the gravel pits?"

And Stone left the storefront police station, not quite slamming the door. On the sidewalk, he looked out on an idyllic small-town scene that might have emerged from the brush of Norman Rockwell—sunshine dappling the lawn of the stately courthouse in the town square, ladies shopping, farmers loading up supplies, lazily flapping flags commemorating the war dead who yesterday the town had honored at the Hopeful cemetery, where Bill O'Reilly had received neither flowers nor gravestone.

But Bill was going to get a memorial, all right—by way of a Richard Stone investigation.

Only nobody in Hopeful wanted to talk to the detective. The supposed "accident" had occurred in the middle of the night, and Stone's only chance for a possible witness was in the all-night diner across from the Civil War cannon in the park.

The diner's manager, a skinny character with a horsey face darkened by perpetual five o'clock shadow, wore a grease-stained apron over his grease-stained T-shirt. Like the chief, he had a cigarette drooping from slack lips. The ash narrowly missed falling into the cup of coffee he'd served Stone, who sat at the counter among half a dozen locals.

"We got a jukebox, mister," the manager said. "Lots of kids end up here, tail end of a Saturday night. That was a Saturday night, when Bill got it, ya know? That loud music, joint jumpin', there coulda been a train wreck out there and nobody'da heard it."

Stone was nibbling at a cheeseburger and fries. "Nobody would have seen an accident, out your windows?"

The manager shrugged. "Maybe ol' Bill got hit on the other side of the park."

Stone craned his neck around. The "park" was just a little square of grass and benches and such; the "other side of the park" was easily visible from the windows lining the diner booths—even factoring in the grease and lettering.

"Seems to me it'd be pretty hard to miss it from here," Stone said, "even across the park."

"Nights get pretty dark around these parts."

"No kidding?" Stone asked, filing that one away as the dumbest response to a question he'd ever received.

Next, the detective talked to a couple of waitresses, who claimed not to have been working that night. One of them, "Gladys" her name tag said, a heavyset bleached blonde who must have been pretty cute twenty years ago, served Stone a slice of apple pie with cheese and a piece of information.

Stone forked a bite of pie, lifted it to his mouth, and said casually, "Bill told me he was going to work as a handyman, for some good-lookin' gal. You know who that would've been?"

"Sure," Gladys said. She had sky-blue eyes and nicotine-yellow teeth. "He was working out at the mansion."

"The what?"

"The mansion. The old Riddle place. You must've passed it on county road seven, comin' in to town."

Remembering, Stone nodded. "I did see a gate and a drive, and got a glimpse of a big old gothic brick barn. . . ."

She nodded, refilled his coffee. "That's the one. The Riddles, they owned this town forever. Ain't a building downtown that the Riddles ain't owned since the dawn of time. But Mr. Riddle, he was the last of the line, and him and his wife died in that plane crash, oh, ten years ago. The only one left now is the daughter—Victoria."

"What was Bill doing out at the Riddle place?"

She shrugged. "Who knows? Who cares? Maybe Miz Riddle just wanted some company. Bill was a handsome so and so, even minus a limb or two." She sighed, her expression turning wistful. "He coulda put his shoe under my bed anytime."

"This Victoria Riddle—she's a looker, then?"

Gladys rolled her eyes. "A real knockout. Like a movie star. Imagine getting born with that kinda silver spoon—money *and* looks."

"And she isn't married? She lives alone?"

"Alone except for that hairless ape."

Stone put his fork down. "What?"

"She's got a sort of butler, you know, a servant? He was her father's chauffeur. Big guy. Mute. Comes into town, does the grocery shopping and such. We hardly ever see Miz Riddle, 'less she's meeting with her lawyer, or going to the bank to visit all her money."

"What does she do out there?"

"Who knows? She's not interested in business. Her daddy, he had his finger in every pie around here. Miz Riddle, she lets her lawyer run things and I guess the family money, uh, under-what's-it? Underwrites, is that the word?"

"I guess."

"Underwrites her research."

"Research?"

"Oh, yeah. Miz Riddle's a doctor."

"Medical doctor?"

"Sort of, but not the kind that hangs out a shingle. She's some kind of scientific genius."

"So she's doing medical research out there?"

"I guess." She shook her head. "Pity about Bill. Such a nice fella."

"Had he been drinking heavy?"

"Bill? Naw. Oh, he liked a drink. I suppose he shut his share of bars down on a Saturday night, but he wasn't no alcoholic. Not like that other guy."

"What other guy?"

Her expression turned distant. "Funny."

The back of Stone's neck was tingling. "What's funny? *What* other guy?"

"Not funny ha ha. Funny weird. That other guy, don't remember his name, just some tramp who come through, he was a crip, too."

"A crip?"

"Yeah. He had one arm. Guess he lost his in the war, too. He was working out at the Riddle mansion, as a handyman—one-handed handyman. That guy, he really *was* a drunk."

"What became of him?"

"That's what's funny weird. Three, four months ago, he wound up like Bill. They found him in the gutter on Main Street, all bunged up, deader than a bad battery. Hit-and-run victim—just like Bill."

The wrought-iron gate in the gray-brick wall stood open and Stone tooled the Chevy coupe up a winding red-brick drive across a gentle treeless slope where the sprawling gabled tan-brick gothic mansion crouched like a lion about to pounce. The golf course of a lawn had its own rough behind the house, a virtual forest preserve that seemed at once to shelter and encroach upon the stark lines of the house.

Steps led to an open cement pedestal of a porch with a massive slab of a wooden door where Stone had a choice between an ornate iron knocker and a simple doorbell. He rang the bell.

He stood there listening to birds chirping and enjoying the cool breeze that seemed to whisper rain was on its way, despite the golden sunshine reflecting off the lawn. Then he rang the bell again.

Stone was about to go around back, to see if there was another door he could try, when that massive slab of wood creaked open like the start of the *Inner Sanctum* radio program; the three-hundred-and-fifty-pound apparition who stood suddenly before him would have been at home on a spook show himself.

He was six four, easy, towering over Stone's rangy six; he wore the black uniform of a chauffeur, but no cap, his tie a loose black string thing. He looked like an upended Buick with a person painted on it. His head was the shape of a grape and just as hair-less, though considerably larger; he had no eyebrows either, wide, bulging eyes, a lump of a nose, and an open mouth.

"Unnggh," he said.

"I'd like to see Miss Riddle," Stone said.

"Unnggh," he said.

"It's about Bill O'Reilly. I represent his family. I'm here to ask some questions."

His brow furrowed in something approaching thought.

Then he slammed the door in Stone's face.

Normally, Stone didn't put up with crap like that. He'd been polite, and the butler had been rude. Kicking the door in, and the butler's teeth, was what seemed called for. Only this boy was a walking side of beef that gave even a hardcase like Richard Stone pause.

And Stone was, in fact, pausing, wondering whether to ring the bell again, go around back, or just climb in his coupe and drive the hell away, when the door opened again and the human Buick was replaced by a human goddess.

She was tall, standing eye to eye with the detective, and though she wore a loose-fitting white lab jacket that hung low over a simple black dress, nylons, and flat shoes, those mountain-road curves Bill had mentioned were not easily hidden. Her dark blond hair was tied back, and severe black-frame glasses rode the perfect little nose; she wore almost no makeup, perhaps just a hint of lipstick, or was that the natural color of those full lips? Whatever effort she'd made to conceal her beauty behind a mask of scientific sterility was futile: The big green eyes, the long lashes, the high cheekbones, the creamy complexion, that full high-breasted, waspwaisted, long-limbed figure all conspired to make her as stunning a female creature as God had ever created.

"I'm sorry," she said, in a silky contralto. "This is a private residence and a research center. We see no one without an appointment."

"The gate was open."

"We're expecting the delivery of certain supplies this evening," she said, "and I leave the gate standing open on such occasions.

You see, I'm shorthanded. But why am I boring you with this? Good afternoon. . . ."

And the door began to close.

He held it open with the flat of his hand. "My name is Richard Stone."

The green eyes narrowed. "The detective?"

He smiled. "You must get the city papers up here."

Several of Stone's cases had hit the headlines.

"We do," she said. "Hopeful isn't the end of the world."

"It was for Bill O'Reilly."

Her expression softened, and she cracked the door open wider. "Poor Bill. Were you a friend?"

"Yes."

"So you've come to ask about his death."

"That's right." Stone shrugged. "I am a detective."

"Of course," she said, opening the door. "And you're looking into the circumstances. A natural way for you to deal with such a loss. . . ."

She gestured for him to enter, and Stone followed her through a high-ceilinged entryway. The hairless ape again appeared like an apparition and took his trench coat; Stone kept his fedora, but took it off, in deference to his hostess.

In front of him, a staircase led to a landing, then to a second floor; gilt-framed family portraits lined the way. On one side was a library with more leather in bindings and chairs than your average cattle herd; on the other was a formal sitting room where elegant furnishings that had been around long enough to become antiques were overseen by a glittering chandelier.

She led Stone to a rear room and it was as if, startlingly, they'd entered a penthouse apartment—the paintings on the wall were strikingly abstract and modern, and the furnishings were, too, with a hi-fi console and a zebra wet bar with matching stools; but the room was original with the house, or at least the fireplace and mantel indicated as much. Over the fireplace was the only artwork

in the room that wasn't abstract: a full-length portrait of his hostess in a low-cut evening gown, a painting that was impossibly
lovely with no exaggeration on the part of the artist.

She slipped out of her lab coat, tossing it on a boomerang of a
canvas chair, revealing a short-sleeve white blouse providing an
understated envelope for an overstated bosom. Undoing her hair,
she allowed its length to shimmer to her shoulders. The severe
black-frame glasses, however, she left in place.

Her walk was as liquid as mercury in a vial as she got behind
the bar and poured herself a martini. "Fix you a drink?"

"Got any beer back there?"

"Light or dark?"

"Dark."

They sat on a metal-legged couch that shouldn't have been
comfortable but was; she was sipping a martini, her dark nyloned
legs crossed, displaying well-developed calves. For a scientist, she
made a hell of a specimen.

Stone sipped his beer—it was a bottle of German imported
stuff, a little bitter for his taste, but very cold.

"That's an interesting butler you have there," Stone said.

"I have to apologize for Bolo," she said, stirring the cocktail
with her speared olive. "His tongue was cut out by natives in the
Amazon."

"Ouch," Stone said.

"My father was on an exploratory trip, somehow incurred the
wrath of the natives, and Bolo interceded on his behalf. By offering
himself, in the native custom, Bolo bought my father's life—but
paid with his tongue."

With a kisslike bite, she plucked the olive from its spear and
chewed.

"He doesn't look much like a South American native," Stone
said.

"He isn't. He was a Swedish missionary. My father never told
me Bolo's real name . . . but that was what the natives called him."

"And I don't suppose Bolo's told you, either."

A smile flickered on the full lips. "No. But he can communicate. He can write. In English. His mental capacity seems somewhat diminished, but he understands what's said to him."

"Very kind of you to keep somebody like that around."

"Like what?"

He shrugged. "Handicapped."

"Mr. Stone . . ."

"Make it Richard—and I'll call you Victoria. Or do you prefer Vicki?"

"How do you know I don't prefer Doctor?"

Stone offered up another shrug. "Hey, it's okay with me. I played doctor before."

"Are you flirting with me, Richard?"

"I might be."

"Or you might be trying to get me to let my guard down."

"Why—is it up?"

She glanced at his lap. "You tell me."

Now Stone crossed *his* legs. "Where's your research lab?"

"In back."

"Sorry if I'm interrupting. . . ."

She shook her head no, and the dark blond hair shimmered some more. "I'm due for a break. I'd like to help you, Mr. Stone—Richard. You see, I thought a lot of Bill. He worked hard. He may not have been the brightest guy around, but he made up for it with enthusiasm and energy. Some people let physical limitations get in their way. Not Bill."

"You must have a thing for taking in strays."

"What do you mean?"

Stone waved a hand. "Well . . . like Bolo. Like Bill. I understand you took in another handicapped veteran, not so long ago."

"That's right. George Wilson." She shook her head sadly. "Such a shame. He was a hard worker, too."

"He died the same way as Bill."

"I know."

"Doesn't that strike you as . . . a little odd? Overly coincidental?"

"Richard, George was a heavy drinker, and Bill was known to tie one on himself. It may seem 'coincidental,' but I'm sure they aren't the first barroom patrons to wobble into the street after closing and get hit by a car."

Stone raised an eyebrow. "Nobody saw either one of them get hit by a car."

"Middle of the night. These things happen."

"Not twice. Not in a flyspeck like Hopeful."

The green eyes narrowed with interest and concern. "What do *you* think happened, Richard?"

"I have no idea—yet. But I'll say this. Everybody seemed to like Bill. I talked to a lot of people today, and nobody, except maybe the police chief, had an unkind word to say about Bill. So I'm inclined to think the common factors between Bill and this George Wilson hold the answer. Frankly—you're one of those common factors."

She touched her bosom. "But surely not the only one."

"Hardly. They were both war veterans, down on their luck."

"No shortage of those."

"And they were both handicapped."

She nodded, apparently considering these facts, scientist that she was. "Are you staying in Hopeful tonight?"

"No. I have a court appearance in the city tomorrow. I'll be back on the weekend. Poke around some more."

She put a hand on his thigh. "If I think of anything, how can I find you?"

Stone patted the hand, removed it, stood. "Keep your gate open," he said, slipping on his fedora, "and I'll find you."

She licked her lips; they glistened. "I'll make sure I leave my gate wide open, on Saturday."

He laughed. "You flirting with *me*, Doctor?"

"I might be. Must I call you Richard?"

"Why?"

"I think I might prefer Dick."

Stone was still contemplating Victoria's final double entrendre as, under a darkening sky, he tooled back into Hopeful, to talk to the night shift at the diner. He got nowhere for his efforts and headed toward the city, in the downpour, annoyed at how little he'd learned.

Now, with his car in the ditch, and rain lashing down relentlessly, he found himself back at the Riddle mansion well before Saturday. The gate was still open, though—she must not have received that delivery of supplies she'd talked about yet.

Splashing through puddles on the winding drive, he kept his trench-coat collars snugged around him as he headed toward the towering brick house. In the daytime, the mansion had seemed striking, a bit unusual; on this black night, illuminated momentarily in occasional flashes of lightning, its gothic angles were eerily abstract, the planes of the building a stark ghostly white.

This time he used the knocker, hammering with it. It wasn't all that late—maybe nine o'clock or a little after. But it felt like midnight and instinctively Stone felt the need to wake the dead.

Bolo answered the door. The lights in the entryway were out and he was just a big black blot, distinguishable only by that upended Buick shape of his; then the world turned white, Bolo along with it, and when the thunder caught up with the lightning, Stone damn near jumped.

"Tell your mistress Mr. Stone's back," he said. "My car's in a ditch and I need—"

That was when the son of a bitch slammed the door in Stone's face. Second time that day. A flush of anger started to rise up around the detective's collar but it wasn't drying him off, even if the shelter of the awning over the slab of porch was keeping him from getting wetter. Only Stone wasn't sure a human being could be any wetter than he was right now.

When the door opened again, he drew back a fist to let that big bastard have it—only the figure standing there was Victoria.

She wore a red silk robe, belted tight around her tiny waist. The sheen of the robe and the folds of the silk conspired with her curves to create a dizzying display of pulchritude.

"Mr. Stone . . . Richard! Come in, come in."

He did. The light in the entryway was on now, and Bolo was there again, taking Stone's drenched hat and coat. Even without them, he formed puddles at his feet as he quickly explained to her what had happened.

"With this storm," she said, "and the bridge out, you'll need to stay the night."

"Love to," he said. Mother Stone didn't raise any fools.

"But you'll have to get out of those wet things," she continued. "I think I have an old nightshirt of my father's. . . ."

She took him back to that ultramodern sitting room and Stone was soon in her father's nightshirt, swathed in blankets, sitting before the fireplace's glow, its magical flickering soothingly restful, and making her portrait above the fire seem alive, smiling seductively, the bosom in the low-cut gown seemingly heaving with passion.

Shaking his head, wondering if he'd completely lost his sanity, Stone tucked Sadie—his best girl, which was to say, his trusty .38—behind a pillow. Hardware like that could be distressing to the gentle sensibilities of some females.

When she cracked the door to ask if he was decent, Stone said, "That's one thing I've never been accused of, but come on in."

Then she was sitting next to him, the red silk gown playing delightful reflective games with the firelight.

"Can I tell you something terrible?" she asked, like a child with an awful secret.

"I hope you will."

"I'm glad your car went in the ditch."

"And here I thought you liked me."

"I do," she said, and she edged closer. "That's why I'm glad."

She seemed to want him to kiss her, so he did, and it was a long, deep kiss, hotter than the fire, wetter than the night, and then his hands were on top of the smoothness of the silk gown. And then they were on the smoothness underneath it, and she opened the robe, letting the silk folds gather at her waist, as the soft nipples of her high, firm breasts hardened under his lips.

Soon she was on his lap, and he was in hers, and the inside of her was as smooth and silky as the red robe, shades of red, reflected firelight, dancing on the creaminess of her flesh as she moved slowly at first, eyes hooded, head back. His hands on her hips, she began to grind, almost savagely, shaking the dark blond hair, a shimmering mane that fell across her lovely face, a jungle tangle her green eyes glittered through. Her hands were on his shoulders and sharp nails dug into his flesh, and he kept up with her, oh yes, as she reached a furious crescendo, but when she came, her cry was almost a scream, and as he emptied himself into her, Stone experienced something he never before had at sexual climax.

Fear.

"There's a guest room upstairs," she said huskily, into his ear, sitting next to him again, silk robe tied shut, tied tight.

"This is fine right here," he said, easing away from her, feeling sudden shame. He was, after all, engaged to Katie—though, goddamnit, it was *her* idea he take this case, wasn't it?

But there was something wrong here, aside from running around on Katie. Stone was well aware that his dark good looks had made him popular with the ladies; but usually not *this* popular, not *this* fast. . . .

"Are you sure? It's no problem, to make the bed up. . . ."

"I'll just couch it right here," he said. "Anyway, I like the fire."

Victoria floated off the couch like sexy smoke and soon was

making herself a drink behind the bar, and got him another German beer.

She handed him the bottle, its cold wetness in his palm contrasting with the warmth of the room. Sitting next to him, close to him, she sipped her drink.

"First thing tomorrow," she said, "we'll call into town for a tow truck, and get your car pulled out of that ditch."

"No hurry."

Her brow lifted. "Don't you have a court appearance tomorrow?"

"Even judges consider acts of God a good excuse," he said, and rested the beer on an amoeba-shaped coffee table nearby, then leaned in and kissed her again. Just a friendly peck.

"Aren't you thirsty?" she asked, nodding toward the beer.

Why was she so eager for him to drink that brew?

He said, "Dry as a bone," and reached for the bottle, lifted it to his lips, and seemed to take a drink.

Seemed to.

Now she gave Stone a friendly kiss, said, "See you at breakfast," and rose, sashaying out as she cinched the silk robe back up. *If she could bottle that walk*, he thought, *she'd really have something worth researching.*

Alone, he sniffed the beer. His unscientific brain couldn't detect anything, but he knew damn well it contained a mickey. She wanted him to sleep through this night. He didn't know why, but something was going to happen here that a houseguest like Stone—even one who'd been lulled into a false sense of security by a very giving hostess—shouldn't see.

So he poured the bottle of beer down the drain and quickly went to the couch and got himself under the blankets and pretended to be asleep.

But Stone couldn't have been more alert if he'd been walking a tightrope. His eyes only seemed shut; they were slitted open and saw her when she peeked in to see if he was sleeping. He even saw her mouth and eyes tighten in smug satisfaction before the door closed, followed by the click of locking him in. . . .

The rain was still sheeting down when, wearing only her daddy's nightshirt, Stone went out a window and, Sadie in hand, found his way to the back of the building where a new section had been added on, institutional-looking brick with no windows at all. The thin cotton cloth of the nightshirt was a transparent second skin by the time he found his way around the building and discovered an open double garage, also back behind, following an extension of the original driveway. The garage doors stood open and a single vehicle—a panel truck bearing the Hopeful Police Department insignia—was within, dripping with water, as if it were sweating.

Cautiously, Stone slipped inside, grateful to be out of the rain. Along the walls of the garage were various boxes and crates with medical supply house markings. He could hear approaching footsteps and ducked behind a stack of crates.

Peeking out, he could see Chief Dolbert, in a rain slicker and matching hat, leading the way for Bolo, still in his chauffeur-type uniform. Dolbert opened up the side of the van and Bolo leaned in.

And when Bolo leaned back out, he had his arms filled with a person, a woman—in fact, a naked one.

Then Bolo walked away from the panel truck, toward the door back into the building, held open for him by the thoughtful police chief. It was as if Bolo were carrying a bride across the threshold.

Only this bride was dead.

For ten minutes Stone watched as Bolo made trips from the building to the panel truck, where with the chief's assistance he conveyed naked dirt-smeared dead bodies into the house. Stone's mind reeled with the unadorned horror of it: Norman Rockwell had given way suddenly to Hieronymus Bosch.

Richard Stone was shivering, and not just from the water-soaked nightshirt he was in.

Somehow, being in that nightshirt, naked under it, made him feel a kinship to these poor dead bastards, many of them desiccated-looking souls, with unkempt hair and bony ill-fed bodies, and finally it came to him.

Stone knew who these poor dead wretches were. And he knew why, at least roughly why, Chief Dolbert was delivering them, the "supplies" Victoria had been awaiting.

When at last the doors on the panel truck were shut, and the ghastly delivery complete, the chief and Bolo headed back into the building. That pleased Stone—he was afraid the chief would take off into the rainy, thunderous night, and he didn't want him to.

Stone wanted Dolbert around.

Not long after they had disappeared into the building, Stone went in after them.

And into hell.

It was a blindingly well-illuminated hell, a white and silver hell, resembling a hospital operating room but much larger, a hell dominated by the silver of surgical instruments, a hell where the walls were lined with knobs and dials and meters and gizmos, a hell dominated by naked corpses on metal autopsy-type tables, their empty eyes staring at the bright overhead lighting.

And the seductive Satan who ruled over this hell, Victoria Riddle, who was back in her lab coat now, hair tucked in a bun, was filling the open palm of Chief Dolbert with greenbacks.

But where was Bolo?

Stone glanced over his shoulder, and there the butler was, tucked behind the door, standing like a cigar store Indian, awaiting his mistress's next command, only she didn't have to give this command: Bolo knew enough to reach out for this intruder, his hands clawed, his eyes bulging to where the whites showed all around, his mouth open in a soundless snarl.

"Stop!" Stone told the looming figure, who threw his shadow over the detective like a blue blanket.

But Bolo didn't stop.

And when Stone squeezed Sadie's trigger and Sadie blew the top of Bolo's bald head off, splashing the white wall behind him with the colors of the inside of the butler's head, red and gray and white, making another abstract painting only without a frame, that didn't stop him either, didn't stop him from falling on top of Stone, and by the time Stone had pushed his massive dead weight off, the fat corpse emptying ooze out the top of the bald blown-off skull, he had another fat bastard to deal with, a *live* one: the chief of the Hopeful police department, whose revolver pointed down at Stone.

"Drop it," Dolbert said.

The chief should have just shot Stone, because the detective took advantage of Dolbert taking time to speak and shot him, in the head, and the gun in the chief's hand was useless now, since his brain could no longer send it signals, and the fat former police chief toppled back on top of one of the corpses, sharing its silver tray, staring up at the ceiling, the red hole in his forehead like an extra expressionless eye.

"You fool," Victoria said, the lovely face lengthening into a contorted ugly mask, green eyes wild behind the glasses.

"I decided I wasn't thirsty after all," Stone said, as he weaved his way between the corpses on their metal slabs.

"You don't understand! This is critical research! This will benefit humanity. . . ."

"I understand you were paying the chief for fresh cadavers," Stone said. "With him in charge of the state's potter's field, you had no shortage of dead guinea pigs. But what I *don't* understand is, why kill Bill, and George Wilson, when you had access to all these riches?"

And Stone gestured to the deceased indigents around them.

Her face eased back into beauty; her scientific mind had told her, apparently, that her best bet now was to try to reason with the detective. Calmly. Coolly.

Stone was close enough to her to kiss her, only now he didn't feel much like kissing her and, anyway, the .38 he was aiming at her belly would have been in the way of an embrace.

"George Wilson tried to blackmail me," she said. "Bill . . . Bill just wouldn't cooperate. He said he was going to the authorities."

"About your ghoulish arrangement with the chief, you mean?"

She nodded. Then earnestness coated her voice: "Richard, I was only trying to *help* Bill, and George—*and* mankind. Don't you see? I wanted to make them *whole* again!"

"Oh my God," Stone said, getting it. "Bill was a *live* guinea pig, wasn't he? Wilson, too. . . ."

Her head tilted back in a gesture that was both proud and defensive. "That's not how I'd express it, exactly, but yes. . . ."

"You wanted to make them living Frankenstein monsters . . . you wanted to sew the limbs of the dead on 'em. . . ."

Her eyes lighted up with enthusiasm, and hope. "Yes! Yes! With the correct tissue matches, and my own research into electro-chemical transplant techniques . . ."

That was when the lights went out.

God's electricity had killed man's electricity, and the cannon roar aftermath of the thunderbolt wasn't enough to hide the sound of her scurrying in the dark amongst the trays of the dead, trying to escape, heading for that door onto the garage.

Stone went after her, but she had knowledge of the layout of the place and he didn't; the detective kept bumping into bodies, and then she screamed.

Just for a split second.

A hard *whump* had interrupted the scream, and before Stone even had time to wonder what the hell had happened, the lights came back on, and there she was.

On her back, on the floor, her head resting against the metal underbar of one of the dead-body trays, only resting wasn't really the word, since she'd hit hard enough to crack open her skull and a widening pool of red was forming below her head as she too stared up at the ceiling with wide-open eyes, just another corpse in a room full of corpses. Bolo's dead body, where Stone had pushed his dead weight off of him, was—as was fitting—at his mistress's feet.

Stone grimaced.

Bolo may not have had many brains in that chrome dome of his, but he'd had enough to slip her up.

They didn't wait for the next Memorial Day to come around. Stone and Katie stood close together, the detective's arm around the pretty girl's slender waist, and admired the flowers on the fresh grave in St. Simon's cemetery. Fall wind whispered through Katie's red-tinged locks and ruffled and rustled the many-colored flowers.

The old lady in the wheelchair, on a rare afternoon outing from the county hospital in Hopeful, was dabbing tears from eyes in a face that reminded Stone of his late friend; but the old girl, for all her tears, was smiling.

Sailing to Atlantis

ED GORMAN

1

Matt Shea always smiled when he walked into the house he'd bought his mother. It was a perfectly fine little house, a standard development little house, central air, attached garage, core appliances including self-cleaning oven and ice-making machine in the fridge.

But she'd turned it into a church. And the thing was, she wasn't of that generation. You know, you see them at Mass all the time, those generations of Irish and Czech and Hispanic women for whom it was common to turn houses into shrines or grottos. Framed religious pictures everywhere. Palm drooping from behind the pictures. Crucifixes large and small throughout the house. Three or four Bibles scattered around. Holy cards on end tables. Even, on certain occasions, the scent of incense.

Incense, Matt associated with covering up the smell of grass in his college dorm room.

The funny thing was, his mother had been a regular normal human being all the time he was growing up. There was even the family suspicion that she'd had an affair or two back in the seventies when it seemed *everybody* was having affairs. She walked around in halter tops and Levi cutoffs. She liked Clint Eastwood movies. She and his father put away a goodly amount of wine most weekends, and could frequently be heard banging around on their bed upstairs while he and Don were downstairs watching sci-fi on the tube.

But then his father got a brain tumor, forty-one years old and a fucking brain tumor, and his death was so agonizing, so prolonged that Cassie just flipped out. Couldn't deal with it. Was drunk a lot. Threw up a lot. Stayed in bed and slept a lot. Anything to escape the fact that her beloved husband—and even if she had had those affairs, it was clear that she loved Rick above all others—was dying. And then he was dead and she went even more to shit, it was her college-age boys carrying her instead of the other way around, and then one day, they were never sure why, she got religion, maybe some minister she saw on TV or something, and started wearing dowdy dresses and telling the boys to watch their language and admonishing them not to practice "free love" or to use drugs. She was living in the old house at the time, the big Tudor that had been lawyer Rick's pride and joy, but it was too much house as the realtors liked to say, and so she sold it and put the profits in the hands of stockbroker Matt, who saw to it that she'd never have to worry about money. This being the end of the eighties, Matt was hauling ass financially, making so much in fact that he could afford to make the grand gesture of setting Mom up in her own little tract house.

The house that was now a religious shrine.

The house Matt stood in now, warmed by late-afternoon May sunlight.

His mom was on the couch. She'd aged, many long years past her halter and cutoffs stage. She wore a faded house dress, prim little white anklets, and brown—if-you-could-believe-it—oxfords. She'd gone all the way, had Mom, fifty-one years old, a child of the upper middle class, now looking like a cleaning woman in somewhat ill health.

"Do you ever watch channel 28?" she said.

His smile. "You always ask me that, Mom."

"I just think Sandy and you and the boys should make a point of watching it. You know, as a family." Channel 28 was the religious channel.

"We're pretty busy."

"You should never be too busy for God."

And just how are you supposed to respond to that?

"You're right, Mom," he said, "we should never be too busy for God."

"I just wish Sandy was more religious."

Another running battle. "She's religious in her way, Mom. She really is."

"She doesn't go to church."

"That doesn't mean she's not religious."

"She doesn't take the boys to Mass. And you don't either."

"Sandy's Jewish, Mom. If she attended any kind of services, she'd go to synagogue, not to Mass."

"Then why doesn't she go to synagogue? There's nothing wrong with being Jewish." Mom's first major love affair had been with a Jewish kid.

"I'll talk to her about it."

"People should go to church. If they're truly good people, I mean." How could the college girl who'd spent many, many long hours smoking dope and listening to Led Zeppelin possibly have turned out this way?

"I brought you something," he said. He reached in the suitcoat pocket of his gray Armani and brought forth a small white jeweler's box. "I got your necklace fixed."

For her thirty-fifth birthday, Dad had given Mom a beautiful old chain necklace. But it had gotten broken and Mom had never gotten around to getting it fixed. She held it now, smiling. "I can still feel your father putting this on my neck. It was the first time he'd ever been able to afford anything really nice. He had such big fingers."

"I thought you'd like it." He leaned down and kissed her on the forehead. She was getting older, the texture and feel of her flesh was changing, and it startled him a moment. She was getting older, and just now that realization scared and saddened him. "Say, would you let me use your bathroom if I gave you a dollar?"

This was an old gag between the two of them. "Dollar and a half."

"Dollar and a half it is," he said. Then, as he started back toward the bathroom, "You hear from Jim lately?"

"Just the other day."

"How's he doing?"

"He says he likes his new job. I just hope he can last at this one."

Matt and Jim Shea were as different as brothers could be. Matt, handsome, self-confident, family man. Jim, pale, nervous, luckless. He'd worked sales in the computer department of a number of different local department stores. He was running out of stores. He always got fired and for reasons that were at best vague. He always seemed vaguely relieved, too. He didn't mind living in his drab little apartment on unemployment insurance. Matt was always suggesting motivational speakers whom Jim should go see but Jim always just grinned and shook his head. Though Matt thought of himself as a major player in the world of the local establishment, Jim saw him as just one more Mercedes-driving Nazi. Jim called a lot of people Nazis.

Matt came back after a few minutes. He'd freshened up. He had a meeting at the club with some potential investors for a small shopping mall he was trying to develop. Time for a little hair spray, a little breath spray, a few eyedrops to take the red out.

Mom was still holding the necklace when he came back. "Say hi to that brother of mine."

"I just wish you two boys got together more often."

"Oh, that'll happen as we get older, Mom. I'm sure it will."

"Why don't you take that box of paperbacks in the closet to Sandy? They're Harlequins. She reads almost as much as I do."

He smiled. "You two and your Harlequins." He said it not with contempt but with a kind of awe. He had, in his life, finished reading exactly two novels, *The Great Gatsby* and *Ethan Frome.* *Gatsby* he liked—even though the narrator sounded sort of fruity—because of the love story, which he had to admit made him tear up a time or two, having had a terrible love affair once himself; and *Frome* he liked simply because it was short and because of the irony of the ending. Every other novel he'd "read" had come in the yellow-and-black form of Cliff Notes. He'd been a 4.0 student. He just preferred nonfiction was all. He got the box from the closet, kissed his mom once again as she opened the front door for him, and was then out the door.

He liked the way the new Mercedes four-door sedan stood so proudly in Mom's driveway. He liked the way the men and women driving home from work to their little housing development here glanced at it. Envy. That, not imitation, was the sincerest form of flattery. Envy. I want what you have. He couldn't think of a higher accolade, and hell, he'd be the first to admit he felt it, too, the way Giff McBride, ass-bandit of all ass-bandits out at the club, wheeled around in that little Brit classic car of his, Austin-Healey it was called, wheeled around and got 20 percent of the married women at the club to spend time with him, not to mention an even higher percentage of the waitresses. Even, it was rumored, a few of the college gals who worked there during the summers. College gals, sleek and slender and sun-brown. Now that was something to *really* envy, Giff McBride being in his early fifties.

He opened the trunk and set the box of romances inside. He had to be careful not to knock over the sloshing full red can of gasoline. It had already spilled some on the newspaper it rested on. He looked at the headline. Talk about irony.

THIRD DANCE CLUB FIRE SAID TO BE ARSON
One injured seriously; two others rushed to hospital

Numbers one and two—the black dance club and then the gay dance club—one fatality each.

No fatality this time.

They'd all been lucky enough to get out alive.

He took another look at the red gas can. It looked so harmless most of the time sitting in garages to run power mowers and clean up paint spills.

But there were other uses for it, too. Yes, indeed.

2

They didn't like me much and I guess I didn't blame them. Nobody likes "experts" brought in from the outside to tell you that you're doing a lousy job.

There were four of them, detectives, two male, two female, one black, one Hispanic. They sat at a plain table in a plain room and listened to me as long as they could stand. Then their eyes would look out the window that displayed the downtown across the narrow river and they had to be thinking longing thoughts about this gentle and colorful Iowa autumn afternoon. Football weather. They could be raking leaves, playing touch football with their kids, washing the new car, or sitting in a cop bar talking about the recent union meeting about the unpaid overtime hassle with the city council.

Instead, like school children being punished, they had to sit here, a narrow room painted city-sanctioned green, listening to me play at being a psychological profiler and private investigator for a large law firm.

While they had their own individual cases, Captain Davidson, who'd introduced me, had put them all on the arson case, which was why I was here. The arsonist had burned his third dance club to the ground three nights ago. The first fire, two people had been killed, trampled in the melee. The second fire, nobody had died, but a number of people were in the hospital. The third fire, there'd been one more fatality, a just-divorced suburban housewife out celebrating with her girlfriends. An upscale downtown dance club; a gay dance club; a black dance club. No pattern.

I said, "One thing distinguishes the arsonist from other serial murderers. The typical serial killer wants direct contact with his victims. So direct that sometimes he'll reach in and take out a vital organ with his bare hands. He'll also photograph or videotape what he's done. He wants to remember the moment. He'll masturbate to it later. The arsonist, however, wants the impersonality of setting a building on fire and standing back and watching what happens. A lot of the time, he'll hide across the street so he can masturbate while watching the fire. Totally impersonal. Except for the fluid he uses to ignite the fire, he never gets his hands dirty, as it were, never faces the victims. There's an interesting note here. When you look into the background of the average serial killer, you see a dysfunctional boyhood often marked by cruelty to animals. You find that with serial arsonists, too. But with them you have to add bed-wetting. We don't know why this is but from the hundreds if not thousands of cases we've catalogued, we've seen it play out time and time again."

Detective Gomez raised her hand. "Who does this arsonist think he's killing when he sets these fires?"

"Good question," I said. "I just wish I had a good answer. As we know, many if not most male serial killers have real relationship problems with females. Even killing their victims isn't enough. They'll defile the corpses—make hideous slashes and cuts in the faces, cut off breasts, mutilate the genitals. So while we don't know which female *exactly* the serial killer is destroying—a girl he is attracted to, his mother, maybe even his sister—we do know that in general he has a real problem with women.

"This particular arsonist, though, we just don't know. Even in the male gay bar there were a few dozen women. But that still doesn't tell us a lot. Based on what we know generally, we know he's angry, we know he wants to kill people, and we know that in all likelihood, he'll do this again."

Detective Henderson, who looked like the poster boy for clean-cut WASP detectives everywhere, said, "I take it he's shy and with-drawn."

"That's probably right. Every profile I've ever seen on this kind of arsonist, he doesn't have many social skills and he's frequently unnoticed, even though he may hang around a lot. Almost invisible in some ways."

They were paying attention now that the afternoon had gotten interactive. I should've done this earlier.

Detective Wimmers, the black man, said, "Are there any kinds of jobs this arsonist would be attracted to?"

"No job category, if that's what you mean. But they're likely to be low-level, relatively unsuccessful, whatever line they take up. These aren't aggressive people. Not usually, anyway."

Detective Holden, a red-haired, bulky man in shirtsleeves, loose tie, and an air of belligerence, said, "What if we waste our time looking for somebody like this and it turns out he isn't anything like this at all?"

"Then he can sue the city," I said. Nobody laughed. "This isn't an exact science. I make mistakes, no doubt about it. But generally profiling is helpful. And I think it'll be helpful to you here. Any questions?"

There weren't, of course. They just wanted out of here. All but one of them, anyway. Detective Wimmers, the black man. "Don't pay any attention to them."

I smiled. "Kind of hard not to. They always this pleasant?"

"They just don't like outsiders." He was tall, tending to beef, with a large, imposing face and a gold-toothed smile. With his red regimental-striped tie and herringbone slacks and polished black loafers with the tassels, he looked more lawyer than cop. Except lawyers don't wear guns and badges on their belts. He pinched some skin on the thick black arm shooting from his short-sleeved white shirt. "I bring my sorry black ass in here six years ago—first black detective this city ever had—and you should've heard 'em, man. Always whisperin' and jokin' and pokin' each other in the ribs. I coulda written all their jokes myself. Lots of watermelon and pork chops in the jokes, you know what I'm saying. They'd even leave notes in my locker. Death To Niggers. Shit like that."

"I'm sorry." And I was. That had to be a special hatred, to be singled out and despised that way.

"My wife and kids, they'd cry and beg me to quit. But I wouldn't, 'cause I just wanted to piss these guys off. Stay in their faces. You know what I mean? I just wore 'em down. I didn't go to the civil rights board. I didn't complain to the police review board. I just stayed in their faces. And one by one, they started bein' nice to me. The first guy, when he was nice, they started givin' him more shit than they gave me. But one by one, we started bein' friendly. And now they pretty much accept me. Our wives and kids get together. And we bowl and stuff after work. So it's pretty good here, now. And the young black cops comin' up say they aren't havin' much trouble at all, especially with the cops their own age."

"I guess I'll have to take your word for it, that these are really swell people."

He grinned with his gold tooth. "I guess they weren't real friendly, Mr. Payne. I'm sorry. Maybe if you could spend a little more time with 'em."

He held up a manila envelope.

"What've you got?" I said.

"Photos from the crime scene. I was going over them this morning and I found something. Captain Davidson said you were going to be here the next few days consulting on the case so I thought you might want to ride along with me this afternoon. I'll tell you about it on the way."

"Fine."

3

Wimmers handed me a manila folder while we sat at a traffic light. He was a fast, savvy, and aggressive driver. At one point he'd grinned and said, "You want to wear a crash helmet, fine with me."

I'd said, "And I want to make sure my insurance is paid up."

"I grew up in Chicago. My old man was a cabbie. He taught me how to drive."

I'd spent three years working out of the Chicago FBI bureau— before going private as a profiler and investigator—so he didn't need to say any more.

Just as the traffic light changed, I said, "Same guy."

"Same guy at all three fires. Just standing around watching things."

We were off. Wimmers wanted to be in the right-hand lane so we could get on the interstate that cut through the city. God help anybody in his way.

"How many people you killed in your lifetime?" I said.

"Killed? You kidding, Payne? Hell, I've never even drawn my gun."

"Not with your gun. Your car. You didn't even notice that you ran over a couple of nuns back there."

"Yeah?" He smiled. "Serves them right for wearing black. They should wear brighter colors."

I decided to give up on my subtle drive-safely messages.

He said, "I know who the guy is."

"In the pictures?"

"Yeah. Matt Shea. Country club set. Runs his own brokerage. Lots of money, lots of clout. Reporter on the *Gazette* I know happened to notice Shea while filing the photos. He sent them over to me."

"Maybe Shea just likes to look at fires."

"Maybe. But what's he doing out so late, pillar of the community, family man, all that happy horseshit? The earliest of any of those fires were set was one A.M."

"Good point. So where we going?"

"His brokerage."

"God, can it really be this easy?"

"Seems wrong, don't it?" he said.

"You see a guy in some photos—"

"—and you drive over to where he works—"

"—and you ask him some questions and—"

"—case is closed. And you got your man."

"I've never even *heard* of it happening like this."

"Well," he said, wheeling the police car into the parking lot of a new six-story steel-and-glass building, "there's always a first time."

The decor was designed to do one thing: intimidate you with its quiet good taste, right down to the quiet, gold-framed Rembrandt reproductions and the quiet Debussy on the office music system. The receptionist complemented her setting perfectly, lovely in a slightly fussy and disapproving way, the only hint of earthiness or carnality found in the oddly erotic sag of her bottom inside the discreet gray Armani upscale fifty-year-olds were wearing this year.

Matt Shea did not fit quite so well into his hallowed surroundings. There was a roughneck quality to his movements that no high-tone suit, no one-hundred-twenty-five-dollar haircut, no twenty-five-dollar manicure could quite disguise. It wasn't a class thing, it was a testosterone thing. He'd look roughneck in a tutu.

He said, "Sit down, sit down."

Old-firm law school office was the motif in this particular room, cherry wood wainscoting, built-in bookcases packed with tomes bound in leather for theatrical effect. The small fireplace snapped and popped with autumnal balm, the woodsmell sweet and melancholy.

"Police, huh?" Shea said. "Wow, now this *is* a surprise." Despite his linebacker size and his big-man poise, he sounded nervous.

I didn't like him in the way you abruptly do or don't like somebody you've just met. He was too much obvious cunning and too much obvious aftershave. The perpetual overachiever who was not without a certain frantic sweaty sadness.

After we were all seated, he said, "So how can I help you?"

"Those fires," Wimmers said. He was the man here.

"Fires?"

"Dance club fires?"

"The dance club fires in the papers."

"Right."

He looked at me and shrugged his shoulders and smiled his practiced cunning smile. "Hey, I'm a family man." He winked at Wimmers and smiled. "You can ask my rabbi." He wasn't, of course, Jewish. He was just a lounge act. "I don't even go into places like those."

Wimmers carefully set the manila envelope on the desk and pushed it across to Shea. "How about looking inside?"

The smile again. He couldn't sustain it for much longer than two seconds. "You going to be reading me my rights or something?"

"I'd appreciate it if you'd just look inside the envelope, Mr. Shea."

"Sure. Be glad to."

He looked inside, then pulled the photos out one at a time. When he'd seen all three, he said, "Wow. I can see why you wanted to talk to me." He held his arms up in the air. He was still doing stand-up. "I'll come along peacefully, Officer, sir."

"This isn't funny, Mr. Shea. Two people died in those fires. Another one is clinging to life."

"I was coming home. Just saw the fire trucks and stopped by."

"I see. All three times?"

"Working late. Honest. As innocent as that."

"The fires took place in different parts of the city, Mr. Shea. You take different ways home every night?"

"Fuck." Shea looked grim. He shook his head, as if chiding himself. The way you do when you've done something really dumb.

"Pardon me?"

"I said fuck," Shea snapped. "I take it you've heard the word before."

Ugly, awkward silence. Shea stared down at the two big fists he'd planted on his desk. "I didn't set those fires," he said after a while.

"I didn't say you did."

"No? You just came out here to show me these three photos but not to make any accusations?"

"I'm trying to figure out who *did* set the fires. You being there doesn't necessarily mean it was you."

"It doesn't, huh?"

"No. But it may mean that you know something I should maybe know."

Shea looked at me. Fellow member of the white race. "You probably think I'm one of those candy asses."

"Which candy asses would those be, Mr. Shea?"

"You know. Inherited wealth. The right schools. You know something? I grew up on the west side of this city—and in those days, you told people you were from the west side, they started treating you just like you were some inferior species." He looked back at Wimmers. "Something you're probably familiar with, Detective Wimmers."

Wimmers smiled sadly. "I've heard rumors about some human beings treating other human beings that way."

"You know damned well what I'm talking about. Well, that's just how it was when you were from the west side. No Choate. No Wharton School of Business. That's where my two best friends at the club went—Choate first, then Wharton. But not me. I went to the community college here before I could afford the university in Iowa City. I bussed dishes there at the frat houses. All the rich fraternity boys." To me, he said, "I've worked for every dime. Every dime. And now my pathetic fucking brother goes and spoils it."

"Your brother?" Wimmers said.

"Yes, my brother," Shea said sadly. "Who do you think's been setting those fires?"

4

The middle of a vast, calm sea on a sun-golden day on a sun-golden ship. The destination was Atlantis or some other fabled land where they would know peace and security and love for the rest of their lives, where their children would prosper, and their children's children, and all would meet again in the sunny, leafy paradise that lies just beyond death.

The sound of a distant siren woke Jim Shea.

The dream vanished. The perfect dream.

Sway and jerk of moored boat. Stink of river water. Voices up on the dock. At day's end everybody with a houseboat here descended on this place. One of the last few warm days before harsh prairie winter. Most of them didn't even take their boats out. Just hauled out the aluminum tube chairs and sat there on Ellis landing listening to the Cubbies on the radio and laughing well into the work night. It was a pretty democratic place, the houseboat marina. You had lawyers talking with guys who worked on the line at Rockwell, doctors talking to guys who sold electronics stuff at Best Buys.

The boat belonged to Ella. It'd been her dad's. She'd inherited it when he died a few years back. Jim kept the curtains closed. They had as little to do with their neighbors as possible. Couple months back a few of the kids who belonged to a houseboat down the way laughed at Ella. Saw her face and laughed at her. She stayed in the houseboat bed for four days. Kept the place totally dark. Wouldn't eat. Wouldn't even talk. Just kept herself unconscious with sleeping pills. Finally, he forced her to take a shower and eat the oatmeal and toast and strawberry jam he'd fixed for her. She couldn't take it when people laughed at her. Unlike Jim, Ella had never had any practice at being ugly, at being the outsider. Indeed, she'd always been the beauty. Cheerleader. Homecoming queen at Regis. Prime U of Iowa heartbreaker. Two rich husbands, both of whom had begged her to stay. And then a year and a half ago when her rich friend (and possible husband #3) had been all coked up and accidentally smashed his big-ass Caddy convertible into a bridge abutment north of Iowa City, her life changed. How it changed. He'd died instantly. The seat belt had saved her life but hadn't done anything for her face. She'd gone into the windshield. Nearly a thousand stitches in her head and face. You ever see anybody with a thousand stitches in her head and face? We're talking your basic Frankenstein's monster here. The face now a series of slightly puffy sewn pockets, angled scars, red remnants of stitching. Snickers from little kids. Gasps from adults. She stayed in bed a lot. A *lot*. They were supposed to fly to Houston next month—there was a plastic surgeon there who'd developed some new techniques he thought might possibly help her—but in the meantime Jim was still trying to get her to resume something like a normal life.

You're beautiful to me, Ella. That's all that matters.

You know, I don't even notice the scars any more, Ella. I really don't.

Don't worry, Ella. I'm paying them back. Every one of them.

These were the things he said to her over and over here in the course of their dark houseboat days.

He lived for that gentle drifting time after they made love and just held each other. Complete peace. The golden ship on the ancient sea, drifting toward Atlantis, just the two of them.

He wanted to be thinking of Atlantis right now—even awake

he could sometimes conjure up that ship and that sea—but instead all he could think of was the missing gas can and that stack of *Cedar Rapids Gazette*s he'd kept about the fires he'd set. Somebody had gotten into the trunk of his car and taken them. He wondered who. He wondered why.

Four days ago, it had been. Opened the trunk to put some groceries in and—gone. He hadn't told Ella, of course. She didn't need any more grief. It was up to him to find out what was going on here. But how to start? Who to suspect?

He wanted to be one of them, one of the children running along the dock outside, laughing and having a good time. He wanted that for Ella, too. God, if only this Houston surgeon could do what he said he could do.

He eased himself off the bed, not wanting to wake her. He had a lot to do tonight. Time to visit the fourth and final dance club. Now, he'd have to buy a new can and fill it with gasoline. He'd also have to scope the place out. There were sure to be extra cops posted around clubs these days. He might even have to wait a few days until the story faded from the headlines. He'd just have to see.

5

Matt, Jim's older brother, said, "It was pretty funny to us—to me and Mom and Dad, I mean—for a while anyway. We lived in this real bad part of town and this really beautiful little girl named Ella Casey moved in down the street and Jim—he and Ella were both in sixth grade at the time—it changed his whole life. He was obsessed with her right from the start. And he didn't care who knew it, either. I mean, you know how boys don't like you to know that they've got a crush on somebody? He'd come right out and tell you. I can still hear him sitting in the kitchen with Mom after school, talking about all his plans for when he and Ella got married. Mom tried to help him with it—tried to make him see that she was just too, you know, beautiful for him, I mean, Jim isn't a handsome guy, I got the looks and he got the brains our dad always said—but he didn't listen. He got this paper route and he spent all the money he earned from it on Ella. He was always buying her stuff. She'd take the stuff but she'd never go to a movie with him or go for a walk with him or anything. She was so beautiful, she's in ninth grade and she's got senior boys literally fighting over her. She was the fucking trophy, man. She was the trophy. And Jim was always there for her. Always. She'd invite him over when she was depressed or didn't know which boyfriend to choose or had some errand she needed run. And, man, he'd do whatever she wanted. He was like her shrink and her servant rolled into one. We thought maybe once he got out of high school, maybe one of them would go away to college. But Jim stayed here and went to the community college and she stayed in town and married this rich kid two days after she got out of high school. Eloped, because the kid's parents were against it. [Grinning.] They were part of the Cedar Rapids jet set, you know what I'm saying? And they just didn't want their very special little boy laying it to white trash every night. All the time they were married, poor Jim was her confidant. She was always calling him, crying and bitching about how unhappy she was. He got so caught up in her problems, he dropped out of school. He lived at home so all he'd have to have was a part-time job. He wanted to be there when Ella needed him. Finally, Ella couldn't handle the rich boy's family any more, so she divorced him and got a very nice settlement out of it.

"That's when she first started hitting the bars and the clubs. She'd never really done that before. Hadn't had to. But she was midtwenties now and starting to slip, looks-wise, just a little. Still very, very sexy, but not the new kid on the block any more, either. She becomes the queen of the local clubs. Guys literally line up along the bar to talk to her. Only the best clubs, only the best guys, young lawyers and young docs and young investment bankers, guys like that.

"She ends up finding hubby number two in a club. Advertising guy who'd just sold his agency to a bigger shop out of Chicago. Plenty of cash and recently divorced. Midforties. Real fading ass-bandit type. But with pretensions. Guys like him used to get involved in charities so they could show everybody how cool they were. This decade, they dabble in the so-called arts. Local art museum board. Symphony board. Reading endowments for the underprivileged. Previous wife had been big in the Junior League so he's connected that way, too. And our little Ella is really taken in by all this. She thinks it's very sophisticated and elegant and all. She asks Jim—she's told her husband that Jim is gay, you know how a lot of women have male gay friends, and this fits right in with Hubby's image of himself, the local *New Yorker*-type is how he sees himself, tells him Jim's gay even though he's not because this is the easiest way to explain the friendship—she asks Jim to start giving her some background on all the great painters and composers and like that. And he does, of course. And that's how things go for a few years until she starts having this thing with this college kid who buses dishes out at the club. Everybody in the club knows this is happening except her husband. She's one of those women who doesn't hit thirty well. The rich ones head to the plastic surgeons; the poor ones just have affairs. Ella does both. And then the new husband finds out and dumps her. He's cheated on every woman he's ever known but the one time he's the cheatee, his ego absolutely can't handle it. He gives her a lot of money on the condition that she gets out of his life immediately, which she does. But she's already sick of the college boy, even though he's real serious about her.

"She's kind of in a panic, actually. Needs reassurance. This is the first time she ever lets Jim sleep with her. He told me about it, said she was having her period and everything, but he didn't care, even had oral sex with her, told her he wanted their blood to 'commingle.' Of course, he had to explain to her what 'commingle' meant but that was all right because she said it was 'beautiful.' She went back to the clubs. Of course, by this time, there's a whole new raft of beauties younger than she is. She's still got men lined up along the bar but the lines aren't quite as long as they once were. She's thirty-one now. And there's one thing she can never be again—and that's new. And that's what clubs like these always want. The new band. The new girl. The new drink. You know what I'm saying?

"Then she does the dumbest thing she's ever done in her life, she falls in love with this bartender who's putting it to every babe in the place. He's got lines of women around the block, including all the newest and the hottest. And she falls in love with him. He goes out with her a few times—hammers her like she's never been hammered in her life—but then he dumps her. She's not used to being treated like this. In *her* life, it's supposed to be the other way around. She panics. Getting dumped undermines her whole life. She has money, a nice house, she can have all the plastic surgery she wants—but she knows that her time has passed as babe-of-the-moment.

"She starts stalking the bartender. She calls him night and day, she e-mails him, sends him flowers and candy, even gives him a car—a frigging Firebird, if you can believe it—and two or three times, she breaks into his apartment while he's hammering some other babe in his bedroom. One night, he's so frustrated, he punches her, gives her a black eye. Another night, she literally attacks his date in this restaurant. Throws her down on the floor and starts kicking her like some homeboy would. And the coup de grace. She hides in his car, the car she bought him and he was asshole enough to accept, and at gunpoint forces him to take her for a long drive. She is very, very drunk. They drive around and around and she tells him all these plans she's got for when they get married. The first thing she wants with him, she says, is children. One boy, one girl. She's got access to enough cash to set him up in his own bar. An upscale one. No more club bullshit working for bosses who deal coke out their back door. And all of a sudden, he starts laughing at her. Which is not a good idea, somebody has a

gun on you the way she does. By this time, they're up in the red
clay cliffs. And she grabs the wheel from him and stomps her foot
on his on the gas pedal and they go shooting right off the cliff.
And we're talking a forty-foot fall to the road below. He dies, her
face is totally destroyed.

"Six, seven plastic surgeries in three years and there's not much
improvement. The last one, though, she kind of convinces herself
that she's looking better. And that's when she starts going back to
the club scene. And it's a catastrophe. I only saw her once but she
looked like a monster in a bad sci-fi flick. I mean, a dollar-ninety-
eight monster. But this monster is for real. People are so repelled
by her, they don't even laugh at first (she tells Jim all this later on),
they just shy back from her like she's got something contagious.
Or she's like an omen that's going to bring them bad luck or
something. Anyway, every place she goes, they just stare at her.
The waitresses come over and they kind of smirk at her. And then
people start getting mean. All the hotshots start asking her to
dance. And some chick comes up and asks her what kind of
makeup she's wearing. Not even the people she used to think of as
friends want anything to do with her. She was a pretty ruthless
little bitch when she was young and beautiful, and they're not all
that sad to see her cut up this way. And every night, she goes up
to her nice fancy lonely house and tells all this to Jim, who is by
this time sort of her live-in shrink. And Jim is so pissed by what
she's telling him—how she was treated in these clubs—that he
starts setting the places on fire, the clubs I mean. For her, that's
why he's doing it. For her. Because he wants her to know how
much he loves her, how much he's willing to protect her. Because
he knows that she'll marry him now. Ever since he was a kid, that
was all he wanted. For her to marry him. And now it's finally going
to happen."

6

Wind rattled the warped wood-framed windows. The linoleum
was so old it was worn to floor in several places. The one big room

smelled of cigarettes and Aqua Velva and whiskey, and a bathroom smelled of hair tonic and toilet bowl cleaner. There were doilies on the ragged armchair and the wobbly end tables and even on top of the bulky table model TV that dated from the sixties. The windows were so dirty you could barely see outside. If you listened carefully, you could hear the spectral echoes of all the lonely radio music that had been played in this shabby for-rent room down the decades, Bing Crosby in the thirties and Frank Sinatra in the forties and Elvis in the fifties, and God only knew what else since then. A lot of animals crawl away to die in hidden shadowy places; this was a hidden shadowy place for humans.

"It's only a hundred and fifty dollars a month is why he lives here," Matt Shea said.

"They should pay him," I said.

"Yeah, it is pretty grim."

We'd spent three hours trying to find him and Ella. No luck. The times we'd called the landlady, she'd said he wasn't home. I finally said we should check out his apartment anyway. Shea agreed and here we were.

"We need to go to the police," I said.

"I know." He made a sour face. "This gets out, I'm going to have a hell of a time holding on to some of my clients. You don't want your lawyer having a god damned whacko for a brother."

He didn't seem unduly concerned about the people who'd died, or what fate awaited his brother.

He said, as if reading my mind, "I know I sound pretty selfish. But I came from the west side. I just don't want to see it all go to hell."

I started looking through the faded bureau. The mirror atop it was yellow. There were ghosts trapped in the mirror. You could sense them, dozens, maybe scores, of working men and women who died out their time in this room, staring at their fading lives in this mirror.

There was a bundle of photographs inside a manila envelope. There were maybe thirty pictures and every one of them was of the same person. Ella at ten, Ella at fifteen, Ella at twenty, and so on. She was a true beauty, all right. Her smile could jar your teeth loose and give you a concussion. She was innocence and guile in equal measure, and she probably couldn't tell the difference between the two, and neither could you, not that you gave a damn anyway. She was trophy blonde, eternal blonde, slender and supple goddess blonde, with just enough sorrow in the blue eyes to give her an air of fetching mystery, not ever completely knowable or possessable, this Ella girl and Ella woman, not ever.

I found it significant that there were no photos of them together. Ella was always alone. Beautiful and alone. The stuff of myth.

"Maybe he left town," Shea said.

"Maybe."

"She's got plenty of money. They could go anywhere."

"He isn't finished yet."

"Finished with what?"

I showed him the piece of Yellow Pages I'd just found in the bottom drawer. It had been ripped out, jagged. Under Dance Clubs, there were six names. He'd crossed off three of them.

"Looks like three to go," I said.

"That crazy sonofabitch."

"We need to find him fast."

Then I saw the edge of another photo sticking out from beneath a sack of cheap white socks that were still in their plastic bagging.

"You find something else?" Shea said, as I stooped over.

"Uh-huh."

I snatched the photo and stared at it. "He a fisherman?"

"No way. Why?"

"He's got a photo of the marina here."

He took the photo from me. "Hey, I forgot about her house-boat."

"Ella's?"

"Yeah."

"Big-ass houseboat. Really fancy. Out at the Ellis marina."

"Sounds like it'd be worth checking out," I said.

"Yeah," he said. "It does."

7

Ellis Park was the place to go to see summer girls. At least it used to be when I'd visit my Cedar Rapids cousins back in the sixties and early seventies. The girls came in all colors and shapes and sizes and they were probably just as afraid of you as you were of them but their fear was more discreet than ours, and they passed by on bare sweet grass-flecked feet and tire-thrumming ten-speed bikes and in the backs of shiny fine convertibles and on the rear ends of motorcycles driven by boys with biceps like softballs.

The summer girls were long gone now. Autumn was on the land, and on the water too, and the bobbing boats, mostly cabin-style or houseboats, looked lonely in the dusk and the first faint light of winter stars. Here and there you saw cabin lights. In the summer they would have been welcoming and beacon bright but now there was something faded and desperate about them.

We pulled up on the ridge above the marina. Matt said, "I want to go down there alone first." Wimmers had been pulled on an emergency case, a bank robbery.

"The one you pointed out, there aren't any lights on."

"She doesn't want any lights on. Ever. Her face. He told me that. She gets pissed when he turns lights on." He shook his head. "All this shit comes out at the trial, I'm fucking dead meat. My father-in-law's a wheel at the country club. They're gonna be all over his ass."

"Maybe you should concentrate on your brother right now."

He glared at me. "Oh, I'm concentrating on him, all right. He's some psycho and he's going to destroy everything I built for myself in this town. So don't fucking tell me about concentration, all right, Payne?"

He got out of the car and then ducked his head back in. "If he's down there, I'll bring him back. You got any handcuffs or anything like that?"

"No."

"Great," he said. "Fucking great."

8

Every so often, Jim'd realize the significance of the moment. How long he'd loved her. How long she'd been denied him. And now, how free she was with him.

Lying in the big double bed on the houseboat. In the darkness so she didn't feel bad about her face. Right next to her in that silk sleeping gown of hers. God, her body. Such a perfect body. No reason for her to feel bad about her face when she had a body like that. No reason for her to feel bad about her face when he loved her so much. And someday, she'd *understand* that. That her face didn't matter as long as he was there to protect her and comfort her.

Slight sway of boat, lying there; slight wind-cry outside in the night sky.

He worked himself against her spoon-fashion; a perfect match. Her sleeping. Careful not to wake her.

And then he heard it.

Somebody on the wooden walk of the marina. Footsteps coming this way.

Somebody.

He reached down to the floor where he kept the gun.

Somebody coming.

She'd argued with him about the gun at first. Guns scaring her. Guns going off when you didn't want them to and accidentally killing people. Guns something only bad people owned. (Forgetting that she'd pulled a gun on the loverboy bartender.)

Now, he was glad he'd talked her into letting him keep it.

9

By the time Matt Shea reached the dock, he was lost in the dusk. Only as he passed lighted boats did I get a glimpse of his silhouette.

I wanted to be somewhere else. In a nice restaurant with a nice lady. Or with my cats in my Cedar Rapids apartment reading a book and dozing off under the lamp.

But not here with Matt Shea and all his country club concerns, and his sad crazed brother, and the once beautiful Ella. Sometimes, it's fun, the pursuit; but sometimes it's just sad, you learn something (or are reminded of something) you'd just as soon *not* know—the knowing changing you in some inalterable way—and then you wish you drove a cab or bagged up people's groceries.

He was gone fifteen minutes before I started to think about going down there.

All sorts of possibilities presented themselves. I'd kept the window rolled halfway down so I could hear shouts or screams. The marina was settling in for the night. A few cars wheeled into the parking lot. Men and women with liquor bottles tucked under their arms trekked from cars to boats. They laughed a lot and the laughter seemed wrong, even profane, given the moment, crazy Jim and scarred-up Ella. I waited another few minutes and then went down there.

The board walkway pitched beneath my feet. I could glimpse people behind houseboat curtains. They were searching for summer, even if it was only the memory of summer their boats offered them.

Ella's boat was three slips away from its nearest companion. This gave it a privacy the others lacked. No lights as I approached, no sound except the soft slap of water, and the tangle of night birds in the tangle of autumn trees.

I jumped aboard and went to the door. Locked. I walked to the window to the left of the curtain. The curtains were pulled tight. I listened carefully. Nothing.

And then I heard the sobbing. Male sobbing. Throaty and uncomfortable, as if the man didn't *know* how to sob, hadn't had sufficient practice.

I went to the door. Tried the knob again. Uselessly. "Matt? Are you in there?"

The sobbing. Barely audible.

I got out the burglary tools I keep in my pocket most of the time. I went in and clipped a light on.

Smell of blood and feces. And something even fouler. He brought it with him when he staggered up off the chair and fell into my arms. Matt Shea.

The knife was still in his chest. Just to the right of his heart. A long, pearl-handled switchblade. The sobs were his. "This is really going to look like shit in the papers tomorrow." All this, and his primary concern was still his rep with the country club boys. "Sonofabitch stabbed me. His own brother."

I half carried him back to the chair he'd been in and sat him down. There might still be time for an ambulance. I went to the phone and dialed 911.

The boat was laid out with bunks on both sides, a tiny kitchen, and a living room arrangement dominating the center of the room. The couch had been opened up to become a bed and now there were two people in it. One of them was alive. That was Jim Shea. The other was dead, six, seven days into death judging by what I could see of the lividity and rigor mortis. The body was bloated and badly discolored. There were flies and maggots, too. The facial flesh itself had separated and spoiled but even so you could still see the scarring. Jim Shea didn't seem to notice any of this. He wore a black T-shirt and chinos. He lay up against her, an arm wrapped around her hip with great proprietary fondness. She was his woman, the woman he'd dreamt of most of his life, and he wasn't going to let go of her even now. He probably didn't even know she'd been dead for nearly a week. Or maybe he didn't care. She wore a white blouse and a dark skirt. No blanket covered them. There was a bullet wound in her right temple. I was going to say something to him but then I looked at his eyes and saw that it was no use. Certain mad saints had eyes like his, and visionaries, and men who believe that God told them to go down to the local school and open fire on the children on the playground.

The note was still on the small dining table. Simple enough. She couldn't handle it and killed herself. But he'd kept right on taking care of her, killing those who had made fun of her at the clubs.

"I work my ass off and make something of my life and this is what I fucking get for it," Matt Shea said somewhere behind me.

10

After the DA decided to go with a plea bargain and a reduced sentence—Jim Shea's defense attorney deciding to drop the insanity defense even though Jim was clearly insane—I got a call from Matt Shea thanking me for everything. He said things hadn't gone so badly for him, after all. In fact, ironically, some of the members feeling badly for him, he'd been nominated to sit on the board of the country club. First time a west sider had ever been nominated.

Then he said, "You hear about Jim?"

"No."

"Killed himself."

He was so calm, I thought he might be talking about some other Jim. "Your brother?"

"Yeah. Started squirreling socks away in jail. Made a noose for himself." Pause. "I know you think I'm a callous bastard, Payne. But it's better for everybody."

"He belonged in a psychiatric hospital."

"You know what that fucking trial would've done to me? All those headlines day after day? They wouldn't've done my mother any good, either, believe me."

"That's touching, you caring about your mother and all."

"Believe it or not, Payne, I do. And Jim was never anything but a burden to her. His whole life. If he'd lived, she would've had to go up to the penitentiary and see him every month."

"You wouldn't have?"

"Sure, sometimes. When I had the time, I mean. But prisons spook me. Like hospitals. Or graveyards. I just think it's bad luck to be anywhere around them. Well, I just thought I'd catch you up on some things. You get my check by the way?"

"Very generous. I appreciate it."

"You helped me, Payne, and I appreciate it. Well, listen, gotta run."

My first thought was to have one of those dramatic little moments you see in bad movies and tear his check up into a thousand pieces. Moral outrage.

But then I realized that I badly needed the money, the old cash flow not being so hot lately.

I went down and deposited it right away. Just the way Matt Shea would have.

Intimate Obsession

ROBERT J. RANDISI

1

It was dark as Marta and Elizabeth stood outside the apartment building. They had watched the doorman open and hold the door for a dozen people in the past hour, but over the last few minutes no one had come along.

"How much longer?" Marta asked, nervously.

"About twenty minutes," Elizabeth said. "Let's make sure everything's really slowed down. We don't want anyone coming along while I'm distracting him."

Marta didn't understand why Liz was so calm, especially since she was the one who had to approach the doorman. Her own nervousness was understandable because she was the one who had to slip into the building unnoticed, and then open a back door to let Liz in.

Jesus, she thought, how had they gotten themselves in to this?

Marta's hands kneaded the muscles in Paul Barron's buttocks, eliciting a moan of pleasure from him. Some clients preferred to keep their underwear on during a massage, while others chose to go completely naked. Paul was one of the latter—and she didn't mind a bit.

Usually, Marta covered the naked ones from the neck down with a sheet, exposing only that part of the body she was working on at the moment. However, when it came to Paul she found herself exposing more than necessary. Paul was exceptionally built, and Marta—while working on him for the past few weeks—had found her professionalism slipping further and further away.

She placed each of her palms on one of his buttocks and moved them in a rotating motion. His skin was smooth and hairless. She loved the way it felt in her hands. She casually slid one finger along the crack of his ass. If he noticed he said nothing. She sometimes wondered what he would do if she gave into the urge to bite him.

"Oh, yeah . . ." he moaned, and she closed her eyes, pretending they were in bed. "You've got great hands."

She'd given him every opportunity to ask her out. With most of her clients she remained silent while working on them, but with Paul there was too much she wanted him to know about her. She told him that she was single, lived with a roommate, that she was available most evenings because she was so good at what she did she could make her own hours. She'd told him her likes, her dislikes, her hobbies, everything she could to get him interested.

"Oh, Jesus . . . oh, Marta . . . oohh . . ." He groaned as she moved her hands down to his thighs, and then his calves. His pleasure was incredibly erotic. She was becoming excited. She kept the sheet flipped up, exposing him from the waist down. She couldn't help giving his butt some very unprofessional glances.

She was a therapeutic masseuse. Because she was pretty, though, men often made lewd remarks or suggestions to her, treated her like some stupid Swedish masseuse. Those men never got to come to another appointment. Paul respected her as a professional from the beginning. Maybe that was because he'd been referred to Marta by his psychologist. No, she chose to believe it was because he was a gentleman—the *right* kind of man.

She fell in love with Paul Barron during his first visit. Now all she had to do was get him to realize that he loved her, too.

"**Y**ou look very relaxed, Paul," Dr. Elizabeth Tyler-Wallace said.

"I should be. I just came from a session with Marta."

"Ah," Elizabeth said. She touched her pencil's eraser to her lush lower lip. "That would explain it. I guess your visits to her are doing you some good."

"Not as much good as my visits to you, Doc," he said, coming around to her side of the desk.

"Paul—"

"Shh." When his lips touched hers all semblance of resistance on her part melted away. While they kissed he unbuttoned her blouse far enough to reveal her cleavage, and leaned down farther to kiss her breasts, freeing them from the lacy, lavender bra she had put on for him.

Elizabeth knew how unprofessional it was to be sleeping with Paul Barron, but damn it, she couldn't help herself. When he first came to her, unhappy about his loveless marriage, depressed from years of trying to make it work, her heart had gone out to him. Visit after visit she began to realize what a wonderful, sensitive man he was, a man who had been mistreated by a miserable, cold bitch of a wife. She wasn't even sure who had made the first move, but one day they were on the couch together, naked. That first time the door had been unlocked. Alma, her receptionist, could have walked in on them. The realization had made that encounter more exciting, but since that day she had taken to keeping the door locked.

As he lifted her from her chair and carried her to the sofa she wondered why every session did not result in sex. Sometimes they actually just talked, and it was on those days she felt he *truly* needed her, that she was really helping him.

It was on days like this, however, as he peeled her clothes off and ran his tongue over her belly and down into the fragrant, tangled jungle of her pubic patch that she wondered why they ever bothered to talk. . . .

2

"Okay," Liz said, "ready?"

"I'm ready."

"Don't fuck up, Marta," Liz said. "I'm only going to be able to hold his attention for so long."

"Just long enough," Marta said, "and I'll do the rest."

"Okay, here I go. . . ."

"**H**ow's Paul doing?" Marta asked.

"You know I can't talk about my patients, Marta," Elizabeth replied.

They were the perfect roommates, hardly ever home at the same time, which made this evening unusual. Not coincidentally, however, Marta had stayed in because she wanted to talk about Paul.

"I'm not interested in specifics, silly," Marta said. "I just want to know if he's doing . . . better."

"He's doing a lot better," Elizabeth said. "His sessions with you are really relaxing him, and he's opening up to me more."

Marta bit her lip, feeling some jealousy. She wished Paul would open up to *her,* and she wouldn't charge him fifty dollars an hour for it.

Elizabeth and Marta were both professional women, but neither was making the kind of money that would enable them to afford this kind of apartment alone. It was for that reason, after their initial meeting at an art gallery, they had decided to live together.

Marta Desmond was in her late twenties and had been working

for the Therapeutic Center for two years as a technician and therapeutic masseuse. It was the only job she'd ever had that made her feel fulfilled.

Elizabeth was in her early thirties and had opened her own office only a year ago.

Both women had similar tastes in art and films and food, but their fashion sense was totally different. In fact, Marta had none, while Elizabeth seemed to have a natural knack for knowing—as Marta put it—"what went with what."

Marta knew she could never wear what Elizabeth wore. She was slender, of medium height, and worked out to keep herself in shape. Elizabeth had a lovely, full figure and was tall enough to carry her heavy breasts without looking terribly busty. While Marta's chestnut hair was usually straight and short, Elizabeth's blond hair fell in shimmering waves to her shoulders. Marta thought she was "pretty" but knew Elizabeth was beautiful.

Elizabeth, on the other hand, admired Marta's fit and tight body and had joined the same health club—thanks to Marta's sponsorship—to try to tone herself up. She only worked out twice a week, however, while Marta tried to go every day, and usually managed at least five visits a week. In return, Elizabeth had been helping Marta with her makeup and her clothes.

Since they were home at the same time tonight they ordered Chinese takeout. It was while they were eating out of the cartons in the living room that Marta asked about Paul.

Now Marta felt a warm flush when Elizabeth told her how much better Paul was doing since he started coming to her for massage therapy. Maybe it was more than just the massage, maybe it was the conversation, as well, that was helping him.

She hoped.

Marta panicked for a few moments, thinking she was lost in the bowels of the building. Finally, however, she located the back door and opened it.

"What took you so long?" Liz complained, slipping inside.

"I got lost."

"Never mind, we're in now. Let's go up."

"Liz," Marta said, "do we really want to do this?"

"Do you enjoy being made a fool of?"

"No."

"Being laughed at?"

"No."

"Being used?"

"N-no."

"Then what do you think?"

Marta took a deep breath and said, "Let's go."

Several more weeks went by before Paul finally showed some interest in Marta.

She had just finished his massage and offered to leave the room while he dressed.

"I don't think there's any real need for that," he asked, "do you?"

He dropped the sheet to the floor so she could see him completely naked for the first time. She caught her breath. His penis was erect. She'd gotten glimpses of him beneath the sheet from time to time, knowing that her hands excited him, but she never could have imagined how beautiful, how utterly perfect his cock would be. She'd been waiting for this day for weeks. His body was absolutely flawless.

"Marta, have I been reading the signs wrong?"

She glanced around the room, both nervous and elated, her face suffused with blood.

"Look at me."

Once she did she couldn't take her eyes off of him, again.

"Lock the door," he told her.

She did it without a word.

"Come here. . . ."

She went to him and when he kissed her she moaned. He undressed her, then lifted her onto the massage table.

"Someone will come. . . ." she said, resisting feebly.

"If they do they'll knock," he said, with a smile, "and you'll tell them you're almost finished."

"Yes," she said, closing her eyes as his mouth closed over one breast, as his teeth tugged at her nipple, as his hand slid down between her legs to find her wet and ready. "Yes. . . ."

It went on for weeks, Paul Barron having sex with both Marta and Elizabeth. Of course, he might have enjoyed it more if he had known they were roommates, but neither saw fit to tell him, which led, of course, to his ultimate downfall.

3

They weren't sure how many apartments were on each floor. There was always a chance that someone could come out into the hall, but they had watched the building for days, taking turns, and noticed that, during the week, at this hour of the night, very few people came or went.

They ascended the stairs to the fourth floor and Liz peeked into the hall.

"It's clear."

They let the heavy door shut quietly behind them and made their way to apartment 4D. . . .

Another few weeks passed before Marta and Elizabeth talked about Paul Barron again. This time it was a Saturday evening, when neither of them had to work.

Marta had a massage table in the apartment, and every so often would give Elizabeth a massage. The first time she had envied and admired her friend's body. It was so lush and smooth, high breasted and long waisted. There had been times, in between men, when Marta had thought that if she was ever going to *have* a gay experience, it would be with somebody like Elizabeth.

But Marta was used to Elizabeth's body now. She was satisfied with her own body and, obviously, so was Paul. That was all that mattered. Well, almost.

What she found odd, though, was the fact that they only had sex at work. He never took her out, and never invited her to his apartment. Still, it was a small price to pay for the pleasure he gave her.

Lately, however, she'd started longing for more. She wanted time alone with him when they would talk, possibly make plans for the future. She wanted to be in a real bed with him.

She was working on the knotted muscles in Elizabeth's back when she asked, "How is Paul?"

"Still coming along. He's remarkably relaxed when he comes from your sessions with him. Mmmm, that's good. . . . I can't say I blame him. . . . You have wonderful hands, Marta."

Marta laughed to herself, knowing that it wasn't her hands that had been relaxing Paul lately.

Marta wondered if she should confide in Elizabeth. She was her best friend. They rarely talked about the men in their lives, but then they were both so busy they rarely *had* men to talk about. This was special, though, and they *were* both his therapists, weren't they? They both wanted what was best for him.

"Liz, I have to tell you something." She moved her hands down and began kneading Elizabeth's smooth buttocks, easing the aches from a long day of sitting and listening to other people's problems.

"Mmmm," Elizabeth moaned. "What, Marta?"

"I'm . . . involved with someone."

Elizabeth lifted her head.

"Really?"

"Yes."

"Is it . . . sexual?"

"Oh, yes."

"And serious."

"Yes."

"That's wonderful!" Elizabeth said. "I guess I should tell you that I'm seeing someone, too."

"Really? This is wonderful. Are you in love?"

"Yes, I am."

"So am I."

"Who is he?" Elizabeth asked.

"I was just going to ask you the same thing," Marta said.

Excited, they both took a deep breath and said, simultaneously, "Paul Barron!"

"**H**ow do we get in?" Marta asked.

They knew the woman was home. She was always home on a Wednesday night, they'd made sure of it.

"We knock," Elizabeth said.

"Knock? That's your plan? What if someone hears?"

"As long as they don't look out into the hall we're okay."

"And if they do?"

"Then we pretend we have the wrong apartment, leave, and come back another night."

"I don't think I can, Liz," Marta said. "I don't think I could come back again."

"Then we better do it tonight," her roommate said. "Get ready to knock."

"Me? Why do I have to?"

"Because," Elizabeth said, digging into her purse, "I have the chloroform. . . ."

After the initial shock they each took turns comparing their relationships with Paul.

Elizabeth told Marta that she had been having sex with him for three months.

Marta told Elizabeth that it had only been about half that for them. She couldn't help but think that her friend had smirked at that, if only for a moment.

Elizabeth said they only had sex in her office.

Marta said the situation was the same for them.

"Has he told you he loves you?" Elizabeth asked.

"N-no, not exactly," Marta said. "He says he's never felt this way about anyone before."

"Oh, God . . ." Elizabeth closed her eyes. Sitting up on the table she was totally unaware of her nudity, until she felt a chill. Her nipples became prominent and she said, "Can I have my robe, please?"

Marta handed it to her. "He's told you the same things, hasn't he?"

Elizabeth nodded. "I've been such a fool." She hugged herself, still cold despite the robe.

"We both have."

"He's been using us, Marta."

Marta couldn't help wondering, in spite of her anger, why Paul had started having sex with Elizabeth so much earlier than with her. Did he find her so much more attractive?

"Marta?"

"I'm sorry . . . I'm . . . a little shocked."

"I'm more than a little shocked," Elizabeth said. "I'm . . . pissed off!"

"So am I."

"I think we should go and see Mr. Paul Barron."

"You have his home address?" Marta asked. "Of course you do. We probably have it on file, too."

"Now I know why he's never taken me out, or taken me to his apartment," Elizabeth said.

"I wonder how many other women he has?"

"I'll get dressed," Elizabeth said, "and we'll go ask him."

4

The woman answered the knock, looking puzzled. She had no time to speak, however, as Liz quickly covered her mouth with the chloroformed rag.

The woman backpedaled, frantically trying to catch her breath. Liz staggered forward with her, hissing, "Close the door!"

Marta closed the door as quietly as she could, then turned to see Liz and the other woman topple to the floor, the woman's legs kicking. She was wearing a robe and was naked underneath.

"Help me," Liz said.

Marta ran forward and pinned the woman's legs. What did Paul see in her? She was so cheap. She had neither her muscle tone nor Liz's beauty. She was a cow, possessing the obvious attributes men craved for some reason, and hardly any brains at all.

She was disgusting.

It was quite by accident that Marta and Elizabeth saw the bitch. They had gone to Paul's apartment that Saturday night. As they parked they saw him get out of a car with a woman. She was a brassy blonde with big boobs and fleshy hips, wearing stiletto heels, hanging on Paul's arm. They went into his apartment house together, and both Marta and Liz sat watching, stunned.

"This is too much," Liz finally said.

"Did you see her?"

"Cheap."

"Obvious."

"A . . . a centerfold!"

"How could he?"

"All right," Liz said, "help me with her."

Together they dragged the woman into the bathroom and removed her robe. When she was naked both women stood for a moment, inspecting her. Her pubic hair was its natural black, her breasts large and pear-shaped, obviously implants. Her skin was pale, but her nipples were ugly and dark. Crescent-shaped scars marked the spots where incisions had been made for the implants.

"What does he see in her?" Liz asked.

"I have no idea."

"Start the water. I'll look for someplace to put the cuff link and the note. . . ."

For several days they had followed Paul and the other woman, whose name was Tammi, with an *i*.

"Wouldn't you know she'd have a name that ended with an E sound?" Marta asked, a few days after they found out about her. They were in Elizabeth's office.

Once or twice they got close enough to hear Tammi speak, and realized how dumb she really was.

"What do men see in women like that?" Marta asked, in frustration. They were each holding a glass of white wine. The bottle was between them, half consumed.

"She's nonthreatening," Elizabeth said.

"But Paul's an intelligent man."

"Smart enough to fool us into thinking he cares for us." Elizabeth poured more wine into each glass. "Smart enough to be sleeping with three women at one time."

"Oh, God," Marta wailed, "what about AIDS?"

"He used a condom with me," Liz said.

"Me, too," Marta said, then added, "most of the time."

"Marta!"

"Well, the first time we didn't. . . ."

Elizabeth sighed and admitted, "We didn't our first time, either. God, we're so stupid! What should we do now?"

"Well, I know what I'm going to do," Marta said.

"What?"

"I'm not going to have anything else to do with him," she said. "I'm going to tell him off."

"That wouldn't satisfy me," Elizabeth said. "Besides, he could do me some real harm if it gets out I was sleeping with a patient."

"Jesus, I didn't think of that."

They sat silently for a few moments, drinking wine.

Marta finally said, with a drunken giggle, "We should kill him."

She giggled again, then stopped when she noticed Elizabeth wasn't laughing.

"Liz?"

When the tub was full they eased the naked woman into it, sloshing water onto the floor.

"That's okay," Elizabeth said. "The police will expect that."

They both stared down at Tammi, who was now lying in the water, her head floating.

"Who's going to do it?" Marta asked.

They looked at each other. It was silly, but they hadn't thought of that.

"We'll both have to do it, Marta," Elizabeth said, finally.

"I know, it's only fair."

"Are you ready?"

Marta took a deep breath and then nodded.

Both women bent over the tub. . . .

5

Two days later Elizabeth and Marta watched the nightly newscasts together.

"A St. Louis man has been arrested in the drowning murder of a Miss Tammi Blakely. Police said that an anonymous caller reported suspicious sounds coming from the woman's apartment. When the police arrived they found Miss Blakely dead in the tub. An autopsy revealed she had been chloroformed and forcefully drowned. A search of the apartment turned up a monogrammed cuff link, and a typewritten letter telling the woman she wouldn't get away with treating the author, quote, 'this way.' Police assume the motive for the murder was jealousy, and have arrested Paul Barron, a local attorney, and charged him with the murder. Mr.

Barron's fingerprints were found in the apartment, making it impossible for him to deny having been there. He does, however, vehemently deny that he killed her. We'll have more on this story as it continues to break. . . ."

Liz hit the power button on the remote and the TV went dead.

"How do you feel?" Marta asked.

Elizabeth thought a moment, then said, "Vindicated. How about you?"

"I guess . . . I just wonder if we could have done it another way."

"Sure, we could," Elizabeth said. "We could have killed him and framed her. Either way, they were both going to pay. This way, Paul doesn't get off so easy."

"Easy?"

Elizabeth nodded.

"If he was dead he wouldn't suffer."

"And since Tammi is dead, *she's* not suffering."

"Right."

Marta brightened and said, "Well, when you put it that way, I don't feel so bad."

"Me, neither. I think this calls for a toast."

They opened a bottle of champagne and filled two glasses.

"To friendship," Marta said.

"And obsessions," Elizabeth said, "the intimate kind—only never so intimate that we don't talk to each other about them."

"I know," Marta said, "if we'd only talked more this could have been avoided."

Elizabeth sighed and said, "He was a beautiful man, though."

"And," Marta said, mischievously, "a great lover!"

"But there are others out there. . . ."

"I'll drink to that."

They clinked their glasses together.

The Club of Masks

EDWARD D. HOCH

My name, if it matters, is Winston Dover, and the business that brought me to our Paris office in the balmy May of 1933 need not concern us here. Let it only be said that the great French Republic, having weathered the earliest days of the world economic crisis, was finally suffering through a series of financial scandals and bank failures. The government was tottering and a Bourbon pretender to the throne was actually issuing manifestos as King Jean III in exile.

Here I was, away from my comfortable home in London, chained to a desk in a dour financial institution for a month, analyzing countless ledgers. The unique beauty of the blossoming horse chestnut trees along the Champs-Elysées was visible only through a dirty window in my office. Who could blame me for feeling an age-old stirring in my loins?

One day, taking off my reading glasses and laying aside my pencil, I rubbed the fatigue from my eyes and asked the senior bookkeeper, "Where does one go at night for amusement, Pierre?"

He was a man in his forties, at least a decade older than myself, who walked with a slight limp from a wound suffered at the

Marne. My question brought only a puzzled stare and finally the words, "There is a nice little café on the Left Bank. I have never been there myself, but friends tell me the food is inexpensive and quite good."

I was thinking of something a bit more exciting, something to get my blood flowing. Perhaps Pierre's assistant, a young red-haired woman named Claudine, with high cheekbones and darting eyes, sensed that when she suggested, "The Folies-Bergère is always popular with the English businessman." It was the first time I remembered her speaking directly to me during my two weeks in the office.

"Thank you," I replied. "Perhaps I'll give it a try."

But of course I didn't. The Folies was far too ordinary for my tastes. I spent the evening at a Left Bank café, lingering in the company of some Americans who offered to find me a prostitute, but nothing came of it.

The next morning in the office, as I was settling down to business, Claudine asked, "Did you get to the Folies, Winston?"

"No," I admitted. "I just wandered around for a while."

Nothing more was said about it, and Claudine returned to her work.

It was the following morning when she brought up the subject again. "The famous Moulin Rouge has become a dance hall now. You might find some entertainment there if the Paris nightlife still bores you."

"I may try that," I agreed. "Thank you for the suggestion."

But of course I didn't go. I hardly knew myself what I was seeking, but it was something beyond the bright lights, something best kept in the dark.

The following Monday morning I found a large square envelope on my desk. My mail always came from England and it was surprising to find something mailed in Paris. I opened it and took out a formal card almost like a wedding invitation. It was in French and it read, *You are invited to an evening at the Club of Masks, 137 Boulevard de Clichy, Montmartre. 19 May 1933. Eight p.m. Formal dress, masks will be supplied. Admittance by this invitation, between the hours of eight and ten only.*

The date was Friday of that week. I flipped the card over onto Pierre's desk. "What do you make of this?"

His face seemed to pale as he read it. "I know nothing about it," he said after a moment, returning the card to me.

"Have you ever heard of the place?"

"I believe it—" he began, but then fell silent as Claudine entered the office.

It was not until lunch time that I found myself alone with him again and raised the question once more. "The Club of Masks. Is it something I might attend?"

He moistened his lips and said, "There are always rumors of such places, in many cities of Europe. They are mentioned occasionally in fiction, in Arthur Schnitzler's *Dream Story*, set in Vienna, and in John Dickson Carr's *The Waxworks Murder*, set right here in Paris and published in England just last year."

"But those are fiction!" I protested.

"Fiction based on fact. Rumor has it that another Club of Masks exists in Berlin."

"Have you ever been to this place?" I asked, holding up the card.

"Hardly! I am a happily married man."

His meaning was clear. "Why would I be invited to such a place?"

"Perhaps someone you met in a café," Pierre suggested.

"I told no one where I worked."

"It would be best to throw it away, forget about it."

"I think you're right." I dropped the invitation into the wastebasket and went on with my work. But later in the day, when Pierre was out of the office, I retrieved it and put it in my pocket.

* * *

I had brought no formal clothes with me from London, but I located a shop with reasonable prices and by Friday evening I was ready for my adventure. I considered it more of a joke than anything else, imagining half-nude dancing girls and music hall comedians such as I'd experienced back home. Thus I was unprepared for the reality that awaited me.

The Boulevard de Clichy was a wide street in a hilly section on the north side of the city. On Friday evening it was alive with crowded cafés and every sound of life. Traffic moved relentlessly and street hawkers sold their wares while well-dressed gentlemen and their ladies stepped carefully, bound for the Moulin Rouge with its familiar windmill. It had been raining earlier and the puddles still reflected the lights from flashing electric signs. Loud jazz music came from one of the buildings. A garishly painted streetwalker approached me but then turned away when I ignored her. I saw that this was truly Paris by night, and wondered that I hadn't discovered it earlier.

I found number 137 with little difficulty. It was a three-story building without windows on its street side, and only a single entrance was visible. I walked up to the door and pressed a bell at its side. A slender man in evening clothes who wore a plain white mask over much of his face opened the door almost immediately. The mask was such that it covered his nose and cheekbones as well as the area around his eyes. "Your invitation, please," he said in French. I showed him the printed card and he allowed me to enter a foyer area with a cloakroom at one end.

The young woman who accepted my mackintosh also wore a white mask. She was dressed in a long black gown. Her eyes lingered on me as she accepted the coat. "Is this your first visit here?"

"Yes. The invitation said a mask would be furnished."

"Of course." She produced one shaped like her own, covering my cheekbones and the top of my nose. But instead of plain white, it was black with elaborate gold embroidery. In the center of the forehead was a small green gem, perhaps an emerald, perhaps an imitation. I thanked her and put it on. I noticed the doorman was detaining the next arrival until I was masked.

"How much do I owe you?"

"Tonight you are here as a guest. If you are invited to return, you will be advised of the management's fees."

From the foyer I entered a lounge with a bar at one end. The bartender was masked, as were his customers. I realized now that the establishment's employees wore white masks while the visitors, or customers, wore the darker black-and-gold ones. Through another set of doors a trio of masked musicians was playing. Not feeling the need of a drink at the moment I proceeded into the next room, descending a few steps into a spacious promenade hall where some masked couples danced to the music. About thirty feet above my head was a glass domed ceiling, and along the walls were ornate marble pillars with lights aimed upward, leaving the dancers in semidarkness but illuminating open balconies on the two upper floors. I could see rows of doors.

I noticed that the women were also dressed formally, in long black gowns and gloves. Their masks displayed rubies instead of emeralds, but were otherwise identical to mine. Occasionally a couple would leave the floor and disappear through one of the hall's side doors. I assumed I was in an expensive bordello catering to the wealthy and I wondered again who had invited me here. As I glanced about the room, seeking out a lone companion like myself, I was approached by one of the white-masked attendants who handed me a key. "What's this?" I asked.

"Room twenty-four," he said. "It is on the second level." Then he was gone.

I stared down at the key in my hand and decided the answer to the mystery was awaiting me there. I could not have left the place without knowing. Passing through the nearest door I found myself in a dimly lit passageway with a brick floor. There was a line of closed doors here, bearing the numbers one through six. I imagined the numbered rooms continued around the corner to the other sides. An iron staircase spiraled toward the second floor and I went up without hesitation. At the door to room 24 I paused and knocked. When no one answered I knocked again, then realized that I was supposed to use the key.

The lock turned silently and I stepped inside. A masked woman sat at a table smoking a cigarette. There was a vase of red roses on the table and she was playing solitaire with a deck of cards. When she saw me she put down the cards and said, "Good evening. I've been expecting you."

She stood up to shake my hand, and I saw that she wore a black silk gown like the others, with black gloves that reached almost to her elbows. Her bare neck and shoulders were a creamy, flawless white. An overhead light caught and reflected the jewel on her mask, sending an arrow of red darting across the walls. It seemed to match the roses. "What's this all about?" I asked. "I received your invitation."

"You are an Englishman working in the city, away from home. All men are lonely in those circumstances." She was a tall, slender woman with shining black hair done in the helmet style favored by the American movie actress Louise Brooks. The mask hid much of her face from view and I could see only the sweet soft lips that occasionally curved into a cunning smile as she spoke. Her voice, speaking accented English, seemed deep and husky, as if she might be trying to disguise it.

"This place—is it a bordello?"

"Only if you make it so."

"Then what—?"

"May I call you Winston?"

"You know me."

"I have been told about you by others. I have seen and followed you on your aimless nighttime wanderings about the city."

Could that be possible? Had I been followed without my

knowing it, and by such a creature as this? "All right," I said at last. "What should I call you?"

She pointed to her mask. "Ruby is as good as anything."

"What do we do now? Take off our clothes?" I couldn't help noticing the large brass bed against the wall.

"I was thinking of a game of bezique."

"What?"

She held up her hand. "Hear me out. If you agree, we will play a single game and the loser becomes the winner's slave until dawn."

"I see. And what will that involve?"

"If I am the winner, complete unquestioning obedience in all things."

"And if I disobey I suppose that means a caning," I said, remembering my days at boarding school back home.

"Ah, the English vice! No, no, nothing like that here. In some of the other rooms, who knows?" She smiled her cunning smile. "Here, if you obey my wishes until dawn, you will be rewarded. You may do any one thing you want to me, except remove my mask."

"And if I win at the game?"

She picked up the cards and fanned them across the table. "Then I will obey you until dawn. The rules are the same."

I had the growing feeling that I should turn around and leave, but it was something I could not do. Perhaps this was the adventure I'd been craving and I could not turn my back on it. "All right, I agree."

"Good." The smile was back. "Then it will be one game of bezique. A thousand points?"

"Fine."

She set aside the solitaire deck and produced a sixty-four-card bezique deck from a drawer of the desk, fanning the cards faceup as she had the others. The French game was similar to the American game of pinochle. I wasn't particularly good at either one and

I hardly expected to win. The woman known as Ruby would not have chosen a game at which she was unskilled. It lasted three hands, longer than I'd expected, but in the end she was triumphant.

"Now it begins," she said simply, putting away the cards.

I glanced at my wristwatch. "It's a long time until dawn."

"Give me your watch. Time will have no meaning here."

I did as I was told. She stood up and came around the desk to face me. "Kneel down before me."

"All right." She stepped very close, until the black silk of her gown touched my face as she raised it.

"Now kiss me," she said. "Here."

It was soon clear that my only pleasure would come from pleasing her in an endless variety of ways. At times during the next few hours, as it must have passed midnight in our timeless room, I would attempt to relieve the tension growing within me, but always her hand restrained my movements. Her lips played with mine, moving up and down my body while her hands caressed and tickled and tormented, often at the same time. Occasionally, when even she seemed sated, she would rest on the bed while I was instructed to amuse her with exercises or contortions.

"What's the point of this?" I asked her once.

"I like to look at your body. You're very handsome, Winston."

It was during one of these periods, in the hours well after midnight, that a sudden muffled scream was heard from one of the adjoining rooms. I was on my feet at once but Ruby dissuaded me with a raised hand. "It is nothing," she assured me.

"It sounds like she's in pain!" I insisted.

"It was a man who screamed," she assured me. "After a time one can tell the difference."

I stood by her for a moment and realized for the first time that without her high heels she was shorter than I was. Seeing her like this, she reminded me of someone. Had we met one night at a café? "Whoever it is, he might need help."

"He is safe," she assured me. "Lie on your back now, with your right knee raised."

"Who are you? What are you doing here? Is this your only gratification?"

"You ask too many questions, Winston. I might have to gag you."

But I persisted as she positioned herself above me. "Are you married? Does your husband know you come here?" Then a thought struck me. "Or perhaps you both come here. Is that him in the next room?"

She laughed at the suggestion. "You ask about my husband and I will tell you if you really want to know."

"I do."

She rose to her feet and stood above me. The smile had vanished. Perhaps she was remembering. "I was nineteen when I married. My husband Paul was everything to me, a wonderful loving man. I did not know at first that he was a supporter of Jean III. Do you know the name?"

I nodded. "The pretender to the throne of France. No one takes him seriously, do they?"

"My husband did. When the gendarmes came to arrest him there was a fight and Paul pushed one of them over the stair railing in our apartment building. The officer was killed and my husband was convicted of murder. He was sentenced to be guillotined last May, just a year ago. Only a pardon from our president could have saved him. On the day before the execution, a Russian madman trying to provoke a war between France and Russia assassinated President Doumer. Because technically Paul had lost his chance for a last-minute pardon, his sentence was automatically commuted to life in prison. It was the happiest day of my life."

"Is he still in prison?"

She shook her head and turned away. "How cruel life can be

at times! Who would have considered the guillotine to be merciful? Paul was sentenced to Devil's Island off the coast of French Guiana, to be transported there by the French convict ship *La Martiniere* last October. Later I was told he died at sea. I never knew what happened until a fellow convict wrote to tell me. On the ship the prisoners were locked below decks in great iron cages. Overhead were pipes from the furnace ready to pour out live steam in the event of a mutiny or escape attempt. A prisoner overpowered one of the guards at dinnertime and the ship's captain turned on the steam. Paul was one of seventeen men scalded to death."

"That must have been terrible, for him and for you when you learned of it. But why come here, to the Club of Masks? Because of your heartbreak?"

Her eyes darted back toward me. "I come looking for a man with a body as beautiful as Paul's."

I couldn't resist asking, "How do I rate?" As soon as the words were out of my mouth I regretted them.

She ignored the question and went on. "Paul had known the owner of this club, another supporter of Jean III named Dr. Bastian. I went to him with the terrible news of how Paul had died. I said I would never find another lover like him, and Bastian invited me to come here. His suggestion was crazy. I had never been that sort. But after a month of bitter loneliness and another month of prowling the Left Bank I knew I must do something. I started coming here, on Fridays and sometimes other nights as well."

"Do men accept the rules of your game?"

She shrugged. "Some do, some don't. Some are looking for their own little perversions."

"Like the one who screamed next door?"

"Yes."

Before I could say more, a bell sounded from outside the room. She went to the bed and slipped a robe over her bare body. "Stay right here," she commanded. "Don't move."

I lay perfectly still as she opened the door and stepped outside.

She returned almost immediately. "They're having a cutting," she told me. "Get dressed."

"What's a cutting?"

"An amusement to enliven the night hours. A woman is tied to one of the marble pillars and the men in attendance take turns cutting away small pieces of her gown until she is nude. It's harmless enough and the male guests seem to like it. Sometimes even the women join in."

"What do you want me to do?"

"Go down and join them. Bring me back a piece of her gown. I'll watch from here."

I did as I was told, descending the spiral staircase to the main level. About a dozen masked men and women were gathered there, and I could see a few more on their way. A tall woman with curly blond hair had been tied loosely to one of the pillars, her hands held above her head by a length of cord looped around one of the light fixtures. She was barefoot and without gloves, wearing only her black evening gown in addition to the glittery mask. Head bowed, she seemed oblivious to her humiliating situation. The first man had already gripped the gown around her navel and cut out a small rectangular piece. A second man likewise removed a piece from the waist area, this one at the side. It seemed to be a game to cut as much as possible without actually separating the bottom of the dress from its top, thereby maintaining a momentary degree of modesty.

By the time I reached her and accepted the scissors from my predecessor, the masked woman's knees were bent and she was hanging from the rope supporting her wrists. Her eyes were closed and her head was sagging so that I could barely see the emerald mask through the curls of her blond hair. Then I saw her arms stretched out above her, saw the tiny puncture mark with its trickle of blood running down the arm, and I knew.

I turned to the others. "This woman is dead."

*   *   *

A stout man in a white mask immediately took charge, ordering everyone back while he and two other white-masked employees cut down the body. He tried to detect a pulse and held a mirror to her nose, but there was no evidence of breathing. I suspected the stout man was Dr. Bastian, and this was confirmed for me when he spotted the needle prick on her arm and ordered the other two to carry her into the manager's quarters at the rear of the first floor.

By this time Ruby had dressed and come downstairs to join me. "What happened?" she asked.

"The woman was dead when I reached her. That man had her carried into his office."

The stout man was standing by the door and Ruby walked quickly up to him for a whispered conversation. I saw them glance back at me. Then she motioned me to join them. "What is it?" I asked.

It was the man who spoke. "It was you who announced she was dead. How did you know? Are you a medical man?"

"No. But when I saw the recent needle prick in her arm I suspected drugs. Most of the people have been drinking here and a mixture of drugs and alcohol could be lethal, especially heroin."

One of the men who'd carried the body into the office appeared at the door and told his employer, "You'd better see this."

Bastian, if that's who it was, entered the office without closing the door behind him. Ruby and I followed. The masked man who'd summoned him inside walked over to the couch on which they'd placed the body. "Look here," he said, lifting away the mask and wig, baring the chest. "This is a man."

And so it was. A man dressed in woman's clothes. "Did he enter like that?" Ruby asked. "Or did his mistress change clothes with him?"

The stout man had a more immediate concern. "I know him. His name is Veygoux, a former major in the French army. He was to make an important speech supporting Jean III next week."

"Did he come here often?"

"Yes."

"You'd better call the police," I suggested. It seemed like the obvious next step, but perhaps nothing was obvious at the Club of Masks.

"That's out of the question," Bastian said. "A police investigation would mean the end of this establishment. Even if they didn't shut us down immediately, my clientele would be fearful of returning."

Ruby tugged on my sleeve. "Let me speak to you," she said, leading me over to a corner while Bastian followed our progress with a questioning eye.

"What is it?" I asked.

"This is Dr. Bastian, as you must have guessed. I want you to help him investigate. If it was murder, find the killer. The police must be kept away."

"I'm no detective," I protested.

"But you have an analytical mind."

"No. I can't do it."

Her eyes met mine through the holes of the mask. "Are you violating our agreement, Winston?"

"Agreement? A man is dead, for God's sake! Are you still playing games?"

"The future of France is no game. The dead man was a supporter of Jean III."

"As are you," I reminded her.

"That was Paul, not me. Some of Dr. Bastian's patrons support the pretender, but not all."

"Obviously not the person who killed him, if that was the motive."

Her answering smile was almost smug. "Tell him you will help."

I took a deep breath and went over to Bastian. "I may be of service. He died of an overdose of heroin, didn't he?"

"Most likely. It could have been poison."

"Do you supply drugs to your guests?"

"Certainly not! Either Veygoux or his partner must have had the hypodermic needle."

"It was his partner," I said. "The trickle of blood from the needle prick ran down his arm as he hung there, toward his body. If he'd injected himself earlier, the blood would have trickled toward his hand. That means he was already hanging when injected. He couldn't have done that himself. The person who tied him there killed him. Someone on your staff must have seen it."

"I saw it myself," Bastian said. "A cutting wasn't that unusual. So long as no one is harmed, we don't interfere. Of course I didn't notice the injection. It would have been easy to hide the hypodermic in the palm of the killer's hand. It couldn't be done earlier because Veygoux had to walk out to the pillar on his own."

"Was it a man or woman who tied him there?"

"It was someone dressed as a man." He motioned toward the body. "In view of this discovery, I suppose they must have exchanged clothes. That would have been part of the humiliation."

"Could you ask everyone to assemble in the promenade hall?"

The stout man started to object. "They cannot be made to remove their masks. That is our fundamental rule. Once they pass from the foyer into the lounge area, no one ever removes their masks."

"The masks stay on. But I must see everyone."

Ruby had come up beside me. "Do it," she told Bastian. "I trust him."

Most of the house's clients were already downstairs, attracted by what had happened. One of the masked employees checked each room, rounding up a few who'd ignored the commotion in pursuit of private pleasures. Bastian explained to everyone what had happened, and presently I faced their lineup, walking back and forth like a drill sergeant. I silently counted thirty-four men and women wearing the embroidered masks of the guests. Adding

Ruby and myself made thirty-six. "How many were invited to-night?" I asked the proprietor.

He thought for a moment and answered, "Thirty-eight, nineteen men and the same number of women. Most, like Veygoux, were regulars. We have a staff of nine on duty every evening—myself, the doorman, the bartender, the woman in the cloakroom who is also our office manager, a trio of musicians, and these two who handle security."

"In my country and America they would be called bouncers," I told him, eyeing the two who had carried the dead man's body into the office. "Nine white masks, staff all accounted for. But there are only thirty-six guests, counting myself. The dead man makes thirty-seven, still one short."

The masked doorman spoke up. "I collected only thirty-seven invitations. One person did not come."

"Who was that?" I asked.

"We have no way of knowing," Bastian replied. "The invitations are identical. They are not coded in any way. People occasionally pass them on to friends, though we try to discourage that."

"The missing person could have been a man or woman?"

He turned and pointed toward the cloakroom employee. She took her cue and answered, "I passed out nineteen male masks and eighteen female."

"All right." I counted them again. It was all in the numbers. "There are eighteen men, counting myself. The dead man makes nineteen."

"If he arrived as a man," Ruby pointed out. "You don't know that."

"But I do know it," I replied. "I think I was the only one who noticed it because that blond wig was partly covering the top of the mask, but Veygoux had an emerald, not a ruby, on his forehead. Upon his arrival he was given the mask for a man, not a woman. She changed clothes with him, but not masks. The masks are never removed, remember?"

"Then the woman who killed him is here," she said. "Dressed as a man but with a ruby like mine on her mask."

Bastian quickly surveyed the line of patrons. "None of the male guests wears a ruby. Look for yourself."

What he said was true enough. I shifted my gaze to the women. Eighteen of them, including my own if I could call her that. One missing, but all wearing a ruby. "One of these men is really a woman," I said. "They'll have to unmask."

"Impossible! Our rules forbid it."

One of the guests, a bulky man whose stomach strained at his evening clothes, stepped forward. There could be no doubt from his deep rasping voice that he was male. "It's hardly necessary, is it? We paired off, man and woman, at the start. If one woman didn't come, there should have been an extra man. Where is he?"

"Dead in my office," Bastian replied.

"Then where is the woman who killed him? We have eighteen men and eighteen women here now."

Another of the men volunteered a statement. "I was standing quite close when this person in the gown was tied to the pillar. As you say, the wig may have hidden the mask's emerald from view but I certainly saw the other person's emerald. It was a man who tied her, a man who killed her—or him."

"Could two men have gone upstairs together?" I asked.

Bastian shook his head. "There are other places for such sport."

"Winston," Ruby whispered at my side. "There must be an answer."

There was, but perhaps the growing fatigue of the morning hours had fogged my brain. I wanted nothing more than to be back upstairs in the room with Ruby, obeying her wishes, preparing for my promised reward.

"I was given a key to the room where this woman waited," I told them. "Did your attendants deliver a key to the murdered man?" Both of them denied it, insisting that I had been the only one to receive a key that night. "She was awaiting him then, when he entered. Either they went up together or she gave him the key."

And then I knew.

I turned and pointed my finger at her like some final judgment. "It was you! You were the one awaiting his arrival, the one who gave him the key along with his mask, the only one who could have provided herself with the necessary male mask!"

I heard someone shout "Winston!" in warning. The cloakroom woman had broken from the line and lunged at me with her hypodermic needle. In a split second one of the masked guards drew his pistol and shot her dead.

"You shouted a warning," I told Ruby later when we were alone again in room 24. The night had passed and it was almost dawn. "Only my name but I recognized the voice, just as I recognized the darting eyes behind your mask."

"You recognized nothing," she said. "Keep it that way." She lit a cigarette and asked, "How did you know it was her?"

"We had a witness who said the killer wore an emerald mask, a male mask. That was so she could blend more easily with the other males in making her escape from the crime scene. But the mask wasn't the one her victim wore, so how had she acquired it? The injection of poison meant the crime was almost certainly premeditated, but how did she know he was coming? More than that, where had the additional female guest come from? The cloakroom woman had to be the answer. Bastian said she was also the office manager, so she would handle the mailing of the invitations. She made certain Veygoux was invited, then destroyed one of the female invitations. She gave him the key when he entered, and after ten o'clock when the guests stopped arriving she joined him in the room. Exchanging clothes must have appealed to him, and it helped her by adding to the confusion of the crime. She left him dying, procured another black gown that she'd hidden earlier, changed back to her white mask, and returned to the floor. The dead man's attire which she'd worn was hidden here somewhere."

"What was her motive?"

I shrugged. "To keep Veygoux from delivering next week's speech in favor of the pretender. I don't attempt to understand French politics."

"They killed her. They just shot her dead."

"Now your friend Bastian can dispose of her body along with Veygoux. Perhaps he can even make it look like a murder-suicide."

She walked to the window and opened the blinds. "You have found the killer. I will keep my part of the bargain." She spread her arms in surrender. "It is dawn. You may do anything you wish to me."

"Except remove your mask."

"Except that, yes."

"Claudine—"

"That is not my name. You are mistaken."

"Your black hair is a wig, like the victim wore. Underneath is your lovely red hair. I have worked with you all these weeks without realizing the woman you are. For that I apologize."

She undid the black gown and let it rustle to the floor. "What will you do to me? I am at your mercy."

I placed my hand on her head. "I wish to pull your hair."

Her mouth opened in something like surprise. There might have been a sadness in those eyes behind the mask. "I am sorry it must end like this."

I pulled. Her head jerked upward but the hair stayed where it was. She was not wearing a wig. It was not Claudine.

I stepped back, aghast at my error.

"Now get out," she said angrily, turning away from me.

Claudine seemed her usual self on Monday, asking about my weekend but saying little else. One evening I worked up the courage to invite her to dinner. She seemed surprised and offered some excuse for not accepting. On the following Friday I paid another visit to the Club of Masks. The door was locked and a small card advised that the premises were closed for renovation.

A week later I finished my work at the Paris office and took the midday Imperial Airways flight from Le Bourget airfield to Croydon, the London airport. It was just before takeoff when the stewardess brought me an envelope that had been delivered to the gate. In it was a crushed red rose, and I knew at once that it was one of those from room 24. The note accompanying it read simply:

Winston,

If we ever meet again, I hope you will make the correct choice. The black hair is real, the red hair is the wig.

Gators

VICKI HENDRICKS

It was a goddamned one-armed alligator put me over the line. After that I was looking for trouble. Carl and me had been married for two years, second marriage for both, and the situation was drastic—hateful most times—but I could tell he didn't realize there was anything better in the world. It made me feel bad that he never learned how to love—grew up with nothing but cruelty. I kept trying way too long to show him there was something else.

I was on my last straw when I suggested a road trip for Labor Day weekend—stupidly thinking that I could amuse him and wouldn't have to listen to his bitching about me and the vile universe on all my days off work. I figured at a motel he'd get that vacation feeling, lighten up, and stick me good, and I could get by for the few waking hours I had to see him the rest of the week.

We headed out to the Everglades for our little trip. Being recent transplants from Texas, we hadn't seen the natural wonders in Florida. Carl started griping by midafternoon about how I told him there were so many alligators and we couldn't find a fucking one. I didn't dare say that there would've been plenty if he hadn't taken two hours to read the paper and sit on the john. We could've made it before the usual thunderstorms and had time to take a tour. As it was, he didn't want to pay the bucks to ride the tram in the rain—even though the cars were covered. We were pretty much stuck with what we could see driving, billboards for Seminole gambling and airboats, and lots of soggy grassland under heavy black-and-blue-layered skies. True, it had a bleak, haunting kind of beauty.

Carl refused to put on the air conditioner because he said it sapped the power of the engine, so all day we suffocated. We could only crack the truck windows because of the rain. By late afternoon my back was soaked with sweat and I could smell my armpits. And, get this—he was smoking cigarettes. Like I said, I was plain stupid coming up with the idea—or maybe blinded by the fact that he had a nice piece of well-working equipment that seemed worth saving.

At that point, I started to wonder if I could make us swerve into a canal and end the suffering. I was studying the landscape, looking ahead for deep water, when I spotted a couple vehicles pulled off the road.

"Carl, look. I bet you they see gators."

"Fuckin' *A*," he bellowed.

He was driving twenty over the limit, as always—in a hurry to get to hell—but he nailed the brakes and managed to turn onto a gravel road that ran a few hundred yards off the side of a small lake. One car pulled out past us, but a couple and a little girl were still standing near the edge of the water.

It was only drizzling by then, and Carl pulled next to their pickup and shut off the ignition. My side of the truck was over a puddle about four inches deep. I opened the door and plodded through in my sandals, while Carl stood grimacing at the horizon, rubbing his dark unshaved chin.

We walked toward the people. The woman was brown-haired, wearing a loose print dress—the kind my grandma would've called a housedress—and I felt how sweet and old-fashioned she was next to me in short-shorts and a halter top, with my white-blond hair and black roots haystack style. The man was a wiry, muscular type in tight jeans and a white T-shirt—tattoos on both biceps, like Carl, but arms half the size. He was bending down by some rocks a little farther along. The little girl, maybe four years old, and her mother were holding hands by the edge.

"That guy reminds me of my asshole brother-in-law," Carl said in a low tone, as we got closer. I nodded, thinking how true it was—the guy reminded me of Carl too, all the same kind of assholes. Carl boomed out "Hey, there," in his usual megaphone, overly friendly voice. The mother and child glanced up with a kind of mousy suspiciousness I sometimes felt in my own face. It was almost like they had him pegged instantly.

We stopped near them. The guy came walking over. He had his hands cupped together in front of him and motioned with his arms toward the water. I looked into the short water weeds and sticks and saw two small eyes and nose holes rising above the ripples a few yards out. It was a baby gator, maybe four feet long, judging by the closeness of his parts.

"There he is!" Carl yelled.

"Just you watch this," the guy said. He tossed something into the water in front of the nose and I caught the scrambling of tiny legs just before the gator lurched and snapped it up. "They just love them lizards," the man said.

Carl started laughing "Ho, ho, ho," like it was the funniest thing he'd ever seen, and the guy joined in because he'd made such a big hit.

Us women looked at each other and kind of smiled with our lips tight. The mother had her arm around the little girl's shoulder holding her against her hip. The girl squirmed away. "Daddy, can I help you catch another one?"

"Sure, darlin, come right over here." He led her toward the rocks and I saw the mother cast him a look as he went by. He laughed and took his daughter's hand.

The whole thing was plenty creepy, but Carl was still chuckling. It seemed like maybe he was having a good time for a change.

"Reptiles eating reptiles," he said. "Yup." He did that eh-eh-eh laugh in the back of his throat. It made me wince. He took my hand and leered toward my face. "It's a scrawny one, Virginia—not like a Texas gator—but I guess I have to say you weren't lyin. Florida has one." He put his arm across my shoulder and leaned on me, still laughing at his own sense of humor. I widened my legs, to keep from falling over, and chuckled so he wouldn't demand to know what was the matter, then insist I spoiled the day by telling him.

We stood there watching the gator float in place hoping for another snack, and in a few minutes, the squeals of the little girl told us that it wouldn't be long. They came shuffling over slowly, the father bent, cupping his hands over the girl's.

"This is the last one now, okay, sweetheart?" the mother said as they stopped beside her. She was talking to the little girl. "We need to get home in time to make supper." From her voice it sounded like they'd been sacrificing lizards for a while.

The two flung the prey into the water. It fell short, but there was no place for the lizard to go. It floundered in the direction it was pointed, the only high ground, the gator's waiting snout. He snapped it up. This time he'd pushed farther out of the water and I saw that he was missing one of his limbs.

"Look, Carl, the gator only has one arm. I wonder what got him?"

"Probably a Texas gator," he said. "It figures, the one gator you find me is a cripple."

Carl had an answer for everything. "No," I said. "Why would one gator tear off another one's arm?"

"Leg. One big chomp without thinkin. Probably got his leg in between his mother and some tasty tidbit—a small dog or kid. Life is cruel, babycakes—survival of the fittest." He stopped talking to light a cigarette. He waved it near my face to make his point. "You gotta protect yourself—be cruel first. That's why you got me—to do it for you." He gave me one of his grins with all the teeth showing.

"Oh, is *that* why?" I laughed, like it was a joke. Yeah, Carl would take care of his own all right—it was like having a mad dog at my side, never knowing when he might turn. He wouldn't hesitate to rip anybody's arm off, mine included, if it got in his way.

The mother called to her husband, "Can we get going, honey? I have fish to clean."

The guy didn't look up. "Good job," he said to his daughter. He reached down and gave her a pat on the butt. "Let's get another one."

It started to rain a little harder, thank God, and Carl motioned with his head toward the car and started walking. I looked at the woman still standing there. "Bye," I called.

She nodded at me, her face empty of life. "Goodbye, honey." It was then she turned enough for me to see that the sleeve on the far side of the dress was empty, pinned up—her arm was gone. Jesus. I felt my eyes bulge. She couldn't have missed what I said. I burned through ten shades of red in a split second. I turned and sprinted to catch up with Carl.

He glanced at me. "What's your hurry, sugar? You ain't gonna melt. Think I'd leave without ya?"

"Nope," I said. I swallowed and tried to lighten up. I didn't want to share with him what I saw.

He looked at me odd and I knew he wasn't fooled. "What's with you?"

"Hungry," I said.

"I told you you should've had a ham sandwich before we left. You never listen to me. I won't be ready to eat for a couple more hours."

"I have to pee too. We passed a restaurant a quarter mile back."

He pointed across the road. "There's the bushes. I'm not stopping anywhere else till the motel."

We crossed the state and got a cheap room in Naples for the night. Carl ordered a pepperoni pizza from Domino's, no mushrooms for me. The room was clean and the air and remote worked, but it was far from the beach. We sat in bed and ate the pizza. I was trying to stick with the plan for having fun and I suggested we could get up early and drive to the beach to find shells.

"To look for fucking seashells? No."

His volume warned me. I decided to drop it. I gave him all my pepperonis and finished up my piece. I had a murder book to curl up with. He found a football game on TV.

I was in the grip of a juicy scene when Carl started working his hands under the covers. It was halftime. He found my thigh and stroked inward. I read fast to get to the end of the chapter. He grabbed the book and flung it across the room onto the other bed.

"I'm tryin to make love to you, and you have your nose stuck in a book. What's the problem? You gettin it somewhere else and don't need it from me? Huh?"

I shook my head violently. His tone and volume had me scared. "No, for Chrissakes." His face was an inch from mine. Rather than say anything else, I took his shoulders and pulled myself to him for a kiss. He was stiff, so I started sucking his lower lip and moving my tongue around. His shoulders relaxed.

Pretty soon he yanked down the covers, pulled up my nightie, and climbed on top. I couldn't feel him inside me—I was numb. Nothing new. I smelled his breath.

I moaned like he expected, and after a few long minutes of pumping and grabbing at my tits, he got that strained look on his face. "I love you to death," he rasped. "Love you to death." I felt him get rigid and come hard inside me, and a chill ran all the way from his cock to my head. He groaned deep and let himself down on my chest. "It's supernatural what you do to me, dollface, supernatural."

"Mmm."

He lit up a cigarette and puffed a few breaths in my face. "I couldn't live without you. Know that? You know that, don't you? You ever left me, I'd have to kill myself."

"No. Don't say that."

"Why? You thinkin of leaving? I *would* kill myself. I would. And knowin me, I'd take you along." He rolled on his side, laughing "eh-eh-eh" to himself. My arm was pinned, and for a second I panicked. I yanked it out from under him. He shifted and in seconds started snoring. Son of a bitch. He had me afraid to speak.

The woman and the gator came into my head, and I knew her life without having to live it, the casual cruelty and a sudden swift slice that changed her whole future. I could land in her place easy, trapped with a kid, no job, and a bastard of a husband that thought he was God. Carl said he was God at least three times a week. I shuddered—more like he was the devil. First he'd take an arm, then go for my soul, just a matter of time. He'd rather see me dead than gone.

There was no thought of a road trip the next weekend, so we both slept late that Saturday. By then, the fear and hatred in my heart had taken over my brain. I was frying eggs, the bathroom door was open, and Carl was on the toilet—his place of serious thinking—when he used the words that struck me with the juicy, seedy, sweet fantasy of getting rid of him.

"I ought to kill my asshole brother-in-law," he yelled. The words were followed by grunts of pleasure and plunking noises I could hear from the kitchen.

"Uh-huh," I said to myself. I pretended to be half-hearing—as if that were possible—and splashed the eggs with bacon grease like he wanted them. I didn't say anything. He was building up rage on the sound of his own voice.

"The fuck went out on Labor Day and left Penny and the kids home. She didn't say anything about him drinkin, but I could hear it in her voice when I called last night. I can't keep ignoring this. I oughta get a flight over there and take ol' Raymond out."

"How's he doing from his knife wound?"

"Son of a bitch is finally back to work. I should just take him out. Penny and the kids would be fine with the insurance she'd get from G.M."

"Oh?"

"Those slimy titty bars he hangs out in—like Babydoe's—I could just fly into Dallas, do him, and fly back. Nobody would think a thing unusual."

I heard the flush and then his continued pulling of toilet paper. He always flushed before he wiped. I knew if I went in there after him I would see streaky wads of paper still floating. He came striding into the kitchen with a towel wrapped around him, his gut hanging over. He seemed to rock back as he walked to keep from falling forward. He turned and poured his eighth cup of coffee, added milk, held it over the sink, and stirred wildly. Half of it slopped over the sides of the cup. His face was mottled with red and he growled to himself.

I looked away. I remembered that at seventeen he had thrown his father out of the house—for beating his mother. He found out later they snuck around for years to see each other behind his back—they were that scared of him.

I knew going opposite whatever he said would push him. I could barely hold myself back. I pointed to the phone. "Calm down and call your sister. Her and the kids might want to keep Ray around."

"Yeah? Uh-uh. She's too nice. She'll give that son of a bitch chance after chance while he spends all their money on ass and booze. If anybody's gonna take advantage of somebody, it's gonna be me."

I handed him his plate of eggs and went to take my shower and let him spew. I heard him pick up the paper again and start with how all the "assholes in the news" should be killed.

Before this, it didn't occur to me as an asset that he was always
a hair's breadth from violence. I'd tried for peace. I didn't want to
know about the trouble he'd been in before we met, his being in
jail for violating a restraining order. He'd broken down a door—I
heard that from his sister because she thought I should know. I
figured he deserved another chance in life. He had a lousy child-
hood with the drunk old man and all. But now I realized how
foolish I was to think that if I treated him nice enough—turned
the other cheek—he would be nice back. Thought that was human
nature. Wrong. I was a goddamned angelic savior for over a year
and not a speck of it rubbed off. He took me for a sucker to use
and abuse. It was a lesson I'd never forget, learned too late.

This sounds crazy—but something about the alligator incident
made me know Carl's true capabilities, and I was fucking scared.
That alligator told me that a ticket for Carl to Dallas was my only
ticket out. It was a harsh thought, but Penny's husband wasn't
God's gift either, and if Carl didn't get him, it was just a matter of
time till some other motherfucker did.

At first, I felt scared of the wicked thoughts in my heart. But
after a few days, each time Carl hawked up a big gob and spit it
out the car window or screamed at me because the elevator at the
apartment complex was too slow, the idea became less sinful. He
was always saying how he used to break guys' legs for a living,
collecting, and he might decide to find some employment of that
kind in Florida since the pay was so lousy for construction. Besides
that, there was his drunk driving—if I could get him behind bars,
it would be an asset to the whole state. Or maybe I'd only have to
threaten.

One morning he woke up and bit my nipple hard before I was
even awake. "Ouch," I yelled. It drew blood and made my eyes fill
up.

"The world's a hard place," he told me.

"You make it that way."

He laughed. "You lived your little pussy life long enough. It's time you find out what it's all about." He covered my mouth with his booze and cigarette breath, and I knew that was the day I'd make a call to his sister. He wasn't going to go away on his own.

Penny did mail-outs in the morning, so I called her from work. I could hear her stuffing envelopes while we talked. I asked about the kids and things. "So how's your husband?" I added. "Carl said he went back to work."

"Yeah. We're getting along much better. He's cut back on the drinking and brings home his paycheck. Doesn't go to the bar half as much."

"He's still going to that bar where he got hurt?"

"Oh, no, a new one, Cactus Jack's, a nicer place—no nude dancers, and it's only a couple miles from here, so he can take a cab if he needs to. He promised he wouldn't go back over to Babydoe's."

Done. It was smooth. I didn't even have to ask where he hung out. "Yeah," I said. "He gets to the job in the morning. That's what I keep telling Carl."

"He goes out Fridays and maybe one or two other days. I can handle that. I'm not complaining."

She was a good woman. I felt tears well in my eyes. "You're a saint, honey. I have to get back to work now—the truckers are coming in for their checks. Carl would like to hear from you one night soon. He worries."

I had all I needed to know—likely she'd wanted to tell somebody and didn't care to stir Carl up and listen to all his godly orders. She wasn't complaining—goddamn. It was amazing that her and my husband were of the same blood. And, yeah, she was being taken advantage of—I could hear it. Now I had to tell Carl when and where to go without him realizing it was my plan.

That night I started to move him along. "I talked to your sister Penny this morning," I told him at the dinner table.

"Oh, yeah?" He was shoveling in chicken-fried steak, mashed potatoes with sawmill gravy, and corn, one of his favorite meals.

I ate with one hand behind my back, protecting my arm from any quick snaps. "She's a trooper," I said. "Wow."

"Huh?"

"I never heard of anybody with such a big heart. You told me she adopted Ray's son, right?"

"Yeah. Unbelievable." He chewed a mouthful. "Him and Penny already had one kid, and he was fuckin around on her. I'd've killed the motherfucker, if I'd known at the time. I was in Alaska—workin the pipeline. Penny kept it all from me till after the adoption." He shook his head and wiped the last gravy from his plate with a roll. "Lumps in the mashed potatoes, hon."

"She works hard too—all those jobs—and doesn't say a thing about him having boys' night out at some new bar whenever he wants. I couldn't handle it." I paused and took a drink of my beer to let the thought sink in. "He's a damn good-looking guy. Bet he has no trouble screwing around on her."

Carl looked up and wiped his mouth on his hand. "You mean now? Where'd you get that idea?"

I shrugged. "Just her tone. Shit. If anybody's going to heaven, she will."

"You think he's hot, don't ya? I'll kill the son of a bitch. What new bar?"

"Cactus Jack's. I bet you he's doing it. She'd be the last to say anything. Why else would he stay out half the night?"

Carl threw his silverware on the plate. "I ought to kill the son of a bitch."

"I don't like to hear that stuff."

"It's the real world, and he's a fuckin asshole. He needs to be fucked."

"I hate to hear a woman being beat down, thinking she's doing the right thing for the kids. Course, you never know what's the glue between two people."

"My sister's done the right thing all her life, and it's never gotten her anywhere." He was seething.

"She's one of a kind, a saint really." I tucked my hand under my leg—feeling protective of my arm—took a bite of fried steak, and chewed.

Carl rocked back on the legs of the chair. His eyes were focused up near the ceiling. "Hmm," he said. "Hmm."

"Don't think about getting involved. We have enough problems."

"You don't have a thing to do with this. It's family."

I gathered up the dishes and went to the sink feeling smug, though I was a little freaked by the feeling that the plan might just work. I was wiping the stove when the phone rang.

"Got it," Carl yelled.

It was Penny. She'd followed my suggestion to call. I could hear him trying to draw her out. He went on and on, and it didn't sound like he made any progress. By the time he slammed down the receiver, he had himself more angry at her than he was at her husband. He went raging into the bathroom and slammed the door shut. It was so hard I was surprised the mirror didn't fall off.

I finished up in the kitchen and was watching *Wheel of Fortune* by the time he came out, their special Labor Week show.

He sat down on the couch next to me and put his hand on my thigh, squeezed it. "You got some room on your Visa, don't you? How 'bout makin me a reservation to Dallas? I'll pay you back. I need to talk to that asshole Raymond face to face."

I stared at the TV, trying to control my breathing. "He's not going to listen to you. He thinks you're a moron."

"A moron, huh? I think not. Make a reservation for me—"

I was shaking my head. "You can't go out there. What about work?"

"Do it—get me a flight after work on Friday, back home Saturday."

"Not much of a visit."

He squinted and ran his tongue from cheek to cheek inside his mouth. "I'm just gonna talk to the motherfucker."

I'd never seen murder in anybody's eyes, but it was hard to miss. I took a deep, rattling breath. It was too goddamned easy—bloodcurdling easy. I reminded myself it was for my own survival. I needed both goddamned arms.

That night I called for a reservation. I had to make it three weeks in advance to get a decent fare. I'd saved up some Christmas money, so that way I didn't have to put the ticket on my charge. I could only hope nobody ripped Raymond before Carl got his chance. The guy that stuck Ray the first time was out on probation. It would be just my luck.

The days dragged. The hope that I would soon be free made Carl's behavior unbearable. I got myself a half-dozen detective novels and kept my nose stuck inside one when I could. I cooked the rest of the time, lots of his favorite foods, and pie, trying to keep his mouth full so I wouldn't have to listen to it—and throw him off if he was the least bit suspicious of what I had in mind. It was tough to put on the act in bed, but he was in a hurry most of the time, so he slathered on the aloe and poked me from behind. Tight and fast was fine with him. His ego made him blind—thinking he was smarter than everybody else, especially me, and that I could possibly still love him.

Thursday morning, the day before Carl was supposed to leave, he walked into the bedroom before work. I smelled his coffee breath and kept my eyes shut. A tap came on my shoulder. "I don't know where that new bar is," he said. "What was it? Cactus Bob's? Near their place?"

"Jack's. Cactus Jack's. I'll get directions at work—off the computer. No problem—Mapquest."

"Get the shortest route from the airport to Babydoe's, and from there to the cactus place. He's probably lying to Penny, still goin back to Doe's for the tits and ass."

I printed out the route during lunch. It was a little complicated. When I came in the door that evening, I handed Carl three pages of directions and maps. He flipped through them. "Write these on one sheet—bigger. I can't be shuffling this shit in the dark while I'm driving a rental around Arlington."

"Sure," I said. A pain in the ass to the end, I thought. I reminded myself it was almost over. I copied the directions on a legal sheet and added "Love ya, Your babycakes." Between his ego and my eagerness to please, I hoped he didn't suspect a thing. I couldn't wait to show him the real world when I gave him my ultimatum.

I got up in the morning and packed him a few clothes and set the bag by the door. I called to him in the bathroom. "Your ticket receipt is in the side pocket. Don't forget to give Penny my love." I knew he really hadn't told her a thing.

He came out and took a hard look down my body. His eyes glinted and I could see satisfaction in the upturn of his lips, despite their being pressed together hard. I knew there was some macho thing mixed in with the caretaking for his sister. In a twisted way, he was doing this for me too, proving how he could protect a poor, weak woman from men like himself.

I thought he was going to kiss me, so I brought on a coughing fit and waved him away. He thumped me on the back a few times, gave up, and went on out. He paused a second at the bottom of the steps, turned back, and grinned, showing all those white teeth. For a second, I thought he was reading my mind. Instead he said softly, "You're my right arm, dollface." He went on.

I shivered. I watched his car all the way down the street. I was scared, even though I was sure he had every intention of doing the deed, and I was betting on success. He was smarter and stronger than Ray, and had surprise on his side. Then I would hold the cards—with his record, a simple tip to the cops could put his ass in a sling.

I was tense all day at the office, wondering what he was thinking with that grin. Too, I hoped he'd remembered his knife. I went straight to his bureau when I got home and took everything out of the sock drawer. The boot knife was gone. I pictured him splashed with blood, standing over Ray's body in a dark alley. I felt relieved. He was set up good.

I went to the grocery and got myself a six-pack, a bag of mesquite-grilled potato chips, and a pint of fudge royale ice cream. I rented three videos so I wouldn't have to think. I started to crack up laughing in the car. I was between joy and hysteria. I couldn't stop worrying, but the thought of peace to come was delicious.

Carl was due home around noon on Saturday, and I realized I didn't want to be there. I got a few hours sleep and woke up early. I did his dirty laundry and packed all his clothes and personal stuff into garbage bags and set them by the door. I put his bicycle and tools there. I wrote a note on the legal pad and propped it against one of the bags. Basically it said to leave Fort Lauderdale that afternoon and never come back—if he did, I'd turn him in. I wrote that I didn't care if we ever got a divorce or not, and he could take the stereo and TV—everything. I just wanted to be left alone.

I packed a bathing suit, a book, and my overnight stuff and drove down to Key Largo. Carl was obsessed with me in his lurid, controlling way. The farther away I was when he read the note, the safer I'd feel.

I stayed at a little motel and read and swam most of Saturday, got a pizza with mushrooms, like Carl hated. On Sunday morning I went out by the pool and caught a few more rays before heading home. I stopped for a grouper sandwich on the drive back, to congratulate myself on how well I was doing, but I could barely eat it. Jesus, was I nervous. I got home around four, pulled into the parking lot, and saw Carl's empty space. I sighed with relief. I looked up at the apartment window. I'd move out when the lease was up. I unlocked the door and stepped inside. The clothes and tools were gone. I shut the door behind me, locked it, and set down my bag.

The toilet flushed. "Eh-eh-eh-eh."

I jumped. My chest turned to water.

The toilet paper rolled. Carl came swaggering out of the bathroom. "Eh-eh-eh-eh," he laughed. The sound was deafening.

"Where's your car?" I asked him. "What are you doing here?"

"Car's around back. I wanted to surprise my babycakes."

I looked around wildly. "Didn't you get my note? You're supposed to be gone—I'm calling—" I moved toward the phone.

He stepped in front of me. "No. You don't wanna make any calls—and I'm not going anywhere. I love you. We're a team. Two of a kind."

"You didn't do it." I spat the words in his face. "You chickened out."

He came closer, a cloud of alcohol seeping from his skin and breath, a sick, fermented odor mixed with the bite of cigarettes. "Oh, I did it, babe, right behind Doe's. Stuck that seven-inch blade below his rib cage and gave it a mighty twist. I left that bastard in a puddle of blood the size Texas could be proud of." He winked. "I let Ol' Ray know why he was getting it too."

He took my hair and yanked me close against him. He stuck his tongue in my mouth. I gagged but he kept forcing it down my throat. Finally, he drew back and stared into my eyes. "I did some thinkin on the flight over," he said, "about you and me, and how your attitude isn't always the best. I figured I could use some insurance on our marriage. You know? Penny'll remember you askin her about the bars if she's questioned, and she wouldn't lie to the cops. Also, the directions are in your handwriting, hon. I rubbed the prints off against my stomach, balled up the sheet, and dropped it right between his legs. Cool, huh?" He licked his lower lip from one side to the other. "Oh, yeah, I found one of your hairs on my T-shirt and put that in for extra measure."

My skin went to ice and I froze clear through.

"A nice little threat in the works, if I needed it to keep you around. Guess I saved myself a lot of trouble at the same time." His eyebrows went up. "Where I go, you go, baby girl. Together forever, sweetheart."

He grabbed my T-shirt and twisted it tight around the chest. All the air wheezed out of my lungs, and he rubbed his palm across my nipples till they burned. He lifted my hand to his mouth, kissed it, and grinned with all his teeth showing. He slobbered kisses along my arm, while I stood limp. "Eh-eh."

Like the snap of a bone, his laugh shot chills up my spine and the sorry truth to my brain. I was the same as Carl, only he'd been desperate all his life. My damned arm would be second to go—I'd already handed Satan my soul.

Scorpion's Kiss

STUART M. KAMINSKY

Ringerman was almost finished shaving when the doorbell rang. No one had rung his bell or come to his door in the three months he had lived here, but he wasn't surprised by this announcement of his first visitor.

He looked in the mirror. He had been through much in forty-six years. His face still looked youthful and smooth and there was no more than a little gray in his hair.

The doorbell rang again.

He had stepped out of the shower only minutes ago. He wanted to be ready for what he had to do this afternoon. Now he stood barefooted, shirtless. He wiped away the soap and washed his face with cold water. Then he dried.

Ringerman had not worked out with weights for more than four months but his body was still firm and he did do a half hour of push-ups and sit-ups every morning and at night.

The doorbell rang.

He examined himself once more, brushed back his hair with his hands, and went through the door. He had one more thing to do in his bedroom and living room.

The doorbell rang.

Finished with what he had to do, he moved across the wooden floor to the heavy, metal-reinforced door he had installed when he moved in. One of his conditions, which the landlord of the building accepted because he was having difficulty renting in this rapidly declining district, was that Ringerman could put on a new door and install bars on the windows.

Since the apartment was on the fifth floor, the tired-looking landlord in the crumpled suit, head balding, tinged with sweat, agreed. He had nothing to lose. When Ringerman left, the landlord, whose name was Gentry, would use the bars and reinforced door as inducements for a possible tenant.

The doorbell was ringing again as Ringerman opened it after looking through the peephole. On the wall across from his door in the corridor, Ringerman had installed two mirrors three feet apart at angles. The mirrors were small, unobtrusive, and allowed him to see to the end of the corridor both right and left. There was no one outside but a woman looking back at him.

He opened the door.

"Robert Miles Ringerman?" she asked.

She was as tall as he, dark of face as he was, and definitely pretty. Her hair was short and blond. Her dress was dark and fashionably expensive. She looked as if she were no more than thirty-five. He was certain she was older, close to his age. She was holding something in her hand.

"Yes," he said standing in the doorway.

"Here."

She handed the wallet to him.

"You dropped it in the Jewel, near the deli counter."

He took the wallet.

"Thanks," he said.

"You're welcome. You going to count the money, check the credit cards?"

Her smile showed perfect white teeth.

"No, I'm not going to count the money or check the credit cards."

"Then it's all right?" she said.

"Yes, thank you. It's fine."

"Then I'll go."

"Can I offer you—?"

"No," she said with a smile. "I—no, but thank you."

"Please come in. Just for a minute. Let me get you something to drink or . . ."

She looked at the thin, gold watch on her left wrist and puckered her full lips in thought.

"A minute," she said.

He stepped back and she entered. Ringerman closed the door behind her. It clicked shut, metallic, firm. He threw the deadbolt.

She looked at the door, unafraid.

"You're careful," she said.

"Paranoid," he said. "If you're afraid . . ."

He reached over to open the door again.

"No, no."

He nodded and said, "Can I offer you coffee?"

"Coffee would be nice. Black."

She smiled nervously, looking around the room.

Ringerman didn't smile. "I'll have it ready in a minute or two," he said. "Have a seat, please."

She nodded and gave a careful smile.

He went through a door to his right and out of sight.

She looked around the room, glanced at the barred windows. It was late afternoon. The sun was still shining. She looked at the furniture and the polished wood floor. When he moved in, Ringerman had pulled up the dirty carpets and found good oak underneath. He had polished it into respectability. The furniture was simple, consignment, two armchairs, a sofa. They were a rough fabric, gray with a series of black stripes. A small television stood on an oak cabinet against the wall near the door he had gone through. There were three floor lamps and a handmade bookcase about three feet wide and reaching to the ceiling. The shelves were filled with neatly lined up books.

But what really drew her were the paintings, twenty of them, all in simple black frames, some horizontal, some vertical, all of them the same size, about two feet by two and a half feet.

She heard him moving around the kitchen as she moved to the wall, drawn by the paintings. The paint was thick on the first ones to her left, thick, heavy, dark, standing out in three dimensions like irregular mountain ridges. She thought she felt anger in what she saw. As she moved down the line, the paint was laid on less thickly. The colors were brighter. They moved from left to right from abstraction and darkness to sunlight and portraits of men, women, children.

The first six paintings of darkness were of the same room, a room without windows and no people, just furniture. The furniture was simple. There were different angles of the room.

The next set of paintings was less dark but more abstract. The one that held her longest was of a simple balance scale, grayish white against a background of blue. The scale was tipped to the right because the left plate of the scale was empty and the one on the right held a red scorpion, its tail raised, ready to strike.

She moved quickly past the rest of the paintings of people, mostly men, tired men, smiling men, and finally to the portraits of women, four of them, all beautiful; all, she could now see, were of the same woman. The woman's hair was short and blond in one painting, long and dark in another, piled dark and red in the third, and hanging in an almost white ponytail over her right shoulder. She was smiling in all of the pictures. These were followed by another set of four children, each different, ages from perhaps five to twelve.

He was still moving around the kitchen. She moved to the bookcase, pausing to examine the scorpion on the scale for a mo-

ment. The painting held her till she forced herself to look away
and step toward the high bookcase.

There was no pattern to the books. There was a book on Inuit
art; a history of Peru; a thin book on learning to play the banjo; a
book on diplomatic relations with India; biographies of movie
stars, authors, soldiers; a book on clocks and clock repair; and
novels. Mickey Spillane, Tolstoy, Joyce Carol Oates, James Feni-
more Cooper, Hans Helmut Kirst, Albert Camus, Roald Dahl,
Louis L'Amour, Borges, Marjorie Kinnan Rawlings.

She was holding a book on astrological signs in her hand when
she sensed him in the kitchen doorway across the room. She
turned slowly, book in hand.

"You read all of these?" she asked, looking at the rows of
books.

He stood with two mugs, identical, blue, in his hands. He was
wearing a long-sleeved button-down denim shirt now.

"Yes," he said.

She carefully returned the book to the shelf and moved toward
him to take the warm cup. Their fingers touched.

"Your taste is certainly . . ."

"Eclectic," he said. "I read whatever comes to me."

"Have you ever seen *The Manchurian Candidate?*"

"Sinatra? Yes."

"After he's been brainwashed he reads everything, anything,
book after book, piled up all over. He meets Janet Leigh and he
stops the manic reading."

"I remember," he said. "Saw it a long time ago on television.
Guy is brainwashed into killing some friends. Then he kills his
girlfriend and her father and then his stepfather and mother."

"You're right. Does he kill any brothers or sisters?"

"He didn't have any," Ringerman said.

"And you?"

"Brothers or sisters?"

"Yes," she said. "Wife, children, mother? Father?"

"Mother and father are dead," he said. "I have one sister, a twin. I'm not married."

"Are you close? I mean you and your sister?"

"Very," he said. "You?"

"Yes," she said, stepping back to sit on the sofa. She held the mug in both hands. Her long red fingernails formed a jagged pattern. "I have a husband, a fourteen-year-old son, and a brother."

"Are you close?" he asked.

"With my husband and son? Yes. With my brother, not really. I'd say no. These paintings. Yours?"

"Yes," he said, still standing, looking toward the paintings.

"You've done more?"

"Yes."

"Many more?" she asked.

"About eighty more. Some of them went to friends. I've got other ones stored."

Something clattered outside, maybe a truck. They could hear it far away through the closed and barred windows and down five floors. Ringerman and the woman paused.

"That one," she said, pointing toward the wall when the clatter had stopped. "The one with the scale and the scorpion. Before you put your shirt on I saw . . ."

"Scars," he said.

"Yes," she answered. "Scars and what looked like that scale tattooed on your left arm, right by the muscle."

"Libra," he said. "I'm a Libra."

"Your only tattoo?"

She sipped her coffee.

"Yes," he said.

"Coincidence," she said.

"What? You're a Libra?"

"No," she said, "Scorpio."

She put her mug down on a *Time* magazine on the table in front of her and kicked off her left shoe, looking up at him as she did it. She turned her foot so he could see the very small tattoo just below her ankle bone.

"It's a scorpion," she said. "I'm a Scorpio."

"Your only tattoo?"

"Yes," she said, kicking off her other shoe. "That's a scorpion on the scale in the painting."

"Yes," he said, looking at the painting.

"You know a Scorpio?"

"I'm not really into astrology," he said. "That was done a long time ago. A roommate of mine was a Scorpio."

"A roommate. That room in the paintings," she said. "You were in jail, weren't you? It's none of my business, but it looks like a cell."

"Prison," he said. "I was in prison. That's where I got the tattoo. When I first went in. If I flex the muscle, it tips the scale."

"Which way?" she asked with a smile.

"Whichever way I want it to go. You want to leave?"

"No," she said. "No. I haven't finished my coffee. You want to get rid of me?"

He looked directly at her.

"No," he said.

"I've never known an ex-convict," she said. "I got married young, moved to Wilmette with my husband, an accountant. Got a college degree in not much of anything, joined groups. Not a very interesting biography. Your life?"

He still stood looking at her. He stood for a long, slow thirty seconds before he spoke.

"Lived with my mother in Wisconsin," he said. "Small house, right on Lake Michigan, just below the Michigan border. Lots of land. No money. My father died when my sister and I were babies. I wasn't much of a student in school. I wasn't much of a son. I wasn't any kind of a brother. Loner, quiet. Started with small crimes, stealing cars. There was a chop shop in Madison my friend and I used to drive them to. His name was Charlie. He wasn't much of a friend. Spent his money getting drunk . . . and on women. We were kids. Sure you want to hear this?"

"I'm sure," she said, curling her legs under her.

Ringerman could see that she had good, long legs.

"I split with Charlie when we were both twenty-five," he said, leaning back against the wall, not drinking his coffee. "Went on my own. Safer."

"Your mother?"

"She didn't know. I told her I was driving a truck. She worked in a shop that rented uniforms, till her legs gave out. She got disability, read, watched television, mostly game shows. *Wheel of Fortune* was her passion. She actually said that. I just remembered. '*Wheel of Fortune* is my passion.' I'd drive days away, as far as Duluth or outside Chicago or Fort Wayne, put something, cheap mask, stocking, over my face, point a gun in the face of a department store manager or a jewelry store owner, take the cash, and get out of town. I'd wear gloves, do all the right things, and never go near the same town twice. I'd always use a cheap stolen car, a car I stole from somewhere about twenty miles from the place I'd hit. After, I'd drive the car back to where I'd parked my car out of sight, wipe it down. Did all right. Then . . ."

"Then?" she said, looking up at him intently.

"Got greedy, getting older, almost thirty-five, and getting greedy. I was doing fine, but not big fine. I decided to go for a bank. Not inside where they have the alarms you can't stop and people ready to be heroes. Or maybe someone gets scared and runs even with a shotgun leveled at them. I decided to take the armored car at the end of a pickup day. Come at the guard, stick the shotgun in his face, grab what he had in both hands, cut the truck tires, back the guard up to my stolen car to keep the armored car driver from helping, and get away fast. It was all worked out. I checked the bank out for a week, eating at a McDonald's across the street, sitting in the parking lot of the mall where the bank was, reading a book. Had it all worked out."

"But?" she asked.

"But," he repeated. "Everything went down perfectly. Truck, tires, guard, gun, bags. A few people were watching, but I didn't care. None of them moved. You never know. When I was backing up with the guard, a little kid, a boy no more than five or six, got away from his mother who was watching. She screamed. The kid ran at me, grabbed my leg and wouldn't let go. I tried to shake him loose, but I had the shotgun at the guard's neck, two heavy bags in the other hand, and my eyes on the doors of the armored car. The kid bit me."

"Too much television," she said.

"He wanted to be a superhero," Ringerman said, pushing away from the wall and moving to the chair across from her. "I told the guard to get the kid off of me but my time was running out. The whole thing had broken down. The guard made a halfhearted move to get the kid loose, but the kid's mother was running fast at me and only a few yards away."

"And you got caught?"

"Gave up," he said after taking a long drink of coffee. "If I believed in astrology I'd have said the stars and planets were against me. The kid was a hero. They said I would have gotten away with two hundred thousand and change. Instead I wound up with fourteen years and change, the change being three months. They tied me to some of the other, smaller jobs I'd done. I did ten years with good behavior. Could have been worse, much worse. More coffee?"

"I don't think so," she said.

"My mother was seventy-nine and ailing," he said. "She died a few months after I went in. Since the job had been done in Illinois, I did my time in Stateville."

"How long have you been out?" she asked.

"Three months, four days," he said. "Three months, four days."

"And now?"

"I'm on parole. I drive a bus up and down Western Avenue, report to a parole officer, mind my business." Ringerman smiled.

"Am I missing a joke?"

"I don't know. Just kind of funny that I wear a uniform now instead of looking at other people wearing them."

"And you built your own prison cell," she said, looking at the barred window and then at the bolted, reinforced door.

"What did you study in college, psychology?"

"A little of lots of things," she said. "Nothing to make a living with. I think I should be going."

She stood, barefoot, and handed the empty mug to Ringerman, who stood to take it. Then she just stood there looking at him. He looked back.

"Have you . . . it's none of my business, but have you been with a woman since you've gotten out?"

"Yes, twice," he said. "Paid for it."

"You're a good-looking man," she said. "I wouldn't think you'd have to pay."

"That's the way I wanted it," he said.

"This is crazy," she said with a laugh, shaking her head, looking up at the ceiling and then back at him. "Would you like, do you want? I mean with me?"

Ringerman clinked the two empty mugs together.

"You mean . . . ?"

"Yes," she said. "Before I change my mind. I've never done anything like this before, not even remotely like this. We're strangers. We'll never see each other again. One time. No more. Never again."

He stood looking at her and she looked at him.

"Not your type?" she asked.

"My type covers a lot of possibilities," he said. "You're a very beautiful woman."

"Thanks, but?"

"No 'but,'" he said.

"You have protection. I mean . . ."

"I have," he said. "You sure you want this?"

"I'm sure," she said. "I'm very sure."

She moved in front of him, reached for the top button of his denim shirt, paused, and then leaned forward to kiss him. They were about the same height. After a few seconds, he put his arms around her and kissed her, feeling her breasts against his chest.

"I feel you," she said, pulling her face a few inches back.

He saw her full lips, her white, even teeth. He nodded his head.

"Before I panic, before I change my mind, before . . ." She paused. "The bedroom?"

He turned his head toward the closed door next to the bookcase.

"You want to know my name?" she asked.

"Make one up," he said.

"Emma," she said. "Emma Bovary."

"Emma Bovary," he repeated.

"I'll go in first," she said. "Please. I need a minute, just a half minute. This is crazy. . . . I need a minute. Please, wait till I call you."

"I'll wait," he said.

She hurried into the bedroom and began to take off her clothes. She did it carefully, laying each item out on a chair, not taking time to look at the paintings on the bedroom wall. The bed was narrow. A single. She and her husband had a king-size. When she was naked, she looked around for a mirror to examine herself in. There wasn't one. She got into the bed and called, "Ringerman."

He appeared in the doorway, stripped down to his undershorts. She knew he was freshly showered and she knew his body was strong and hard. She searched for the tattoo. He moved to the bed, sat beside her, and touched her breast.

"Oh God," she said, sitting up. "I forgot something in my purse. I'll be right back."

Ringerman sat, back straight, looking at one of the ten paintings in the room. It was of his mother's house, now supposed to be his house, at least as he had remembered it. If it were still standing, it was probably smaller, probably in worse shape than he recalled. Probably not quite so close to the massive cold lake of dead, dark black and blue.

He could hear her go into her purse.

When she came back into the room, he was still looking at the painting. He did not turn his head toward her.

"That was our house," he said.

"I know." He heard her voice, soft, not at all confident.

Then he turned his head.

She stood there with a small gun in her hand. She was quite beautiful. He knew how old she was but her body was young, straight. Her breasts were high, not large.

"I'm going to kill you," she said.

He nodded, unsurprised. His lack of surprise or fear made her shake slightly, but she was determined.

"You're not afraid," she said.

"No," he answered.

"I want you to be afraid," she said.

"I'm sorry," he said. "I'm not much of an actor."

"Don't you want to know why I'm going to kill you? You think I'm just some crazy robber?"

"No," he said.

"I've been having you watched for weeks," she said. "Since you got out. I've been having you watched."

"By a little man, neat, not much hair," he said.

"Ye . . . Yes."

He nodded.

"I wanted to know where you lived, what you did, where you shopped. When I knew, I paid him and ended his services. He told me you were a very careful man."

Ringerman looked at the painting again.

"You learn to be careful in prison," he said. "Still, you get scars. If you survive, you have scars."

There was another rumble beyond the room. The windows in here were also barred. The rumble this time was distant thunder. The sun was still shining.

"When you dropped your wallet, I saw my chance. Are you interested in this?"

"Yes," he said.

"Then look at me. Look at me."

There was a distinct edge to her voice now. Ringerman turned his head to look at her.

"Do you know who I am?"

"You're not Emma Bovary any more," he said.

"I never was."

"No."

"My name is Charlotte Brenner. The name doesn't mean anything to you?"

"No."

"Before I married, it was Charlotte Dianne Glicken, a name given to me by my adoptive parents, and before that for a few days it was Charlotte Ringerman," she said. "I'm your sister, your twin sister. The Scorpio born less than an hour after your sign, Libra, had ended and mine had begun."

She looked at him for a reaction. There was none.

"I was the one they chose to give up for adoption," she went on. "You were the one they chose to keep. The boy. The boy who became an armed robber and went to jail."

"Prison."

"Prison," she repeated.

"So you're going to shoot me because our parents gave you up for adoption and you blame me? You've been holding this inside and now because our parents are dead you hold me responsible?"

"Yes."

"No," he said, shaking his head. "It doesn't make sense. Resentment, maybe, but hate? No, unless you're crazy. I've known people in prison and out who killed for crazy reasons. There was a kid named Ramirez two cells down from me, in for drug dealing. Low level stuff but he got caught and the Dade County attorney wanted numbers. Ramirez was a number. He was twenty-four when he took his sharpened spoon in the yard and started stabbing everyone he could reach who had a wife and kids. He went right by the single guys, young, old, black, Mexicans, me. Just started stabbing. Killed five, hurt the hell out of two more. One of them, Ian Plickwell, lost his voice box. Ramirez went for a guard. Guard was shaking, pissed in his pants. Guards weren't armed in the yard. Ramirez went down and out with two shots from a tower guard."

Ringerman lay back on the bed and flexed the muscle of his left arm. The scale moved first one way then the other. He reached down and ran his finger along a raised pink scar about four inches long, the memory of a prison gang fight he hadn't wanted to be in.

"You're the crazy one," she said, now holding the gun in both hands to try to keep the weapon steady.

"Maybe," he said. "I've thought about it. I mean, whether or not I'm crazy. I don't think so, but maybe. I don't think you're crazy either. A year before I got out I had a friend who got out the year before check on Mom's property. A resort had built up around it. Choice lakefront property. Worth close to a million, maybe more. My friend, Alan, poked around. He was good at it. Con man. Knew how to find out things and use them. Alan found out I had a sister. I had him find you. Not hard. When did you find out you had a brother?"

She had stepped forward now, nearly frantic. "It doesn't matter."

"Does to me," he said, looking at his arm. "Does to me. You're going to shoot me dead. Least you could do is answer and be honest."

"I got a letter from a lawyer," she said. "He was trying to find out who owned the land. I don't know how he tracked me down. He said something about adoption records. That's when I found out about you, about me."

"And you told him you were the only heir?"

"Yes."

"You told him your brother was dead and he believed you? Stopped at that?"

"Yes. He wanted to believe me."

"But you had someone find out I was alive and in prison. I wonder why they couldn't find me. The lawyer. I wasn't that hard to find. But I've known men who've been lost in the system for years. Records lost, misplaced. People mistaken for other people. A guy named Pope released from a twenty-year sentence for tearing a woman's arm out and then raping her. He got out in two years. The Pope who was supposed to get out spent five extra years locked up. Of course, the second Pope was simpleminded. I doubt he knew till another con—"

"Stop it," she screamed. "Stop it. Stop it."

"You got the money," he said.

"I needed it," she said. "We owed almost three hundred thousand. My husband's business went bankrupt."

"It wasn't yours," he said.

"Half of it should have been mine," she said, moving closer, but not close enough so he could come off the bed.

"Half of it should have been yours," he agreed. "You got one million two hundred and fifty thousand. You give me six hundred and twenty-five thousand and we'll be even. Law says it's all mine, but I figure half is yours."

"It's gone," she said, removing one hand from the gun to brush back her short hair, which needed no brushing back. "It's spent. We paid off the debt, bought a new house, invested. There's only a little more than two hundred thousand in the bank."

Ringerman put his hands behind his head and looked at the barred window. She could see the tattooed scale on his biceps quivering, undecided about which way to tip. She remembered that the painting in the other room had the scorpion on the right side of the scale. She watched, sobbing without hearing herself sob, unable to take her eyes from the scale, which moved first one way then the other.

"I have to kill you," she said. "I knew you'd get out, that you'd find out what I'd done, that you'd come for your money, put me in jail, humiliate me. I deserved something."

"Half," he said. "You deserved half. I'll take the two hundred thousand. I'll forget the rest, forgive the rest."

"No," she said. "I can't trust you. I've got a life that . . . I can't trust you."

"Don't pull the trigger, Charlotte," he said, still looking out the window.

"I have to. I have to. Oh God, I have to."

He heard the click of the trigger as she pulled it back. He heard the tripping sound. Nothing happened. She was crying now, crying and firing.

When Ringerman turned his head toward her, she was crying and moaning, the gun at her side, her shoulders sagging. Ringerman got off the bed slowly and went to his closet. He took out a white terry-cloth robe and moved toward her. She saw him coming, let out a whimper like a dog expecting a beating, and backed away. He handed her the robe and took the gun from her hand.

"Put it on," he said quietly.

She obeyed.

"You've had your man watching me," he said. "I had my friend Al watching you. I came to Chicago to serve out my parole so you'd be able to find me. Al said you'd try to have me killed. I didn't want to believe it, but I've been wrong lots of times. You can see some of the scars. I knew you were watching me at the supermarket. I dropped the wallet so you'd pick it up."

He threw the gun on the bed and turned her around, gently guiding her back into the living room.

"I took the bullets out before I came into the bedroom," he said.

She had stopped crying. He sat her down on the sofa, near her shoes. She slumped forward. Her mouth was open. Her face was white and she looked almost her age and his.

"Coffee?" he asked.

"What?"

"You want some more coffee?" he asked again.

"You're going to kill me," she said.

"My only sister? No. Took me too long to find you. You want coffee, water, tea?"

"Tea," she said.

"Stay right there," he said gently. "You won't be able to work the locks on the door and you can't get through the windows. Just sit. I'll get the tea."

She sat. Her eyes moved to the paintings on the wall, the dark cell, the portraits and the scale and scorpion. She stared at the scale and scorpion. Somewhere inside she registered the sound of water from the tap in the kitchen, the sound of a humming microwave oven. No time seemed to pass.

Ringerman stepped back in the room, still clad only in his underpants. He handed her the tea and sat next to her.

"What do you . . . What are you going to do?" she asked.

"Two hundred thousand even," he said. "Talk to your husband, draw it out, cash. I meet you. You give it to me and you don't see me again unless you ride the Western Avenue bus, which I don't see much chance of. I owe Al fifty thousand for his help. The rest goes to . . . I haven't really thought too much about it. The money. You get the money tomorrow. Talk to your husband if you like, but I get it tomorrow or I go to the police. I don't like going to the police. It'll get complicated. You might get by but I don't think so, and a good lawyer'll take the money and your house."

"All right," she said.

"I'd like to see my nephew once, maybe," he said. "You have a photograph?"

She gulped back some tea, put the cup down, and reached for her purse, the purse in which she had carried the gun she had planned to use to kill the man who sat next to her, gently asking about her son. She took out her wallet and handed it to him. Ringerman opened it and looked at the photographs: Charlotte and her husband, a smiling man with a tanned face and white teeth that looked false; Charlotte alone, a candid of her smiling over her shoulder at the camera in front of a tree; three photographs of a boy, one when he was no more than three, another when he was about seven or eight sitting on a white fence and waving his hand, and the last, a tall boy wearing a suit and tie.

"Looks like me," Ringerman said.

"Yes, a little," she agreed.

He removed all the photographs except the one of Charlotte and her husband and placed them on the table in front of him, side by side.

"I'll keep these," he said.

"Why?"

"The only family I've got. I've got one of our mother and father when they were young. I can get you a copy."

"No, thank you," she said, a touch of her earlier anger returning. "No, no thank you. They didn't want me. I don't want them."

"Suit yourself," he said. "You can get dressed and go. I'll meet you at the bank at ten in the morning."

"How do you know which bank?" she asked, getting up.

"I know."

"Your friend Al?" she asked.

He nodded.

"You can take the gun," he said.

It was her turn to nod.

"Don't think about coming back with new bullets," he said. "I had tape recorders running from the second you came through my front door. I'm putting the tapes in an envelope and mailing them to Al right after you leave. You shoot me and . . . well, you understand."

"I won't shoot you," she said. "I'll get your money."

She moved to the bedroom and dressed while Ringerman sat waiting. When she was ready, he watched her take a mirror from her purse and reapply her makeup.

"I . . . You want to hear something crazy?" she said. "Very crazy?"

"I've heard enough crazy in the last hour to last me the rest of my days," he said.

"Maybe . . . I mean, maybe we could be . . . you know, see each other. You could meet my husband, your nephew."

"I'll pick my time to see the boy," he said. "He won't know. I won't bother him. If you hadn't pulled the trigger in the bedroom, I might have considered your offer, but not now. Not now."

He got out of the chair. She watched him walk to the wall and take down the painting of the scorpion on the scale.

"It's yours," he said, holding it out to his sister.

She slung her purse over her arm and took the painting.

"The woman in the other paintings," she said, turning her head toward them. "Who is she?"

"No one," he said, looking at the paintings with her. "I made her up."

Ringerman walked to the front door, threw open the heavy bolt, and turned the other locks. He opened the door.

She stepped into the corridor.

"Tomorrow morning at the bank, ten sharp," he said.

"Thank you for the painting. I wish . . ."

He was shaking his head no, not sure of what she might wish, but certain that he would have no part in making it come true.

"Emma Bovary," he said softly. She didn't seem to hear.

She walked slowly down the hall, painting held out in front of her. Ringerman closed the door and bolted it. The envelope was

ready, addressed and stamped. He got the tapes from the two recorders and dropped them into the envelope.

In a few minutes, he would get dressed, go down, and drop the
envelope in the mailbox a block away. Now, he sat in front of the
table in his living room and looked at the photographs he had
spread out.

They would go in his wallet along with the old snapshot of his
parents, and if anyone ever asked him about his family, he would
show them his collection.

He looked at the photograph of Charlotte for about a minute
and said aloud, "We don't look like either of our parents. Not even
a little."

He would take the bars off of the windows now. He would
remove the bolt lock from his front door. He would not keep
himself locked in or keep others locked out.

Ringerman touched the image of his sister, got up, and moved
to the bedroom to get dressed.

Evil Grows

LOREN D. ESTLEMAN

No, I'm not prejudiced. Well, not any more than the majority of the population. I'm an organic creature, subject to conditioning and environment, and as such I'm entitled to my own personal set of preconceptions. No, I'm not disappointed; relieved is the word. If you'd shown up with cauliflower ears or swastikas tattooed on your biceps, the interview would have been over right then. So let's sit down and jabber. What do you drink? Excuse me? Jack and *Coke?* Don't get defensive, you're young, you'll grow out of it. You grew out of your formula. Miss, my friend will have a Jack and Coke, and you can pour me another Chivas over rocks and don't let it sit too long on the bar this time. Scotch-flavored Kool-Aid is not my drink.

What's that? No, I'm not afraid she'll spit in my glass. She's got miles on her, no wedding ring, she needs this job. People will put up with what they have to, up to a point. Which is the point where my job begins. Or began. See, I'm not sure I'm still employed. It isn't like I go to the office every day and can see if my name's still on the door. I'm talking too much; that's my third Scotch the barmaid's spitting in. You don't mind that I'm a motor-

mouth? I forgot, you're one of the new breed. You want to know
why. I'm down with that. Thank you, miss. Just keep the tab going.

Let's see. You ever watch the news, read a paper? Don't bother,
the question's out of date. You can't avoid the news. The wise man
on the mountain in Tibet picks up Dan Rather in his fillings. But
that's network; it's the local reports I'm talking about, the police
beat. I know what you're thinking. Crime's the last thing I should
be interested in when I get home. Truth is, I can't relate to wars in
eastern Europe, not since I got too old for the draft, but give me a
carjacking two streets over from where I live and you can't pry me
away from the screen. Past forty you get selective about what you
take in. I'm not just talking about your stomach.

Anyway, have you ever noticed, once or twice a month there's
a story about some schnook getting busted trying to hire a hit
man? Some woman meets a guy in a bar and offers him like a
thousand bucks to knock off her husband or boyfriend or her
husband's girlfriend or the mother of the girl who's beating out
her daughter for captain of the cheerleading squad? Okay, it's not
always a woman, but let's face it, they're still the designated child-
bearers, it's unnatural for them to take a life. So they engage a
surrogate. The reason they get caught is the surrogate turns out to
be an undercover cop. I mean, it happens so often you wonder if
there aren't more cops out there posing as hit men than there are
hit men. Which may be true, I don't know. Assassins don't answer
the census.

That's how it seems, and the department's just as happy to let
people think that. Actually there's very little happenstance involved. The woman's so pissed she tells her plans to everyone she
knows and a few she doesn't, gets a couple of margaritas in her
and tells the bartender. Working up her courage, see, or maybe
just talking about it makes her feel better, as if she went ahead and
did it. So in a week or so twenty people are in on the secret. Odds
are pretty good one of them's a cop. I don't know a bookie who'd
bet against at least one of them *telling* a cop. So the next Saturday

night she's sitting in a booth getting blasted and a character in a Harley jacket with Pennzoil in his hair slides in, buys her a zombie and a beer for himself, and says I understand you're looking for someone to take care of a little problem. Hey, nothing's subtle in a bar. People want their mechanics to be German and their decorators gay, and when they decide to have someone iced they aren't going to hire someone who looks like Hugh Grant.

You'll be happy to hear, if you're concerned about where civilization is headed, that many of these women, once they realize what's going on, are horrified. Or better yet, they laugh in the guy's face. These are the ones that are just acting out. The only blood they intend to draw will be in a courtroom, if it ever gets that far; a lot of couples who considered murder go on to celebrate their golden anniversaries. A good cop, or I should say a good person who is a cop, will draw away when he realizes it's a dry hole. It's entrapment if he pushes it, and anyway what's the point of removing someone from society who was never a threat to begin with? It just takes time away from investigations that might do some good. Plus he knows the next woman whose table he invites himself to will probably take him up on it.

Hell yes, he's wearing a wire, and I'm here to tell you Sir Laurence Olivier's got nothing on an undercover stiff who manages to appear natural knowing he can't squirm around or even lift his glass at the wrong time because the rustle of his clothing might drown out the one response he needs to make his case. I was kidding about the Harley jacket; leather creaks like a bitch, on tape it sounds like a stand of giant sequoias making love, and you don't want to hear about corduroy or too much starch in a cotton shirt. Even when you wear what's right and take care, you need to find a way to ask the same question two or three times and get the same answer, just for insurance. Try and pull that off without tipping your mitt. I mean, everyone's seen *NYPD Blue.* So you begin to see, as often as these arrests make the news, the opportunity comes up oftener yet. You can blame Hollywood if you like, or maybe violent video games. I'm old enough to remember when it was comic books. My old man had a minister when he was ten who preached that Satan spoke through *Gangbusters* on the radio. My opinion? We've been fucking killers since the grave.

Lest you think I draw my munificent paycheck hanging around gin mills hitting on Lizzie Borden, I should tell you life undercover most of the time is about as exciting as watching your car rust. When the lieutenant told me to meet this Rockover woman I'd been six weeks raking leaves in the front yard of a druglord in Roseville, posing as a gardener. I never saw the man; he's in his bedroom the whole time, flushing out his kidneys and playing euchre. He's got maybe a year to live, so assuming I do gather enough for an indictment, he'll be in hell trumping Tupac's hand by the time they seat the jury. I don't complain when I'm pulled off. Friend, I'd work Stationary Traffic if it meant getting out of those goddamn overalls.

The briefing's a no-brainer. This Nola Rockover has had it with her boss. He's a lawyer and a sexual harasser besides, it's a wonder the Democrats haven't tapped him for the nomination. It's her word against his, and he's a partner in the firm, so you know who's going to come out on the short end if she reports him. Her career's involved. Admit it, you'd take a crack at him yourself. That's how you know it's worth investigating. The odd thing, one of the odd things about getting a conviction is the motive has to make sense. Some part of you has to agree with the defendant in order to hang him. It's a funny system.

Getting ready for a sting you've got to fight being your own worst enemy. You can't ham it up. I've seen cops punk their hair and pierce their noses—Christ, their tongues and belly buttons too—and get themselves tossed by a nervous bouncer before they even make contact, which is okay because nine times out of ten the suspect will take one look at them and run for the exit. I know what I said about bars and subtlety, but they're no place for a cartoon either. So what I do is I leave my hair shaggy from the gardening job, pile on a little too much mousse, go without shaving one day, put on clean chinos and combat boots and a Dead T-shirt—a little humor there, it puts people at ease—and mostly for my own benefit I clip a teeny gold ring onto my left earlobe. You have to look close to see it doesn't go all the way through. I've spent every day since the academy trying to keep holes out of me and I'm not about to give up for one case. Now I look like an almost-over-the-hill Deadhead who likes to hip it up on weekends, a turtleneck and sportcoat on Casual Friday is as daring as he gets during the week. Point is not so much to look like a hit man as to not look like someone who isn't. Approachability's important.

The tech guy shaves a little path from my belt to my solar plexus, tapes the mike and wire flat, the transmitter to my back just above the butt-crack. The T's loose and made of soft cotton, washed plenty of times. Only competition I have to worry about is the bar noise. Fortunately, the Rockover woman's Saturday night hangout is a family-type place, you know, where a kid can drink a Coke and munch chips from a little bag while his parents visit with friends over highballs. Loud drunks are rare, there's a juke but no band. The finger's a co-worker in the legal firm. I meet him at the bar, he points her out, I thank him and tell him to blow. First I have to reassure him I'm not going to throw her on the floor and kneel on her back and cuff her like on *Cops;* he's more worried she'll get herself in too deep than about what she might do to the boss. I go along with this bullshit and he leaves. Chances are he's got his eye on her job, but he hasn't got the spine not to feel guilty about it.

The place is crowded and getting noisy, the customers are starting to unwind. I order a Scotch and soda, heavy on the fizz, wait for a stool, and watch her for a while in the mirror. She's sitting facing another woman near the shuffleboard table, smoking a cigarette as long as a Bic pen and nursing a clear drink in a tall glass, vodka and tonic probably. I'm hoping I'll catch her alone sometime during the evening, maybe when the friend goes to the can, which means I don't count on getting any evidence on tape until I convince her to ditch the friend. So I wait and watch.

Which in this case is not unpleasant. Nola Rockover's a fox. Not, I hasten to add, one of those assembly-line beauties on the order of Heather Locklear or some other blond flavor of the month, but the dark, smoldering kind you hardly ever see except in black-and-white movies and old TV shows. She's a brunette, slender—not thin, I've had it with these anorexic bonepiles that make you want to abduct them and tie them down and force-feed them mashed potatoes until they at least cast a decent shadow— I'm talking lithe and sinuous, like a dancer, with big dark eyes and prominent cheekbones. You're too young to remember Mary Tyler Moore on *The Dick Van Dyke Show*. I know you've seen her on Nick at Nite, but your generation's got some fixation on color, so I'm betting you're thinking about that thing she did in the seventies. You had to have seen her in capri pants and a pullover to understand what I'm getting at. If you were a man or a boy, you fell in lust with that innocent female panther, and she was all yours. I mean, you knew she was beautiful, but you thought you were the only one in the world who knew it. Well, that was Nola Rockover.

She was sitting there in this dark sleeveless top and some kind of skirt, no cleavage or jewelry except for a thin gold necklace that called your attention to the long smooth line of throat, and she had a way of holding her chin high, almost aloof but not quite, more like she hadn't forgotten what her mother had told her about the importance of good posture. She's not talking, except maybe to respond to something the other woman is saying, encourage her to go on, except I'm thinking she's not really that interested, just being polite. In any case it's her friend who's flapping her chin and waving her hands around like she's swatting hornets. Probably describing her love life.

Yes, miss, another Chivas, and how's yours? Sure? Now you're making me look like a lush.

Nola's friend? Okay, so I'm a chauvinist pig. Maybe she's talking abut the Red Wings. She's got on this ugly business suit with a floppy bow tie, like she hasn't been to see a movie since *Working Girl.* Jogs, drinks bottled water by the gallon and two percent milk, got enough calcium in her you could snap her like a stick. Takes the *Cosmo* quiz on the G spot. One of those goddamn silly women you see walking in sheer hose and scruffy tennis shoes, poster child for penis envy. I'm giving you a better picture of her than Nola, and I never saw her again or learned her name. I'm thinking Nola tolerates her company to avoid drinking alone in public. Maybe she already suspects she's said too much in that condition. You can see I'm kindly disposed to her before I even make contact. There's no rule saying you can't like 'em and cuff 'em. I get Christmas cards, sincere ones from killers and pushers I sent to Jackson. Meanwhile I don't know a lawyer I'd go out for lunch with, and we're supposed to be on the same side.

I watch twenty minutes, my drink's all melted ice, and I'm starting to think this other woman's got a bladder the size of Toledo when she gets up and goes to wee-wee. I give it a minute so as not to look like a shark swimming in, then I wander on over. Nola's getting out another cigarette and I'm wishing, not for the first time, I didn't give up the weed, or I could offer to light her up from the Zippo I no longer carried. Sure, it's corny, but it works. That's how some things stay around long enough to get corny. So I do the next best thing and say, "I hear the surgeon general frowns on those."

She looks up slowly like she knows I've been standing there the whole time, and you'll like what she says. "I don't follow generals' orders any more. I got my discharge." And she smiles, this cool impersonal number, that in a book would be a page of dialogue about what a load of crap the mating ritual is, and why can't we be more like cats and get right down to the scratching and yowling. Either that or she's saying go fuck yourself. I'm not sure because I'm too busy noticing what nice teeth she has—not perfect, one incisor's slightly crooked, but she keeps them white, which is not easy when you smoke, and it's good to know there's someone with the self-confidence to refuse to send some orthodontist's kid to Harvard just to look like a model in a toothpaste ad. Her eyes don't smile, though. Even if I didn't know her recent history I'd guess this was someone for whom life had not come with greased wheels.

I'm scraping my skull for what to say next when she throws me a life preserver. "You like the Dead?"

Copy that. Not, "You're a Deadhead?" Which is a term they know in Bowling Green by now, it's hip no more, but most people are afraid not to use it for fear of appearing unhip. The way she doesn't say it, though, tells me she's so hip she doesn't even bother to think about it. I admit that's a lot to get out of four words, but that was Nola, a living tip-of-the-iceberg. Thanks, honey; I like my Scotch good and orange.

I lost the thread. Oh, right, the Dead. I take a chance. Remember everything hangs on how I broach the subject, and the conventional wisdom is never, ever jump the gun. If opening it up standing in front of her table with her friend about to come back any second is not jumping it, I don't know what is. I say: "I like the dead."

That was it. Lowercase, no cap. Which you may argue makes no difference when you're talking, but if you do, good day to you, because you're not the person for what I have in mind. No comment? There's hope for you. Then you'll appreciate her reaction. Her face went blank. No expression, it might have been enameled metal with the eyes painted on. She'd heard that lowercase *d*, knew what it meant, and quick as a switch she shut down the system. She wasn't giving me anything. Wherever this went, it was up to me to take it there.

"I know about your problem," I said. "I can help."

She didn't say, "What problem?" That would have disappointed me. Her eyes flick past my shoulder, and I know without looking her friend's coming. "Have you a card?"

This time I smile. "You mean like 'Have gun, will travel'?"

She doesn't smile back. "I'm known here. I'll be at the Hangar in an hour." And then she turns her head and I'm not there.

I confer with the boys in the van, who take off their earphones long enough to agree the Hangar is Smilin' Jack's Hangar, a roadhouse up in Oakland that's been around since before that comic strip folded, a trendy spot once that now survives as a place where the laws of marriage don't apply, which is enough to pay the bills even after it gets around that it's not Stoli in the Stoli bottles but cheap Smirnoff's and that a ten-dollar bill traded for a three-fifty drink will come back as a five-spot more often than not. Every community needs a place to mess around.

So forty minutes later, wearing fresh batteries, I'm groping through the whiskey-sodden dark of a building that was once an actual hangar for a rich flying enthusiast under the New Deal, my feet not touching the floor because the bass is so deep from the juke, looking for a booth that is not currently being used for foreplay. When I find one and order my watered-down Scotch, I'm hoping Nola's part bat, because the teeny electric lamp on the table is no beacon.

No need to worry. At the end of ten minutes, right on time, I hear heels clicking and then she rustles into the facing seat. She's freshened her makeup, and with that long dark hair in an underflip and the light coming up from below leaving all the shadows where they belong, she looks like someone I wish I had a wife to cheat on with. I notice her scent: Some kind of moon-flowering blossom, dusky. Don't look for it, it wouldn't smell the same on anyone else.

"Who are you?" She doesn't even wait for drinks.

"Call me Ted."

"No good. You know both my names, and if we do this thing you'll know where I work. That's too much on your side."

I grin. "Ted Hazlett." Which is a name I use sometimes. It's close to "hazard," but not so close they won't buy it.

"And what do you do, Ted Hazlett?"

"This and that."

"Where do you live?"

"Here and there. We can do this all night if you like."

My Scotch comes. She asks for vodka tonic—I'm right about that—and when the waiter's gone she settles back and lights up one of those long cigarettes. Determining to enjoy herself.

"We're just two people talking," she says. "No law against that."

"Not according to the ACLU."

" 'This and that.' Which one is you kill people?"

I think this over very carefully. " 'That.' "

She nods, like it's the right answer. She tells her story then, and there's nothing incriminating in the way she tells it, at least not against her. She's a paralegal with a downtown firm whose name I know, having been cross-examined by some of its personnel in the past. Attends law school nights, plans someday to practice family law, except this walking set of genitalia she's assigned to, partner in the firm, is planning even harder to get into her pants. You know the drill: whispered obscenities in her ear when they're alone in an office, anonymous gifts of crotchless panties and front-loading bras sent to her apartment in the mail, midnight phone calls when she's too groggy to think about hitting the *Record* button on the machine. At first she's too scared to file a complaint, knowing there's no evidence that can be traced to him. Then comes the day he tells her she'd better go down on him if she wants a job evaluation that won't get her fired. These evaluations are strictly subjective, there's nobody in the firm you can appeal to, the decks are stacked in management's favor. The firm's as old as habeas; no rec means no legal employment elsewhere. To top it off, this scrotum, this partner, sits on the board of the school she attends and is in a position to expel her and wipe out three years of credits. Any way you look at it he's got her by the smalls.

What's a girl to do? She's no Shirley Temple, lived with a guy for two years, object matrimony, until she caught him in the shower with a neighbor and threw his clothes out a window—I mean every stitch, he had to go out in a towel to fetch them. So she does the deed on the partner, thinking to hand in her two weeks' notice the next day and take her good references to a firm where oral examinations are not required.

Except she's so good at it the slob threatens to withhold references if she refuses to assign herself to him permanently, so to speak. Sure, I could have told her too, but it's a lot easier from the sidelines. She knew the odds, but she rolled the dice anyway and came up craps.

After stewing over it all weekend, she decides to take it up with the head of the firm, file a complaint. But the senior partner won't sully himself and fobs her off on an assistant, who by the time she finishes her story has pegged her as an immoral bitch who's gone to blackmail when she found out she couldn't advance herself on her knees, if you get what I'm saying; she can see it in his face when he tells her the incident will be investigated. Next day she's assigned to computer filing. It's obvious the investigation stopped with the partner, who is now out to hound her out of the firm, filing being a notorious dead end whether it involves a modem or a bunch of metal cabinets.

But he doesn't stop there. She tries to finance a new car but gets denied for bad credit. Pulls out her card to buy a blouse at Hudson's, the clerk makes a call, then cuts up the card in front of her. Some more stuff like that happens, then late one night she gets another phone call. It's the walking genitalia, telling her he's got friends all over and if she isn't nice to him he'll phony up her employment record, get her fired, evict her, frame her for soliciting, whatever; it's him or a cell at County, followed by a refrigerator carton on Woodward Avenue, choice is hers. He's psycho, no question, but he's a psycho with connections. The refrigerator carton seals the deal. She's his now, and the law is no longer her parachute. What the partner hasn't figured on is that by blocking all the legal exits, he's left her with only one way out.

There's no way I can tell you all this the way Nola told it. She lays it out flat, just the facts, without a choke or a sob. I'm ready for the waterworks; I've seen some doozies, Oscar-quality stuff, they don't call undercover Umbrella Duty for nothing. The only hint Nola's stinging at all is when she breaks a sentence in half to sip her drink, like a runner taking a hit of oxygen before he can go on. Maybe she's just thirsty. What I'm saying is there's nothing to distract from the bare bones of her story. And I know every word's true. I can see this puffed-up fucker in his Armani, ripping up some poor schmoe in court for stepping out on his wife, then rushing back to the office for his daily quickie with the good-looking paralegal. And while I'm seeing this—I can't say even now if I knew I was doing it—I sneak a hand up under my shirt and disconnect the wire.

Nola won't talk business in a bar. She suggests we meet at her place the next night and gives me an address on East Jefferson. I stand up when she does, pay for the drinks—there's no discussion on that, it's an assumption we both make—and I go to the can, mainly to give her a chance to make some distance before I meet with the crew in the van. Only when I leave the roadhouse, I know she's somewhere out there in the dark, watching me. I walk right past the van and get into my car and pull out. I don't even give the earlobe-tug that tells them I'm being watched, because I *know* Nola would recognize it for what it was. And I spend an extra fifteen minutes crazying up the way home, just in case she's following me.

My telephone's ringing when I get in, and I'm not surprised it's Carpenter, from the van. What's the deal, he wants to know, something went wrong with the transmitter and you forgot we were out there freezing off our asses, you get drunk or what? I tell him I'm wiped out, sorry, I must have pulled loose a wire without knowing. Not to worry; the Nola thing didn't pan out, she was just looking for a sympathetic ear, had no intention of following up on her wish-dream of offing the partner. I didn't like the way the bartender was giving me the fish-eye, thought if I was seen climbing in and out of a van in the parking lot I might blow any chance of a future bust involving the high-stakes poker game that went on in the back room Tuesday nights. Which was the only truth I told Carpenter that night.

I don't know if he believed me about Nola, but he didn't question it. Carpenter's not what you call gung ho, would just as soon duck the graveyard shift for whatever reason. It's not for fear of his disapproval I stay awake most of that night wishing I still smoked. I can still smell her cigarettes and that dusky scent on my clothes.

Most of the next day is spent filling out reports on the nonexistent Rockover Case. I log out in time to go home and freshen up and put on a sport shirt and slacks, no sense working on the image now that the hook's in. Understand, I have no intention of whacking the son of a bitch who's bringing Nola grief. In twelve years with the department I've never even fired my piece except on the range, and even if I had I'm not about to turn into Sammy the Bull for anyone. I'm sympathetic to her case, maybe I can help her figure a way out—brace the guy and apply a little strongarm if necessary, see will he pick on someone his own size and gender. Okay, and maybe wrangle myself some pussy while I'm at it. Hey, we're both single, and it's been a stretch for me, what with everyone so scared of AIDS and GHB; I'm telling you, the alphabet's played hell with the mating game. I figure I'm still leagues above the prick in the two-thousand-dollar suit.

She's on the second floor of one of those converted warehouses in what is now called Rivertown, with a view of the water through a plate-glass window the size of a garage door in her living room. Decor's sleek, all chrome and glass and black leather and a spatter of paint in a steel frame on one wall, an Impressionist piece that when you stand back turns out to be of a nude woman reclining, who looks just enough like Nola I'm afraid to ask if she posed for it. I can tell it's good, but the colors are all wrong: bilious green and violent purple and a kind of rusty brown that I can only describe as dried blood, not a natural flesh tone in the batch. It puts me in mind less of a beautiful naked woman than a jungle snake coiled around a tree limb. Just thinking about it makes my skin crawl.

It takes me a while to take all this in, because it's Nola who opens the door for me. She's wearing a dark turtleneck top with ribs over skin-tight stirrup pants with the straps under her bare feet, which are long and narrow, with high arches and clear polish on the toenails. It's as if she knows I'm a connoisseur of women's feet. With plastic surgery getting to be as common as root canals, pretty faces come four-for-a-quarter, and the effect is gone when you look down and see long bony toes with barn paint. Nola's perfect feet are just about the only skin she's showing, but I'm telling you, I'm glad I brought a bottle of wine to hold in front of myself. It's like I'm back in high school.

She takes the bottle with thanks, her eyes flicker down for a split second, and the corners of her lips turn up the barest bit, but she says nothing, standing aside to let me in and closing the door behind me, locking it with a crisp little snick. Bird Parker's playing low on a sound system I never did get to see. She has me open the wine using a wicked-looking corkscrew in the tiny kitchen, and we go to the living room and drink from stemware and munch on crackers she's set out on a tray on the glass coffee table, crumbly things that dissolve into butter on the tongue. I'm sitting on the black leather sofa, legs crossed, her beside me with hers curled under her, as supple as the snakewoman in the picture, giving off that scent. She looks even better by indirect light than she did in the Hangar. I'm thinking the Gobi at noon would be no less flattering.

We start with small talk, music and wine and the superiority of streamlined contemporary over life in a museum full of worm-eaten antiques, then she lifts her glass to her lips and asks me if I approve of the police department's retirement package.

She slides it in so smoothly I almost answer. When it hits, I get the same shuddery chill I got from the picture, only worse, like the time I had my cover blown when I'd been moled into a car theft ring downriver for a month, bunch of mean ridgerunners whose weapon of choice was a welding torch. Don't ask me why. All she's armed with is crystal.

I don't try to run a bluff, the way I did with the car thieves—successfully, I might add. Rivertown is not Downriver, and Nola Rockover is not a gang of homicidal hillbillies, although I know now they'd be a trade-up. I ask her how she doped it out.

"You forget I'm in computer filing. I ran that name you gave me through the system; you shouldn't have used one you'd used before. It came up on the transcript when you testified against one of our clients as arresting officer. Are you getting all this on tape?"

And would you believe it, there's no emotion in her tone. She might have been talking about some case at work that had nothing to do with either of us. All I see in her eyes is the reflection of the wine glass she's still holding up. I look into them and say no, I'm not wearing a wire; I was before, but I yanked it. I want to help.

"Am I supposed to believe that?"

"Lady, if it's a lie, you'd be in a holding cell right now."

Which has its effect. She drinks a little more wine, and then she leans across me to set her glass down on the table. Before I know it she's got her hands inside my sport shirt. She goes on groping long after it's obvious there's nothing under it but me. And in a little while I know there's nothing but Nola under the sweater and pants. It's like wrestling a snake, only a warm one with a quicker tongue that tastes like wine when it's in my mouth and burns like liquid fire when it's working its way down my chest, and down and down while I'm digging holes in the leather uphol-stery with my fingers trying to hang on.

Understand, I'm not one of these fools that regales his friends with the play-by-play. I want you to see how a fairly good cop brain melted down before Nola's heat. I was married, and I've had my hot-and-heavies, but I've never even *read* about some of the things we did that night. We're on the sofa, we're off the sofa, the table tips over and we're heaving away in spilled wine and bits of broken crystal; I can show you a hundred little healed-over cuts on my back even now and you'd think I got tangled in barbed wire. In a little while we're both slick with wine and sweat and various other bodily fluids, panting like a couple of wolves, and we're still going at it. I'm not sure they'd take a chance showing it on the Playboy Channel.

Miss? Oh, miss? Ice water, please. I'm burning up.

That's better. Whew. When I think about that night—hell, whenever I think about Nola—this song keeps running through my head. It isn't what Bird was playing on the record, he died years before it came out. It wasn't a hit, although it should have been, it was catchy enough. I don't even know who recorded it. "Evil Grows," I think it was called, and it was all about this poor schnook realizing his girl's evil and how every time he sees her, evil grows in him. Whoever wrote it knew what he was talking about, because by the time I crawled out of that apartment just before dawn, I'd made up my mind to kill Nola's boss for her.

His name's Ethan Hollis, and he's living beyond his means in Grosse Pointe, but if they outlaw that they'll have to throw a prison wall around the city. I don't need to park more than two minutes in front of the big Georgian he shares with his wife to know it won't happen in there, inside a spiked fence with the name of his alarm company on a sign on the front gate. Anyway, since I'm not the only one who's heard Nola's threats, we've agreed that apparent accidental death is best. I'm just taking stock. The few seconds I get to see him through binoculars, coming out on the porch to tell the gardener he isn't clipping the hedge with his little finger extended properly—I'm guessing, I can't hear him across four acres of clipped lawn—is enough to make me hate him, having worked that very job under the druglord in Roseville. He's chubbier than I had pictured, a regular teddy bear with curly dark hair on his head and a Rolex on his fat wrist, with a polo shirt, yet. He deserves to die if for no other reason than his lack of fashion sense.

I know his routine thanks to Nola, but I follow him for a week, just to look. I've taken personal time, of which I've built up about a year, undercover being twenty-four/seven. The guy logs four hours total in the office; rest of the time he's lunching with clients, golfing with the senior partner, putting on deck shoes and dorky white shorts and pushing a speedboat up and down the river, that sort of bullshit. Drowning would be nice, except I'd join him, because I can't swim and am no good with boats.

These are my days. Nights I'm with Nola, working our way through the *Kama Sutra* and adding footnotes of our own.

The only time I can expect Hollis to be alone without a boat involved is when he takes his Jaguar for a spin. It's his toy, he doesn't share it. Trouble is not even Nola knows when he'll get the urge. So every day when he's home I park around the corner and trot back to his north fence, watching for that green convertible. It's a blind spot to the neighbors too, and for the benefit of passersby I'm wearing a jogging suit; just another fatcat following the surgeon general's advice.

Four days in, nothing comes through that gate but Hollis's black Mercedes, either with his wife on the passenger's side or just him taking a crowded route to work or the country club. I'm figuring I can get away with the jogging gig maybe another half a day before someone gets nervous and calls the cops, when out comes the Jag, spitting chunks of limestone off the inside curves of the driveway. I hustle back to my car. Hollis must need unwinding, because he's ten miles over the limit and almost out of sight when I turn into his street.

North is the choice today. In a little while we're up past the lake, with the subdivisions thinning out along a two-lane blacktop. It's a workday—Nola's in the office, good alibi—and for miles we're the only two cars, so I'm hanging back, but I can tell he's not paying attention to his rearview or he'd open it up and leave me in the dust. Arrogant son of a bitch thinks he's invulnerable.

You see how I'm taking every opportunity to work up a good hate? I'm still not committed. I'm thinking when I get him alone I'll work him over, whisper in his ear what's in store if he doesn't lay off Nola. He's such a soft-looking slob I know he'll cave if I just knock out a tooth.

After an hour and a half we've left the blacktop and are towing twin streamers of dust down a dirt road with farms on both sides and here and there a copse of trees left for windbreaks. Now it's time to open the ball. I've got police lights installed inside the grille, and as I press down the accelerator I flip them on. Now he finds his rearview mirror, begins to slow down. But we're short of the next copse of trees, so I close in and encourage him forward, then as we enter the shade I signal him to pull over.

I've shucked the jogging suit by this time, and am wearing my old uniform. I put on my cap and get out and approach the Jag with my hand resting on the sidearm on my right hip. The window on the driver's side purrs down, he flashes his pearlies nervously. "Was I speeding, Officer?"

"Step out of the car, please."

He's got his wallet out. "I have my license and registration."

I tell him again to step out of the car.

He looks surprised, but he puts the wallet away and grasps the door handle. His jaw's set. I can see he thinks it's a case of mistaken identity and he may have a lucrative harassment suit if he can make himself disagreeable enough. Then his face changes again. He's looking at the uniform.

"You're pretty far out of your jurisdiction, aren't you? This area is patrolled by the county sheriff."

I repeat myself a second time, and this time I draw my sidearm.

"Fuck you, fake cop," says he, and floors it.

But it's a gravel road, and the tires spin for a second, spraying gravel, bits of which strike my legs and sting like hornets, which gives me the mad to make that lunge and grab the window post with my free hand. Just then the tread bites and the Jag spurts ahead and I know I'm going to be dragged if I don't let go or stop him.

I don't let go. I stick the barrel of my revolver through the window, cocking the hammer for the effect, and who knows but it might have worked, except my fingers slip off the window post and as I fall away from the car I strike my other wrist against the post and a round punches a hole through the windshield. Hollis screams, thinks he's hit, takes his hands off the wheel, and that's the last I see of him until after the Jag plunges into a tree by the side of the road. The bang's so loud if you even heard my revolver go off you'd forget about it because the second report is still ringing in your ears thirty seconds later, across a whole fucking field of wheat.

I get up off the ground and sprint up to the car, still holding the gun. The hood's folded like a road map, the radiator pouring steam. Hollis's forehead is leaning against the cracked steering wheel. I look up and down the road and across the field opposite the stand of trees. Not a soul in sight, if you don't count a cow looking our way. Just as I'm starting to assimilate the size of my good break, I hear moaning. Hollis is lifting his head. Lawyers are notoriously hard to kill.

His forehead's split, his face is covered with blood. It looks bad enough to finish him even if it wasn't instantaneous, but I'm no doctor. I guess you could say I panicked. I reached through the window and hit him with the butt of the revolver, how many times I don't know, six or seven or maybe as many as a dozen. The bone of his forehead started to make squishing sounds like thin ice that's cracking under your feet, squirting water up through the fissures. Only in this case it wasn't water, of course, and I know I'm going to have to burn the uniform because my gun arm is soaked to the elbow with blood and gray ooze. Finally I stop swinging the gun and feel for a pulse in his carotid. He wasn't using it any more. I holstered the revolver, took his head in both hands, and rested his squishy forehead against the steering wheel where it had struck. The windshield's still intact except for the bullet hole, so I look around and find a fallen tree limb and give it the old Kaline swing, smashing in the rest of the glass from outside. I settle the limb back into the spot where it had lain among the rotted leaves on the ground, take a last look to make sure I didn't drop anything, get into my car, and leave, making sure first to put the jogging suit back on over my gory uniform. And only the cow is there to see me make my getaway.

For the next few days I stay clear of Nola. I don't even call, knowing she'll hear about it on the news; I can't afford anyone seeing us together. I guess I was being overcautious. Hollis's death was investigated as an accident, and at the end of a week the sheriff tells the press the driver lost control on loose gravel. I guess the cow didn't want to get involved.

I was feeling good about myself. I didn't see any need to wrestle with my conscience over the death of a sexual predator, and a high-price lawyer to boot. As is the way of human nature I patted my own back for a set of fortunate circumstances over which I'd had no control. I was starting to feel God was on my side.

But Nola isn't. When I finally do visit, after the cops have paid their routine call and gone away satisfied her beef with her employer was unconnected with an accident upstate, she gives me hell for staying away, accuses me of cowardly leaving her to face the police alone. I settle her down finally, but I can see my explanation doesn't satisfy. As I'm taking off my coat to get comfortable she tells me she has an early morning, everyone at the firm is working harder in Hollis's absence and she needs her sleep. This is crap because Hollis was absent almost as often when he was alive, but I leave.

She doesn't answer her phone for two days after that. When I go to the apartment her bell doesn't answer and her car isn't in the port. I come back another night, same thing. I lean against the building groping in my pockets, forgetting I don't smoke any more, then Nola's old yellow Camaro swings in off Jefferson and I step back into the shadows, because there are two people in the front seat. I watch as the lights go off and they get out.

"If you're that afraid of him, why don't you call the police?" A young male voice, belonging to a slender figure in a green tank top and torn jeans.

"Because he *is* the police. Oh, Chris, I'm terrified. He won't stop hounding me this side of the grave." And saying this Nola huddles next to him and hands him her keys to open the front door, which he does one-handed, his other arm being curled around her waist.

They go inside, and the latch clicking behind them sounds like the coffin lid shutting in my face. Nola's got a new shark in her school. I'm the chum she's feeding him. And I know without having to think about it that I've killed this schnook Ethan Hollis for the same reason Chris is going to kill me; I've run out of uses. So for Chris, *I'm* now the sexual predator.

That's why we're talking now. It's Nola or me, and I need to be somewhere else when she has her accident. I've got a feeling I'm not in the clear over Hollis. Call it cop's sense, but I've been part of the community so long I know when I've been excluded. Even Carpenter won't look me in the eye when we're talking about the fucking Pistons. I've been tagged.

Except you're not going to kill Nola, sweetie. No, not because you're a woman; you girls have moved into every other job, why not this? You're not going to do it because you're a cop.

Forget how I know. Say a shitter knows a shitter and leave it there. What? Sure, I noticed when you reached up under your blouse. I thought at the time you were adjusting your bra, but—well, that was before I said I'd decided to kill Hollis, wasn't it? I hope your crew buys it, two wires coming loose in the same cop's presence within a couple of weeks. I'll leave first so you can go out to the van and tell them the bad news. I live over on Howard. Well, you know the address. You bring the wine—no Jack and Coke—I'll cook the steaks. I think I can finish convincing you about Nola. Like killing a snake.

Contributors

Lawrence Block

Block is an MWA Grand Master and multiple winner of the Edgar and Shamus Awards. His latest novel is *Hit List,* featuring Keller, the Urban Lonely Guy of assassins. Block has published several collections of short stories, and an omnibus volume of all his short fiction is due this season from William Morrow. He lives in New York.

Max Allan Collins

Max Allan Collins has been called "the Renaissance man of mystery fiction." His Nathan Heller historical novels include two PWA Shamus Best Novel winners, and he is the *New York Times* best-selling author of such tie-in novels as *Air Force One, In the Line of Fire,* and *Saving Private Ryan.* His comics scripting includes the *Dick Tracy* comic strip, *Batman,* and his own *Ms. Tree.* He has written and directed an award-winning documentary about Mickey Spillane and three independent films, most recently *Real Time: Siege at Lucas Street Market.*

Loren D. Estleman

Michigan's Estleman has written forty-five novels since 1976, including the Amos Walker mysteries. His newest Amos Walker novel is *A Smile on the Face of the Tiger.* He is an authority on both criminal history and the American West who has been nominated for the Pulitzer Prize, the National Book Award, and the Mystery Writers of America Edgar Award. He is the recipient of fourteen national writing awards.

Michael Garrett

The Alabama resident is an internationally published author, editor, and writing instructor. His works have been optioned for movie and television productions and he was the co-creator of the *Hot Blood* anthology series. Garrett is also recognized as the first publisher of Stephen King.

Jeff Gelb

Gelb is the co-editor of the ten-volume *Hot Blood* erotic horror anthology series, and the editor of the *Shock Rock* and *Fear Itself* anthologies. The lifelong fan of horror and noir fiction is the author of the novel *Specters,* and of numerous articles on comic books, his other great passion in life. Gelb lives in California with his wife and son.

Joe Gores

The former San Francisco private detective is a past president of Mystery Writers of America, and has won three Edgar Awards. His novels include *Hammett* (filmed by Francis Ford Coppola), *A Time of Predators,* and *Cases.* The DKA File Novels include *Dead Skip, 32 Cadillacs,* and *Cons, Scams & Grifts.* Other work includes some one hundred short stories and articles, and a massive fact book, *Marine Salvage.* Film and TV work includes ten screenplays, two TV longforms, and teleplays for over a dozen dramatic series. Gores lives in California with his wife.

Ed Gorman

Ed Gorman's work has appeared in magazines as diverse as *Redbook,* British *Penthouse, Ellery Queen's Mystery Magazine, Louis L'Amour, The Magazine of Fantasy and Science Fiction,* and *Poetry Today.* Of his crime novels and stories *Kirkus* said, "Gorman is one of the most original writers around. His recent novels include *The Day the Music Died* ("Much more genuinely affecting than many a more high profile thriller"—*Wall Street Journal*) and *The Poker Club* ("Reminiscent of King and Koontz at their sinister best"—*Time Out* UK).

Vicki Hendricks

Hendricks lives in Florida, where she teaches at Broward Community College. She has had several short stories published, and three novels: *Miami Purity, Iguana Love,* and *Voluntary Madness.* Her upcoming novel *Sky Blues* combines murder and skydiving, the latter being a sport she avidly pursues.

Edward D. Hoch

New York's Hoch is a past president of Mystery Writers of America, and winner of its Edgar Award for best short story. He has published nearly 850 short stories and has appeared in every issue of *Ellery Queen's Mystery Magazine* since 1973. For twenty years he edited *The Year's Best Mystery and Suspense Stories*. The most recent collections of his stories include *The Night People* and *The Velvet Touch*. He received the Bouchercon convention's Anthony Award for best short story in 1999.

Stuart M. Kaminsky

Stuart M. Kaminsky is the author of more than fifty published books, forty short stories, and five produced screenplays. He won the Edgar Award for best novel in 1989 and has received a total of six Edgar nominations for his novels and short stories. Kaminsky writes the Toby Peters series, the Porfiry Rostnikov series, the Abe Lieberman series, and the Lew Fonseca series. He has also written two *Rockford Files* novels. He now lives in Sarasota, Florida, with his wife and family, runs an annual film festival, coaches basketball and soccer, and still finds time to write three books and five short stories a year.

Terrill Lankford

Terrill Lankford writes movies when he needs money and novels when he doesn't. His first two books, *Shooters* and *Angry Moon*, were published in 1997. His new book, *At the End of the Day . . .*, will be published later this year. He has more than thirty feature film credits to his (and his various pseudonyms') name. "Detour Drive" is the first short story he has written for publication. He lives in the City of Angles, but hopes he won't die there. He owns the bookstore Mysteries, Movies & Mayhem in Sherman Oaks, California.

Wendi Lee

Former associate editor of *Mystery Scene Magazine*, Wendi Lee writes a female P.I. series featuring Italian-American ex-marine Angela Matelli for St. Martin's Press. Her titles include *The Good Daughter, Missing Eden, Deadbeat*, and her latest, *He Who Dies . . .* She is hard at work on the fifth Matelli mystery, currently titled *Ph.Dead*.

Dick Lochte

The Californian's novels have been nominated for nearly every mystery book award and have been translated into more than a dozen languages. His *Sleeping Dog* won the Nero Wolfe Award. Lochte's most recent books are *Lucky Dog*, a collection of short stories, and *L.A. Justice*, a novel co-written with attorney Christopher Darden.

Annette Meyers

Meyers is the author of seven Smith and Wessin mysteries, including *The Groaning Board*. With her husband, Martin Meyers, using the pseudonym Maan Meyers, she writes historical mysteries set in New York in the seventeenth, eighteenth, and nineteenth centuries. The latest is *The Lucifer Contract*. Her latest novels are *Free Love* and *Murder Me Now*. She is a former president of Sisters in Crime.

Gary Phillips

Phillips writes the Ivan Monk P.I. series, *Only the Wicked* being the latest. He's also started a new series featuring ex-Vegas showgirl Martha Chainey, the first called *High Hand*. His novellas include *Tyson* and *Scarface*, with each book packaged with its own compilation soundtrack CD of Def Jam rap artists. California's Phillips is vice president of Private Eye Writers of America, and is at work on a screenplay.

Robert J. Randisi

Randisi is the author of more than 375 books under fifteen different names over the past twenty-one years. He reserves his real name for his work in the mystery field, such as the Nick Delvecchio and Miles Jacoby P.I. series. His latest novels include *In the Shadow of the Arch* and *Blood on the Arch*. He is the founder of the Private Eye Writers of America. He lives and works with writer Marthayn Pelegrimas in Missouri.

Thomas S. Roche

Thomas S. Roche has written horror, crime fiction, and erotica. His short fiction has appeared in the *Best American Erotica* series and many other markets, and he has written articles for *Experience: The Jimi Hendrix*

Magazine and *The San Francisco Bay Guardian*, among others. His books include the *Noirotica* anthology series and the short-story collections *Dark Matter* and *Moonlight Sonatas*. He is currently at work on a crime novel.

Donald E. Westlake

Donald E. Westlake is an MWA Grand Master. Under his own name, he is perhaps the most celebrated writer of comic crime fiction in the history of the genre; as Richard Stark, he is noted as one of noir fiction's primary proponents. His books have led to such films as *Point Blank* and its recent remake, *Payback*, and *The Hot Rock*, among numerous others; his screenplays include the Academy Award–nominated *The Grifters* and the cult favorite *The Stepfather*.

Introduction copyright © 2001 by Max Allan Collins.

"Sweet Little Hands" copyright © 2001 by Lawrence Block.

"Dirty Pool" copyright © 2001 by Thomas S. Roche.

"Branded" copyright © 2001 by Gary Phillips.

"You Don't Know Me" copyright © 2001 by Annette Meyers.

"In the City of Angels" copyright © 2001 by Dick Lochte.

"Trophy Wife" copyright © 2001 by Jeff Gelb.

"Summer Fog" copyright © 2001 by Joe Gores.

"Candie-Gram" copyright © 2001 by Michael Garrett.

"Detour Drive" copyright © 2001 by Terrill Lankford.

"Dying for Sin" copyright © 2001 by Wendi Lee.

"The Girl of My Dreams" copyright © 1979 by Donald E. Westlake. First
   published in the UK in *The Midnight Ghost Book,* copyright © 1978,
   Barrie & Jenkins, London. First American publication, *Ellery
   Queen's Mystery Magazine,* April 1979.

"Flowers for Bill O'Reilly" copyright © 2001 by Max Allan Collins.

"Sailing to Atlantis" copyright © 2001 by Ed Gorman.

"Intimate Obsession" copyright © 2001 by Robert J. Randisi.

"The Club of Masks" copyright © 2001 by Edward D. Hoch.

"Gators" copyright © 2001 by Vicki Hendricks.

"Scorpion's Kiss" copyright © 2001 by Stuart M. Kaminsky.

"Evil Grows" copyright © 2001 by Loren D. Estleman.